Critical acclaim

"One of the pleasure... ionship, on every page, of a lively mind showing its incidental erudition, its epigrammatic flair, its quick-witted impatience and impudence. But all this would be brittle were it not for her earthiness—her love of our species and its habitat—and her ability to focus on the small, sweaty intersections of mind and body, past and present."

John Updike
The New Yorker

"She puts on quite a show. . . . It has its full share of the author's caustic social wit. It displays her up-to-date skewering of styles and appetites, her careful tracing of the mined frontier between English affections, and her irresistible flashes of comic absurdity."

Los Angeles Times Book Review

"[She] manages to take us by surprise, to entertain. . . . She can give us that old pleasure of reading in her novel of three friends, their false hopes and loss; she can even enchant us with the hard news that the continuing effort of redemption is troubling and deep."

The Boston Globe

"[A] brilliant paean to friendship . . . With economy and wit she takes their story forward and back through three decades in shapely, trenchant vignettes. These short takes dovetail subtly into a smooth narrative. And her characters pass the stiffest test of fiction—they become real to the reader."

Houston Chronicle

"Margaret Drabble is the real thing—a novelist in the great tradition of English writers. . . . Throughout *The Radiant Way*, Drabble's strong suit is richly imagined people whose interior thoughts are as vividly dramatized as the exterior movements of their daily lives. . . . Drabble comes up with a series of bravura twists [in this] sad, brilliantly wrought tale of the decline of contemporary Britain."

USA Today

"As a novelist, Margaret Drabble is the acknowledged heir of Jane Austen and Barbara Pym, the precise chronicler, through close observation of telling detail, of contemporary British middle-class society. *The Radiant Way* is composed of sure, often brilliantly constructed layers, and long after the book is done we ponder their complexities, recognize their passions, their blindnesses, in ourselves."

San Jose Mercury News

Also by Margaret Drabble:

A SUMMER BIRD-CAGE
THE GARRICK YEAR
THE MILLSTONE
JERUSALEM THE GOLDEN
THE WATERFALL
THE NEEDLE'S EYE*
THE REALMS OF GOLD*
THE ICE AGE
THE MIDDLE GROUND*

Nonfiction

A WRITER'S BRITAIN
THE OXFORD COMPANION
   TO ENGLISH LITERATURE, 5th Ed.
ARNOLD BENNETT

*Published by Ivy Books

THE RADIANT WAY

Margaret Drabble

IVY BOOKS • NEW YORK

Ivy Books
Published by Ballantine Books
Copyright © 1987 by Margaret Drabble

All rights reserved under International and Pan-American Copyright Conventions. Published in the United States by Ballantine Books, a division of Random House, Inc., New York.

Originally published in Great Britain by George Weidenfeld and Nicolson Limited, London.

Library of Congress Catalog Card Number: 87-45126

ISBN 0-8041-0365-8

This edition published by arrangement with Alfred A. Knopf, Inc.

Grateful acknowledgment is made to Beechwood Music Corporation for permission to reprint an excerpt from the song lyrics "The Whims of Heventy Time," by Morrow, Ambler, Taylor and Robinson.
Copyright © 1978 by EMI Music Publishing Ltd.
All rights in the United States and Canada controlled by Beechwood Music Corporation.

Manufactured in the United States of America

First Ballantine Books Edition: January 1989
Fifth Printing: February 1990

Cover photo by Suzzane Opton

NEW Year's Eve, and the end of a decade. A portentous moment, for those who pay attention to portents. Guests were invited for nine. Some are already on their way, travelling towards Harley Street from outlying districts, from Oxford and Tonbridge and Wantage, worried already about the drive home. Others are dining, on the cautious assumption that a nine-o'clock party might not provide adequate food. Some are uncertainly eating a sandwich or a slice of toast. In front of mirrors women try on dresses, men select ties. As it is a night of many parties, the more social, the more gregarious, the more invited of the guests are wondering whether to go to Harley Street first, or whether to arrive there later, after sampling other offerings. A few are wondering whether to go at all, whether the festive season has not after all been too tiring, whether a night in slippers in front of the television with a bowl of soup might not be a wiser choice than the doubtful prospect of a crowded room. Most of them will go: the communal celebration draws them, they need to gather together to bid farewell to the 1970s, they need to reinforce their own expectations by witnessing those of others, by observing who is in, who is out, who is up, who is down. They need one another. Liz and Charles Headleand have invited them, and obediently, expectantly, they will go, dragging along their tired flat fleet, their aching heads, their over-fed bellies and complaining livers, their exhausted opinions, their weary small talk, their professional and personal deformities, their doubts and enmities, their blurring vision and thickening ankles, in the hope of a miracle, in the hope of a midnight transformation, in

1

the hope of a new self, a new life, a new, redeemed decade.

Alix Bowen has always known that she will have to go to the
party, because she is one of Liz Headleand's two closest
friends, and she has pledged her support, for what it is worth.
She has promised, even, to go early, but cannot persuade her
husband, Brian, to go early with her. A couple of hours of any
party is enough for me, Brian had said, and we'll have to stay
until midnight, so I'm certainly not turning up before ten. All
right, I'll go alone, said Alix. She thought Brian was quite
reasonable not to want to go early. She herself is not a
reasonable person, she suspects, a suspicion confirmed that
evening in the bathroom as she tries, out of respect to Liz's
party, to apply a little of a substance called Fluid Foundation to
the winter-dry skin of her face. This is what people do before
parties. She has seen them doing it on television: indeed, she
used to do it herself when she was young, when she had no
need of such substances, before she reverted so inexorably to
her ancestral type.

The Fluid Foundation comes in a little opaque beige plastic
container, and is labelled, in gold lettering, Teint Naturel. She
bought it a year ago and recalls that it cost a great deal of
money. She uses it infrequently. Now she cautiously squeezes
the container. Nothing happens. Is it dry? Is it empty? How can
one tell? She squeezes again, and this time a great glob of Teint
Naturel extrudes itself from the narrow aperture onto her
middle finger. She gazes at it in mild dislike. It glistens, pinky
brown, faintly obscene, on her finger. Common sense, reason,
tell her to wash this away down the wash bowl, but thrift
forbids. Thrift is one of Alix's familiars. Thrift does not often
leave her side. Thrift has nearly killed her on several occasions,
through the agency of old sausages, slow-punctured tyres,
rusty blades. Thrift now recommends that she apply the rest of
this blob to her complexion rather than wastefully flush it
away. Thrift disguised as Reason speciously suggests that an
excess of Fluid Foundation on one's face, unlike a poisoned
sausage, will cause no harm. Thrift apologises, whingeing, for
the poisoned sausage, reminding Alix that she ate it twenty
years ago, when she had no money and needed the sausage.

Alix hesitates, then splats the rest of the glob onto her face
and begins to work it in, angrily. She blames the manufacturers
for the poor design of the container: probably deliberate, she
reflects, probably calculated to make people splurge out far
more than they need of the stuff. She is slightly cheered by the

thought of how little reward they would reap from their dishonesty if all consumers were as moderate as she. (She wonders, in parenthesis, how much of the nation's income is spent on cosmetics, and whether the statistics will be provided in the New Year issue of *Social Trends*.) She is more cheered, although at first puzzled, by the fact that as she works the excess of Teint Naturel on her skin, her appearance begins to improve. Instead of turning brick red or prawn cocktail pink, as she had feared, she is turning a pleasant beige, a natural beige; she is beginning to look the same colour that people look in television advertisements. A pleasant, mat, smooth beige. It is remarkable. So this, perhaps, is what the manufacturers had always intended? She apologises to Thrift for having been angry, then remembers that it was Thrift that had dictated her previous parsimonious, sparing applications, and is confused.

She gazes at herself in wonder. Vanished are her healthy pink cheeks, her slightly red winter nose, her mole, her little freckles and blemishes: she is smooth, new made. She dabs a little powder on top, and stands back to admire the effect. It is pleasing, she decides. She wonders what it will look like by midnight. Will she be transformed into an uneven, red-faced, patchy, blotchy clown? An ugly sister? Alix has always felt rather sorry for the poor competitive disappointed Ugly Sisters. Indeed, she feels sorry for almost everybody. It is one of her weaknesses. But she does not feel sorry for her friend Liz Headleand. As she struggles into her blue dress, she wonders idly if she is so fond of Liz because she does not have to feel sorry for her, or if she does not have to feel sorry for her because she is so fond of her? Or are the two considerations quite distinct? She feels she is on the verge of some interesting illumination here, but has to abandon it in search of Brian, to ask him to fasten the back of her dress: if she does not leave soon, she will be late for her early arrival, and moreover she has promised to meet Esther Breuer at eight-thirty precisely on the corner of Harley Street and Weymouth Street. They plan to effect a double entry.

Esther Breuer has decided to walk to the intersection of Harley Street and Weymouth Street. She often walks alone at night. She walks from her flat at the wrong end of Ladbroke Grove, along the Harrow Road, under various stretches of Motorway, past the Metropole Hotel, where she calls in to buy herself a drink in the Cosmo-Cocktail Bar (she is perversely fond of the Metropole Hotel), and then through various

increasingly handsome although gloomy back streets, until she
arrives at the arranged corner. As she approaches it, she cannot
at first see Alix, but she believes that Alix will be there, and
indeed momently she is: they converge, Esther from the west,
Alix from the south, and moderate their pace (Esther accelerating slightly, Alix marginally slowing down) so that they meet
upon the very corner itself. They are both delighted by this
small achievement of co-ordination. They congratulate themselves upon it, as they walk north towards Liz's house in
Harley Street, towards the invisible green of Regent's Park.

Liz Headleand sits at her dressing table in her dressing room.
Her gold watch and her digital clock agree that it is nineteen
minutes past eight. At half past eight she will go downstairs to
see what is happening in the kitchen, to see if Charles is in his
place, to see if any of her children or stepchildren have yet
descended, to prepare to receive her guests. Meanwhile, she
has eleven minutes in hand. She knows that she ought to ring
her mother, that there is still a faint possibility that she might
ring her mother, but that possibility is already fading, and as
the admonitory red glare of the clock clicks silently to 20:20 it
gasps and dies within her. She will not ring her mother. She
has not time.

Instead, she sits there and for a moment contemplates the
prospect of her party, the gathering of her guests. She knows
them, their reluctance, their need, their larger hopes. She can
hear their conversations, in cars, in bedrooms, in restaurants,
at other parties, as time draws them nearer to her, to one
another, to her house. She eats a pistachio nut, and fastens her
necklace. New Year's Eve. A significant night, at least in
journalistic terms, and there would be journalists here this
evening, no doubt comparing their analyses of the bygone
seventies, their predictions for the 1980s. And for her, too,
significant in other, superstitious ways. Since childhood, since
her early school days, New Year's Eve had possessed for her
a mournful terror: she had elected it to represent the Nothingness which was her own life, the solid, cheerful festival which
had seemed to be the lives of others. New Year's Eve in those
early years had possessed a dull religious sheen, a pewter
glimmer, which by much effort and polishing and dedication of
the will could bring her a little light, a little hope, a little

perseverance; but she had longed for the flames and the candles, the cut glass and the singing. Disproportionately she had longed, in the interminable wastes of adolescence, in the grey and monotonous steppes, and some of the longing had attached itself to this night, this one night of the year, when others (she knew from school friends, from the radio, from novels), when others went to parties and celebrated whatever was about to be. She had longed to be invited to a party, a longing which presented itself to her as a weakness and a wickedness, as well as an impossibility. She had comforted herself with her own severity. Finally, after long years, she had become a party goer. How those oblong cards with her own name upon them had delighted her! Crazily, disproportionately. And now she was a party giver as well as a party goer.

Her dressing table glitters and shimmers, it is festive like the night. It is white and gold, quietly ornate. Beneath the protective glass lies, imprisoned, flattened, a circle of Venetian lace, elaborate, fine, rose-embossed, cream-coloured, expensive, hand-worked, beautiful, useless: a gift, though not of this year's giving. On the table lie a silver-backed hand mirror, a silver-backed brush, an ivory paper knife with a silver handle. Over a little carved corner of the large oval mirror into which she absently stares, not seeing herself, hang necklaces: amber, pearl, paste. She rarely wears them; she wears her little locket, superstitiously. The blonde shells of the pistachio nuts, with their seductive little green gleaming cracks, repose in a small Sheffield plate dish on a stem, an oval dish which echoes, satisfactorily, elegantly, the shape of the nuts; the surface of its lining is tinily scratched, pitted and polished, golden, antique, dull but shining. Behind the dish stands this year's Christmas gift, from her oldest stepson, Jonathan: a tiny, cut-glass snowdrop vase which holds a posy of cold hothouse snow drops, white and green, delicately streaked, fragile, hopeful, a promise of futurity. Liz Headleand is known to like cut glass, so people give it to her, on occasions, pleased to have their gift problem thus simply solved.

Liz Headleand stares into the mirror, as though entranced. She does not see herself or the objects on her dressing table. The clock abruptly jerks to 20:21.

She and Charles have never given a party on New Year's Eve before. They have given many parties in their time, but on New Year's Eve they have always gone out to the gatherings of

others—sometimes to several gatherings in the course of the
evening, and some years separately, not always meeting even
for the magic chimes. A modern marriage, and some of its
twenty years had been more modern than others. Maybe, Liz
reflects (for this is what she contemplates, through the oval
mirror), maybe this is why they decided to have such a party,
this year, at the end of this decade: as a sign that they had
weathered so much, and were now entering a new phase? Well,
why not? After twenty years, one is allowed a celebration.
Charles is fifty, she herself is forty-five. There is a symmetry
about this, about their relationship with the clock of the
century, that calls for celebration. And therefore grumbling
couples complain in cars on their way to Harley Street from the
Home Counties and beg one another not to let them drink too
much; therefore Esther and Alix meet and laugh on a street
corner a few hundred yards away; therefore stepchildren
muster and stepparents-in-law assemble; therefore Liz Headleand's mother sits alone, ever alone, untelephoned, distant,
incomprehending, incomprehended, remote, mad, long mad,
imprisoned, secret, silent, silenced, listening to the silence of
her house.

Charles and Liz, naturally, did not construct the notion of a
New Year's Eve Party in this spirit, as a portent, as a symbol,
as a landmark in the journey of their lives. As far as Liz can
remember the idea came upon them rather more casually, one
Saturday morning in early November before breakfast. Charles
and Liz rarely breakfast together, they are both far too busy:
Liz often sees patients at 8:00 in the morning and Charles's
working hours are wildly irregular. But at weekends, they
attempt to rendezvous over the Oxford marmalade, and on this
occasion had succeeded. Charles, eating his toast, opening his
mail, had suddenly exclaimed with a parody of fury, "Christ,
it's the Venables again!" "What have they done to you now?"
she had mildly enquired, looking up from a photocopy of an
article, "The Compulsion to Public Prayer: A Study of
Religious Neurosis in a Post-Christian Society," which she
had just received in her own post, and Charles had said,
"Asked us to a New Year's Eve party."

"What, now, in November?"

He pushed the invitation over to her. She regarded it with
mock distaste.

"It's got pictures of little cocktail glasses and tinsel spots
on," she observed.

"I could see that for myself," said Charles.

"I refuse to invite them to dinner," she said.

"Of course we don't have to invite them to dinner. Ludicrous couple. Ludicrous."

Liz smiled. She enjoyed Charles's little displays of anger, especially when she was in sympathy with them—as, on matters such as the Venables, she usually was. A good judge of character, Charles, she would sometimes with surprise reflect.

"I think we should retaliate," she said, a few minutes later, after skimming through public prayer and the leaders of the *Telegraph* and the *Guardian* (*The Times*, it will be recalled, was on strike at this time). "I think we should have a New Year's Eve party of our own. That would serve them right."

"It certainly would," Charles agreed. "Yes, it certainly would." And they smiled at one another, collusively, captivated by this broad new concept of social vengeance, and began to plan their guest list. They owed hospitality to half London, they agreed; it was time for a party, it would kill many birds with one big stone. A vision of dead, flattened, feathered guests rose in both their minds, as they plotted and planned.

That was how it had been, perhaps, that was where it had started, thought Liz, as she stared into past and future, before jerking herself back into the present, which now stood at 20:22. The red clock from the bedroom reflected in the dressing-room mirror, at an interesting, an unlikely angle. Her eyes focussed upon her own image. She looked all right, she concluded, without much interest. She bared her teeth at herself, pointlessly. Her teeth were quite large, but there was not much she could do about that now. Her interest in cosmetics, like that of her friend Alix Bowen, was minimal, but, like Alix Bowen, she decided that it was after all a festive occasion, and she began at this late moment to apply a little mascara. Her mascara container, like Alix's Fluid Foundation, was rarely called upon, and appeared to have dried up. She licked the little curved brush, and tried again. A big black dry grainy nodule stuck itself unobligingly to her lashes. Impatiently she reached for a tissue and wiped it off. It left a small black smear. She licked the tissue and removed the black smear, restoring herself to her former state, which had been, and still was, in her own view, quite satisfactory.

20:23. In a few minutes she would go down. She could have borrowed some mascara from her daughter Sally, but it was too late. She should have rung her mother in Northam, but it was too late. Seven minutes of solitude she had, and then she would descend. As she sat there, she experienced a sense of what seemed to be preternatural power. She had summoned these people up, these ghosts would materialize, even now they were converging upon her in their finery at her bidding, each of them willing to surrender a separate self for an evening, to eat, to drink, to talk, to exchange embraces, to wait for the witching hour. Soon their possible presences would become real presences, and here, under this roof, at her command, patterns would form and dissolve and form again, dramas would be enacted, hard and soft words exchanged, friendships formed, acquaintances renewed. The dance would be to her tune. A pity, in a way, that the dancing would be merely metaphorical: this was a house large enough to accommodate dancing, but their friends were not of the dancing classes, would gaze in astonishment, alarm, sophisticated horror, intellectual condemnation, at dancing in a private house . . . another year, perhaps, for the dancing. This year, the dying year, the social dance would suffice.

It would be a large assembly: some two hundred had accepted, and more would come. She had encouraged her stepchildren and her daughter Sally to invite their friends: they would add colour, diversion, eccentricity, noise. She liked the mixing of ages, she even liked a little friction, and friction there would be: Ivan Warner alone was usually enough to raise the temperature of any social gathering to conflagration point, and Ivan in conjunction with Charles's Fleet Street friends and television moguls, with a few publishers and poets and novelists, with an actress or two, with a clutch of psychologists and psychotherapists and art historians and civil servants and lawyers and exactly journalists politicians would surely manage to set the place on fire. Surely this night the unexpected would happen, surely she had summoned up the unexpected. She had, of late, felt herself uncannily able to predict the next word, the next move, in any dialogue: she could hear and take in three conversations at once; she could see remotely as through a two-way mirror the private lives of her patients, sometimes of her friends; she had felt reality to be revealed to her at times in flashes beyond even the possibility of rational calculation, had felt in danger (why danger?) of too much knowledge, of a kind of powerlessness and sadness that is born of knowledge. For these reasons, perhaps, was it that she had decided to multiply the possibilities so recklessly, to construct a situation beyond her own grasping? A situation of which not even she could guess the outcome? Had she wished to test her powers, or, a little, to lose control and stand aside? To be defeated, honourably, by the multiplicity of the unpredictable, instead of living with the power of her knowingness? With the limits of the known?

She had thought, back in November, that the party was merely a celebration, a celebration of having survived, so long, with Charles: twenty-one years, unique in the circle of their acquaintance. Battle and bloodshed and betrayal lay behind them, and now they met peacefully in this large house, and slept peacefully in their separate rooms, and met at weekends over the marmalade, and would continue to do so until Charles's new appointment took him, in a couple of months, to New York. He would return to visit her, she would fly out to visit him, they would speak on the telephone, they would not miss one another. This was understood. Nobody expected Liz to uproot herself, like a woman, like a wife, and follow her husband to America: she was expected to stay where she was, pursuing her own career and pursuing her own inner life, whatever that might be. A modern marriage. Charles and Liz Headleand. Liz knew how they were regarded: as a powerful couple who, by breaking the rules, had become representative. They represented a solidity, a security, a stamp of survival on the unquiet experiments of two decades, a proof that two disparate spirits can wrestle and diverge and mingle and separate and remain distinct, without a loss of brightness, without a loss of self, without emasculation, submission, obligation. And the image, the public image, is not wholly false, although naturally its firm talismanic outlines conceal a great deal of past pain and confusion, of dirty bargaining, of occasional childishness, of outright disagreements; and the present is not wholly peaceful. If it were, it would be dead, Liz tells herself. Conflict is invigorating, it renews energy. So she tells herself. She disapproves of a great deal of Charles's life, these days. She thinks his ambitions misplaced, his goals suspect, his methods dangerous, his new political alignments deplorable; but she is loyal to Charles, to Charles himself, to the man that these manifestations in her view misrepresent. She believes in Charles, in her own fashion, and believes that he believes in her. Their past, with all its secrets, is solid behind them, and cannot be disowned. Their union has a high, embattled, ideological glamour; their dissent is a bond. Her loyalty, she believes, is worth a great deal to Charles: it gives him plausibility.

Or is this line of thought simply a rationalization of the truth, which is that these days she and Charles disagree about almost everything?

A celebration, a farewell party. Charles will be away for at least a year. She is glad he is going, she thinks. The strain of living up to the lofty concept of marriage that they have invented is tiring, at times, and she is a busy woman. A year off will not come amiss. It will give her peace, privacy.

She eats another nut, and needlessly, absently combs her hair. She finds it hard to think clearly about Charles. The time span of the thinking is too long, it makes the present moment arbitrary, a point on a graph that is in itself meaningless. She looks down at her shopping-and-memo list, to find a nearer focus. *Perrier water*, it says. *Poinsettia. Prunes. Remind Deirdre about Tabasco. Japanese seminar, Metropole Hotel. Ask Ivan about R.P.* R.P.? Who or what was R.P.? She must have known last night, while constructing this list. Maybe it will come back to her, when she sees Ivan. She suspects that Charles suspects that she had once had an affair with Ivan, but of course she had not, though she concedes that Ivan is so unpleasant that only a degree of past sexual intimacy could plausibly explain the kind of friendship that he and Liz have over the years established. Charles had not wished to invite Ivan to the party. Wherever that man goes, there is trouble, he said. But that is the *point* of him, Liz had replied. Liz prided herself on her tolerance of Ivan's appalling behaviour. Anyway, she said, we'll have to ask him, or he'll be even ruder about us in his next article. I don't give a damn about Ivan's ridiculous rag, said Charles, but of course he did, he cared much more than she did, and with reason, for Ivan usually managed to deliver her some backhanded compliment, whereas Charles always got it in the neck: Headleand Crashes Headlong had been the headline of Ivan's latest piece of gossip, which had consisted of a dangerous account of Charles's behaviour at a meeting of a board of directors, laced with unfounded but inventive innuendo about a country house which he and Liz were said to be purchasing as a tax dodge. There had also been offensive remarks about Charles's ageing toothless bite. Charles had been particularly annoyed about the toothlessness, she could tell, although he tried to conceal it; he had in fact

been without his two front teeth that week, while having their
thirty-year-old caps replaced, caps that marked a heroic accident long ago in a swimming pool in Sevenoaks. He had
proved remarkably (to her, touchingly) sensitive about their
temporary absence. Losing two front teeth, even two false
front teeth, at the age of fifty, even if only for a week, had
distressed him: he had sat opposite her at the breakfast table
with a napkin over his mouth, and she knew that it had taken
some courage to go to the board meeting at all. No, Charles
certainly did object to Ivan's insults, and Ivan's divination of
Charles's weak spots was uncannily accurate.

She, for her part, was of the opinion that she did not object
to Ivan's insults at all. She saw them as emanations of his own
tormented, neurotic, anally fixated personality, and nothing to
do with herself. She was convinced that he was in reality quite
fond of them both. Particularly of herself. He was grateful to
her for her power of forgiveness, she suspected, for the
absolution she continued to extend. Such an ugly, red-faced,
no, worse, *blue*-faced little man. Small, squashed, snub, stout.
She had known him for many years. One would have thought
that the principle of people living in glass houses not throwing
stones would have warned Ivan off a career as a journalist,
gossip, and so-called satirist, but it did not seem to occur to
him that he was asking for trouble of a kind that she knew
would cause him the most intimate anguish; but, in fact, so
appalling were Ivan's features and physique that comment on
them was rare, even his worst enemies (and he had hundreds)
not considering them fair game. Comment on his dreadful
behaviour, by contrast, flourished. Maybe, she idly wondered,
as she drew a red ball-point daisy by Metropole Hotel, maybe
he chooses to be so offensive verbally in order to divert
attention from his appearance? An interesting conjecture.
Though Ivan claimed success with women, despite or because
of his natural handicaps, and Liz herself, though she had not
slept with him, had on one occasion in the early years of her
marriage to Charles found herself, to her own surprise, sitting
on a table in a flat in Belsize Park Gardens with Ivan's hand
inside her bra. She could remember the incident quite clearly,
although the circumstances surrounding it had vanished into
oblivion, beyond recall of any form of analysis: it had been
early afternoon, so clearly not a party incident—maybe they
had had lunch together?—and she had been anxious about
picking up children from school. She kept telling Ivan that she

had to leave, and he kept telling her that he was a great lover although his prick was only six inches long. Or something to that effect. And all the time his hand had been inside her bra. She could remember the bra, it had been rather a good black lace wired Kayser Bondor, of a line that appeared to have been discontinued, as she'd never been able to find another. But why had they been sitting on a table? And in whose flat? These were mysteries now known only to God.

She had not slept with Ivan, nor ever would, but was deriving a secret satisfaction from the knowledge that present at her party that night would be all the men with whom she had ever slept—or all save one, and he had been from another country, and she had not known his name. There were not so many of them: five, to be precise, and one of those was Charles, and another her first husband, Edgar Lintot, to whom she had remained married for less than a year. Of the other three, one had been revenge, one an escapade, and one half-serious, but all had now merged into a sentimental distance, an affectionate presence. She had set much store by retaining or restoring her relations with these men, and thought she knew why, after the sickening shock of the rapid deterioration of her first childish marriage, she had been so afraid of ever again being engulfed by hatred and violence that she had maintained a resolute pleasantness even through the worst of times, even with Charles, who was not an easy man. She had called it maturity, this pleasantness. She was determined never again to be a party to the hideous transformation which overcomes the partners of a bad marriage, who grow fangs and horns and sprout black monstrous wolfish hair, who claw and cling and bite and suck. There would be no more of that: she would see the person as he was, and see him steadily, setting aside her own long shadow as it fell. Her success in this enterprise had fortified her in her career as psychotherapist, had given her confidence in her right to pursue it, in the rightness of her pursuing it. Even her first husband she had regained from that dreadful hinterland of marsh and bog and storm cloud; and now they were good friends, she and Edgar, in the sunlight, harmlessly friends, and on some subjects (the National Health Service, the pathology of multiple murderers, the ethics of reporting violent crime) had struck up alliances that excluded, that increasingly and dramatically excluded, her husband, Charles.

So there they would be, all friends together. Edgar, Roy,

Charles, Philip, and Jules. A pity about that Dutchman: their union had taken place in a narrow cabin on the North Sea, crossing from The Hague to Harwich in a Force Nine gale, and they had omitted to exchange names and addresses. Would he have enjoyed her party? Would he have raised a knowing glass? They had rolled around in the narrow berth on the unanchored sheet, slipping on the shiny much-worn cheap leatherette surface of the bunk, lurching in and out of one another in a determined kind of way, the only passengers on the boat not to be paralysed with sea sickness. The selection of the fittest. The crossing had lasted eighteen hours instead of eight. An epic. Did he remember, where was he, who was he? Too late to recall him now, he was one ghost who could not obey her summons.

Edgar, Roy, Charles, Philip, and Jules. She had finished with them all. Maybe she had finished with sexual intercourse forever, maybe it was this possibility that gave her this peculiar conviction of strength, this sense of invulnerability, of certainty, of power. They would attack her no more, weaken her no more. She had closed the gates. This was not orthodox, but then, although a Freudian, she was not an orthodox Freudian, and her vision of futurity did not exclude celibacy. From within herself, she would survey. An observer, a non-combatant. As a child, reading her mother's collection of Victorian novels, Edwardian novels, she had wondered how women could bear to renounce their position in the centre of the matrimonial stage, the sexual arena, how they could bring themselves to consent to adopt the role of chaperone, to sit at the edge of the dance on little gilt-legged chairs gossiping and watching, spectators, as the younger ones innocently paired, as the older ones not so innocently paired, in the ever-changing formations of the floor. How could one bear to be on the sidelines? Not to be invited to the waltz? Not ever again to be invited to the waltz? But now she could see the charm, could read the ·meaning, of the observer's role, a meaning inaccessible to a sixteen-year-old, to a thirty-year-old—for the observer was not, as she had from the vantage, the disadvantage of childhood supposed, charged with an envious and impotent malice, and consumed with a fear of imminent death: no, the observer was filled and informed with a quick and lively and long-established interest in all those that passed before, in all those that moved and circled and wheeled around, was filled with intimate connections and loving memories and hopes and concerns and prospects. Nor was the observer impotent, for it was through the potency of the observer that these children took their being and took the floor. Actual children, children of the heart and the imagination, old friends, new friends, the children of friends, they circle, they weave, and the pattern is both one's own and not one's own, it is of the making of generations. One is no longer the hopeful or the despairing guest: one is host in the house of oneself.

So thought Liz Headleand, as she sat at her dressing table, in her yellow-walled, her yellow marble-veined dressing room, eating nuts. She put her glasses on to peer once more at the vanished smear of mascara, and was amused to see the print of her face leap into sharp relief: a new trick, for her glasses are quite new. She dabbed again with the tissue. Her glasses amused her. So did the amusing little sag of her incipient double chin, the veining on her cheeks (which, unlike Alix, she does not think to cover with Fluid Foundation), the slight plump soft dimpling of her upper arm, the raised veins in the back of her hands, the broadening of her hips, the decreasing flexibility of her joints. These signs of age, of the ageing process, she greeted and greets with curiosity, with a resolute welcome. One might as well welcome them, after all: there is not much point in rejecting them. It is all intended, it is all part of the plan. There is a goal to this journey, there will be an arrival, Liz Headleand believes. It is only by refusing to move onwards that we truly die. She truly believes this. She has good reason to believe it.

Her mother sits in Northam, listening to what?

Liz stands up, regards herself, inspects her hemline, adjusts the safety pin fastening her gold leather belt, admires her gold sandals, pats her silver buckets and smooths the limp, arum anti loose-woven cream Moroccan cotton over her broadening hips. She looks upon her broadening hips as an affirmation of life. (Her mother is a scraggy old thing, starved and skinny.) She pulls in her stomach, smartly, as she will remember to do, episodically, throughout the evening, when not too deeply engaged in other pursuits.

Now Charles, he is a different case, she acknowledges. For him, weight is no longer perhaps a laughing matter. He ought to take more care. He is getting solid, even fat, and that reddish tinge to his face has become permanent rather than intermittent. Too many lunches, too many dinners, too many glasses of port at the club beam betrayal from Charles's complexion, bulge from his shirt front. His hair is receding, too. She wonders where he is. She has not seen him since half past six, when they met in the kitchen over a salami sandwich. He was preoccupied, and spoke of trouble with the Home Office and a documentary on prison conditions. The fatter and balder Charles becomes, the more formidable he looks. She supposes that this is only natural. He is probably downstairs, knocking back a stiff gin and tonic before submitting himself to the milder offering of champagne.

20:35, says the little red clock. She has lost five minutes, somewhere. It is time to go downstairs, to see how Deirdre is getting on in the kitchen, to make sure the hired butlers are not drinking too much.

So down the wide staircase she goes, past the oak chest with its bowl of white roses on the half landing, past the pastel sequence of Albers, past the dim varnished portrait of a full-bosomed crimson-gowned pearl-decked eighteenth-century woman whom some take to be an ancestor, though she had in fact come with the house, down through the black-and-white-tiled hall with its marble and gilt claw-legged table strewn with Christmas cards, gloves, and glossy free advertising magazines, and into the broad high first-floor drawing room, where sat Charles, drinking a gin and tonic, which she had expected, and talking to Esther and Alix, which she had not.

Three floors up, on the top floor of the large house, Sally Headleand sat on her bedroom floor painting her toe nails a pale silvery green and listening to her stepbrother Alan trying to explain about inflation and unemployment and monetarism and the economic implications of the new rhetoric praising the Victorian values of family life. In the background, Tom Robinson on a new Christmas cassette sang "The Winter of Seventy-Nine." Sally liked listening to Alan, though she understood only one word in a hundred. He was loyal to the old left, was Alan, unlike their turncoat father, who had in recent years been wooed by, and had, it seemed, espoused, the radical right. The unions had driven him to infidelity. Alan reassured her. Her father upset her. Her mother said it was stimulating to be upset, and maybe it was, but that didn't prevent her from preferring the solace of the old wisdom. It had surrounded her at her progressive private school, it surrounded her still at her fashionable newish university, but she herself lacked economic grasp and was uncomfortably aware of having lost, of late, a few arguments with outsiders, of having been thrown back on arguments about personalities. She was too intelligent to enjoy this position, and too much of a feminist not to be made uncomfortable by its sexist implications. So it comforted her to see Alan lying there on her bed, his huge ancient unpolished cracked shoes nestling comfortably in the tangled mess of her grey sheets and leaking duvet and discarded purple socks, his eager owl face shining with enlightenment as he spoke abstractly of public spending projects and the American New Deal and tight fiscal policy. One could never tell when or whether Alan was wholly serious, for he found ideas exciting in themselves, too exciting, perhaps, ever to be put into practice; there he lay, smoking, waving, occasionally running his fingers through his thick black curly hair, and dropping cigarette ash through the slit into an old Coca-Cola tin. He spoke of the state as mother, of the history of those who clung to the state as mother, of the psychology of those who wished to orphan themselves from the mother, of the novel oddity of a woman Prime Minister who was in fact a mother but was not nevertheless thereby motherly. Sally listened, entranced. She didn't see enough of Alan, now he had moved to Manchester. She needed a regular fix from Alan, to reassure her that the world was still familiar, manageable, subject to known laws.

Alan himself had never known his mother. His mother had died in a car crash when he was three months old. He, with his two elder brothers, had been brought up by a nanny, until, three years later, his father married Liz. Liz had taken on Alan and his brothers. The three boys had always assumed, as soon as they reached the age for such assumptions, that Charles had married Liz in order to provide the three motherless babes with a proper family life. Sally, of course, had never assumed anything of the sort.

*   *   *

It was shortly after Sally's birth, in 1960, that Charles had purchased this larger house. It had seemed, at the time, a daring gesture. Forty thousand pounds he had paid for it, a sum which now seemed laughably small, but which in those days had been a vast amount to pay for a private house, even in such a prime position. It had been financed by blood money, blood money from the wealthy parents of Charles's dead wife. Liz had been keen on the transaction. The house had been in an appalling condition, full of junk and rubbish, its elegant lines unreadable through years of accretions and demolitions. It had been used for many years as a staff hostel for an Oxford Street department store. Five floors, and broad, with an eighteenth-century spaciousness. A challenge. They needed a large house, with four children already, possibly more to come, with a housekeeper and an au pair girl; impossible to survive much longer in their cramped, narrow, bijou terrace in Fulham. From Fulham to Harley Street was an extravagant removal, not the kind of move that young professional couples made, in those days, but the Headleands, ambitious, imaginative, self-appointed pioneers of they knew not what, had done it, and with aplomb. The house, in 1980, was worth, their friends enviously muttered, perhaps a million, perhaps more. True, the rates had soared, but so had the Headleands' incomes. It now lodged not only what was left of the Headleand family, but also the private part of Liz's practice, and the practices of two of her colleagues; a shared secretary had taken over what had once been the au pair girl's flat. A going concern, a successful enterprise.

Liz loved the house, she loved the neighbourhood. It gave her great delight to see her children and Charles's, here, thus, in the centre. Her own childhood had been lived on the margins; she had wanted theirs to be calm, to be spared the indignities of fighting unnecessary territorial and social wars. They would have greater freedom thus, she argued. Charles shared this faith. His own childhood, though markedly less strenuous, less arduous than Liz's, had not been without its privations, its humiliations. He liked the centre as much as Liz herself.

Liz still, after all these years, found satisfaction in giving her address. Each time a shop assistant or a clerk or a tradesman wrote down Dr. E. Headleand, Harley Street, the same thrill of self-affirmation, of self-definition would be re-enacted. Liz Ablewhite of Abercorn Avenue had become Liz Headleand of

Harley Street, London W.1. Nobody could argue with that, nobody could question it, it was so. Her largest dreams, her most foolish fantasies had been enacted in bricks and mortar and mantel shelves and tiled floors and plaster ceilings. It seemed improbable, but it was so. The Headleands of Harley Street. Resonant, exemplary. Myriad uncertainties and hesitations were buried beneath that solid pile, banished by the invocation of a street name. Vanished suburbia, vanished the provinces, vanished forever solitude and insignificance and social fear. No wonder that she and Charles felt that they led a charmed life, that the times were on their side.

It was not fairy gold that had fallen into their open laps: the first Mrs. Headleand, it was true, had conveniently died, but Charles and Liz thereafter had worked for their position. They had studied long hours, both of them, they had burned the midnight oil while munching their way through textbooks and qualifications, through overtime and late-night meetings. They had taken professional risks, had survived personal disasters. And now they inhabited their house.

It had taken some labour to restore: a gang of builders had spent months ripping down hardboard partitions, taking out gas meters, attempting to rescue old parquet flooring, refitting windows, stripping paint from tiles. The most unpleasant discoveries were made during the process of clearance: cupboards full of urine-encrusted chamber pots, of ancient patent medicines, of dead mice, of moth-infested garments, of fossilized scraps of nineteenth-century food: Hogarthian, Dickensian relics of an oppressed and squalid past. In one room there was a plastic sack full of used sanitary towels. Liz had joked that they were sure, in the rafters, to discover a dead baby, and indeed they did find there a mummified cat, which a pathologist friend invited to be at least a hundred years old. Uncertain, profoundly and with reason uncertain of her own taste, she had entrusted redecoration to a professional, then an acquaintance of Esther's, now Liz's friend, who had transformed the glum greens and browns into white and cream and yellow and gold. This vision she had adopted, cultivated, and now it seemed her own, although she would never have conceived of it herself. She sometimes remembered this and gave it thought.

Others sometimes pondered it too. White and cream and yellow and gold did not to everyone seem entirely appropriate shades to represent the Headleands, whose natural colouring, as in a party game, might have been supposed to be more primary, more violent, more extreme, more robust.

The untransformed house had contained treasures as well as horrors, including the portrait on the stairs, and the restored chandelier which now hung, glittering and refracting, from the centre of the ornate ceiling, above the heads of Charles and Alix, who sat disposed, glass in hand, at either end of one of the long settees, and above Esther, who stood by the fireplace reading the Headleand invitations to parties and lectures and public meetings.

"Esther," said Liz, in the doorway. "Alix. I didn't know you were here. You should have called me."

"You said to be early, and we were," said Alix. She did not rise, nor did Liz cross to greet her; they were the oldest of old friends, and did not kiss on meeting. Esther put down the Venables' invitation, and turned into the room.

"You were talking to Charles," said Liz, accusing, as she crossed to the sideboard to pour herself a drink.

"We don't often get the chance," said Alix. "The opportunity, I mean."

All four of them laughed, for no very evident reason, and Charles shifted his weight on the settee.

"We were saying," said Charles, "that it must be over a year since I last saw Esther. And six months since I saw Alix."

"And now Charles is off to New York," said Esther, crossing the room to perch on a low stool by Alix's knee. "In a couple of months. Or less, possibly. So he says."

"So he says," echoed Liz, with a note of mild surprise. They spoke of Charles as though he were not there, as though he belonged to another world of logic from their own, as though he belonged, almost, to another species. It was an affectation that had developed over the years. It appeared that Charles did not find it offensive.

"Men," said Esther, "are an unpredictable lot. One has no way of knowing how their minds work."

"If they have minds," said Charles, who knew the rules of the game.

"Well," said Esther, changing tack abruptly, as was her way, "what do we think we are going to think of the 1980s? I think I might go to live in the country, in the 1980s. I've had enough of the town."

"You've said that before," said Liz. "You probably said it at the end of the 1960s."

"Yes, I probably did. But I didn't mean it then, and who knows, I may mean it now. I could go and live in the country. Or I could go and live in Italy."

"You could, but you won't," said Liz, comfortably.

"One can live very cheaply in Italy," said Esther.

"One can live very cheaply in London," said Liz.

"Yes," said Esther. "Some do. I do, for one." And she looked round, ostentatiously, at the large drawing room, the heavy tasselled curtains, the pale shining cushions, the cut glass, the silver trays, the paintings, the flowers, the deep white rugs. Alix's eyes followed Esther's. They enjoyed teasing Liz about her pretensions, and rarely had an opportunity to tease her in the presence of Charles.

"This evening," said Liz, leaning forward, lowering her voice confidentially with mock importance across the yards of space, "we have *butlers*. And what I think is called catering. And vintage—I think it's vintage—champagne. Is that right, Charles, is there such a thing as vintage champagne?"

Esther laughed. Charles, who appeared momentarily not to have been listening, laughed absently.

"In fact," said Liz, "I'd better go and see what the butlers are up to. They are foreigners and they appear to be drinking. I've a feeling that they might be the same lot that I saw at Geraldine's party last month. One of them fell over a coffee table and threw a whole trayful of bits and pieces on Carrie Donovan and Harry Pritchett. Crudités and avocado dip. Quite messy. We don't want too much of that. Or not too early in the evening. No, you both stay here and talk to Charles. Esther can tell him what paintings to look at in New York. Charles is not as indifferent to paintings as he pretends. Are you, Charles?"

And she made her exit, to the kitchen, where her real worry was not so much the butlers as the cook, Deirdre Kavanagh, ex girlfriend of her oldest stepson Jonathan, a mad and dreadful girl with a talent for puff pastry and a conviction that she was a femme fatale, a conviction alas supported by her authentic Irish beauty and her seductive Irish brogue. Deirdre was not her real name, but her billowing copper red hair was real enough, and so was her solid even dun-cream skin and her lavishly presented bosom. She was somewhere in her thirties; Jonathan had been nineteen when she seduced him. They would never, as a family, be rid of her now, for she had now fallen in love with Liz and moped sadly and dangerously when excluded from Harley Street for too long. Now she stood there, one hand on her hip, the other holding a knife dramatically poised over an oblong platter of an anchovy-and-pepper-covered layered confection, watched by an admiring audience of Mediterraneans. She was wearing a low-cut green silk dress, partially covered by a charming little white broderie anglaise nonsense of an apron, the sort of apron that features in blue movies. Really, thought Liz, really. Deirdre was exactly the kind of neurotic that she did her best, professionally, to avoid—narcissistic, exhibitionistic, selfish, manipulative, childish, unreliable, unpunctual, self-satisfied even in the depths of self-reproach, and yet there she somehow managed to stand, in the middle of Liz's own kitchen, brandishing a pie knife. She had not yet noticed Liz's arrival. "One, two, *three*," said Deirdre, and the knife descended. The inner layers were perfect. One white, one green, one red. "Now look at that now," exclaimed Deirdre triumphantly, "now look at that, isn't it a darling?" The audience nodded, and Liz from the doorway nodded, for she had to admit that for the moment at least everything looked under control: pretty parsley-sprigged snacks awaited distribution, bottles of wine stood in attentive ranks, glasses were lined up, dusted, and polished, piles of white napkins lay neatly folded in readiness. Deirdre had a sprig of parsley tucked jauntily behind one ear. Her real name was Nora Molloy. She had confided this to Liz in a tearful moment, not long after Jonathan had run off with the Williams girl. Now, seeing Liz on the threshold, she waved her knife in greeting. "So there you are, Liz darling," she cried, "and a Happy New Year to you, and I'll be telling you something about 1980, you mark my words, you mark my words, all of you—broccoli will go out of fashion, that's what will happen in 1980, and no mistaking!"

And she proceeded to press upon Liz various samples of her skill, but Liz was unable to eat, nervous, wishing that it would all begin, that the curtain would rise, that the house would fill and the thick conversation rise like smoke through the thin, empty air.

When she returned to the drawing room, she found that Charles, Alix, and Esther were discussing, with much animation, the Italian economy. They did not pause on her arrival, though Alix, ever polite, waved obliquely to welcome her back; watching them, it occurred to Liz that perhaps in all the years they had known one another, this was one of the very few occasions on which they had all been in the same room. She,

Esther, and Alix had known one another since their Cambridge days, and often met, but an evening with them necessarily excluded Charles; Esther and Alix did not much care for the world that Charles represented, and his presence inhibited all three of them. Did they despise Charles's world? She did not know. But suspected that they enjoyed their glimpses of it, on occasions such as this. A male world, a world of suits and ties and speeches, of meetings and money. Charles had conquered it. First he had mocked it, then he had exposed it, then he had joined it, and now he represented it. A normal progression. Whereas Esther, intellectually more gifted than Charles, chose to live in a small flat just off the bad end of Ladbroke Grove, earning a pittance from odd lectures, odd articles, a little teaching. Perversity, purity, cowardice, dedication—no, none of these. There she sat, in her familiar party outfit, an eccentric, much-worn, embroidered Chinese garment, her neat, solidly cut, smartly sloping black hair as tidy as a doll's, looking perhaps faintly Chinese rather than Jewish, diminutive as she was, and with those high cheekbones; and there sat Alix, also by Charles's standards impoverished, though not by her own, which were more austere. Alix was wearing a deep bright blue Indian dress with smocking. She looked exceptionally well, glowing with health, almost as though she had been on holiday, which Liz knew she had not. Liz wondered if Brian would come later.

None of us, thought Liz, is wearing a dress made in England. Moroccan, Chinese, Indian. I wonder what that means, thought Liz. It was the kind of thought that Alix might have been more likely to articulate. She quite often found herself thinking Alix's thoughts. Esther's more rarely.

And Esther, now, suddenly tired of the Italian economy, dismissed it and Charles ("You don't seem to realize, Charles, that I live below the reach of the economy, as an economic unit I simply don't exist"), and peremptorily turned on Liz, demanding to know details of the guest list. Esther's mind moved quickly, apparently at random; she had a habit of introducing subjects and growing bored, within minutes, of the interchanges she had herself provoked. Abruptness was her most familiar mode, and Liz sometimes fancied that she practised it with peculiar pleasure on Charles, whenever she got the chance; and Charles, accustomed to being listened to with reverence, took it in good part. Though now, as Liz recited names of guests, she saw Charles drift away into what she took to be some private realm of financial speculation and morose managerial debate; he started to bite the inside of his lip, as he did when preoccupied, and to drum his fingers on the silvery yellow brocade of the settee. These tics, these traits, had become more pronounced since he had given up smoking. Was it a freak of physiognomy that even in such off-moments he looked so pugnacious, so determined? The square set of his British jaw was hardly disturbed by the neurotic chewing. A gift from nature, such a countenance. It expressed resolution. She could not read it; what was he turning over in there, on the eve of their party? The social life of New York? The restrictions on independent broadcasting? The possibilities of cable television? Or whether or not to have another gin and tonic? Who could tell? The faces of Esther and Alix were mobile, expressive, changeable; they were open to the weather, responsive, at least superficially, even if their darker motives remained obscure. Her own face was also open, she fancied. They had no public faces, the three of them, no public talk. So she fancied.

Impossible to tell, however, despite this openness, what Alix and Esther really made of Charles. They teased him, tolerated him, avoided him. Women were easily captivated by Charles, when he bothered to make any effort to captivate: they humbly smiled when he turned his head to pay them attention. But not Esther and Alix. They were impervious both to his charm and to his aggression: they had neutralized him. And so he sat there, a tame lion, drumming his fingers, while Esther and Alix and Liz his wife chattered on, about scandals and liaisons, about breaking marriages and delinquent children, about Ivan the terrible, about the Post-Impressionist exhibition at the Royal Academy, about the Arts Council, about the Beaubourg, about modernism in architecture, about Brian Bowen's views on his reactionary boss at the Adult Education Institute, about what the word quango might be said to mean (does it stand perhaps for Quasi Governmental Non-Governmental Organization?), about Kate Armstrong's latest article on the single-parent family and child benefits: chatter, chatter, female chatter, unstructured, shimmering, malicious, appreciative, acute, indulgent, shifting, rapid, unpunctuated, glancing, a light bright surface ripple on a deeper current, and Charles sat on, biting his inner lip. "You don't mean to say that this chap Edward Lazenby we keep reading about and hearing on the radio is the same chap as that

persistent creep Teddy who used to edit *Focus* when we were
at Cambridge?'' Esther was saying, returning to the guest list,
recalling scores not settled a quarter of a century ago. ''Yes,
the very man, he's a something or other in the DES, he's a
very important chap now, you ought to have a go at him,''
Liz replied, and as she spoke the doorbell rang, and there was
the first guest, on the dot of two minutes past nine o'clock,
tall, thin, grey, anxious, clutching a bunch of yellow roses,
ex-priest turned analyst Joseph O'Toole, standing stranded on
the black and white marble tiles, not knowing where to turn,
how to divest himself of his coat, to whom to deliver his
roses, a lost man, gazing mildly at the unexpected butler,
waiting for the arrival of familiar Liz Headland, who
advanced upon him, took the roses, embraced him, restored
him, and led him in to Charles, Alix, and Esther; a quarter of
an hour earlier she had predicted the time of his arrival
accurately, to the minute, and now smiled triumphantly as she
effected the introductions, a smile of complicity in which
Joseph O'Toole, who was acutely aware of his own
punctuality problem, was able with a pleasant relief to share.
Here he was, safely: the party could begin.

By half past ten, Deirdre (Molloy) Kavanagh had parted with
all her little triangles of tricoloured pastry, taken off her
apron, drunk a few glasses of champagne, told several guests
that broccoli was out of fashion, and was busily engaged in
conversation with a television journalist who had just returned
from making a programme for Charles in Iran. He was telling
her about the Ayatollah, and she was telling him about her
convent days. Their words fluttered between them like
lubricious little doves. At Deirdre's elbow stood the faithless
Jonathan Headland, who was trying to explain to his
stepmother's first husband, Edgar, why he'd decided, after all
his protests, to follow in his father's footsteps, while
simultaneously trying to keep one eye on Deirdre (for whom
he felt responsible) and the other on his girlfriend, Kate
Williams, who was being harangued by a Tory backbencher
about Marxist infiltration of the Open University. The Open
University was also the subject of debate between Alix Bowen
and Teddy Lazenby of the Department of Education and
Science; Alix's face was expressing a most delicate mixture of

disbelief, disapprobation, and polite attention as Teddy, somewhat indiscreetly presuming on their long, if long-interrupted, acquaintance, revealed what were clearly his own opinions on the inadvisability of wasting money on the education of housewives and taxi drivers. In other corners and other rooms, dozens of other topics floated gaily on the lively, slightly choppy waters, their pennants bobbing and fluttering in the end-of-year, the terminal breeze: the approaching steel strike, the brave new era of threatened privatization, the abuse of North Sea oil resources, the situation in Afghanistan, the Annan report, the prospect of a fourth television channel, the viability of Charles's attempt to conquer the United States, the Cambridge Apostles, the disarray of the Labour party, the deplorable vogue for Buck's Fizz as a party drink, the Yorkshire Ripper, the Harrow Road murderer, the Prince of Wales. In a doorway, wedged between a *Guardian* leader writer and a Kleinian analyst, Alan Headleand and his ex-tutor Otto Werner from the LSE were debating with a fine abstraction and a noble disregard of interruption the question as to whether or not a television programme was a primary product or a service, and whether, by implication or extension, Charles's production company, Global Information Network (Telex GIN), was allied in ideological terms with the manufacturing or the service industry; with equal commitment Esther Breuer and Jules Griffin (colleague of Liz Headleand) were discussing the nature of ancestral voices in schizophrenic patients and in the Homeric and Biblical epic, and the portrayal of the Holy Ghost in Anglo-Saxon manuscripts.

Liz, moving from group to group, surveying from the stairway, engaging and disengaging, tacking and occasionally swooping, was pleased with what she saw. They were mixing and mingling, her guests; the young were speaking to the old, men were speaking to women, left was speaking to right, art unto science, and only a few impossible old dullards of the financial world had drifted together to talk about pay comparability and public sector borrowing and the GNP. She left them to it: interventionist though she was, she knew the limits of her power. Nothing would stop them, nothing would prise them apart, and she was glad to have them there: she liked to think that she and Charles had a comprehensive acquaintance, that in one house they could assemble representatives of most of the intersecting circles that make up society. One needed a little dullness to set off the buoyancy, the festivity, the movement.

And there, at last, was Alix's husband, Brian; she was glad he had turned up, had not spurned her party, had paid her this respect. Brian came from her own home town, though she had not known him there; this had some significance, both acknowledged, though Liz could not have said what it was. Brian did not like parties, according to Alix, and had expressed fears that he would know nobody at the Headleands', but this was not so, for he had already engaged himself with his habitual courtesy with old Sir Anthony. She saw him as he listened attentively to Sir Anthony; she caught his eye, waved at him across the sea of heads, abandoned him to the tide. He was an old friend of Otto Werner's, whom he could seek out if in need of relief. The tide was flowing to the right, according to Charles; could one feel, here, now, its tug, its undertow? She paused, wondered. Brian was a gentleman of the left; what of this new breed of non-gentlemen of the right? She moved on, overhearing talk of broccoli, of death in Kabul, of the phenomenal transatlantic success of Pett Petrie's new novel, and there was Petrie himself, talking to that little monster Ivan about his meeting with Norman Mailer, whooping with laughter, and hitting his own bald head with emphatic glee. There was Charles, talking to the new proprietor of the *Informer* (plotting no doubt), and there was her daughter Sally, arm in arm with Nat Higsby from the Tavistock; they seemed to be singing a duet. There was Roy Strangeways, who was now, implausibly, surely prematurely, a High Court judge, talking to—no, it couldn't be, but it was. Liz fell silent in mid-word of a vague murmured greeting to stare. Yes, it was, how extraordinary, it was her own ex-patient Hilda Stark, diseuse, comedienne, and would-be infanticide, whose career had been violently interrupted when in a fit of madness (in put it non-technically) she had nearly strangled her baby in its cradle, and here she was, laughing and drinking champagne, a guest. How improper, how indiscreet; was she married to somebody, had she come as somebody's *wife*? How brave of her, how bold of her, was she perhaps even now reciting to Roy the interesting medical and legal details of her case? There she stood, in a dove grey suede dress, looped and hung with a dozen necklaces of amethyst and rock crystal and pearl, her thick black-grey hair piled heavily, pinned with silver, attending a party in the very house where as patient she once in many hour-long sessions had disclosed to

Liz on the ground floor the very secrets of her murderous mother's heart? How could she have come here, who could have brought her, and would Roy feel compelled to divulge his and Liz's own smaller, milder secrets in return? Should she intervene, should she break them up, or should she ignore her uninvited guest, pretend, professionally, never to have set eyes on her before? As she considered this, Hilda intercepted her gaze, saluted her, and majestically, graciously, demonstratively, voluptuously blew a kiss across the room; Liz waved back, less flamboyantly but with equal composure, for what did it matter, after all, that Hilda Stark was there, was it not a tribute to them both, to the efficacy of the cure? Hilda brought no shadows with her, she smiled innocently in her dove grey; the scandalous rumours had been, as Liz had predicted, forgotten. It was a credit to them all. And the nearly murdered baby, how was it, where was it, Liz wondered, and found herself involuntarily doing a head count of her own stepchildren and children: she could see Jonathan, Alan, and Sally; her younger daughter, Stella, was away in Florence studying Italian, for her A levels, and staying safely and respectably as paying guest with art-historical friends of Esther's; but where was her middle stepson, Aaron? She had not seen him for an hour or more; he had been here earlier, had he left in a fit of boredom, was he sulking in his bedroom, she asked herself, and on cue, he appeared, at the bend of the hall stairs, beneath the fake ancestor, waving down and shouting at her: "Liz, Liz," he called, "it's the telephone, it's Stella, she wants to wish you a Happy New Year, she's on the upstairs line."

The energy imparted from running upstairs and laughing with Stella in distant Florence flowed over into the impulse to ring, in turn, her own mother—a pointless act, but one that nevertheless in the context seemed pious, necessary, propitiatory, and a gesture at least towards her sister, who bore so much heavier a filial burden, who would (in theory at least) be pleased to know that Liz had remembered. When Liz came downstairs again to her party, after a ritual exchange (how could her sister bear such intercourse? how could it go on?), she found that she had lost her velocity. The brisk social wind that had driven her lightly from guest to guest had dropped, stilled by telephonic contact with the tiny scratching clicking

silence of the voiceless house of the long ordeal of her
childhood; she found herself becalmed, for a whole dull
stretch, talking to old Peter Binns, a charming old boy, but a
bore, and so slow of speech that Liz could hardly restrain
herself from finishing all his ponderous sentences. When she
finally shook herself away, she found herself sailing into yet
more stagnant waters, for there, directly in her way, unavoidable, smiling passively, uncomfortably, yet unavoidably, was
Lady Henrietta, dutifully offering herself for an exchange with
her hostess. Lady Henrietta knew what was right: everything
about her was right, from her tightly bound dark hair to her
dark blue satin slippers. The sight of her filled Liz with a
subdued and dreary panic. Henrietta (Hetty to her friends, of
whom Liz was not one) embarrassed her, she could never say
why. She represented pain, failure, tedium, though not in her
own person: somehow, magically, she managed to transfer
these attributes to those with whom she conversed, while
herself remaining poised and indeed complacent, secure of
admiration. Liz had never admired, and had at times expressed
somewhat freely (and in her own view wittily), her lack of
response to Henrietta's frigid style and vapid conversation, but
nevertheless felt herself, in Henrietta's presence, rendered
almost as dull as Henrietta, and moreover uneasily aware that
in other houses, in other milieus, at a distance, in other circles,
she had seen Henrietta sparkling, laughing, surrounded by
life—vacuous life, feverish small talk, no doubt—but life, a
life that froze in Liz as she contemplated her guest's stiff blue
taffeta gown (this was surely a gown, not a dress, and, worse
than English, probably French), her exposed white bosom, her
diamond necklace (well, probably diamonds, why not?), her
high white forehead, her thin dark red lips. Henrietta's brow
was high, and her hair was scraped back from it and secured by
an intricate velvet ribbon in a smooth, elaborate chignon, a
Bambi head, a skull head, a too, too thin head, an over-bred
head, a painful head. Liz's own forehead was villainously low,
coarsely low. She did not know how to address Henrietta, she
felt the fault her own, she knew herself to be disadvantaged. A
chill, heavy waste of water lay between them, and in it floated
the drowned empty skins of past attempts at rapport. Across
this, the neat Henrietta politely presented a hand and a cheek.
Cheek brushed against cheek. Each muttered some conventional phrase. It appeared that more was required and Liz,
resenting the inanity thus forced upon her even as it passed her

lips, found herself saying, "And how are you looking forward to the 1980s?"

"Oh, yes," said Henrietta, smiling meaninglessly, confirming Liz's view that she never listened to a word that Liz said to her. Silence fell, during which Liz inspected Henrietta's blue dress: it was poutily, boldly cut, made of the kind of shot, stiff, shiny non-absorbent kind of fabric that Liz herself avoided, for it made her sweat; indeed it made her sweat to look at it. She was given to sweat; Henrietta, clearly, not. Perhaps the upper classes did not sweat? She was herself, biologically, a peasant, but was rarely made to feel this to be an eccentricity as she now felt. Gazing at the blue fabric, she noted that Ivan, ever present when least wanted, was intently watching this less than interesting encounter from a position just behind and below Henrietta's left shoulder. His frankly delighted countenance spurred her on to effort: "I myself," she heard herself saying, "am very much looking forward to going to Japan for the first time. Have you ever been to Japan?"

"No," said Lady Henrietta, unhelpfully. Ivan laughed.

"I am attending," continued Liz, "a conference."

"Really?" said Lady Henrietta. "How long do you go for?"

This seemingly innocuous question acted upon Liz with the effect of an instant anaesthetic: as she began to answer, she could feel her jaw growing rigid in mid-word. "Two weeks," she managed to articulate, and then stood there, mouth clamped, feet rooted, as though turned to a pillar of salt, as though the deep deep boredom of childhood had reclaimed her, had rendered her helpless and speechless and powerless, the child in the attic, playing for time to pass and blood to flow. Which, of course, momentarily, it did. "Two weeks," she boldly and brightly continued, breaking the trance-like stillness with a frisky movement of her head and braceleted right arm, "yes, two weeks, in Kyoto and Osaka, it should be quite fascinating, quite an opportunity to see a completely different culture; of course it relates to our own work at the Institute in a very particular way, it seems that there has been a considerable amount of research done in the department we are visiting on the problems of adoption and stepparents. . . ." And on she prattled, watching with some satisfaction the slight tightening professional impatience of Lady Henrietta's lip and the altering glaze of her china blue eyes. Honour was satisfied, the courtesies had been observed, they could smile and part. Though I really cannot imagine, thought Liz, as she turned away, rubbing her hands together as though the cold had truly bitten her, as though the Ice Queen had truly touched her, why we continue to ask her round. Is it just because everyone else does, because she is the kind of person that people ask to parties, because her name inscribes itself by automatic writing on guest lists? Are Charles and I really so susceptible to propriety, to the conventional? Do we like to have people with titles at our parties? What on earth *is* her title? Who *is* she? What a mystery it is, the way we carry on, thought Liz, as she moved on to more congenial entertainment: remembering, suddenly, the oft-repeated claim of an Austrian refugee analyst of her acquaintance, who frequently and unashamedly rejoiced in having had in his house at one time no less than five Nobel Prize winners—a claim which she had always found endearing, ridiculous, foolish, alarming, comic, in its naïveté, its precision, its ruthlessness—remembering the alarms and excitements of her own early encounters with the famous, the great, the titled, the rich; remembering the ancient yearning to crowd her life with people, with voices, with telephone calls, invitations, children, friends of children; remembering, in short, the dread of solitude, the dread of reliving her mother's unending, inexplicable, still-enduring loneliness. And across these memories, flitting in a half-second, as she made her way, for light relief, towards Kate Armstrong, fortifying Kate, came the question—why did Henrietta Latchett, who must have been invited to a hundred parties tonight, who could never have known a lonely evening, why did she choose to come to *us*? Liz smiled to herself, triumphant, and ploughed on towards Kate.

Conventional, unconventional: in the last half hour of 1979 several of Liz and Charles Headleand's guests attempted to formulate what, for them, had seemed to be the conventions of an eclectic, fragmented, purposeless decade; some attempted to prophesy for the next. The house was full of trend spotters, from gossip columnist Ivan Warner and irritable feminist Kate Armstrong to Treasury adviser Philip, worried about pension projections in an increasingly elderly society; from information vendor Charles Headleand to epidemiologist Ted Stennett, across whose horizon the science fiction disease of AIDS was already casting a faint red ominous glow; from forensic psychiatrist Edgar Lintot (who had not yet heard of AIDS, but who had heard rumours about changing views in high places on the sentencing of the criminally insane) to Alix Bowen, worried on a mundane level about the future funding of her own job and on a less selfish level about the implications for the rehabilitation of female offenders of cuts in that funding; from theatre director Alison Peacock, anxious about her Arts Council subsidy, to Representative Public Figure Sir Anthony Bland, the aptly named Chairman (or so Ivan alleged) of the Royal Commission on Royal Commissions, who was thinking that for various reasons he might have to resign, and from more bodies than one, before the jostling and the hinting pushed him into an undignified retreat.

Not all were anxious, apprehensive, ill at ease. Many congratulated themselves on having found a new sense of purpose, a new realism; after years of drifting, of idle ebb and flow, there seemed to be a current. Tentatively, some dipped their toes to test the water. Others had already leaped boldly in the expectation that others would follow, that it would prove wise to have been seen to take the plunge first. Old opinions were shed, stuffy woolly shabby old liberal vests and comforters were left piled on the shore. Some shivered in the cold breeze of change; others struck out boldly, with a sense of freedom, glad to be unencumbered by out-of-date gear and padding, glad to cast off notions that had never seemed to themselves to be smart or necessary: naked into the stream, exhilarated, the new emerging race. Cutting, paring, slimming, reducing, rationalizing: out swam the slim hard new streamlined man, in the emperor's new clothes, out of the gritty carapace, the muddy camouflaged swoon, casting off the old ways, the old crawling, sinking ways. The conventions were changing, assumptions were changing, though not everybody was to enjoy or to survive the metamorphosis, the plunge, the leap into water or air; change is painful, transition is painful, and the social world had not yet reached a stage which could have greeted as conventional, precisely, even at a much-mixed, smart, bohemian-flavoured cosmopolitan New Year's Eve party, the excessively raised voices of two journalist-historians, once friends and allies and fellow contributors to the current of immortal truth and to the *New Statesman*, now locked in bitter dispute about that ghastly, trailing, decaying albatross-corpse of the left, Public Ownership and Clause 4. "You squint-eyed git, you treacherous, turncoat, lying, statistic-faking git," shouted Giles, the man of the left, who appeared to be losing the argument, his voice rising above the more amiable party hubbub in a shriek of despair, a shriek that summoned to his side Liz Headleand, with Kate Armstrong and Ivan Warner in quick attendance. Giles's straw-yellow hair was fierce above his veined brick-red face, his grey eyes glittered with truculent frustrated aggression, the rage of a thousand ideologically committed drinking sessions in dirty pubs surged in his weeping Camden Lock–shirted chest. "Giles, Giles," cried Liz, "don't shout so, it's nearly the New Year, we can't bring in the New Year howling like *wolves*." "Giles, Giles," echoed Kate, throwing restraining arms around him. "Wolves!" shouted Giles drunkenly, "wolves, that's what they are, the pack of them, they're traitors to the human race, scavengers, look at them, look at them, wolves is too good a word for them, jackals, hyenas, that's what they are, hyenas!"

"Oh, don't be ridiculous, Giles, calm down, calm down, come and have a nice Perrier water," said Liz, taking his other arm, and, with Kate, attempting to lead him away from the fracas, as one would a child in a playground from its tormentor (for Giles's antagonist, Paul Hargreaves, pale faced, dark suited, silver-grey tied, was smiling calmly with a horrible amusement at this distressing scene); but the desperate Giles was beyond leading, and fell back heavily as he attempted to disengage himself from his two intercessors, crashing into a large fern and some pots of bulbs and sending earth and splashes of champagne over the carpet.

"There go the 1970s," commented Hargreaves, "there go the drinking seventies," a comment which earned him a slap in the eye from Giles's girlfriend Venetia. "Drunkard yourself!" she shouted, "drunkard yourself!"—whereupon Hargreaves threw his arms around Venetia and kissed her violently, pausing for breath only to make some comment about Public Ownership, as Giles sprawled upon the floor. Ivan Warner was delighted. He looked as though he had stage-managed the whole incident. Liz Headleand stared at the scene with a marked lack of dismay, as Kate Armstrong knelt down and started to dust the earth off Giles, looking up to ask anyone who might be interested about the little blobs of white polystyrene that always seem to come mixed with bulb fibre: "What *is* this stuff," asked Kate, "I've often wondered," as she proceeded to repot a hyacinth with one hand while stroking

Giles's shoulder with the other. Giles's girlfriend Venetia, meanwhile, encircled by the arms of Hargreaves, had started to laugh, and Giles began to laugh too. "Oh Christ, sorry, Liz, sorry, Kate," he declared, as he organized himself into a sitting position, his arms around his knees, "I should never have had those two whiskies at the Venables'."

"Breathe deeply," said Liz, "breathe deeply and relax, and I'll get you a Perrier to drink in the New Year."

"Calm down, calm down, Giles," said Hargreaves. "Calm down, young chap."

"Now you keep *out* of this," said Liz and Venetia simultaneously to Hargreaves, while, in another corner of the room, Deirdre Molloy lifted her voice in an Irish lament.

"Mother, it's ten to midnight!" called Sally from the doorway, and Liz, looking around the confusion she had summoned into being, the scattered earth, the scattered people, the murmuring, the singing, the clustering, thought, yes, this was a party, yes, this was living rather than not living, this was permitted, this was planned disorder, this was cathartic, this was therapeutic, this was admired misrule.

"Piano, Aaron, piano!" she called, and her middle stepson, with his mobile thin white clown's face, emerged from the crowd and seated himself at the instrument, as Liz called to Deirdre and the butlers to fill glasses and then join the guests for a toast. Jonathan turned on the radio, the eagle-crowned clock over the marble mantel shelf struck, some joined hands and some did not, Aaron struck up "Auld Lang Syne," Big Ben struck, some sang and some did not, voices rose straggling, pure and impure, strong and weak, tuneful and tuneless, there were cries and embraces. Two hundred people, solitude and self dispelled; Liz, at the magic moment, found herself unexpectedly clutching the hot hand of Ivan Warner, which seemed wrong but ordained. She looked for Charles, and saw that the poor man had managed to find himself in the icy palm of Lady Henrietta. Such were the random dispositions of fate. But Alix and Brian had found one another, and so had Otto and Caroline Werner; Esther was caught between lofty Edgar and little Pett Petrie, herself the smallest of all. Should old acquaintance be forgot, they sang, bravely, recklessly, tunelessly, and as the singing stopped, Ivan kissed Liz's hand. "Liz," he said, "Liz, I've always admired your style, but this was something else."

She took it, for the moment, as a tribute, beneath the chandelier.

Beneath the chandelier. From it fell refracted light, on balding heads and shaven heads, on Mohican plumes and Gelloed spikes, on neatly barbered and dressed locks, on neglected middle-aged wispy bobs, on plaits and loops and layered body waves. The plural, the eclectic seventies. Dark suits, pale blue suits, Indian kurtahs worn not exclusively by Indians, Viyella shirts, striped mother-knitted pullovers, designer-monogrammed pullovers; cheap ethnic dresses, expensive ethnic dresses, long skirts, short skirts, exclusive French dresses, hand-stitched English dresses, Oxfam thirties dresses, prim high mandarin collars, plunging necklines, slit skirts, glimpses of suspender belt, clown pantaloons, dungarees, studded belts, limp leather belts, crackling metal belts, belts slung round waists, hips, bellies. Disparate, disparate, a hundred opinions, a hundred cross-currents, in this blonde Georgian drawing room: ancestral echoes of ancient Victorian philanthropy of the Clapham school mingled with *louche* ghosts of Bloomsbury, public school public servants held hands with hybrid tieless entrepreneurs of the television aristocracy, new modes of moneyed brutality addressed old shrinking brutality, the educated sons (well, let us not exaggerate, one educated son) of one skilled manual worker maintained an exchange with one exhausted feudal North-umbrian homosexual neurosurgeon, and the accents of North London raised themselves melodiously, classlessly, in-comprehensibly, from the throats of the variously reared young, from the singing birds of the future, in their indeterminate, as yet unidentifiable plumage. There they gathered, the employee who lacks employment, the faithless priest, the investor about to hang himself in the expectation of plenty, the physician who will not be able to heal herself, the director who lacks all direction, the historian who denies the existence of history, the Jewish scholar of early Renaissance Christian iconography, the deaf man who hears voices, the woman about to be taken in adultery. A mingling, of a sort, in this exclusive, this eclectic room, this room full of riddles.

* * *

"I don't believe it," said Sally to Alan ten minutes after midnight in the kitchen, amidst the empty bottles and the crumpled napkins. "How could they? I don't believe it."

"Don't ask me," said Alan, and bravely, coolly drank a glass of water from the tap. "I've never known what they were up to. And anyway, it's nothing to do with us. Not now."

"No, I don't suppose it is."

But panic filled Sally's twenty-year-old heart, for it was, she thought, something to do with her. Now, and always.

Aaron sat on the roof and stared at the sky. Five floors up. The London skyline, the Post Office Tower, the sounds of distant merriment. He lit a cigarette. He had seen what he should not have seen. He was sitting, moreover, where he had often been told not to sit. As children, they had not been allowed on the roof. And were not now. Aaron brooded. He had been in the habit of brooding, up here, as a child. It had frightened Liz. Understandably. He remembered when she once had to beg him to come down. He could see her now, in the room below, under the skylight, gazing up. Imploring. Sweetie, come down, she had begged ridiculously. He had felt power in her distress. He had backed away, had stood perilously on the parapet. Her face had been distorted, ugly, foreshortened, all teeth and mouth. He had been frightened of himself, of her, of the height, of the sky, of the necessity of daring.

He had brooded over his dead mother. Jonathan and Alan never mentioned her. He had meditated upon her, up here. He could not remember her, of course.

The London streets stretched away. As a small child, he had been taken to see *Peter Pan*. The old-fashioned backdrop painted with its winking windows had been remarkably similar to this view, his view. He had thought he could fly, if he willed it enough.

Sweet Hamlet, cast this nighted colour off,
And let thine eye look like a friend on Denmark.

"Sweetie, please come down. Come down and we'll all have supper. It's on the table. It's going cold. Come down, sweetie."

Poor Liz. He had teased her. The others would not: they were good, compliant. Somebody had to tease, to sit on dangerous edges, to affect melancholia.

The dark night surrounded him. He had seen what he should not have seen. But would not speak. Therefore, having played the piano for the people, he sat in the dark.

In the early hours, in the first hours of 1980, gossip spread. Some did not want to listen. Alix, who had no idea of what the gossip was to be about, but who could sense its ominous crackling in the distance, wanted to go home, but tiresomely Brian, the party hater, had managed to find his old friend Otto Werner and was deep in conversation about English social class, European intellectuals, the German education system, public schools, and the appointing of JPs and magistrates, a rich vein which they might have been able to explore for another hour at least, had Alix not been at their elbow, murmuring of departure. In other circumstances she would have been more than willing to engage in this conversation herself, for it was one she had frequently enjoyed; she liked Otto, she had always mildly fancied that he liked her, she was amused by the offhand continental gallantries with which he interspersed, absent-mindedly, the rigour of his argument. But tonight she was tired, her eyes were closing, she had had four hours of party already, had not enjoyed the Hargreaven drama, had not enjoyed her talks with Ivan Warner and Teddy Lazenby, had been polite enough for long enough, and wanted to go home; so stood at Brian's elbow, dully, a reproachful wife, slightly annoyed that neither of them took much notice of her, as Otto invoked the name of Max Weber, a name which meant nothing to her at all, a name which excluded her, exhausted her, and provoked her into prodding, yet again, but this time successfully, Brian's arm, and murmuring of baby sitter Sharon, who was only sixteen.

Esther also left not long after midnight. Esther knew what she knew, had seen what she had seen, but like Aaron chose to say nothing. She rather thought that Charles knew what she knew, and it was this suspicion that prompted what was, for her, an early departure. She had planned to walk home, but accepted, on the front steps, an offer of a lift from Teddy Lazenby and his wife, Delia, who lived in Camden Square and could easily drop her off. Esther had not seen either of them since her days at Cambridge, and listened with a connoisseur's ear to Delia's laments about time passing, times changing, the difficulties of keeping in touch. Esther, who had always been deeply bored by Delia and had no wish whatsoever to keep in touch with her, sat quietly in the smooth, upholstered, comfortable, large toffee-brown Volvo, which smelled of dog. She said nothing, except to give directions. She got home quickly, smoothly, easily, said good night politely, and went in and firmly shut the door.

In their wake, the party in Harley Street continued and rumours thickened. Looking back, Liz would try to remember the moment at which she had known rather than not known; she would have liked to think that she had known always, that there was no moment of shock, that knowledge had lain within her (the all-knowing), that she had never truly been deceived, that at the very worst she had connived at her own deceit. Surely Ivan's first sentence of the New Year had alerted her? (Though that would have been late, late, late.) Surely she had taken it as an ill omen? But no, she had taken it at its face value—from Ivan, of all people, who spread malice as his trade. She had thought herself exempt. Slow she had been, unbearably slow, she who could hear many strands of speech at once; trusting she had been, she who had been reared in the bosom of suspicion. She had thought herself invulnerable. She had been possessed by pride.

Hints, glances, sliding words, oblique smiles, incomprehensible references. Why had she not received them earlier? Had she been too preoccupied with butlers, with introductions, with orchestration, with champagne? Or had the guests waited until midnight, the witching hour, before turning into swine? Pig-faced, snub-nosed, bristling broad-jowled Ivan, snouting disaster. That ominous expression of sympathy from pebble-glassed Jules, who took her hand and asked her meaningfully how she was? Esther's strange allusion to a hornet's nest? That look of frank dislike and satisfaction from Antonia Haycock? Hilda Stark's excessively theatrical departing conspiratorial embrace? That odd, bitter, comradely crack about men from Kate Armstrong? That glance of panic from her daughter

Sally? All these messages had been sent forth, and she had received none of them, had continued to consider herself in charge, in control, the prime mover. Until, under the mirror, after many a circle and feint, after many a playful retreat and renewed approach, Ivan at last cornered her, and even before he opened his mouth she felt the smell of fear from herself: her pores broke open, she stood there panting slightly, her hair rising on the back of her neck in terror, her heated skin covered in icy sweat. "And when," asked Ivan pleasantly, "are you two going to make the announcement? Is it to be tonight, or do we wait?"

The words meant nothing, or should have meant nothing. She smiled, foolishly. Her mind leaped. It ran, it leaped, it scrambled for cover. It turned.

"And why not tonight?" she said.

"You've kept your *own* plans very dark," said Ivan.

"Ah well, you know me," she said, knowing nothing.

"I can't say I'm surprised," said Ivan. "I think you two stuck it out pretty well, in the circumstances. How long has it been? Twenty years?"

The utterly expected, the utterly unexpected, can they be the same thing? she wondered.

"*Your* name," Ivan continued, "has been linked with Gabriel Denham's, but I don't even see him here tonight."

She stood there; he stared at her. She could say nothing. A pillar of salt. She was dependent on him. She could not move until he released her.

"Whereas Henrietta, I see," Ivan continued with a remorseless pity, "is very much at home here."

"Henrietta?" Liz echoed. It was the moment she was most to regret. It betrayed ignorance. Only a second's ignorance, but ignorance. Had Ivan noticed? Desperate, she found again the faculty of speech, heard her own voice, familiar, natural, even powerful: "Ah yes, Henrietta. Yes, we see a good deal of Henrietta." She had no notion of what her words meant, but they sounded good, they fortified her, and she continued bravely, "But as for Gabriel, whose name has *not* been linked with Gabriel's? I think you must find a more interesting candidate than Gabriel. What about, for example"—and she cast her eyes around her assembly, seeing reprieve, in the approaching form of Edgar Lintot, her first husband—"what about Edgar? Now that *would* be an interesting plot, for us at least. I see a great deal of Edgar these days, you know. We often lunch together. Well''—and the plausibility of her own tone, at the moment, amazed her—"sometimes."

"What's all this?" said tall, beaky, dedicated Edgar. "Gossip, is it? I've come to say good night, Lizzie. I've got a long drive tomorrow. Very nice party, very nice. See you at the meeting."

"Yes, gossip," said Ivan tenaciously. "We were talking about Charles and Henrietta. I wonder what New York will make of Henrietta."

Edgar was not listening. Ivan did not interest him, gossip did not interest him, he had given up the personal life. He kissed Liz on the cheek. "I think it's on the thirtieth, isn't it? Have a good time with the Japanese tomorrow. Don't say I didn't warn you."

"Give my love to your mother," said Liz. She managed to edge herself out of her corner, away from Ivan, back into the current. She followed Edgar a few paces across the room. Ivan, behind her, was accosted by a fellow journalist. He wanted to retain her, to keep her, to tease her, to worry her, to kill her, but he could not; she escaped. Escaped to a comforting, numbing succession of thanks and farewells, for the party was beginning to break up. "Happy New Year," echoed again and again, as Liz searched vaguely for Charles but could not find him, Happy New Year, see you soon, goodbye, say goodbye to Charles for me, goodbye. And there, in a conspicuous lull, was Lady Henrietta herself, extending her hand and cheek. Seeing her, Liz saw it all. The certainty inspired her. She drew breath.

"And when," she asked politely, "do *you* go to New York?"

Henrietta looked back, with a frigid calm, beneath which lay a hesitation.

"Ah," she said. "Yes. I thought February."

"Yes," said Liz.

"Perhaps we could talk some time? May I ring you? We could have lunch?"

"Yes," said Liz. She had won, temporarily: she had managed to give the impression that she knew. Though what it was that she knew, she could not at that moment have said.

The two women kissed, again, and drew apart.

*　　*　　*

It was to be a long night. The hard core of party goers stayed on until the small hours, drinking coffee, sprawled on settees, sinking into morose abuse and gloom, surfacing occasionally to laugh, to chatter, relapsing, rising, sinking again. Joseph O'Toole (always among the last to leave any party) sat in a corner with Anthony Keating talking of God. Kate Armstrong came in with another tray of coffee. The young people had gone upstairs, to bed, or not to bed; strains of music drifted from the upper regions plaintively. Charles reappeared, after half an hour's absence, and threw himself into an armchair, where he lay back for some time with his eyes shut. Liz thought he looked appalling, and wondered why she hadn't noticed it before. Blotchy, middle-aged, fat. She was frightened of him. She had always been frightened of him. That was why she had fallen in love with him. He had power over her. And now he was going to divorce her and marry Lady Henrietta Latchett. She knew it all, now; she had divined it all. Too late for self-respect, but not too late to exact a little vengeance. No wonder he looked so crumpled. He was about to embark on a new life in New York with the most boring woman in Britain. And she, at her age, what was she to do? A terrible, drunken tiredness filled her and she too sat back and shut her eyes. The room turned, as it had done in the parties of her youth.

The sight of both host and hostess apparently sleeping rallied the laggards, eventually, and with apologies they began to stumble to their feet. Liz and Charles rose too. Little was said; it was too late. Only one interchange could Liz later remember: "A very good party, a better party than ever," said the recently felled historian Giles, now fully recovered, to which Liz heard herself reply, "Well, it's as well you made the most of it, for it will be the last."

The announcement was greeted with mute and grave acceptance by the departing guests. Cold air drifted in through the front door. Liz shivered. The door shut. She and Charles returned to the drawing room. They sat down. Ceremonially, as it were; to attention, as it were.

"I'm going to bed," said Charles, but did not move.

Liz stared at him. She could see that he was frightened of her. He looked lamentable, disadvantaged, weak. His eyes were bloodshot.

"You didn't dare to tell me," said Liz.

"I think we should get divorced," said Charles.

"Why didn't you tell me? Did you think I'd try to stop you? Did you think I'd plead with you to stay?"

"No," said Charles, dully. "It wasn't that. Not that at all. Anyway, I thought you knew."

"If you thought I knew, why didn't you tell me?"

He laughed, briefly.

"This was a very expensive charade," she said, pursuing her advantage. She was beginning to think she knew where she was. He nodded agreement, muttered that he thought a grand finale would be her kind of thing, better to wrap it up in style, he said, echoing Ivan. And then he suddenly said, in a more natural tone, in an everyday tone that she rarely heard from him these days, "And anyway, I thought it wouldn't matter to anyone, now the children are grown up."

"What?"

Patiently, he repeated, as though perhaps she had not heard: "I thought it wouldn't matter to anyone, now the children are grown up."

"What on earth has it got to do with the children?"

"Oh, well. You know. One wouldn't have wanted to split up the family."

This banal observation astounded her, though she did not know why. It seemed to come from another world of reference, an older, ordinary world, of platitude and cliché, of pattern and familiar family ties, a world that she had thought they had never entered, for many good reasons never entered; and now here was Charles himself, invoking its terms, as though it had been there always, as though they had always inhabited its domain.

"Do you mean to say," she ventured, disliking the silence, "that in your view we've only stuck it out together all these years because of the children? Because of the so-called children?"

Charles shrugged. "I don't know what I thought. I thought that was what you thought. I knew you'd rather have been off on your own, if it hadn't been for the children. You've been very good with the children, I wouldn't deny that. But I knew you were getting restless. Wanting to be off."

"Whatever made you think that?"

"You."

"Me?"

"You."

"*I* made you think that?"

"Yes, you," he said, patiently, irritably, still with that relentlessly everyday, normative tone, as though this whole discussion were the most ordinary event, the most expected of interchanges. "You're not going to start pretending you want to move to New York, are you? You've always made it quite clear that you were staying here and that I could fuck off to the other end of the world for all you cared. You're too busy to speak some days. You won't even notice I've gone."

He spoke without embarrassment.

"That's not quite fair," she said cautiously. "It's not as though you're not quite busy yourself. You haven't had much time for domestic life of late, have you? Or ever. Come to that."

"We're not a domestic couple. Though I must say, you did a good job with the boys. Considering the problems."

The elegiac note sounded ominously, unanswerably, offering calm and collusion; as if aware of the risks, Charles struck suddenly out, moving out into dangerous white water, tipping over the edge into a new reach.

"And anyway," said Charles, "then there was Henrietta."

"Ah," said Liz, feeling herself begin to glitter and crackle and spark, striking out herself, away from sadness and regret, "yes, of course, that's a point. There was Henrietta. *When* was there Henrietta? *When?* Tell me *when?* How long has all this been going on, behind my back?"

A new reach, but the words were banal here too. How could she be uttering them?

"I'm not telling you," he said, in a manner that later she condemned as sheepish.

"When? This month? This year? Last year? Go on, don't just sit there, tell me," she demanded, in a manner that later she condemned as shrewish.

He covered his eyes with his hand and moaned. "For God's sake, sweetie. Let's leave it till morning, shall we? I'm knackered. Let's leave it till morning."

But she heard herself saying, still in shrewish style, that on the contrary there wasn't any time in the morning, that she had to go to a psychoanalytical conference at the Metropole Hotel with a bunch of Japanese in the morning, that she wanted to talk now, that he couldn't just announce that he wanted to get divorced and then decide he was too tired to talk about it. On and on she heard herself ranting (could it be that she heard echoes of her own past self, the speaking, ranting, resurrected ghost of that ephemeral figure Liz Lintot) and heard his vague, evasive grunts and answers: yes, he said, he and Henrietta would marry as soon as possible, Henrietta wanted to go to New York with him, she'd had a thin time herself lately, he needed her in New York, Henrietta hadn't been well, needed to settle . . . And as Liz spoke and listened she was aware of a simultaneous conviction that this was the most shocking, the most painful hour of her entire life, and also that it was profoundly dull, profoundly trivial, profoundly irrelevant, a mere routine, devoid of truth, devoid of meaning: nothing.

"Honestly," Charles was saying, after more than an hour of beleaguered explanation, or semi-explanation, "I didn't think you'd take it like this, old thing, I thought you'd—well, I thought you'd be relieved, to tell you the truth. Relieved to be rid of me. You know me. Worthless kind of chap, in my own way. What did you expect? Good of you to put up with me so long. You'll have more scope on your own."

"You lying hypocrite," said Liz, exhausted, without rancour. "You feeble, contemptible, cowardly two-faced cheat."

"There, there," said Charles.

"I'll never forgive you," she heard herself say.

"Why not?" said Charles, with admirable, with deadly equanimity. "I've always forgiven you."

"Ah yes," she heard herself cry, "but then I never *went away*, did I? I stayed, I stayed with you. I never *went away*!" And suddenly, astonishingly, astonished, she began to weep, great sobs bursting out of her, tears leaping from her eyes, a kind of howling noise in her nose and throat, and Charles got up and came and sat by her and took her in his arms as she howled like a six-year-old. "There, there," he kept saying, until she lay calm against his shoulder, calm and sodden. "Come to bed," he said, and pulled her to her feet, and supported her up the stairs, past the paintings and the roses, and into her bedroom, where she lay motionless as he began to take off her sandals, her tights, her dress. He found her new white Christmas-present nightdress hanging on the back of the dressing-room door, and heaved her into it, then opened the bed, and pushed her between the sheets. He found a sleeping pill, a glass of water, and put them on the table by her side. Then he undressed and lay down beside her and took her in his arms. They had not slept in the same bed for nearly two years. "There, there," he said, soothingly, "hold on to me, hold on." She held on to him, because he was there, because he had been there. He was very solid. She held on to twenty years of him. Heavy, solid, smooth, adult. Safe. The man who had never been safe became, upon leaving her, safe to her. So it was. The death of danger. No harm to come, no more harm to come. Calm shore. He rocked her in his arms. They slept.

London nights. Aaron lay awake at the top of the house. He had overseen, foreseen, overheard. The night was still. The party was over. London, West One. He made himself levitate over the capital. Dark street. Would they have switched off the cold fountains in Trafalgar Square? The owls hooted in Highgate, in Wimbledon, in Dulwich. Drinking men lay huddled in newspaper on benches, in railway stations, beneath the arches, beneath the Festival Hall. Aaron listened to the silence, and to the faint music of a cassette: the fifth symphony of Sibelius. Where the swan drifts upon the darkening flood. He communed with his mother, he implored her to drift with him. Was she there, was it *she* that was with him? Two floors below, his stepmother lay in his father's arms, *for the last time*. Sweet Hamlet, cast this nighted colour off. The party was over. Where would he drift now? The soft cool currents of the air lifted him above the sleeping city, swirled him gently. The music gathered its strength. He lay in its arms. It was the first morning of 1980.

Meanwhile, up in Northam, that figurative northern city, the New Year had also advanced, ignored by some, welcomed by others, bringing suprises to some, and a deadly, continuing tedium to others. The Other Nation, less than two hundred miles away, celebrated in its own style. In a renovated Georgian terrace house less than a quarter of a mile from the Civic Centre, actors, actresses, arts officers, leisure officers, artists-in-residence, playwright-in-residence, and a visiting jazz musician gathered together to laugh, to sing, to eat spinach salad and green bean salad and mackerel pâté and whole meal bread and curried brown rice; they played games, word games, charades, quotation games. Northam's poet sat glumly in a corner with a plateful and a pint and watched with silent outrage, as was his way. Next door, an old woman in her seventies read aloud to her ninety-two-year-old mother, as she had read aloud of an evening for decades. Their house had not been renovated; it belonged to another age. Solid provincial comfort, a little shabby now, but solid. They had stuck it out, as the area stormed around them: they had stood their ground, resisting all offers of rehousing, uprooting. They would die in their own beds. Their high-smelling dog lay on the hairy ancient rug before the smokeless fuel fire. Round the corner another old woman in her seventies awaited the departure of the year, huddled in bed for warmth, clad in layer upon layer of old nylon nightdress, woolly cardigan, matted flannel dressing gown, gazing at an unsatisfactory black-and-white television flickering at her from a chair by the bed. She could see nothing, could make out nothing, but it was a comfort, it was company, she heard its voices, they spoke to her. In the flat below, a teenage couple quarrelled about whether it was safe to leave the baby and go down to the pub. The baby cried, as babies do. The more it cried, the more they wanted to leave it, and the less safe it seemed to leave it. The girl began to cry, as girls do, and the teenage father went out on his own, slamming the door behind him. The girl shouted abuse after him, then picked up her baby for comfort, and settled down to watch telly with the remains of a bag of cheese and onion crisps.

Farther out, in the fashionable village-suburb of Breasbrough, civic spirits were high at a New Year's Eve party, where left-wing councillors, left-wing teachers, left-wing journalists, left-wing social workers, and a few agnostic entrepreneurs raised their glasses and looked forward to the exhilarating confrontation of the approaching steel strike: they were high on a recent freak by-election in the neighbourhood which had reversed the national trend to the right and given, in their own view, a renewed popular blessing to their defiant, daring programme of high social expenditure. Socialism begins at home, they told one another as they filled their glasses with Oake and Nephews Special Christmas Offer Beaujolais. Northam's elderly historian and honorary ideologue sat glumly in a corner with a plateful and a pint, and watched with silent outrage, as was his way. He did not trust this new wave of optimism. He had seen too many waves fall harmlessly upon the shore. He did not approve of wine drinking. He was going deaf: on purpose, he sometimes thought.

Half a mile up the hill, spirits were also high in the home of

Eddie Duckworth, that plump, much-loved, avuncular manager of Pitts and Harley, newly elected President of the Chamber of Commerce, who had faith that at last a government had been elected that would put a stop to inflation, high interest rates, rocketing domestic and industrial rates, shameful capitulation to the unions, centralized bureaucratic planning, and the consequent decay of the manufacturing industries: the writing is on the wall at the Town Hall, he told his guests, as their glasses were refilled with Oake and Nephews Beaujolais. Eddie Duckworth smiled and sparkled and shone. There was much laughter in both Breasbrough houses. There were one or two guests that had been invited to both Breasbrough parties. Northam is a small city, a parochial city. Mrs. Eddie Duckworth did not laugh, although she tried to smile. She was not very good at smiling these days, and the unease disseminated by her unconvincing efforts led Eddie Duckworth to mutter to her in a corner, with a mixture of sharpness and sorrow, that perhaps she'd better go to bed. He didn't know what had come over her, of late.

Shirley Harper, Liz Headleand's younger sister, was at none of these parties, and had been invited to none. She had been expected to invite people in. This was now, at forty-three, her lot. Though in the old days it had been she who had braved her mother's disapprobation and slipped out to enjoy herself, while her sister stuck grimly to her books and her duty and her long-term plans. Shirley had been the rebel, the self-willed, the unappeasing. She had lied and deceived, she had painted her lips with toxic red paint from a box of water colours or with the less toxic red dye of rationed Smarties, she had darkened her lashes with shoe polish and perfumed herself with sample offers of cheap perfume solicited through sycophantic correspondence with cosmetics manufacturers. She had visited coffee bars with boys. She had been to the cinema with boys. She had left school against her mother's wishes, had married against her mother's wishes.

Yet while Liz, the good daughter, the dutiful daughter, was taking a deep hot bath on New Year's Eve before changing for her party, Shirley the rebel was serving up a hot meal for her mother in the old house in Abercorn Avenue before rushing back (without appearing to rush) to see what was happening to her own oven at home, where she was cooking a goose for her husband, Cliff, his brother, Steve, and his wife, Dora, her own mother-in-law and father-in-law, and Dora's uncle Fred. While

Liz was nibbling pistachio nuts, surveying dominions, Shirley, hot, red, and angry (but not appearing to be angry), was listening yet once more to her mother-in-law's description of her digestive system and what the doctor had said about the swelling of her legs, a commentary which followed closely upon her complaints about the absence of her two older grandchildren, who had (in Shirley's view very wisely) buggered off to a disco at Maid Marian's New Year's Superdisco. "In my day," she was saying, "New Year's Eve was a *family* evening; young people didn't just suit themselves. We all used to be together on New Year's Eve, didn't we, Dad?"

Her husband, thus addressed, did not reply; he rarely did. Since his second stroke he had found the effort of conversation hardly worth the meagre rewards. Whatever he said was always ignored: for years, even when in health, he had been used by his wife as a ventriloquist's dummy, in support of an endless succession of mutually contradictory banalities, and whenever he had risked an original or even a conciliatory remark he would be firmly rebuffed. So now he sat there, his napkin tucked around his chin, smiling gently: a mild-natured, weak, weakened old man, loyal to his bully of a wife, glad to be included, glad Shirley hadn't found it all too much for her, grateful to sit there in the warmth of the nice oil-fired 1970s central heating. It made a change. He didn't get out much.

Steve replied for him. "Well, we're all together still, aren't we?" said Cliff's brother, Steve, with some asperity; he could have thought of better ways of spending the evening, given a choice.

"Applesauce?" asked Shirley, who was dishing up, with her back to the table, from a hotplate on a trolley.

"It all depends what you mean by family," said Dora's uncle Fred, who tended to pedantry. He looked round, moved his fork cautiously to a different angle on the best embroidered cloth. "I'm not family, strictly speaking. Here courtesy of Dora. And of our charming hostess, of course."

"Gravy?" asked Shirley, and poured it on without waiting for an answer. Family. She had lacked family as a child, had missed it. And now she'd got it with a vengeance. The source of murder, battering, violence. How ever had it happened?

"Red cabbage?" asked Shirley.

"Red cabbage? Red cabbage? I thought it was sprouts. We always have sprouts." An angry interjection from the oldest Mrs. Harper.

"It's sprouts as well," said Shirley. "I thought I'd do some red cabbage too. As a change."

"He won't like it. He won't want any. He likes his red cabbage pickled." So pursued the oldest Mrs. Harper. Her husband smiled and nodded.

"Yes," mused Uncle Fred, "families aren't what they were. It's all this moving around the country. Thank you, Shirley, that's grand. By the way, Brian asked me to London again, but I thought I'd wait till the weather's better."

"All what moving about the country?" asked Cliff, largely to avert further discussion of sprouts and red cabbage, which he could see was imminent from the suspicious manner in which his mother was turning over the vegetables on her heaped plate.

"Oh, all this moving around for work."

"Go on," said Steve. "No one moves round here. They stick fast, round here. Never been south of Nottingham, half the folks round here."

"I think it's nice for the young folks to get out," said Fred. "I always encouraged my Brian. I didn't want to stand in his way."

Shirley smiled sourly to herself as she poured gravy. Somebody was going to have to ask after Brian soon, ask what he was up to, how he was getting on, but nobody wanted to. They resented Brian. He had got away. They hadn't even the satisfaction of knowing that he treated his poor old dad badly, because all things considered he didn't. It was probably true that he'd asked him down to London.

"Is that a clove?" asked Mrs. Harper, triumphant.

"Yes," said Shirley.

"The cabbage is delicious," said Dora, quickly. She and Shirley exchanged glances.

"And how's your mother, Shirley?" asked Mrs. Harper, carefully and conspicuously laying her clove on the side of her plate; taking the offensive.

"She's much the same as ever," said Shirley. "Thanks."

"Pity she couldn't be with us," said Mrs. Harper, dangerously. But Shirley hadn't the energy to fight back; she helped herself to a spoonful of sage and onion stuffing and sat down to begin her meal. Those served earlier had nearly finished: they didn't believe in standing on ceremony, in the family. They ate what was in front of them. While it was hot.

"She doesn't get out much," said Shirley flatly: a statement at once accurate and wonderfully, gloriously misleading. *"She doesn't get out much,"* an acceptable phrase, a dull little coin, an everyday coin, suggesting a mild, an ordinary, a common-place disinclination, for in Northam "getting out" was in many circles regarded as suspect, as improper, as leading to no good (those making merry in Breasbrough, for example, were undoubtedly up to no good)—a freak tolerated in the young, though with much grumbling, but considered dissolute, way-ward, against nature in their elders. "She doesn't get out much," a phrase that Shirley had learned to use of her mother to forestall inquiry, impertinence, sympathy: a middle-aged phrase that she heard in her own voice as parody—indeed, she had noticed that when "the family" gathered together all of them spoke in parodies of clichés, and some of them knew quite well that they were doing it. Dora knew, Cliff knew, Fred knew. And everybody there at the table knew that in the case of Shirley Harper's mother, the phrase "she doesn't get out much" conveyed the distilled essence of a withdrawal so extreme that the term agoraphobia would hardly do it justice.

"No, she doesn't get out much," she repeated, almost defiantly, wondering if her sister, Liz, would bother to ring their mother that night, and if she didn't, if it mattered. What an extraordinary childhood they had survived. Odd that both of them had turned out almost normal. "Her eyesight's not too good now," she continued, as though that might somehow render her mother's behaviour less odd, as though by mere words she could be converted into a harmless, ordinary, ageing old lady, just like other people's mothers. And indeed, with old age, Rita Ablewhite was beginning to appear slightly less abnormal: behaviour strange in a healthy thirty-five-year-old was more acceptable at seventy. "She's even agreed to have Meals On Wheels," Shirley volunteered, as nobody else was saying anything.

"That must take a bit of the burden off of you," said Mrs. Harper, lining up a peppercorn by the clove.

"Oh, yes, it does," said Shirley. "It's a wonderful service, you know."

This innocent remark, which Shirley had injudiciously thought platitudinous enough to pass without comment, stirred her brother-in-law Steve to speech: he launched into an attack upon the City Council and the high rates, an attack guaranteed to annoy Uncle Fred, upset his mild dumb father, and plunge his brother, Cliff, into the deepest financial anxiety. It had been a bad year for Cliff, and it was as easy to blame the Council as anyone. On they went, the men, talking men's talk of rates and the threatened steel strike and the Marxist lunatics at the Town Hall; of the closure of the Timperley works, of the three hundred made redundant at Brook and Partridge, of the folly of running courses of lectures at public expense in the Hartley Library on nuclear disarmament and feminist opportunities in local government. "It's disgusting," contributed Mrs. Harper from time to time, presenting her flat, mean, worthless little counter simply because she could not bear to remain silent, to sit back while others played, although she recognized herself temporarily outnumbered, "disgusting, I call it," and Shirley, hearing this phrase for the millionth time, had a vision of households all over Britain in which censorious, ignorant old bags like her mother-in-law, who had never done anything for the public good, who had nothing positive ever to contribute to any argument, passed judgement on others while stuffing themselves with goose and roast potatoes and sprouts and applesauce. The backbone of the nation, the salt of the earth.

And there was poor Fred, speaking up for the reviled council block in which he, unlike any of the others, lived: "Nay, it's not that bad, it's a lot of it exaggeration," he interposed mildly, as Steve repeated the time-worn allegation that it wasn't safe to walk under the deck walkways for fear of having a television set or an old mattress chucked on your head. "Nay, it's not that bad at all."

"You'd have thought your Brian could have found you somewhere a bit more comfortable," interposed Mrs. Harper, seeing her opportunity of introducing Brian to his disadvantage. "He must know a few folk; it's not only money that counts . . ." and her voice trailed away, as she simultaneously managed to imply that Brian had the Town Hall in the palm of his hand, and that he had enough money to buy his father a comfortable bungalow in a nice suburb whenever he felt like it. Shirley watched Fred return Mrs. Harper's grease-smeared red-nosed gaze: affable, broad, patient, he stared at her, and wiped his mouth on his table napkin. She could see his decision not to bother to try to explain that Brian hardly knew anybody in Northam Town Hall, and that Brian's salary as Head of Humanities of an Adult Education College hardly rose to paying his own mortgage, let alone to buying a house for his ageing father. She applauded this decision. It was not worth presenting reasoned arguments to Mrs. Harper. When they appeared before her, she shifted her ground, with an agility that occasionally suggested to Shirley that perhaps she was not after all impenetrably stupid, but on some dismal level quite intelligent. "Nay," said Fred, "I like it where I am, it suits me where I am, I wouldn't want to be moving at my age. I've been in that block since it was built, it suits me fine. There's a grand view, you know." He looked at his niece Dora. "Your auntie loved it. We used to sit in the evenings and watch the lights come on." He looked back at Mrs. Harper. "You ought to come and visit me one day. You'd be surprised." Mrs. Harper sniffed and moved her clove half an inch.

You could see she thought Fred had cheated by mentioning his dead wife; any minute now if she didn't watch her step he might drag in his dead daughter too. The conventions prevented her from heaping any further abuse on Chay Bank, a housing project which she had frequently and loudly denounced, but near which she had never set foot: the precariousness of her own social position would forever prevent her from visiting Fred Bowen, and this yearly ritual meeting on neutral ground was as much as she would ever dare risk.

"You'd be surprised," Fred insensitively urged. "My Brian's Alix thinks it's lovely. She invited her mum and dad over from Leeds specially to have a look last time they were up here. We had a very nice tea."

Now that was almost cruel, thought Shirley, as she offered second helpings. Fred had gone too far, had widened the discourse unfairly. Alix, whom Brian had so unexpectedly married, represented a world beyond articulate resentment, too remote to attack. Brian they could get at, but not Alix. They didn't understand her well enough. They didn't like her, but they didn't know why.

Celia Harper, youngest child of Shirley and Cliff, too young to be allowed to escape to the disco, sat silent throughout the meal. She ate minimally. Sometimes her lips would move slightly, as though she were repeating something to herself. Nobody paid her any attention at all.

Shirley began to stack the plates. Nobody wanted any more, which was just as well, as there wasn't much left and she couldn't face hacking at the carcase.

Cliff would never carve. His father hadn't carved before him, so Cliff wouldn't carve. Fatherless Shirley knew perfectly well that most British men carved, and that it was a bit of bad luck that she happened to have married into a family where the

women were expected to wield the knife. She wondered if her
sister, Liz, carved. Probably not. That dreadful Charles would
be brilliant at the job. She wheeled the trolley into the kitchen,
and took the plum tart out of the oven. The oven clock said it
was only five to eight. It felt like midnight, and they'd have to
sit up till midnight. She'd persuaded the old folk to eat far later
than usual anyway and it was still only five to eight. She
wondered if there was any hope of getting them to play cards
after supper instead of watching telly. She herself would much,
much rather play cards. In the old days they had all played
cards. They'd enjoyed a game of snap or whist or gin rummy.
But gradually, over the years, they had defected, as weak as
the teenagers they so relentlessly criticized: they'd let the old
ways lapse in order to slump like dummies in front of appalling
chat shows and glimpses of the Sugar Plum Fairy and obsequious shots of the Royal Family and its corgis and babies, to
goggle at old movies and new dance routines and to sit back
sucking sweeties while sneering at pop stars and newscasters
making fools of themselves at televised parties. The medium
had been too strong for them, they had taken to it like
aborigines to the bottle. Only her mother had resisted. But her
mother, of course, was mad.

Two hours later, as they sat watching an Irish comedian
telling jokes that she herself considered quite unsuitable for
family viewing, jokes that she hoped were incomprehensible to
Celia and her grandparents, the telephone rang: it was her
mother, to report that Liz had not telephoned. "Maybe she's
waiting to ring later," Shirley said feebly, as a tide of rage with
Liz, far away in distant London, washed through her; too
absorbed in her own life, too selfish even to spend five minutes
talking to her own mother.

"She knows I don't stay up," said Rita Ablewhite.

"She may ring later," repeated Shirley. "How was your
chicken?"

A short silence ensued. "I said, how was your chicken?"
Shirley repeated. She could hear the drone of the television
from the drawing room, the snores of her father-in-law, and her
mother's deliberate silence at the other end of the line. She
could have murdered the lot of them, Irish comedian included.
"Look, I've got to go now, I've got the kettle on for coffee,"
said Shirley.

"The chicken was very nice," said her mother.

Half an hour later, the telephone went again. It was for Fred, Fred's Brian.

"Hello, Brian," said Shirley, who was feeling marginally more cheerful, having managed to bring out the card table in the midst of an argument about the relative demerits of the offerings on BBC and ITV. "Happy New Year, when it comes."

"And to you, Shirley," said Brian. "I'm not ringing too late, am I? I thought you'd still be up. Is Dad there?"

"Yes, he is, I'll get him for you." She could hear a lot of background noise, the noise of life. "Are you having a party?"

"No," said Brian, "we're not having a party, but I'm at one, I'm at your sister's." He laughed his big, round, comfortable but oddly high-pitched laugh: his inoffensive laugh, defusing the reference to Liz: the soul of tact, as ever, Brian: "I'm at Liz's, Alix would come. Funny world, isn't it? You're very good to my dad, Shirley."

"Is it a good party?"

"It's a very up-market party. Champagne flows."

"How's Alix?"

"She's fine, thanks. And Cliff?"

"Not so bad. I'll get your dad, shall I?"

"Thanks a lot, Shirley. I just thought I'd have a word with him. The silly old bugger still won't have a telephone installed, you know. Barmy, that's what he is. That's what I tell him." Brian spoke with affection. She heard its authentic note. Brian could afford to be affectionate, from over a hundred miles away.

She went to get Fred, who was overcome with nervous confusion and pleasure. He hated the telephone, it frightened him. "That you, Brian? How are you, Brian?" he shouted. "What's that? What was that?" Technological alarm deafened him. "What was that? You spoke to Barbara? What's that? Did she really? Happy New Year to you, love to Alix and Sammy. Yes, I'll tell Dora. What was that? What was that? What?"

Triumphant, he returned to the card table. "That was my Brian," he announced, unnecessarily. "Fancy that. He had a phone call from our Barbara in Australia. Fancy that. She told him to tell Dora she'd written to Auntie Flo to thank her for the cake. She says why don't I go out there on a visit. And I don't know that I won't. You get that, Dora? Barbara's written to Auntie Flo about the cake."

And he picked up his hand of cards, and surveyed it with a bewildered distracted satisfaction.

"Whose turn is it?" he said.

"Yours, of course," said Mrs. Harper, grimly: so grimly that her reply seemed like wit.

"Sorry, all," said Fred, and threw away a club.

"I don't fancy Australia, myself," said Dora. "My trick, I think. They say it's very rough, Australia." She gathered in the cards, laid them neatly, criss-cross, upon her last gain.

"It is a country with opportunities," said Steve; and off they went again, with their secondhand opinions, their echoes of overheard conversations, their phrases from advertisements and tabloid newspapers: and yet to Shirley there was perhaps something comfortable, despite all, something reassuring about the hands of cards, the button and matchstick money, the green baize of the table, the predictable, ancient jokes, the cigarette ends in the big red ashtray: there was safety here, of a sort, safety in repetition, safety in familiar faces and frustrations, and warmth of a sort, warmth and communion of a sort, society of a sort: the society she had discovered as a teenager, when she would slip surreptitiously out of the icy silence of Abercorn Avenue, where the clock ticked relentlessly on the kitchen wall, where Liz propped her textbooks against the Peak Freen biscuit tin on the kitchen table, where her mother sat in the front room listening to the radio, cutting up newspapers; she would let herself quietly out the back door and creep down the passage, past the outside lav, through the back gate, round the corner, and then she would run for it, along Hilldrop Crescent, down The Grove, up Brindleford Drive, and across the main road at the lights to Victoria Street, where Cliff and Steve and their sister, Marge, lived. Cliff and Steve and Marge were allowed to have friends in. They even had a playroom of their own, an attic under the eaves. A gang of them would meet there, graduating from Meccano and toy farms to risqué games of Dare, illicit cigarettes, speculation about sex. Wildness and safety combined, Shirley had discovered there; they had made her welcome, they called her Shirl. Spirited she was, in those days, and she played one boy off against another, teasing, bold, *louche*, at times wildly immodest, shocking, provoking, drooping a ciggy from her wide wicked lip, dropping her blouse from bare shoulders, playing cards for forfeits, egging them on to experiment with Ouija, inventing naughty messages from the spirit world. How had she known these things, what models had she copied from films she had never seen, what spirit spoke through her, informing her impatient flesh?

Safety and danger, danger and safety. "A bad girl, that Shirley Ablewhite." Nobody ever said this, but she half hoped they would. She had longed to be a bad girl in those post-war years, those austerity years. But she couldn't quite manage it: she remained a nice girl, just this side of safety. A nice girl. A small, suspicious caution held her back: a small caution teased Cliff, teased Steve, teased their friends, kept them on a hook, watching, waiting, to see how far she dared go. She was deceitful, was Shirley: downstairs, with Mr. and Mrs. Harper, she would be another girl, helpful, quiet, obsequious, prim, in her neat, absurdly old-fashioned blouses and skirts, her hair tied neatly back in bunches. She liked her downstairs self too, she liked the unfamiliar familiarity, the bickerings and grievances, the small change of domestic life.

Cliff and Steve both fancied Shirley. They watched her switch from the attic Shirley to the downstairs Shirley with appalled, enthralled admiration. Her inventiveness astounded them. She was the spirit of subversion. Mr. and Mrs. Harper thought she was a very nice girl.

Sometimes, after acquisition of a television set in Coronation year, they would all watch television together. Shirley had enjoyed that. Mr. and Mrs. Harper had sat in their respective armchairs, Marge had sat on a red leather pouf and she, Steve, and Cliff had occupied the two-seater settee of the three-piece suite. Cliff liked to get her in a corner but she liked to sit in the middle. There, by small wrigglings and the exercise of will, she could encourage them both to insert their hands into different parts of her clothing, her body, sometimes simultaneously. Steve's hand would cup her breast inside her blouse, while Cliff's would explore her suspenders, her knickers. She learned to control these manoeuvres with great expertise. The Harper parents never noticed, but continued to watch the programmes: *What's My Line?*, *Down You Go*, *Animal, Vegetable, Mineral?*, *Twenty Questions*, *Science Review*. Shirley watched the programmes too, but was occasionally distracted by an intensity of experience that sometimes approached orgasm. A communal event.

And her sister, Liz, sat at home, missing all the fun, deaf to the call of the flesh, with her alternative mathematics, her chemistry and her biology, wasting her youth, wasting her opportunities, obeying the will of their mother, programmed, docile, chaste, pale. One autumn night, when Liz was preparing for Oxford and Cambridge entrance, Shirley had come home at ten from the Harpers', flushed from sexual excitement and from running through the cold streets under the yellowing smoke-scented suburban trees, her body on fire, and had found Liz still sitting where she had left her, two hours earlier, at the kitchen table, staring at the pale green wall, as though in a catatonic trance. Shirley had clattered noisily on the linoleum, had huffed and puffed and banged about, and finally had said with some passion, "You're barmy."

And Liz had slowly swivelled her head round, and stared at her as though from a great way off, and had said dreamily, "If you really want something badly enough, do you think you get it?"

"I haven't the faintest," said Shirley, taking off her outdoor shoes and putting them on the rack, putting on her indoor slippers, and guiltily, belatedly, bending down to wipe the shoe marks off the linoleum with spit and hanky. She assumed her sister was referring to getting into Cambridge, which she herself considered a poisonous, disreputable fantasy, and one unlikely ever to be fulfilled: the number of girls who had achieved Cambridge places from Battersby Girls' Grammar in the last ten years could be counted on the fingers of one hand. She sat back on her haunches, as the smear dried. "I don't know," she repeated, more solemnly, "I don't know if the amount of wanting has anything to do with the getting."

"It *must* have," said Liz, who sat there, burning, burning, eaten up with longing for words beyond her sister's guessing: a pale effigy, locked up in imaginings. "It must have." She sighed. The imaginings were so potent that they took wing and rustled round the room, little winged souls, small bird-faced holy ghosts, emanations: the whole room was suddenly dense with the vibration of their rustling, the old-fashioned white tiles with their rounded edges glinted with their reflections, the linoleum shimmered, the kitchen cupboards shook, the morbid whiteness and greenness of the paintwork quivered, the exposed pipes trembled and knocked. The two girls held their breath, Liz sitting there with her mock examination papers, Shirley crouching by the shoe rack—their prison kitchen filled with presences. These moments came, but they came rarely.

"I think," Shirley said, softly, catching her sister's low, dreamy, drugged tone, "I think it has. Yes, I think it has. What we want, we do get."

"If we want, for example, eternity, we get it," said Liz.

"Yes. Or if we want this world, we get it."

"But we have to suffer for our wanting," said Liz.

"Ah, that's what I can't stand, the suffering," said Shirley, jumping to her feet, her fifteen-year-old voice reasserting, boldly, fraily, the tones of elsewhere, of normality and new Bird's-Eye peas and modern kitchenettes, of television and hands fumbling inside brassières. "I can't stand the suffering, I won't suffer, I've had enough of suffering."

Liz stared at her, coldly.

"Then you won't get," she said. "You won't get."

At this moment they heard their mother turn off the radio in the other room. They looked at one another.

"What if one suffers, and suffers, and suffers," said Shirley, deliberately, vengefully, "and doesn't get? What then?"

And Liz had shaken her head in pain at the mystery in the next room.

And still that mystery in the front room continued, reflected Shirley on New Year's Eve 1979, as she examined the handsome features of the dangerous queen of spades, and wondered if the king had come out in the deal. It was a little deaf, and a little blind, the mystery, and its only friend, Miss Mynors, was dead, but it continued. On and on it went. There was no mercy. Whereas Liz, by some immense, visionary effort had invented her own mercy, under cover of obedience, had drawn up a secret map of escape, and had departed, and was now at this instant giving a party for hundreds of guests where champagne flowed. How could these things be? How could it be that Liz, so young, had known her way out of the maze? Was it true that the mind was wiser than the body? Shirley took a risk and played her queen, but Cliff had the king, and she lost the trick.

She must forgive Liz. Liz was right to vanish, as the boys were right to congregate at the Maid Marian and avoid their grandmothers. It was by her own choice that she sat here. It was by her own choice that she had married Cliff, not Steve; it was she herself who had seduced Cliff, in a field of cow parsley on a May evening. She had obeyed her body, she had opened her legs, had pulled him into her, and said, Now, come, now. What was, what could have been wrong about that? She had thought to free herself, through nature, through the violence of nature. But nature was cunning and had kept her trapped. What did it want her for? She had obeyed sex, she had trusted sex, she had loved sex, and it had betrayed her, had deceived her, had left her sitting here, a middle-aged housewife, mother of three, playing cards, with nothing before her but old age. Was it so? Could it be so? How had it happened? Was there maybe some other event, some other metamorphosis awaiting her? Or was this it? Shirley, sitting there mildly, the downstairs Shirley, thinking these thoughts, remembering the peremptory demands of the old, the attic Shirley, felt trembling in her, deep deep buried in her drawing-room centrally heated flesh, a wild improper memory, an admissible echo, the faintest thrill of a shudder of remembered desire: Shirley Ablewhite, the bad-good girl, called to her through the knot of her body, painfully, angrily, buried, buried alive, and Shirley Harper half heard her, bent her head, and acknowledged with mixed fear and relief the stirring, the tremor, the sulking, menacing, sweet, and half-despairing plea.

Cliff was winning. His pile of matchsticks was considerable. He had had a succession of good hands and won the kitty twice. Now he was playing recklessly, sportingly, trying to let the others in, but he couldn't help winning, it seemed. His mind wasn't on the game at all: it was on balance sheets and interest rates and VAT and cash flow and overdraft facilities. Over-extended, that's what they were, too many orders and not enough money to buy the gear. Borrow, said his partner, Jim, borrow, but look at the price of borrowing. Sums flitted through his head as he won another unlikely trick with a paltry knave. Jim was all for going on, for expanding, for advancing rather than retreating, but Cliff was beginning to think that after all he hadn't the temperament for it, he couldn't stand the anxiety, he didn't enjoy the suspense: all he wanted was security, independence, freedom from worry, being his own man. That was all. Nothing too extravagant. But it was true, what Jim said, in business you can't stand still, you go up or you go down; you can't just sit comfortably in your own 1972 executive four-bedroomed plate-glass-windowed centrally heated wall-to-wall-carpeted gadget-equipped house, with your Rover and your wife's Mini in the two-car garage, and your pot plants in your loggia, and your electric lawn mower in the shed. You can't sit still and enjoy it, you can't call it a day and call a halt when you own it all and don't owe anyone a penny;

you have to go on and on, relentlessly onwards, juggling with larger and larger sums, owing more, paying out more, until finally perhaps the whole thing comes tumbling round your head like a pack of cards. Jim was right: you had to go on. Risks were part of the game. He'd enjoyed them himself when he was younger. Always ready to accept a challenge, his school reports had said. It wasn't the hard work he minded; he liked work, he liked long hours, he didn't want to slack off. It was the anxiety he couldn't stand. Where was it going to end? Inflation made one run to stand still. What if one ran and slipped backwards? A nightmare world. Maybe after all he'd have been better off like his dad, quietly pushing papers round a desk in an office at the Gas Board for nine hours a day for nearly fifty years. A living death, it had seemed to him and Jim, but maybe it hadn't been so bad. It had been safe, at least.

They were still talking about Australia, the land of opportunity. Fred's Barbara had gone out there with her bricklayer husband and now he had a building firm and employed ten men. Cliff and Jim employed twenty, making screw-on wing mirror attachments and assembling picnic sets.

"It's coming up for midnight," said Shirley, with some relief, pointing at the quartz carriage clock on the mantelpiece. They consulted watches, nodded agreement. "Somebody ought to go out and come in again with a lump of coal," said Dora. "Isn't that what we usually do?"

"We didn't last year," said Mrs. Harper. "We forgot. We were watching that Scottish comedian in Trafalgar Square on telly."

"A dark-haired man, it has to be," said Dora. "That's you, Steve."

Cliff looked at Steve, ran his hands through his own hair, and said, "That's right, Steve. I've got plenty left, but it's the wrong colour. Yours is bearing up well. Touch it up, do you? What's that stuff called? Grecian?"

Steve hit his brother playfully but rather hard on the shoulder.

"Where's the coal, Shirley?"

"We haven't got any coal. Oil-fired, we are."

"What's the next best thing?"

"Some people," said Shirley, "have those fake gas fires

now, you know, they look like real coal fires, with lumps of stuff like real coal, and real ashes. But it's all fake. They're quite nice. Something to look at.''

"Go on, out you go, Steve," said Dora. "Take something black. It's for luck. You're to bring it in in a shovel.''

"We never used to do this when I was a girl," said Mrs. Harper. "Did they in your family, Dad?''

Her husband nodded and smiled, but whether he had heard the question or not, who could say.

"What does it mean?" said Shirley.

"It's for luck," said Dora. "First footing. It's for luck.''

"They do it up in Newcastle," volunteered Fred. "It's a Geordie custom, I've heard say. Go on, Steve, we could all do with a bit of luck. Out you go.''

And Steve obediently went off, taking with him a jar of Marmite in a garden trowel as a substitute for coal in a shovel, and he stood out there on the front porch in the cold listening to the silence and looking at the stars, waiting for them to let him in on the last stroke of Big Ben on the radio: a faint, feeble echo of some once meaningful ritual, though what it had meant or now could mean nobody there knew or had ever known. And thus, all over Northam, all over Britain, ill-remembered, confused, shadowy vestigial rites were performed, rites with origins lost in antiquity; Celtic, Pict, Roman, Norse, Anglo-Saxon, Norman, Elizabethan, Hanoverian, Judaic rites: mistletoe dangled from drawing pins and picture rails, golden stars shone on the Christmas Trees of Prince Albert and geese and haggis and hams lay heavy on the digestion of some, while others laughed themselves silly or sick on rum and Coke at the Maid Marian New Year's Superdisco. Steve Harper, haulage contractor, stood outside alone for a grateful crisp smokeless moment of silence, and when they opened the door to him a strange shadow of the night sidled in with him from prehistory. Shirley Harper touched the locket at her throat, for luck, a superstition she had had since childhood. "Happy New Year," they said to one another, inadequately, shivering a little. Something was absent, yet something was present. The shadow filled the corners of the broad bright hallway. A pitiful exhalation, an obscurity, a memory. A homeless ghost. The eight-year-old house perched precariously on the raw earth, amongst other isolated, precarious, detached houses, their lights shining on the dark hillside. No one had lived on that hillside for nineteen centuries. The Brigantes had held it once, against the Romans, but they had retreated to the mountains and left it to gorse and the bracken. And so it had remained until the scoops and cranes and bulldozers of 1970s Post-Industrial Man had moved in to uproot the scrub and to build the suburb known as Greystone Edge. A few Bronze Age artifacts were turned up in the dark soil, but they had meant nothing to those who had seen them, and they had been turned back into the earth. Here Benutius, leader of the Brigantes, had crouched in the night by his camp fire, dwelling on the treachery of his faithless queen, Cartimandua, who had sold her people to the Romans. A tragic theme. Here the Harper clan gather, a small tribe, frail, ageing, on the threshold of 1980, in the presence of the sky; here thirteen-year-old Celia, young, aspiring, judgemental, reflects upon the past, as, long after her usual bedtime, she looks up at the stars and plots her own future. On the threshold of Brock Bank the Harpers gather, bidding one another good night beneath the moon. What obscure blood runs in their veins? Who could have drawn the roots, the branches, the fibres, the tendrils that have fed them and bound them? Ancestral voices whisper from the young dry garden hedge, as Steve starts up his Ford Cortina. Shirley keeps her finger on her locket, which rests on her throat like a warm stethoscope. She thinks of her mother. She thinks of her father, whom she has never known, of whom she knows nothing, almost nothing, but whose image, it is alleged, is in that locket: an image which also hangs in an identical locket at this moment around her sister's neck. A prized possession. Shirley is tired, fatigue has overwhelmed anxiety and desire; she hopes her two boys will come home soon, and go to bed quietly. She waves goodbye.

In 8 Abercorn Avenue, Rita Ablewhite lies in bed in the dark. She is not asleep. She is waiting for the clock downstairs to strike twelve. When it strikes, she will shut her eyes. When she was a girl, at midnight on New Year's Eve she could hear the celebratory steam trains whistle beyond the crossing down Station Road. Now she hears nothing but the sounds of her own house. When she was a girl, she could lie in bed and hear her mother and father talking in the next room. When she was a young woman, she could hear distant laughter down long corridors, as she lay in her bed. Now she hears nothing but the sounds of her own house. And she does not hear them as well as she did once. She lies there in the dark, with her eyes open, keeping watch.

When Liz Headleand woke on the first day of 1980 and found herself in bed with her husband, she remembered instantly the scene of the night before, and wondered how she could ever have been so upset by it. Lying there at seven o'clock in the morning, suddenly wide awake, as was her manner, it seemed to her quite obvious that she and Charles should get divorced: it had surely long been inevitable, and if Charles really wanted to marry that woman (or had he perhaps been *joking*—no, perhaps not), well then, let him. She had plenty to get on with meanwhile. Why ever had she taken it so badly? She had an embarrassed recollection of having burst into tears, of having demanded to know how long the affair with Henrietta had been going on. I must have been tired, she said to herself reasonably. Tired and a little drunk. All those people in the house. That's what it was.

Charles was still heavily asleep. Unlike her, he was not good in the mornings. He lay solidly. She left him there, and went to have a bath, dressed briskly, went downstairs to inspect the damage, had a coffee, looked at her list for the day. It was New Year's Day, bank holiday, but, bizarrely, for her a working day. She had to attend a conference at the Metropole Hotel organized by a group of Japanese psychoanalysts and psycho-therapists. They did not recognize the British calendar. Their first choice of conference date had been Boxing Day, but from this they had been dissuaded. The group were admirers of the dissident English Freudian Jay Spenser, who was unaccount-ably famous in Japan. They had invited Liz to give a paper, "Theseus and the Minotaur: Spenser's Version of the Family Romance." She wondered what they would make of it as she got out the vacuum cleaner and started to run it over the drawing-room carpet. Would they understand her? Would she understand them? Foster children, stepchildren, institution children. She had no idea of how these patterns were formed in Japan, nor why the Japanese should have any interest in her paper, or in Karl Auerbach's, or in Gertrude Feinstein's. Step-children. What would her own stepchildren say to her divorce from their father? The vacuum cleaner ran smoothly, efficiently over the rich dark yellow pile, collecting cigarette ash, canapé crumbs, scattered bulb fibre; her mind sang with a faint clear high-pitched hum like a well-serviced machine. She listened to it with an expert ear. It sounded all right, but was there perhaps something slightly odd about the tuning, some as yet almost imperceptible new thin whine? She tested it with the concept of Henrietta, and yes, undoubtedly it responded, changing its frequency to an angry buzz before returning to its smooth hum. Henrietta. Zezeee, zezeeee. Henrietta. Zezeeee, zezeeee. Like stepping on an accelerator. The buzz of jealousy. But how *could* one be jealous of a stick, a statue? The vacuum cleaner, sensing her lack of concentration, took advantage of it to munch and slaver up a long strand of rug fringe: there was a smell of burning rubber. Shit, said Liz, and knelt down to unwind it. She had learned bad language from her stepsons. She struggled with the string of rug. Would they continue to be her stepsons, if she and Charles were to divorce? Would they become the stepsons of Henrietta? Of course they would. Rage possessed her and her mind zinged furiously, smelling of burning rubber. She did not worry about Sally and Stella: they were hers, her blood and body, forever. But Jonathan, but Aaron, but Alan. Her boys, and not her boys. What was her claim to them now? What sudden right had Henrietta Latchett to her three boys? Calm down, calm down, she told herself, they are all grown up, they need neither of you, this has nothing to do with them, they will not even notice. But rage continued. The buzz of jealousy. So this was it. She had seen something of it professionally, and had thought herself exempt.

For her predecessor, Naomi, she had felt none. It had not been required. Naomi Headleand, who had been killed so tragically, so tragically young, when driving herself quietly and soberly home from Glyndebourne one night. Young, beautiful, innocent, rich, she had, it was claimed, been killed instantly when an oncoming overtaking car had lost control and collided, head-on, with hers. She had died instantly, of internal, invisible injuries. When the police arrived, ten minutes later, her car was still singing: from the radio swelled the fifth symphony of Sibelius, representing eternity. Where could jealousy enter here? A young, a beautiful, a fairy story mother, dying with the greatest of grace, as immortality asserted itself and pledged its reassurance in the night air of her departure. A potent myth, but a friendly one. Liz had felt herself to be close to Naomi, as she nursed Naomi's children,

slept with Naomi's husband, took tea or sherry with Naomi's
parents, helped to form the childish letters which her stepchildren wrote to Naomi's parents thanking them for presents, for
outings. She had never met Naomi in her life, but in death she
grew to love her; she had taken her into herself, had learned her
likings, had read her books and tried (although not herself
musical) to listen to her music, she had spoken much of her to
the children, had insisted upon treating her as an ally, as a
friend beyond the grave, had reinvented her and kept her close
to them—oh, not without awareness of the dangers, of the
necessary distortions and consolations, but then all life is
danger, and Liz had embarked willingly upon its full tide with
those three small boys, with that ambitious, importunate
widower and that friendly ghost. A great adventure, a fitting
enterprise for one who had known herself from infancy to be
set apart for some rare destiny, and one that she had thought
herself to have pursued courageously, successfully, with a
redeeming love that had rescued even the anguished, complex,
hostile Aaron, and had saved him from his wilder flights. How
magically her love for the boys had developed into, contrasted
with, reinforced her different but equally powerful passion for
her daughters: how strange but inevitable had appeared the
five-pointed constellation of their heroic family.

Accomplished. Yes, well, perhaps that was the point. She
collected glasses on a tray. She picked a dying leaf from a
branchy green-pink flecked begonia. She answered the telephone, thanked the Martellis for thanking her for the party. She
would look for their gloves, would ring back if she found them.
She restacked the dishwasher. The whole house was still
sleeping, although it was half past nine. She read the paper.
She was not due at the Metropole until twelve. She would walk
there. The morning gaped, endless. She switched on the radio
and switched it off again. She heard Charles move across the
landing to his own room and run a bath. Of course they should
divorce. She had often thought of it herself, had once or twice
in low or high moments suggested it. But was nevertheless
outraged, outraged, that the suggestion should have come from
Charles. Had he meant it? Yes, he had meant it, she had no
doubt. It was up to her, quickly, to forge herself a manner that
would give her an advantage in whatever negotiations were to
come; and she had done so, by the time he came down for his
breakfast. She greeted him with a pot of coffee and a brisk,
slightly mocking, offhand smile. She would treat him as a

delinquent, a time-waster, a bad child, whose offences could only be petty. She would refuse to allow that the matter was serious, or that its consequences could affect her profoundly. A minor irritation. Yes, that was the line.

But it did not, she found, come very naturally to her. Breakfast was not pleasant. They spoke of indifferent things, but her mind, resenting too tight a control, kept whining away with its own questions. What would happen to the house? Whose house was it, anyway? Legally, morally? What would the children think? What would Edgar think? What would the world think? What was it like, life in the 1980s for a woman on her own? How much would it devalue her? Whatever could a man like Charles see in Henrietta? What had been lacking in her that he had found in Henrietta? What had she done wrong? Should she feel guilt? Should she feel shame? What would her solicitor say? Was it true that she had *neglected* Charles, as he sometimes claimed? She had always thought he was joking. How could one neglect a man who was never there? Was he never there because she had neglected him?

And these questions pursued her, buzzing like mosquitoes, as she walked up Marylebone High Street with her briefcase, as she crossed the Edgware Road, as she joined the conference group for sherry in the Westminster Suite, as she discovered that Edgar had rightly warned her that conversing with Japanese was not easy, as she ate her indifferent luncheon of Maryland chicken, as she listened to Professor Yamamoto speak on Spenser's reinterpretation of Freud's interpretation of *folie à deux* in the classic case of Orphan Eva and her mother, as she delivered her own paper, as she attempted desperately to follow the ensuing discussion, of which she could grasp only one word in ten; all through this crazy jumble of non-language and misunderstanding, of erudition and impenetrable obscurity, of meaningless signs and uninterpretable eye contact, the mosquitoes buzzed and nipped and drew blood. By six, at the end of the session, she was exhausted, demoralized. She took a taxi home. She felt herself, beneath the pricks and stings, to be growing ill. Charles had made her ill. She needed comfort, reassurance. She would ring Alix. She would tell Alix. She knew that in speaking to Alix her voice would find its normal level, her mind would return to its normal tuning. She could rely on Alix. But when she got back and dialled Alix's number, Alix was out. Liz replaced the receiver and tried to keep calm, but she could feel panic, fever, tears approaching. Charles had

gone out. To see Henrietta, to his club? He had left no word.
She sat in her study and stared at the telephone. If I were my
patient, she asked herself, would I prescribe myself a tranquil-
lizer? Is this what people feel like when they request tranquil-
lizers? She rang Esther. Esther too was out. She went back into
the drawing room and poured herself a whisky and soda. She
switched on the television.

Alix Bowen was out because for her, too, New Year's Day was
a working day, of sorts. She had to go to the Garfield Centre,
where she taught one day a week, to see the inmates perform
their Christmas entertainment. She had promised to go. They
would be angry with her if she did not go. But when she got
into the car at five, ready for the fifteen-mile drive across
London, it wouldn't start. The battery felt flat. It clicked and
died on her. No life in it at all. It hadn't been such a cold night,
what had happened? She did not understand cars. She sat there
crossly. There was absolutely no way of getting from Wandsworth to Wanley except by car, or none that did not involve at
least four methods of public transport. It was not easy even by
car. In fact, it was a ridiculous journey, and one that annoyed
her regularly once a week. The car had been behaving all right
the night before, when Brian had driven them back from Liz's.
It always behaved for Brian. She switched it on again. A faint
but more hopeful splutter, this time. She switched off, quickly.
She would have to get Brian. Brian wouldn't mind being got,
but he would laugh. Her feet were cold. Perhaps she would put
on another pair of socks. But it was always so hot in the
Centre.

   Brian did laugh. He patted her on the shoulder, then he
hugged her, and laughed.

   "You look *so* miserable," he said. "It's wonderful. It's
only a car."

   "I know it's only a car," she said, peevishly, shifting from
one foot to another on the damp pavement. "And it won't
bloody well start. What's the point of a car that won't start?"

   It started at once, for Brian. They listened to it. It sounded
perfectly well, for Brian.

   "There you go," he said, getting out, putting his arm round
her.

   "I'm a fool," she said.

"We're all fools," said Brian. "It's a foolish world."

"You're not a fool," said Alix. "You're a saint."

"No, you're the saint," he said. "And you look very nice in your new woolly hat. Off you go, they'll be howling for you."

"Don't forget about the boiled potatoes."

"I've got plans for those potatoes."

"Fry-up plans?"

"That sort of thing."

"I'll see you later."

"Drive carefully."

And off she went, driving carefully, through South London, and east, and under the river, and north, and up the A113, towards the Garfield Centre, thinking of Brian frying up the cold boiled potatoes for himself and their son, Sam, chopping parsley, frying eggs and bacon, delicious. Brian handled the frying pan as confidently as he handled the car; eggs never broke for Brian. He had a firm grasp of the material world, of pan handles and gear levers and of her own warm body, of garden spades and wayward boilers, of carving knives and power drills and saws and scissors and invisible screws, he treated all these things as his friends and allies, an Ideal Husband, she sometimes teased him; and yet, and yet, he spent his days and his nights teaching abstractions, he spent his time with words, words, words. To this he had aspired. How could it be otherwise? From paradox to paradox we travel, onwards, from ourselves. And what on earth was she herself playing at, crossing the urban wastes so regularly to teach a bunch of delinquent girls, a bunch of criminals, for £15.60 a night? It hardly covered the petrol. It probably didn't cover the petrol, if she sat down to work it out, which she didn't. What an ill-organized, hotchpotch, casually assembled, patchwork life. Everything seemed to have happened by accident, even the things that lasted. Her job at Garfield, her three days a week in Whitehall, the house in Wandsworth, her furniture, Sam's school, a series of accidents. None of it had been intended. She could have done such things. But she had always been, it seemed, too busy to stop to take stock, too busy to plan, too busy to rationalize. How ever did people manage to discipline themselves and stick to a single line for long enough to gain control, to come out on top, to become the boss instead of the employee? At Liz's party, last night, there had been bosses: Charles himself was an archetypal boss, and if one didn't know

Liz so well one might think she was one too. That chap
Lazenby appeared, improbably, to be a boss, despite his
glaring character defects. Of course, Brian himself was a boss,
if one counted being Head of Humanities in a poorly funded
and now much-threatened Adult Education Institute as being a
boss. One couldn't so count it, in her view. He employed
nobody; he was employed, and precariously employed at that.
Not even his so-called students thought of him as a figure of
authority. But at least Brian had a job with a name. Whereas I
scurry aimlessly from this to that, thought Alix, as she drove
through the dark evening; they block one path, I try another,
and so it goes on, thought Alix, who at times thought no such
thing, and was not thinking it now with much conviction. It
was the car that had annoyed her.

But the car now proved obedient, and the north-east London
suburbs received her, soothing her as they usually but not
invariably did with their eloquent monotony, their repetitive
regularities, street after street of semi-detached houses, their
lights lit, their curtains drawn, their television sets humming,
their inhabitants safe within. An orderly life on either side of the
dual carriageway, the illusion of an orderly life. In spring there
would be pink blossom at regular intervals. Nice, quiet, safe,
dull, desirable. Desirable residences. How the owners of these
desirable residences had complained ten years ago when
they found that the Garfield Centre was going to be built in their
neighbourhood. Nobody wants prisoners or lunatics on
their doorstep, and there had been a well-fought campaign to
demonstrate that the women of Garfield would be both prisoners and lunatics. Even an optimist like Alix found people
depressing when they revealed themselves in this manner. She
made excuses for them, but she found them depressing.

Mile after mile, ribbons of roads. What was going on,
behind those closed curtains? Were people peacefully frying up
potatoes, or were they hitting one another on the head with
their frying pans? Alix liked to let her mind wander over the
map of Britain, asking herself which interiors she could
visualize, which not. She aspired to a more comprehensive
vision. She aspired to make connections. She and Liz, over
supper together, often spoke of such things. Their own stories
had strangely interlocked, and sometimes she had a sense that
such interlockings were part of a vaster network, that there was
a pattern, if only one could discern it, a pattern that linked
these semi-detached houses of Wanley with those in Leeds and

Northam, a pattern that linked Liz's vast house in Harley Street with the Garfield Centre towards which she herself now drove. The social structure greatly interested Alix. She had once thought of herself as unique, had been encouraged (in theory at least) by her education and by her reading to believe in the individual self, the individual soul, but as she grew older she increasingly questioned these concepts—seeing people perhaps more as flickering impermanent points of light irradiating stretches, intersections, threads, of a vast web, a vast network, which was humanity itself; a web of which much remained dark, apparently but not necessarily unpeopled; peopled by the dark, the unlit, the dim spirits, as yet unknown, the past and the future, the dead, the unborn. And herself, and Brian, and Liz, and Charles, and Esther, and Teddy Lazenby, and Otto and Caroline Werner, and all the rest of them at that bright party, and in these discreet anonymous dark curtained avenues and crescents were but chance and fitful illuminations, chance meetings, chance and unchosen representatives of the thing itself. We are all but a part of a whole which has its own, its distinct, its other meaning; we are not ourselves, we are crossroads, meeting places, points on a curve, we cannot exist independently for we are nothing but signs, conjunctions, aggregations.

Liz and Alix sometimes talked of this vision. Liz had a more robust notion of the self, and took another line on the individual's place in the structure. Each suspected the other (each suspected) of personal, biographical reasons for arguing the case that each, by and large, argued; and the difference between them was in itself odd, as in the great graph of time and place their paths had oddly crossed and oddly coincided. How strange it was, after all, that Alix out of the whole of Britain should have married Brian Bowen, whose father was the uncle of Liz's sister's sister-in-law. Or was this perhaps not odd at all? Alix was not sufficiently numerate to be able to calculate the odds against such an apparently odd relationship, though she could not help but feel that its component, accidental parts were startlingly combined. Was there, could there be, a computer that could work out these things? That could prove, perhaps, that it was yet *more* odd that Liz's sister's sister-in-law had *not* met and married, for instance, Teddy Lazenby? She must ask Otto Werner of this one day; Otto had a new passion for computers, and loved to speculate on their possibilities.

Otto's wife, Caroline, for instance, was alleged to be Edgar Lintot's cousin, though this had not emerged in the days when Liz Ablewhite had been briefly married to Edgar Lintot. At the thought of Caroline Werner, a small shadow of anxiety crossed over Alix's party recollections; the Werners were coming to dinner at the Bowens' the following week, and what should she give them to eat? Otto did not care, did not notice what he ate, which was rather a waste, really, as Caroline Werner was a first-class cook, and wrote cookery books. Alix found this daunting, although Caroline took great pains not to daunt, and was on other, non-culinary matters, a perfectly acceptable non-competitive person. But the knowledge of Caroline's expertise hung heavily, at times, on Alix; heavily, too, hung the knowledge that Caroline was such an unpretentious, agreeable woman that she would be quite happy to eat a plateful of fried-up boiled potatoes, parsley, bacon, and scrambled eggs.

Liz had sidestepped the problem, last night, with caterers, and with Deirdre Kavanagh. Alix could not have afforded this solution, and would have thought it cheating had she been able to afford it, although she thoroughly despised herself for these scruples.

Female roles, female inadequacies, parties, social life. Liz's chandelier had glittered bravely. Gatherings, glitterings, a faint perfume. How had Liz managed it, this assembly? It was against the laws of nature, unnatural. Alix arrived at the gates, at the high wall, with its discreetly disguised barbed wire, at the porter's lodge. There was Stanley, one-handed Stanley, hook handed Stanley, listening in his little hut to his radio, Stanley loves music, as he often says. A Viennese waltz drifted into the January night. Stanley greeted her, wished her a Happy New Year, glanced perfunctorily at her pass, admitted her. Alix drove on to the staff car park, as Technicolor Viennese figures in ball gowns, wearing ruby pendants, flowered corsages turned in her mind, in a scene that derived less from Vienna (where she had never been) than from Tolstoy's descriptions of balls in *War and Peace*. Once, long ago, Otto Werner's father had danced with Esther Breuer's mother, on New Year's Eve, in Vienna, in 1925; but neither of them remembers the incident, and therefore, perhaps, it does not exist? What computer, what analysis, could ever retrieve it? Alix's godmother, also named Alix, had once been to a ball in Vienna. Alix herself had been to a May Ball or two in

Cambridge, in her dancing days. These are now over, thank God, she thinks, as she makes her way towards the discreetly locked, discreetly monitored side gate.

The temperature is high in Garfield on Tuesday, January 1, 1980. Here also it is party time, here also there is glitter. Alix could feel the heat at once, embodied in more than the pink and green balloons, the paper chains, the tinsel. Garfield, of all the institutions in which she had ever worked, was most responsive to mood, to atmosphere; it shifted and changed from day to day, from week to week, for it had, like the larger society of her larger imagining, its own corporate, its own embodied spirit, all the more powerful for its caging, its high barbed wire, its high walls. On some evenings, the place was dull, impassive, stifled, solid with boredom; on some evenings it grumbled ominously, with violence waiting for Lights Out; on some evenings it was studious, attentive, solemn; and on other evenings, like this, it sang with a high, sweet, feverish erotic intensity, a claustrophobic glamour, an emotional throb. This was a sweet evening. Alix found herself embraced, caressed, her hand held, her hair stroked, her new striped woolly hat with its purple bobble extravagantly admired. These liberties were permitted. This was a liberal régime, the only régime of its kind in the country. Sometimes Alix shook off the liberties irritably, but tonight she submitted, responding to the petting, intimate, female warmth; she kissed and was kissed, she thanked them for their Christmas cards, she wished them a Happy New Year, she shook hands with the older women, she laughed and felt safe with her friends, she made no effort to repel their eager affection. (It did not always go this way: sometimes they sulked and abused her, sometimes they threatened her and one another, sometimes they would not attend class.) The wardens, Eric and Hannah Glover, welcomed her with more restraint but equal friendliness and introduced her to a man from the Home Office who had come to visit—well, to inspect, in effect, but the mood was holiday, informal, and the man from the Home Office smiled with the rest of them. There were sandwiches and cups of coffee. The half hour's entertainment was due to begin at eight-thirty; some relatives, waiting now patiently in the hall, had been admitted, but were not allowed backstage to mingle. Freedom, but not too much freedom. Some of those taking part were already in costume: Jilly Fox was wearing what looked like an Iranian chador, contrived from a sheet, Karen Gray was dressed up as a nurse,

and Bob Saxby, who taught pottery, was encased in a
Michelin-man spacesuit which he claimed was an Arctic
explorer's sleeping bag. "Imagine, man, trying to kip in this,"
he kept asking, to anyone who would listen, as he demonstrated
the inconvenience of his garb. Innocent, innocent, like schoolchildren, the thieves and murderers. Toni Hutchinson stroked
Alix's arm, possessively, affectionately, wheedling out of her
the story of the party of the night before: "So you wore your
blue dress? And did you put your hair up? Did it *stay* up?" She
liked to tease Alix about her hair, which was forever wispily
descending from its large wooden slide: Toni's own curled
neatly in angelic dyed blonde braids, and sometimes on request
she had given Alix lessons in hair management, but Alix could
not, would not learn.

The entertainment reminded Alix of the end-of-term pantomime at school, a regular feature of her own girlhood. The
same rows of uncomfortable chairs, the same improvised
curtains, the same primitive lighting effects, the same take-off
versions of popular songs, the same in-jokes, the same
attempts at topicality, the same satirical renderings of figures of
authority. One girl produced a more than passable imitation of
Hannah Glover's dress and mannerisms, in a sketch in which
the pseudo-Hannah reprimanded a contrite inmate for
"smoking in the bog": the shapeless woolly cardigan over the
wrongly buttoned blouse, the broad-seated tweed skirt, the
slipping petticoat, the spectacles constantly removed and
polished on the slipping petticoat and replaced, the sensible
shoes, one with a trailing shoelace, the repeated exhortation to
"help us to help you," the earnest smiling and the short-
sighted blinking, the flat Midlands accent. Cruel, a little, but
not savage: Alix could see Hannah smiling gamely, taking it in
good part, and wondered if she was also taking in the rather
subtle sub-text of allusions to drugs other than nicotine. One
could never tell how blind Hannah's blind eye really was. It
was Eric's turn next: his presenter appeared in jogging track
suit, and false beard, and needed to do little more than puff
heavily round the stage several times intoning, "No, not on the
roof, no, not on the roof," to bring the house down, rousing
laughter even from those who did not know that these were the
mysterious words that the warden had uttered in a loud cry
when abruptly roused from slumber during a session of group
therapy. One or two of the visiting psychiatrists were brought
forth in a psychiatric chorus, singing in psychobabble; Bob

Saxby was presented giving a learned discourse on the nature of the pot, insisting reassuringly in a phrase that needed no exaggeration, so frequently was it heard from him in real life, that "a few irregularities add charm to a pot." An example of a charming pot was produced, to much mirth. Alix herself was not mimicked, or not that she could see; she did not know whether this was a sign of affection, contempt, or indifference. Jilly Fox did a rather well-informed feminist sketch comparing the chaplain's sexist attitudes to those of the Ayatollah; it wasn't very funny and the chaplain was not amused, although he wisely pretended to be. Then Jilly cast off her chador and sang, a plaintive rendering of "The Winter of Seventy-Nine," and suddenly, as happens on these occasions, the knockabout mood changed, people stopped laughing, tears stood in eyes, as Jilly's harsh, grating flat voice lamented the year and deplored the future, as her white, beaky, angry face gazed fiercely at the audience, as the confined energy of months swelled up in self-pity around the room, orchestrated by Jilly's incantation:

> *"All you kids that just sit in line,*
> *You should have been there back in seventy-nine.*
> *In the winter of seventy-nine,*
> *When all the gay geezers got put inside,*
> *The coloured kids were getting crucified,*
> *A few fought back and a few folks died,*
> *Yes, a few of us fought, and a few of us died,*
> *In the winter of seventy-nine,*
> *Back in seventy-nine,"*

sang, angrily, menacingly, Jilly Fox. Jilly Fox had been educated at an expensive boarding school. She was doing time for several rather serious drug-related offences. She was having an affair with Toni Hutchinson of the blonde braids, who was the daughter of a pharmacist in Hendon. Jilly had passed her A level in English Literature the summer before, having notably failed to acquire any qualifications except a Pass in O level Divinity at her expensive school; now she was hoping to qualify for a course at the Open University. Jilly Fox had once said bleakly to Alix Bowen on a bad evening that her release would be the death of her. Alix feared this might be true.

Alix, driving home, thought that Hannah Glover probably had been rather hurt, despite her appearance of good humour.

She was vulnerable, still, after years of inevitable disappoint-
ments, years of failure. She said she liked to think that the
younger women looked on her as a mother, but of course they
didn't: they found her faintly ridiculous, old-fashioned, gullible, naïve. She would never have been able to operate without
her husband, Eric, who for all his bluff and jolly manner was
in practice a hard man, a no-nonsense man, who sent trouble-
makers back where they came from, into the main prison
system, without any heart searchings or regrets. Maybe,
thought Alix, that mild, concerned approach of Hannah's is all
a front, devised between them over the years, consciously or
unconsciously, to mediate, to palliate, to distract attention?
Her own parents had played such a game, but in their case it
was her father who had played the mild, the foolish role. God,
what a fool he had been, was. Many times during the past
evening he had returned to her, in ludicrous, colourful, brightly
painted effigy, all his embarrassments clustered and clanging
round him, all his mannerisms protruding, projected, en-
hanced: the sharp red nose, the usually broken bifocal spectacles, the striped woolly lunch-spattered waistcoats, the bald
shining brown freckled Professor Brainstorm brow, the pockets
full of string, the green socks and brown sandals, the little
pedantries, the favourite quotations, the antiquarian commentary, the hydrometer, the tufts of hair in his ears, the batty,
potty, dotty, hurt, persistent grin. Dotty Doddridge, Deputy
Head, French teacher. What a buffoon, what a butt, what a
caricature. How she had suffered for him, for her poor pitiable
ridiculous father, how she had hated her cruel peers for their
relentless mocking, how she had dreaded each Christmas
pantomime, each school-leavers farewell, each assembly that
she knew her father was due to conduct, each occasion on
which she heard him open his mouth in public. The disorder,
the whisperings, the giggles, the open contempt! And her
mother, in revenge, in reaction, brusque, tart, offhand, cutting,
fearful, fearing and avoided, uneasily detached, dismissively
remote. Large conspicuous wooden figures, Dotty and Dolly,
and beneath their knees skulked little Alix Doddridge, creeping
quietly, smiling obsequiously, keeping a low profile, longing
to be ordinary, longing with such passion to be unnoticed, to be
accepted, to be one of the crowd, not Dotty's Daughter, with
all that that implied.

Ah well, her parents were old now, and retired, and nobody
thought them funny any more: indeed, it was only the intensely

conventional world of a Yorkshire boarding school that had made them seem so eccentric in the first place. They were now revealed as what they had always been, not figures of fun, not left-wing political extremists, not loony vegetarians (though they were vegetarians), but harmless, mild, Labour-voting, CND-supporting, Fabian-pamphlet-reading intellectuals, of a species that Alix now knew to be far from extinct. Odd, though, that they had once seemed so odd, so isolated, for the school at which Dotty Doddridge vainly endeavoured to teach French had been nonconformist, faintly progressive, certainly egalitarian in its religious and social complexion; it had offered a liberal, secularized, healthy coeducation, and had on its foundation in the 1860s set out to attract the children of vegetarians, Quakers, free-thinkers, pacifists, Unitarians, reformers. Its academic success had been such that it had become progressively less progressive, its original zeal swamped by the fee-paying prosperous solid northern conservatism of parents and offspring: it had become a bastion of respectability, its one-time principles upheld by stray survivors like Doddridge, who appeared blithely not to notice that at election time the entire school, with one or two flamboyant exceptions, howled its enthusiasm for the Tory party. A rum evolution, Alix had often thought, though it had not seemed strange at the time: what had then seemed strange, in her girlhood, had been her parents' quaint socialist ideals, which had caused her such embarrassment, and, partly because of that embarrassment, had inspired in her such undeviating loyalty. "I say, does your dad *really* vote Labour?" had been one of the politer questions addressed to her at elections and other periods of heightened political interest. "My dad's a Socialist," Alix would mumble in reply, aged eleven, twelve, thirteen, fourteen, thinking that the word Socialist sounded somehow more acceptable, more intellectual, than the dreadful word Labour, with its connotations of manual toil and prison routine. From the age of fifteen onwards she became more defiant, and would sometimes even attempt a half-baked account of some of the notions she had heard discussed at home in the Deputy Master's Lodge. She began to affect, in history lessons, an interest in the Soviet Union; such was the climate of opinion in this progressive boarding school in the north of England in the early 1950s, amongst the sons and daughters of tradesmen and doctors, industrialists and university lecturers, dentists and estate agents, lawyers and farmers, that her interest was regarded

with awe and alarm or with frank disbelief by those who did
not dismiss it as the affectation which, in fact, at this stage it
was. Nobody, during the Cold War, was interested in the
Soviet Union, not even Alix herself, not even her parents, who
never mentioned the place. It was taboo. Indeed, her father had
shocked her by breaking this silence and by advising her, when
she went up to Cambridge, not to join the Communist party: a
joke's a joke, he told her, but you don't want trouble with visas
if ever you want to go to America. A surprisingly worldly
comment from so innocent a man, she had thought this.

Cambridge had been different. There had been Communists
there. There had been the lot, or so it had seemed, at
Cambridge: Socialists, Communists, socialites, die-hard
dinner-jacketed Pitt Club Tories, bohemians, Christians, lacrosse and rugger players, sloggers, poets, actors, Leavisites,
wits, bores, eccentrics, homosexuals; to Cambridge they
flocked, from ancient grammar schools, upstart grammar
schools, progressive schools, public schools, private schools,
even from private tutors in the south of France. God's plenty.
Looking back from the eclectic seventies, the essentially
post-sixties seventies, these youngsters of the fifties might well
appear a deeply conventional, timid, duffle-jacketed wasp-
waisted narrow-based crew, but to Alix, newly emerging from
the all-too-personal matrix or patrix of The Heights, they had
seemed richly various. Her own college, at first encounter,
struck her as somewhat dimly conformist, with long brown
corridors and an unexpectedly high proportion of young women
apparently wrapped up in the triumphs of yesteryear on the
hockey field or in the prefects' Common Room, but even there
she had discovered part of what she was looking for: in the
persons of Liz Ablewhite (now Headland) and Esther Breuer
(still Breuer) she had discovered it, and rediscovered it there
each time she met them, which was, these days, on average once
a fortnight. She had found it in them perhaps more securely than
in the friends she had made in other colleges, with whom her
relationships had been complicated by sex. She had married one
of these complications, for that is what young women did in
those days: educated young women married, straight out of
college, as she and Liz had done. Liz's first marriage had lasted
all of ten months: Alix's had lasted slightly longer, and had been
terminated not by divorce but by death.

And now she is married to Brian Bowen, towards whom she

drives home through the January night. It is a happy marriage. They have one son, Sam. He is eleven. Alix also has a son by her first husband. He is twenty-two, and his name is Nicholas. Liz Headleand suspects that Alix Bowen is in love with Nicholas Manning, and wonders if she knows it. Brian Bowen suspects that Alix Bowen is in love with Nicholas Manning, and wonders if she knows it. Alix Bowen, for her part, has strong suspicions about Liz's relationship with her three stepsons, but considers her own feelings for Nicholas entirely natural. Esther Breuer is not much interested in the distinction between the natural and the unnatural. Both Alix and Liz are of the opinion that Esther's relationship with her niece, with whom she shares her flat, is very odd indeed, but it is not to their advantage to discuss this with one another, or with Esther herself, and they never mention it.

When Alix arrived home in Wandsworth, she found Brian and Sam sitting comfortably in front of television on the ancient sofa with their socked and shoeless feet up watching a Len Deighton movie. She told Sam it was time he was in bed, but without conviction. She sat down with them. Brian told her that Esther phoned and wanted her to ring back. Alix said it is too late. She started to watch the movie.

In the morning Alix was about to apply herself to a file of Home Office statistics when the phone rang. It was Esther, with the news that their friend Liz had rung her the night before to tell her that she and Charles were getting divorced, and that Charles intended to marry Henrietta Latchett. I thought something was going on, said Esther, and it appears I was right. Good God, said Alix. I had absolutely no *idea*, said Alix, how ever did *you* guess? I saw Charles and Henrietta at a Private View in the National Portrait Gallery, said Esther. Last month. That's no evidence, said Alix. Well, you know how fond Charles is of painting, said Esther. And evidence or not, I was right, said Esther. Good God, said Alix, what a surprise. She tried to ring you but you weren't in, said Esther. Well, I don't know what to say, said Alix, I thought they'd stuck it out so long they'd stay stuck, didn't you? I mean to say, Charles is an absolute prick, but he's been a prick for twenty years, why divorce him now?

Esther pointed out that Charles was the one who wanted the divorce.

"To marry *Henrietta*?" asked Alix, in a tone of incredulity. "How could he? I mean, he may be a prick, but he's not an absolute fool."

And they continued to discuss the personality of Lady Henrietta, or rather her apparent lack of personality, for some time, until Alix, almost as an afterthought, got round to enquiring how Liz was taking it. "She sounded fine to me," said Esther. "Well, of course, she would be," said Alix. "But why didn't she tell us earlier?"

"Apparently she didn't know earlier. He sprung it on her."

"Good God. What a bastard. I'd better give her a ring, I suppose."

"I asked her to supper on Friday. Can you make it?"

"Of course," said Alix. "I'll see you then."

Esther, having thus fulfilled her obligations to her friends, forgot them both instantly, and returned her attention to a volume called *The Vegetation of Medieval Europe* and a German monograph on Sodoma; works which she was reading and annotating by her own interleaved system, a system which had evolved from her inability to concentrate fully on any one topic for more than ten minutes. It had thrown up some very challenging cross-references in its time, and she was at the moment pursuing a connection between the nature of quattro-cento pigmentation, and lichenology as a method of dating the antiquity of landscape: a gratifyingly pointless and therefore pure pursuit which enabled her mind to wander in the direction of Italy and to hover about the abstraction of a particular shade of green-blue which she had noted in many a painted Italian scene as well as in the lichens of ancient English woodland. A pale, delicate, hard, metallic, heavenly, shocking, suggestive green-blue. It tinted dry artistic Italian cypress trees and the undersides of vine leaves, it lived on the damp bark of English oaks and thorns. It expressed both distance and presence: it was both of the background and of the sharpest proximity. An enigmatic colour, speaking of metaphysical correspondences. Signifying nothing but the search for itself. But an essential shade. Italian farmers claimed that some of its modern mani-festations were inspired by pesticide, but pesticide would not account for the hue of those ravishing little sprigged seaweed trees on the Tuscan hillsides in the frescoes at Monte Oliveto, of Sodoma and Signorelli. Badgers and magpies featured also in those frescoes, and frequented the hillsides to this day. So that vegetable blue also must then and now have had a natural home? Esther Breuer made a note to order Oxenholme's monograph on Signorelli, and read on, waiting for some little current to leap from one open page to the other, from one lobe of the brain to the other, and to ignite a new twig of meaning, to fill a small new cell of the storehouse of her erudition. She was content with twigs and cells, or so it seemed. Sometimes, when accused of eccentricity or indeed perversity of vision, she would claim that all knowledge must always be omnipresent in all things, and that one could startle oneself into seeing the whole by tweaking unexpectedly at a surprised corner of the great mantle. At other times she conceded that her interests were pointless but harmless. I am not ambitious, I do not seek answers to large questions, she would say. This would baffle her friends and her students, who had the impression that she was engaged in some vast if imprecise enterprise. No, I prefer precision, Esther would say. They did not know how to take it.

Jane Austen recommended three or four families in a country village as the thing to work on when planning a novel. Esther Breuer might well have been expected to approve this advice, with its implication that depth rather than breadth is of importance, and intimate knowledge of a corner more valuable than a sketchy acquaintance with the globe. In fact, perversely, Esther Breuer disliked the only Jane Austen novel she had ever read (which was, perversely, *Sense and Sensibility*) and frequently boasts of her inability to tackle the others. "Too English for me," she will sometimes add, in her impeccably English middle-class intellectual's voice.

Esther, Liz, and Alix, who in Jane Austen's day would never have met at all, met in Cambridge in 1952. Just before Christmas, when they were up for interview from their respective schools. Alix was applying to read English Literature, Liz to read Natural Sciences (with a view to medicine), and Esther to read Modern Languages. This should have safely prevented any rapport between them, but did not. There were, it is true, many awkwardnesses in their first communications, for none of them was much used to speaking to strangers, but this lack of practice was balanced by a strong desire on the part of all three of them to enter upon a new life in which speaking to strangers was possible. Otherwise, each had separately recognized, the future was circumscribed. Somehow, haltingly, over dinner in Hall (chicken, leeks, and tinned spaghetti, a mixture delicious to each after years of post-war whale meat and school meals) they lurched into conversation, having found themselves for no good reason sitting together; Liz and Alix discovered that both came from Yorkshire, and that neither played lacrosse, nor had ever seen it being played, and Esther joined the discussion by volunteering that she had herself managed to avoid playing netball for the past three years on the grounds that she was too small. "I said I was unfairly handicapped, and they let me do extra Latin instead," she said. The fact that both Liz and Alix seemed to accept that extra Latin might be preferable to netball indicated that further interchange might be possible, and they continued to talk, through the fruit tart and custard, of the nature of intellectual and physical education, of matter and spirit, of Descartes (brought up by Esther), of T. S. Eliot (brought up by Alix), and of schizophrenia (brought up by Liz). The matter was abstract, for none of them knew anything other than abstractions, and the tone lofty. It was what they had expected of university, but had not hoped so soon to find. Esther, at the end of the meal, expressed her satisfaction with her new companions by inviting them to go with her to visit a friend already attending the college, an old girl of her school. They accepted with alacrity the prospect of a glimpse of the world inside, and all three of them went along dark portrait-hung corridors and up panelled staircases to the room of one Flora Piercy, a second-year history student of considerable sophistication, who offered them a glass of wine. Had they known how rare such a commodity was in a woman's college at that date, they might have been even more astonished, but in a sense, looking round Flora's room, with its bright scatter cushions and Picasso prints and posters for plays at the Amateur Dramatic Company, with its invitations on the mantelpiece, with its gas fire and clutter of old shoes, with its romantic piles of what looked like lecture notes and essays, with its candle in a pewter stick and its wilting rose in a vase, they were beyond astonishment. The glass of wine went quickly to each head, for Alix's family was teetotal, and Liz's alcohol consumption to that date comprised perhaps three glasses of brown sherry and one (celebrating her A levels with her teacher) of Liebfraumilch: Esther seemed better connected with drink as with friends, but even she became confiding under the mild influence. They shared their dreams and aspirations, encouraged by the benevolent, admonitory, tutelary spirit of ample broad-faced Flora. "I would like," said Liz Ablewhite, after midnight, staring into the white flaming chalky cracked pitted flaring columns of the gas fire, "to make sense of things. To understand." By things, she meant herself. Or she thought she meant herself. "I would like," said Alix, "to change things." By things, she did not mean herself. Or thought she did not mean herself. "You reach too high," said Esther. "I wish to acquire interesting information. That is all."

Liz, at that time, was pale and fair and thin, a colourless creature, unmade-up, drooping and slightly stooping, ill-complexioned, cardiganed, dull, yet glowing with a greenish pallor that compelled attention. Alix was mousy, square faced, healthy of complexion, and, even then, extraordinarily pleasant of expression, with a pleasantness that was at times radiant, and almost always irrefutable: she was wearing, as girls who had them did for their Oxbridge interviews in those days, a two-piece middle-aged suit of an oatmeal mix, with square shoulders and a straight skirt. Esther was small, neat, brown of skin, smooth, tidy, even (almost) elegant, yet somehow at the same time pugnacious of aspect, subversive, aggressive, commanding, Napoleonic of manner. She was wearing a severe school uniform, olive green, from an expensive private school. It looked ironic, satiric, suggestive on her small frame.

Flora Piercy was wearing black velvet trousers, and a large white cable-knit sweater. Her eyelids were painted blue with a blue greasy paste called eye shadow. Alix bought some the next day, on her free half day in Cambridge before she took the Bletchley route to her Oxford interview (for she was a clever girl, Alix)—but she never dared to apply it, save in the privacy of her own room, until she went to Cambridge herself as a bona fide student the following autumn.

Liz, Alix, and Esther all obtained places at the college of their choice, in Cambridge, and there were reunited, to gossip there and elsewhere over subsequent decades of their fortuitous friendship. They lost touch for some time with Flora, their first presiding deity, but even she was to reappear in another context, another life.

Liz Ablewhite was offered, and graciously accepted, the Alethea Ward Scholarship in Natural Sciences (an annual college award specifically designated by Dr. Ward, 1853–1935, for female students of medicine from the County of Yorkshire, her own home county), the goal towards which her mother had been directing her for the past ten years. Great Expectations. Is there anything more peculiar, more idiosyncratic, more circumscribed in these expectations than in those of Pip, or of Dickens himself, towards being a gentleman? In the 1950s, one of the surest ways forward for an intellectual young woman from the provinces, for a socially disadvantaged young woman from the provinces, was through Oxford, through Cambridge. Not through Manchester, or Leeds, or Durham, or Bristol; but through Oxford or Cambridge. Dr. Alethea Ward had known this, and thus had left her money, some of which eventually Liz Ablewhite had inherited. Rita Ablewhite knew this, though how she knew it remained, to Liz, a mystery which she did not think, did not care to question. As Pip cared not to question too closely the sources of his own endowment. Between them, the deceased Dr. Alethea Ward and the surviving Rita Ablewhite directed Liz Ablewhite towards Cambridge, and Liz in her turn handed the same knowledge on to her stepsons and her daughters.

Alix was offered places at both colleges of her choice. In fact, she was offered a better deal (let us not go into too many historic technicalities) in Oxford, but she chose Cambridge because of Flora Piercy's eye shadow, and because of Dr. Leavis. At Cambridge she met her first husband, Sebastian Manning, who introduced her to a world in which socialism, far from being ridiculous, was natural, chic, colourful, confident, artistic. Sebastian's parents were artists of some repute, one a painter, the other a potter, and they did not think much of the austerities of Dr. Leavis. Bloomsbury and St. Ives were more their style. Now Sebastian is dead, long dead, and Alix is married to Brian Bowen, son of a saw polisher, grandson of a furnaceman, and often sits with him on an old settee in her stockinged feet. Brian Bowen admires Dr. Leavis, with some respectful reservations.

Esther was also offered places at both universities, and chose Cambridge because it offered her a scholarship, and because her brother had been at King's, and because she heard an owl hoot thrice in the college garden when she retired to her narrow bed after the glass of wine with Flora Piercy. This last explanation for her choice is the one she most frequently proffered. In Cambridge she quickly established herself as a cult figure of mysterious portent: she claimed to be in love with her brother, whom nobody had ever seen, and went in for gnomic utterances and baroque clutter. Now she lives in a small flat in Ladbroke Grove, with a young woman she says is her niece. She sits in her bed-sitting-room-study reading books. Her walls are painted bright red. Not Pompeian red, as she sometimes points out: it is less blue, slightly more flame, more orange coloured. She is not sure whether it could accurately be described as Venetian red. She is still surrounded by baroque clutter.

These three women, it will readily and perhaps with some irritation be perceived, were amongst the *crème de la crème* of their generation. Illustrious educational institutions not merely offered them places, but also attempted to entice them. Their initial meeting at dinner in Hall was not quite accidental: the nature of the *placement* was such that strong scholarship candidates were more likely than not to find themselves sitting together. They did not, of course, know this at the time.

Narratives, in the past, related the adventures of the famous and the wealthy. Kings, queens, emperors, warlords. In *The Tale of Genji*, which has a claim to be considered the world's first novel, an emperor weeps for lost love in the opening pages. (Do pages open in a Japanese novel? Probably not.) In Jane Austen, to come nearer home, the protagonists are not, it is true, titled, but they are privileged. By youth, by wit, by beauty, and sometimes by wealth. The princesses of their country villages.

Liz, Alix, and Esther were not princesses. They were not beautiful, they were not rich. But they were young, and they had considerable wit. Their fate should, therefore, be in some sense at least exemplary: opportunity was certainly offered to them, they had choices, at eighteen the world opened for them and displayed its riches, the brave new world of Welfare State and County Scholarships, of equality for women; they were the élite, the chosen, the garlanded of the great social dream. Adventure and possibility lay before them, as they had not lain before Liz's sister, Shirley, who married at nineteen and stayed on in Northam, or before Dora Sutcliffe, who left school at

fifteen and sold sweets in Woolworth's until she married
Shirley's husband's brother, Steve.

Brian Bowen's sister Barbara went to Australia and married
a building contractor, but that is another story. Brian himself,
had he not done his National Service, would, arguably, still be
working at Pitts and Harley and might have continued to work
there until 1981 when this ancient, well-established firm
closed, with the loss of six hundred jobs. But that is another
part of this story, and not to be pursued here, for Brian is not
a woman and reflections on his prospects or lack of prospects
in 1952 would at this juncture muddy the narrative tendency.
Forget I mentioned him. Let us return to Liz, Alix, and Esther.

Liz, Alix, and Esther were reunited in Cambridge in the
autumn of 1953. They had spent their "year off" in highly
dissimilar circumstances. Esther paid her first visit to Italy,
where she spent three months at the Università per Stranieri in
Perugia, learned some Italian, drank a great deal of wine, took
up with a middle-aged American art historian and began to
look at paintings. Alix spent three months working as an au
pair girl—working very hard, for no pay—in a suburb of Paris,
bored out of her mind most of the time, but strangely,
surprisingly consoled by the youngest member of the large
family, a baby, which, unlike its larger siblings, seemed to like
her. Alix, then as ever, liked anybody who liked her. She spent
her rare afternoons off visiting the sights of Paris, or lying in
the Luxembourg Gardens alone, reading Dostoevsky and
Sartre and Camus, and sending out contradictory messages to
idle young men who wondered if it would be worth trying to
pick her up.

Liz stayed at home in Northam, studying. Her mother (she
knew without asking, there was never any possibility of her
asking) expected her to stay at home. Liz had a calendar and
she crossed off the days in black ink. She read Victorian novels
and studied textbooks of anatomy. She started to read Freud
(*The Psychopathology of Everyday Life, Totem and Taboo*),
without understanding, yet without misunderstanding. She
tried to learn the Book of Job by heart, but never got safely past
the end of the second chapter; the first two chapters were on the
dull side, overloaded with yoke of oxen and she-asses, with
Eliphaz the Temanite, Bildad the Shuhite, and Zophar the
Naamathite, Job's comforters. Liz wanted to get on to the
exciting bits, in which Job demanded why light was given to
him that was in misery, and life to the bitter in soul: in which

Job desired to argue with his God: in which the Lord answered Job out of the whirlwind: but she knew it would be cheating to miss out the she-asses and skip to the livelier parts, so she plodded dully on with the dull narrative. Obsessional behaviour: she determined that one day she would find an explanation for it, and, meanwhile, pursued it.

Esther sent Liz a postcard, from Perugia. Liz put it under her bedroom mantelpiece, and touched it, every morning on rising and every night as she went to bed. Esther sent a card to Alix, too, but Alix's mother forwarded it accidentally-on-purpose to the wrong address possibly because she did not care for a rather elaborate allusion to Lachrymae Christi in the text, nor for the brightly coloured shiny modern Madonna which the card portrayed. Alix's mother, broad-minded though she was, did not approve of Catholicism, and was hardly to know that Esther was Jewish.

It would be wrong to give the impression that Liz, Alix, and Esther fell into one another's arms with cries of delight when they met again that October, or to suggest that they proved thereafter inseparable. But they were, nevertheless, pleased to rediscover one another, and sat up late on their first evening in Esther's room, which had already begun to put out hints of its later decorative eccentricities. They talked of their summer adventures, of their hopes for the future, but mostly of their own provenance. Liz attempted her first sketch of her mother, her first outline for the outside world of the domestic ghost with which she had lived so long; Alix spoke of her relief at escaping from the small boarding-school world in which her parents and her contemporaries all knew one another far too well; Esther conjured up visions of both deprivation and splendour in her own past. They did not know then, were not to know for many years, were never fully to understand what it was that held them together—a sense of being on the margins of English life, perhaps, a sense of being outsiders, looking in from a cold street through a lit window into a warm lit room that later might prove to be their own? Removed from the mainstream by a mad mother, by a deviant ideology, by refugee status and the war-sickness of Middle Europe? None of this would have meant anything to them, then, as they drank their Nescafé, which in those days came not in granules in jars but in powder in tins with brown, cream, and white labels; tins which cost 2/6d. each. They thought they found one another interesting. And so they became friends.

They also made other friends, of course, both inside and outside their own college. Liz, like a pale convent girl too long mewed up, went wild in her first year, as she discovered the world of parties she had hitherto known only by reading and by hearsay. In those days, such was the imbalance between the sexes, women were much in demand as status symbols, as sleeping partners, as lovers, as party ballast, and Liz went out a great deal, her appearance improving dramatically as she did so. She had little money for clothes, but that did not matter; it did not even matter, much, to her, though sometimes she wished she had more than two dresses, one pink, one grey. She hung herself around with cheap earrings and necklaces and bangles. Her stockings were always laddered. She was much invited. Men accosted her on bridges, in lectures, in bookshops. She tried them all. But she never disobeyed the rules by spending a night, illicitly, out of college. Like Cinderella, she returned at midnight. In the mornings, in the long vacations, she worked.

In her second year, she met Edgar Lintot. He was a conspicuous high-profiled figure, in those days, a medical student and a man of the theatre, famed for his Footlights appearances and his impromptu wit. Liz also dabbled with acting, and played several roles rather well—an inventive Helena in *A Midsummer Night's Dream* and a curiously haunting, poignant Bellario in *Philaster*, directed by Edgar. Wounded loyalty and dignified pathos were her line onstage, although offstage she grew increasingly self-assertive. Her social world, in Cambridge, was largely theatrical. After midnight, in college, she would discuss it with Alix and Esther.

Alix's social world was somewhat different. Having been to a coeducational school, she did not find men a novelty, and in theory ought to have been able to discriminate better than Liz (who endured some fairly dreadful experimental evenings in her search for entertainment), but her natural kindness made it almost impossible for her to refuse any overture, however offensive, however *louche*. A mixture of gratitude and pity held her captive through many a long, polite, sad, dull declaration of admiration, and kept her smiling through many an impolite drunken assault on her brassière straps. "What *will* become of me?" she would sometimes ask Liz and Esther, in mock alarm.

What became of her was Sebastian Manning and his friends

and relations. She met Sebastian at a political rally. Alix continued to attend such things, in unbroken allegiance to her upbringing. Sebastian was there in allegiance to his upbringing, too. She knew who he was, for she had observed him at lectures and had been informed of his parentage. The names meant nothing to her, as her own family austerity eschewed, in characteristic northern professional manner, any interest in the visual arts, but she picked up what they were meant to mean. Of more interest to her was Sebastian's appearance, which was delightful—wide-eyed, golden-red-haired, sunny, surprised— and his manner, which, as they fell into chat, was even more attractive. Never had she met anyone of such mildness, such ease, such openness of heart, such certainty of pleasing. Sebastian liked everybody. He said so. He certainly liked Alix, and after the demo he took her off for lunch in a pub and then for a walk to his room in King's, where he showed her his pots and his paintings. He also made her a piece of toast. People dropped in and more toast was eaten. In no time at all Alix became his intimate friend. Sebastian appeared to believe that the world was a place full of sunshine and enjoyment. He had been educated at a progressive, artistic school in the south, with a radical tradition very different (despite its ostensible similarities) from the one in which Alix had been reared. She loved this new climate. She basked in it, she took off her clothes and browned herself in it. It was so easy to be with Sebastian. He never called upon one to doubt one's welcome. Nervous Alix, sycophantic Alix, diffident Alix found in his undemanding ease the simplicity of Paradise. He had, in fact, had something of a Rousseauesque upbringing, much of it in Provence: his parents too liked the sun, and had defected from St. Ives at an early stage. Ripe tomatoes, red, green, and yellow peppers, artichokes, olives, courgettes. These vegetables were not then, in the 1950s, part of the staple British diet. They were symbols, glowing, of plenty, of the plenty that Sebastian's uncle (a Labour MP, no less) believed and somehow expected could and should belong to all, regardless of the rigours of a northern European climate and a war-crippled economy. They featured in still-lifes on Sebastian's walls. Alix began to think that perhaps, after all, it was not wrong to be happy. In her heart of hearts she still suspected that it was, but the charmed garden of Sebastian and his friends opened to her so easily, so seductively, that what could she do but step inside? It was not as though there was anything *wrong* with

Sebastian's ideas. He was a child of nature, a romantic, not an élitist. His happiness made others happy. What could be wrong with that?

Esther led a slightly less straightforward social life. Much of it was conducted from her own room, which soon acquired a shrine-like notoriety, both on account of its furnishings and its occupant. Young men and women, not-so-young men and women wended their way across Cambridge to sit for an hour with Esther Breuer, sipping coffee, tea, or, if they were favoured, vermouth or wine, as they gazed at the red draped walls, the crowded bookshelves, the umbrella stand, the hat stand, the cabin trunk, the medley of different-patterned fabrics, the little figurines that marched along the shelves in front of the books, the carefully assembled strip of photographed Roman frieze, the little glass doves in front of the tiny mosaic fountain. (The fountain did not play; Esther was not a magician, and college rooms did not rise to running water for people, let alone fountains.) Outside college, Esther's life was eclectic, fragmented, secretive. The American art historian whom she had met in Perugia reappeared as professor on a sabbatical from his East Coast university, and was to be seen dining with Esther in restaurants beyond the reach of the undergraduate purse: the Arts Theatre Restaurant, Miller's, the Garden House Hotel. She went out with other, older, even weightier men. But she also had alliances with people nearer her own age, notably with a wild young postgraduate architect, a hard-drinking, reckless, one-off character called Colin Lindsey, who was already provided with a wife and a baby, but who would nevertheless take his turn to sit on Esther's beaded rug. Throughout this, Esther maintained the fiction that she was in love with her older brother, Saul, and maintained it so well that not even Alix and Liz knew the truth of the matter. The brother existed, for they saw him once; he was an unlikely object of incestuous passion, a small, dark, worried-looking lawyer, with a curiously compelling speech defect. Esther hinted that it was the grim circumstances of their childhood that had drawn them together with a love that dared not speak its name. Saul had been born in Vienna, in 1931; Esther, in Berlin, in 1935. They were both lucky to be alive. They had huddled together, small exiles, refugees, in a boarding house in Manchester, while their mother looked for work and their father hung on in Berlin trying to assemble his papers. He assembled them: he got out just in time, he joined his wife and children: he re-established himself as manufacturer of optical devices: but those early years left their mark. Or so Esther said.

It took Liz over two decades to read the signals of Esther's room, and to recognize the affinities of its décor. Through her Cambridge years and long afterwards she simply accepted them as evidence of Esther's eccentricity and originality—and it was not, after all, difficult to be original in a period when most female undergraduates, fresh from school and far from well off, ventured little further in terms of home-making than a cushion or a Chianti bottle, a photograph or a teddy bear, a gingham frill round an orange box or a postcard collage on the wall, a modernist paper mobile or an arrangement of seaside pebbles. But, years later, Liz found herself visiting the Freud museum in Berggasse in Vienna, and there she suddenly saw it all—the red walls, the figurines, and, perhaps more distinctively, the predominance of red carpet-cushions, the characteristic mixture of Persian geometric patterns on floor and couch—a Jewish mixture, a Viennese mixture, a Freudian mixture? Liz did not know, and doubted if Esther knew. She had noticed earlier, of course, Esther's particular liking for red. The walls of Freud's consulting room were red also. Liz found this very interesting, but did not comment on it to Esther. Esther claimed not to be interested in Freud.

And so these three densely packed, formative years passed, preparing these three highly selected young women for their respective careers. Liz's education was to take more than three years: she had already decided to specialize in psychiatry, and knew she still had a long journey ahead of her. This did not prevent her from becoming engaged, in 1956, to Edgar Lintot, who was about to leave Cambridge to take up a pre-registration post at St. Michael's Hospital in Lewisham. He had decided to opt for medicine rather than the stage, and had felt virtuous, mildly sacrificial, a little self-important while making this choice. His rejection of the overtures of a smooth-faced, smooth-tongued, camp, high-powered theatrical agent coincided with his offer of marriage to Liz. The high-minded, the dedicated, the serious path. They joked about this, but so it was. He bought her a ring, with little seed pearls and a sapphire. The world lay all before them and, from Liz's point of view most importantly, its roads did not lead back, to

Northam. She would never have to go home again. (And who is to say that she was not a little piqued that her younger sister, Shirley, was already planning marriage?)

In the same month, in what was for her the last term of her formal education, Alix became engaged to Sebastian Manning. It seems odd, now, but so it was: this is what young people did in those days. Sebastian was not quite clear about his own job intentions at this stage, nor did he have to be so. There were plenty of jobs. His family did not take jobs seriously. None of them had ever had one, except for his MP uncle, who had once been a journalist. Sebastian thought he might be a journalist. Or go into the BBC. Or something like that. Anybody, he knew, would be glad to have him. For Alix, marrying Sebastian was an alternative to a job. She did not feel entirely at ease about this, and even went to consult the careers adviser in Cambridge, who gave her various leaflets, told her about trainee courses at the BBC, and sent her off for a two-day inspection of the Civil Service. Alix, I regret to say, did not take the Civil Service seriously as a prospect. She looked at the sample examination papers with alarm and concluded that she was lamentably ignorant about the way the world worked. Wordsworth, Blake, Chaucer, George Eliot she knew well, but not the name of the president of Chad or the number of trade-union-sponsored MPs in the House of Commons. She did not care for the serious young men who toured the Home Office and the Treasury with her. In their early twenties, before taking their finals, they were already worried about their pensions, and their wife's pension. "Have you got a wife?" Alix wished to ask, of one particularly baby faced, prematurely anxious candidate, who was contemplating the allowance that he might leave to his wife should he predecease her, but did not dare. It would have been impolite. Grasshoppers three a-fiddling went, Alix hummed to herself, as she ran down Whitehall for the bus, swinging her shoulder bag in the cold, bright, showery, uncertain sun of late April. She was happy. She would marry Sebastian, she would never have to go back to cold and sooty Leeds to drink brown soup and eat gristle stew with dark greens and mashed potatoes. Sebastian bought her a ring, with a little gold heart and an inscription. "Forever," it said, in Victorian script.

Esther had elected to take a higher degree, in the History of Art. Art history as a subject was not yet available at Cambridge: she would attach herself to the Courtauld Institute.

There was plenty of money around to finance such choices. Esther was encouraged to continue her studies. She would return to Perugia for the summer, to learn more Italian.

Both Liz and Esther went to Alix and Sebastian's wedding, in early July, in Leeds. It was a sunny day, and the garden party in the grounds of the school was a success, for Deborah and Stephen Manning, alerted by Sebastian and Alix, had insisted on presenting champagne (you won't get anything to drink otherwise, they had been warned) and it went quickly to the heads of those unaccustomed to drinking at all, while Sebastian's contingent had primed themselves at their hotel before arriving, in double defence. Laughter and a smell of cut grass rose from the lawns, and in the distance children played tennis. High seriousness mingled with amiable bohemianism, provincial spoke to cosmopolitan, Fabian joked with hedonist, and teachers of mathematics admired the hats of potters from Cornwall. Alix wore a white dress bought ready-made from a department store, her younger sister was a sort of bridesmaid in a flowered print, and her little brother wore a grey suit with short trousers and a pale blue tie, on which he spilt some strawberry ice cream. The headmaster, who had offered for the occasion his own private stretch of garden, was unusually gracious. The ceremony had taken place in a register office as both families were agnostic. Photographs were taken. Everybody said that Alix looked lovely. Sebastian smiled at everybody, and the Doddridges thought he was wonderful. Not a cloud, not a shiver of cold air, though Liz for one could have done with a little less heat, as she wiped the sweat from her brow and sought the shade of a chestnut tree. Her turn next, people said to her in a slightly menacing manner, but she protested she and Edgar would wait until he had qualified. They were the sensible couple, the forward planners; Alix and Sebastian the children of the hour.

Alix smiled and thanked people for saucepans and toast racks and ironing boards. She and Sebastian were off on a long honeymoon, to spend two months in Tuscany in an old farmhouse belonging to friends of Deborah and Stephen; it was temporarily in need of a caretaker. They did not intend to take the saucepans and toast racks and ironing boards to Tuscany. Esther planned to visit them there, on her way to Perugia. The thought of a visit from Esther slightly cheered Alix, who was feeling, despite her smiles, extremely unhappy, extremely apprehensive. In the garden in her white dress, she knew she

had done the wrong thing. She should not have married
Sebastian. She doubted Sebastian. She had betrayed herself
and Sebastian by marrying Sebastian.

Deborah Manning liked Alix very much. She hoped she
would be good for Sebastian. Alix seemed to her to be both
practical and highly intelligent. Deborah also doubted Sebastian, although she never let it show, or hoped she did not let
it show.

Alix went upstairs to her old bedroom to take off her white
dress and to put on her pale blue linen Jaeger going-away
dress. The white dress lay on the bed. Alix was a virgin. She
had tried to disembarrass herself of her virginity, and had been
certain, once she started "going steady" with Sebastian, that
this would be accomplished. But Sebastian had not seemed
eager to take the final step. She had suggested to him, although
of course not in words, that it would be a good idea to alter
their pattern of lovemaking to something a little more adult, but
he had moved away: shrunk, dwindled, and moved away. And
since that movement, that rejection, Alix had felt her own
desire diminish. So here she was, married to a man she no
longer wanted, at the age of twenty-one.

She put on her pale blue linen Jaeger dress and, believe it or
not, a little hat. Yes, a little hat. She stared at herself. Then she
went to look for Esther to make plans, for at least there would
be Esther in these appalling two months of honeymoon ahead.

When Esther visited Alix and Sebastian, they had been
married for three weeks, and the marriage had been consum-
mated. Alix, although she did not know it, was pregnant. They
did not seem entirely happy, to Esther, but Esther put her
suspicions down to jealousy. But they made Esther very
welcome, and they passed pleasant afternoons by the swimming pool and pleasant evenings on the terrace eating salami,
cheese, sausage, and salad. One did not have to cook, in
Tuscany. Back in England, in the autumn, the saucepans came
into their own, as Alix, in a small basement flat in Islington,
struggled to learn the rudiments of domesticity. Sebastian got
a job, as easily as he had said he would, working for an
intellectual left-wing magazine. Alix applied for jobs until she
found she was pregnant, then gave up and sat at home. She was
deeply depressed, and felt guilty about her depression. Sebastian seemed as cheerful as ever, but what she now saw as
the unthinking, meaningless nature of his good nature irritated
her almost beyond bearing. She contemplated suicide. She told

herself she was suffering from hormones, that she would cheer up soon. She did not want a baby. She never wanted to sleep with Sebastian again.

She played house, with her saucepans. Loyalty sealed her lips, even with Liz and Esther, whom she at this period rarely saw. Sebastian dropped his clothes on the floor, she picked them up and washed them. She cooked meals, they both ate them, though often the meals were not very nice.

The baby, Nicholas, was born in April. Alix fell helplessly, hopelessly, recklessly in love with the baby. He was all the world to her. She no longer knew if she was happy or unhappy, cheerful or depressed, as she gazed at the infant lying in his pram, asleep in his cot, kicking on a rug before the fire. She was obsessed, in love. Sebastian spent more time out of the house. Alix did not care.

They went to Tuscany to the same house again, that summer. They invited friends to stay, to alleviate their couple-loneliness. Liz came, briefly, with Edgar, whom she had just married; Esther for a night, alone; then a couple of Canadians, who stayed for weeks. They were painters, perhaps, or poets, perhaps, casual acquaintances picked up by friendly Sebastian at a publisher's party in Bedford Square. They had long hair and said they knew Jack Kerouac. They thought that life was holy. They also smoked dope. Sebastian was not used to dope and one night he drowned in the swimming pool. Nobody was quite sure how it happened, but there he was, suddenly, dead. Alix was asleep upstairs at the time, with Nicholas.

Everybody was very sorry for Alix. Widowed at twenty-two, left with a small baby. Sebastian cut off in the glory and promise of his youth, with all the world before him.

Alix, naturally, was almost (but not quite) overwhelmed with guilt, at not grieving enough, at not having been the perfect wife, at having ceased to love Sebastian. Maybe her love would have kept him alive. Maybe she had killed him. The sympathy of others was hard to bear. She felt a fraud, as the letters poured in. She hugged Nicholas in her arms and rocked him backwards and forwards in the basket-backed rocking chair, in the damp Islington basement, night after night, morning after morning, holding on to him in his little cream Viyella nightdress and blue sleeping bag. Her tears flowed onto him. He was all she had. Little mother, little widow. Everybody had loved Sebastian. Alix felt herself growing mean and spiteful.

Sebastian's mother, Deborah, was the only person who
seemed to suspect the disarray of Alix's emotions. She made
friendly overtures, invited her to stay in their large, warm,
scenic, colourful, untidy house in Sussex, told Alix to live for
herself and look to the future, offered to look after the baby
whenever Alix needed a break. She would willingly have
engulfed the baby. Alix suspected this, and clung to him the
more tightly, rejecting Deborah's support, rejecting everything
except a little money "to see her through." She was too fragile
to form an alliance with large, strong, fully made Deborah. She
had to find her own way, in the damp, in the shadows, by the
light of 40-watt bulbs, in the solitary evenings. She would not
visit her own family, except as a formality, and then as briefly
as decency permitted. Their pity, their concern rubbed her raw.

She pushed the pram round Islington, speaking to shopkeep-
ers and other mothers on street corners and in playgrounds. She
had tried to enter the world of light, but it was not for her.

She saw even less of Liz and Esther. Liz was at this stage
engrossed by the dramatic, blinding, smoky disaster of her own
marriage, which after only six weeks managed to transform
herself and Edgar into mockeries of their former selves, loud
puppets mouthing insults on an unreal battlefield. Later, she
could hardly remember what the issues were that had so roused
them to mutual abuse. Her own domestic incompetence (which
was indeed extreme, but what had Edgar expected from a wife
with an upbringing like hers?), Edgar's male chauvinism
(though this was a phrase not yet current) and his expectation
that his work was always, would always be of greater importance than her own these were aspects of their mutual
dissatisfaction, no doubt, although both were, decades later, to
concede that Edgar at this time was paying a high psychological
price for having renounced his theatrical ambitions (old Cambridge friends of his already had their names in lights in the
West End, while he was a mere house officer) and that Liz was
still suffering from the trauma of confronting her mother with
her total, final defection.

Not a happy marriage, and not one that could take on the
extra burden of a weeping widowed friend. It could not bear
the bright inspection of another's sorrow. So Alix and Liz kept
their distance.

Esther, unmarried, appeared happy. She pursued her studies.
She planned a thesis on the works of Carlo Crivelli, so briefly
mentioned in 1894 by Berenson, so little mentioned since. She

did not expect to see much of Liz and Alix, who had married and made their own lives after another pattern. She had a flat in Camden Town. She continued to go out to dinner with academics, to receive the hard-drinking architect. She embarked on a new and even more enigmatic liaison with an Italian anthropologist of satanic reputation who in the fullness of time turned out to be—indeed, for some time, unrecognized by the British, had been—a structuralist. He too was a married man. His interest in witchcraft was said to be more than scholarly. He instructed Esther in the interpretation of medieval Italian iconography.

Liz's marriage broke up after eight months. Edgar, chivalrously, moved out of the flat they rented in New Cross, though he could hardly afford to do so, and into a large shabby house in Greenwich which he shared with several old Cambridge friends. He was much happier there. He paid her a small allowance, as she, as a married woman, was no longer eligible for the grant that had supported her at university. Liz was humiliated by this, rather than enraged, but she knew that she had to qualify in order ever to be free and accepted the conditions. She did not tell her mother that she and Edgar had separated. She continued her clinical training at St. Michael's and qualified in 1959. In 1960, while she was doing six pre-registration months as house physician at St. Michael's, she met Charles Headleand. Seven months later, after divorcing Edgar, she married Charles, a widower with three small boys. She was twenty-five, he thirty. She informed her mother after the event.

Her second marriage somewhat disrupted her postgraduate career. It also renewed her interrupted friendship with Alix. She sought out Alix, to tell her of her plans to remarry, and they spent a long evening, over spaghetti and Hirondelle, talking of what already seemed to them the distant past. Alix admitted what Liz already knew, that she and Sebastian had been less than happy, that the idyll had been less golden than it looked. Liz deplored her own appalling behaviour towards Edgar, confided his towards her. Why ever did we marry so *young*, they asked one another. And why are *you* doing it *again*, asked Alix. Oh, this is different, said Liz. At twenty-five, she felt mature. She had seen people die, she had seen them give birth, she had chopped them into little pieces; more significantly, with Charles she had achieved orgasm, which she had never managed with Edgar. She knew it was all right, this

time. So she told Alix. I will never marry again, said Alix. But
how do you manage, said Liz. Oh, I teach a little, I mark exam
papers, I scrape by, said Alix. Liz was embarking on a world
of wealth, with Charles Headleand. Naomi's parents, in grief
and regret, had been generous to their grandchildren. Liz,
whom they liked, whom they wished to like, whom they were
obliged to like, would profit, although she would work hard for
her rewards. So it was calculated, so it was arranged.

Liz had pulled herself together, on the domestic front, she
told Alix, as she looked around Alix's brass-railed, shabby,
cluttered, plastic-toy-littered flat, where clothes hung drying on
an ancient fireguard. Some of the things Edgar had said had
struck home. I'm going to be efficient, this time, she said. But
three babies, said Alix, it's impossible. No, it's not, said Liz,
a manic glitter in her eyes. *One* is exhausting, said Alix. I shall
come to you for advice, said Liz.

And so Liz Headleand was born, out of guilt, out of chance,
out of sexual felicity and complicity, out of ambition, and Liz
Lintot passed away, as Sebastian Manning and Naomi Headleand had passed away.

Alix Bowen was slower in the making. She put together
slowly the bricks of her new self. She reconsidered, slowly, the
privileges and disadvantages of her childhood, of the three
years of Cambridge, of the brief interlude of her marriage, of
the streets of Islington where she pushed her pram. She
dismantled, she rebuilt.

In the streets of Islington, she observed poverty. She
experienced it, also. A one-parent family, living on scraps
from the educational world, too proud to seek refuge and warm
her hands on the tepid thickly painted radiators of Leeds, to
cast off her jersey and socks on the radiant central heating of
Sussex, to lie half naked in that ill-starred farmhouse in
Tuscany. Fifties pride possessed her. She had read her Henry
James. She made no appeals. She renounced the role of tragic
widow with an austerity that irritated her would-be saviours.
She would not go out, though she occasionally made a martyr
of herself by pointing out that because of the price of
baby-sitting, she could not afford to go out; this was as far as
she went towards self-pity.

Leeds, Sussex, Cambridge, Provence, Tuscany, Islington.
There was a lesson in it somewhere, if she had eyes to see, ears
to hear. Semi-chosen austerity: a rich cultural life in green
pastures with fruit: unchosen semi-hardship. Ugliness: beauty:

ugliness. Alix turned these things over in her mind. Admired discomfort; cultivated ease; semi-comfortable squalor.

Alix had been told about poverty, in Leeds, at school, and at home. (In her case school and home were not easily separable.) She had knitted woollen squares to raise money to sink wells in India (and had knitted them very badly too). She had donated pittances of pocket money to buy tractors for India. She had attended slide-illustrated talks on the agricultural problems of vast and distant continents. Poverty nearer home had been less vividly presented to her, and indeed it had been less colourful, less extreme. It was grey, shabby, and somehow infectious: to be avoided. It was also rough and noisy and unmannerly. It lived in back streets of terrace houses and on sprawling housing estates. It wasted what money it had on drinking and it spoke with rough accents. It was feckless, unthrifty, sluttish, violent, loud-mouthed, and materialistic. Its children taunted nice little middle-class children in school uniform who strayed into its terrain. It did not need wells dug or tractors purchased. Poverty was an attribute of the working classes in England. Those who worked were poor. Those who did not work were better off, therefore? No, it was not quite like that. The equation, to Alix's schoolgirl mind, had already proved confusing. Her father worked hard, for example, but was not a worker. Nor was he poor, in terms of the poverty portrayed in the coloured slides, where black children with hunger-distended bellies stared at the camera, where lepers crouched by begging bowls. But he was poor when compared with the parents of many of the children who attended his school, even when compared with some of the other teachers. Poverty, therefore, was comparative. One measured it by a sliding scale. One was always poor, in terms of those who were richer.

This puzzled Alix. She was hungry for absolutes. The question which had most intrigued her in her childhood— where does space end?—was joined by another unanswerable question. What happens if people go on demanding pay rises and getting them? (This was the 1950s, the early 1960s.) Do they get richer, or do they merely appear to get richer? Do others get poorer if some get richer? Do the rich need the poor? Will the poor be always with us?

And if so, Alix thought sometimes, have I joined them?

Alix was, at this stage, perhaps perversely, perhaps naturally, attracted by poverty. It seemed to her less alarming than it had seemed to her parents. She got on speaking terms with it. She discovered the art of sinking. She sank. Not very deep, but she sank. She and Nicholas, in Clissold Park, eating crisps on a bench, feeding the ducks with crusts. Indistinguishable from her neighbours. Unrecognizable to her Cambridge friends. She walked for miles with Nicholas round North London tiring herself and him so that they would both sleep in the long nights.

Gradually her fears of the rough and the unmannerly faded, her expectations of the world adjusted. As a child, she had always had a secret yearning to enter the other city, the unknown city beyond and within the suburbs, where nobody, middle-class folklore declared, read books or washed or cooked proper meals. She had sometimes, even as a child, wondered if it could be as fearful as its reputation. She disliked fear. Particularly she disliked being made to feel fear of her fellow men and women. Now she lived with these people, and was no longer afraid, for they were like herself in more ways than they were unlike herself. She faded into the background.

Inconspicuous, accepted, she discovered new talents. She found she could teach. At first she took a few private students, through Gabbitas and Thring (her first-class Cambridge degree came in handy at last) and found that she enjoyed coaching them for their English O levels and A levels. She understood so well what it was that they did not understand. Then she taught one or two illiterates on an illiteracy scheme. Then she started to teach two classes a week at a College of Further Education: aspiring caterers on day release. Cambridge visitors, visitors from outer space, childless visitors, asked her how she could bear to teach such stupid, such dull, such unambitious, such ill-read folk. She did not answer that intelligence is relative, like poverty. She did not think her students stupid, just different. She herself was stupid. She had been stupid to marry Sebastian and to drown him in the swimming pool.

Little Nicholas was minded, during Alix's working hours, by a woman whom her visitors did not consider acceptable: they were familiar with the shortcomings of Swiss and French and Swedish au pair girls, but drew the line at Mrs. Parfitt, a grey-haired, bedroom-slippered, floral-aproned, skinny, ill-spoken old grandma with sunken cheeks, a rasping smoker's cough, stick-like legs, and an agile mind.

At the end of Alix's road was a little patch of grass, on the corner in front of the launderette and the pub. A small patch, smelling of dog shit, in a heavily built area. On it was a bench, and on the bench sat, in fair weather and sometimes in foul, a row of strange-complexioned men, not all of them old though most of them looked it, with bottles of wine, cider, and beer, sometimes with a half bottle of spirits. They accosted Alix as she passed, not for money—she no longer looked as though she had any money—but for company. "Come and sit down for a minute, darling," they would wheedle. And sometimes Alix sat down with them, in the feeble London sunshine, to pass the time of day. To pass the time of day. "It's a grand day," they would say, when it was. She would agree. Idle, derelict, washed-up, full, as often as not, with a deep, deep sentimentality, a strange despairing optimistic emotion, which would flow from them in praise of young Nicholas, in praise of Alix, in praise of the goodness of the Lord, in praise of the odd flower that managed to bloom in the much-trampled flowerbed. They rarely seemed drunk to Alix. They were past drunkenness, washed up on some far beach of harmless universal being, ground down to the bedrock of being, unstruggling, undemanding, unresentful. Dirty, ragged, high-smelling, communing with the Lord. They told her not to worry, the worst would never happen.

She made more acceptable friends among her colleagues at the College of Further Education.

She tried a job in a comprehensive school in Holloway, but the hours were too long and she abandoned it after a year. She started to teach a course at a polytechnic. She taught an evening class. She taught a class in a women's prison. After a few years, she began to see Liz and Esther again, regularly, and they resumed their conversations: they talked a good deal, in the 1960s, about psychotic art, a subject which combined several aspects of their three separate interests. They talked of writing a book together, but did not.

In 1968, Alix married Brian Bowen, one-time beater of circular saws in Northam, now lecturer in Adult Education and novelist. They met at a meeting in the Conway Hall. Alix went to live in Wandsworth. She continued to see Liz and Esther regularly, having recognized the importance of friendship. Brian encouraged this; it would not have crossed his mind to do anything other. Unlike Charles Headleand, Brian was a good man, and instantly recognizable as a good man.

Esther Breuer continued unmarried. She completed her thesis. She wrote the catalogue for an exhibition of the works of Crivelli, which was shown in Paris and New York. She declined to pursue a proper academic career, for it would have meant, initially, leaving London, where she preferred to live. Instead, not unlike Alix, she picked up bits and pieces. She taught a course at the Courtauld, and another at the City Lit. She wrote an introduction or two here, contributed a chapter or two there, reviewed for learned journals and even for some paying periodicals. She toyed with various ideas for various original full-length books but did not commit herself to any of them. She lectured at the National Gallery, at the Tate. She gained a reputation, as a lecturer, for making startling, brilliant connections, for illuminating odd corners, for introducing implausible snippets of erudition. When invited to deliver slightly grander lectures, which she occasionally was, she declined, and thus, as the years went by, was no longer invited. She lived very modestly, never taking a taxi, never eating an expensive meal out, yet nevertheless maintaining the halo of mysterious privilege that she had worn at university: unlike Alix, who had made herself ordinary by hard work, Esther made herself extraordinary by hard work, with the result that her friends and students continued to consider her attention a favour not universally granted. The married satanic anthropologist and the married architect (now an even more hard-drinking architectural journalist) continued to pay court to her. Long evenings of great intensity would be spent with each, separately: the two suitors never met. Esther talked of them to Liz and Alix, even joked about them, relaying titbits of eccentricity and horror from their domestic and professional lives; Liz and Esther got to know Claudio's hypochondriac wife, Roberta, quite well by repute, were well versed in Claudio's obsession with lift doors, grilles, grids, and railings, and spent many an hour trying to analyse Colin Lindsey's drinking habits and bouts of amnesia, one of which landed him one night, to his own perpetual bewilderment, in a police cell in Dorking, where he claimed he had never been in his life, and whither he had no reason to go. They laughed a good deal, Esther, Liz, and Alix, about the odd behaviour of Claudio Volpe and Colin Lindsey, yet Liz and Alix, despite this, felt that beyond the oddity some serious drama was being enacted from which they themselves were excluded, debarred, but which might in time perhaps be played in public instead of in that red room, behind those thick drapes.

In 1978 Esther's niece Ursula arrived in London from Manchester to study, and took up residence in Esther's small spare dark blue room. Esther said she needed the rent. Esther and Ursula became the best of friends, and spent much time visiting galleries, parks, and parties together, and talking in the red room.

Liz, Alix, Esther. No, it was not an unbroken friendship, they did not become inseparable; they had distant patches, patches of estrangement that lasted for years at times, when they met rarely, or distantly. Alix and Esther did not care to see much of Charles, nor he of them, as we have seen, and there were periods when the Liz-Charles alliance was dominant in Liz's life and excluded other interests. Alix sometimes removed herself into her work, sometimes simply went silent, and answered the telephone forbiddingly. Esther went abroad for months at a time, or took up a new acolyte who absorbed her attention for a while. But by the end of 1979, when this account opens, they had settled down into what looked like a semi-permanent pattern. They would meet for an evening meal, once a week, once a fortnight, once a month—if a monthly gap occurred, each would feel the need for apology, explanation. They met alone, without their men, as over the years they more often than not had done: a pattern of relationship that was considered mildly eccentric by some, mildly avant-garde by others, but to themselves was natural.

They would eat, drink, and talk. They exchanged ideas. Sometimes they exchanged them so successfully that a year later Alix would be putting forward a proposition that she had energetically refuted when Liz had proposed it a year earlier; only to find that Liz, influenced by Alix, had subsequently shifted her ground and herself rejected it. It can only have been through Esther that Liz and Alix began to look at paintings at all, that the pastel sequence of Albers hung on the Harley Street stairs. Some of their notions swam, unallocated, in the space between them. The origins of some of their running jokes had been forgotten.

Their professional worlds overlapped and, between them, their frame of reference was quite wide, although they had been educated at the same college of the same university.

Liz's patients were, largely, middle class or upper middle class (for she had become fashionable); they included, as we have seen, lawyers, priests, politicians. But she also saw a random selection of first referrals, from the public sector, to keep her on guard. (This was one explanation she gave for her mixture of private and public practice, but Alix found it suspect. Alix likes to raise with Liz the question of the class content of psychological disorder and fantasy. Do princesses dream that they are princesses, for example, or that the queen is coming to tea? Liz is not much interested in this line of thought. Alix sometimes accuses Liz of believing in universal human nature.)

The objects of Alix's concern are less advantaged, although by and large less neurotic. They include law-abiding young Asian girls seeking a few qualifications; middle-class women attending evening classes in order to get away from their children or their husbands or the emptiness of their apartments; elderly autodidacts of both sexes and all classes; an illiterate, handsome, paranoid building site manager; a garbage collector; and, of late, the criminal inmates of Garfield—heroin addicts, thieves, prostitutes, muggers, infanticides, a couple of forgers—all of them selected because they are considered suitable for the experimental psychiatric approach of Garfield unit. Alix teaches all these people English language and literature.

Esther, either because of her personality or because of her subjects (the quattrocento, Palladian architecture, the history of the early Italian Renaissance), attracts a much better-heeled class of student than Alix, students who like to spend their holidays in Florence or Siena or Perugia or Venice. Esther is indifferent to their class origins, indeed indifferent to her students as a mass altogether, and rarely bothered to learn their names, although she occasionally took an interest in an individual case. Esther was interested in her subject, and expected her students to be interested in it too. Esther's professional acquaintance also included a strange assortment of European intellectuals, not all of them art historians: one of these (to create another link in the circle) once consulted Liz professionally about his relationship with his temperamental stepdaughter, but Esther did not condone this link: she tended to argue that her own grasp of the norm was so weak that she would not see what distinguished the sick from the healthy. We are all very, very sick, and it does not matter much, was Esther's line.

But one cannot, really, wholly differentiate these three women. In their mid-forties, after more than half a lifetime of association, they share characteristics, impressions, memories, even speech patterns; they have a common stock of knowledge, they have entered, through one another, worlds that they would not otherwise have known. They have pooled their discoveries, have come back from other regions with samples of leaf, twig, fruit, stone, have turned them over together. They share much. The barriers between them are, they think, quite low.

As their professional worlds overlap, so do their diversions—or one, at least, of their diversions. They share, perhaps surprisingly, a love of walking, of the English countryside. This might have been expected from Alix, whose parents had patronized Youth Hostels long after their youth, and who like to boast of long pioneering rambles in the 1930s. But Esther too, essentially an indoor person, likes to walk. The countryside, she says defensively, is an aesthetic experience. She is knowledgeable about flowers, trees, even grasses. Liz, the most reluctant recruit to this wholesome pursuit, has become its most enthusiastic addict and of late tends to take upon herself the role of organizer.

They have been on some good walks, in their time. Along the Dorset coast path, on the short nibbled turf, spotting ancient field patterns, rare yellow poppies, and hopefully identifying the Lulworth skipper. Along the Berkshire Downs, above Wantage, in a white milky-gold autumnal harvest haze, through beech woods with bluebells in Sussex, through Norfolk mud, and, for a brave two days, along the Pennine Way. When they have not time to go farther afield, they study the Ordnance Survey map of the Dorking and Reigate region, of Outer West London, and discover rural back ways, almost forgotten routes through neglected cow parsley, past the back of allotments. They have walked the towpath at Barnes, have explored the Hackney marshes.

They make an odd trio, to the eye of the observer. They refuse to dress seriously for their walking expeditions. Alix favours a pair of gym shoes, socks, and a skirt; she does not like wearing trousers. Esther wears trousers, but they are not the right sort for walking in: velvet, loose silk, or striped cotton, with a smart little pair of somewhat indoor boots. Liz wears proper trousers, jeans or khaki land girl's trousers from Lawrence Corner Army Surplus, but she rather spoils the effect by the ill-assorted sunhats, Indian headsquares, Liberty scarves, and ski helmets with which she protects herself from the variable English weather, and by a pair of everlasting Dr. Scholl's clogs which ought to be unsuitable for long tramps but which, according to Liz, serve very well. Off they trudge, with a picnic, happily, once or twice a year. Happily, innocently.

Alix has a string bag, bought in an Oxfam shop, in which

she is allowed to carry the map. Sometimes they speculate on the number of miles the bag has walked. Like Liz's clogs, it never perishes.

Men are not usually invited. Charles is a sporting man, or was once a sporting man, but he is not a walker. Esther's friends have rarely been seen out of doors, even by Esther. Brian has accompanied them once or twice, for Brian loves to walk, but the women tease him about his walking boots. "How can you lift your feet up, in those great things?" they mockingly wonder. They refuse to let him carry the picnic in his rucksack. So Brian does not often go, although they sometimes invite him. Alix has a photograph, taken by Brian on one of these expeditions; it shows the three of them crouching under a hedge, in the roots of hawthorns, in driving rain, eating wet sandwiches. None of them is looking at the camera; they are looking in different directions, wetly, miserably. Liz has her back to Alix; Esther is sitting some way away staring at the ground. They are very fond of this dismal photograph; the essence of the English landscape, Esther declares. The essence of togetherness.

But, more commonly, England being England, they meet indoors, and thus they meet, on Friday evening, the first Friday of 1980, in Esther Breuer's flat in Ladbroke Grove. Ursula is not there: she is still up in Manchester for the vacation. Esther, Alix, and Liz drink red wine and eat tomato and mozzarella, while Alix describes the New Year's party at Garfield. They drink more red wine, and eat liver with haricot beans, while Liz tells them about the Japanese at the Metropole. They eat green salad, and Esther tells them about a foiled attempt to snatch her handbag as she was waiting for a bus on the Harrow Road. They then discuss the Harrow Road murderer (acclaimed by the press the Horror of Harrow Road) and the ethics of reporting murder trials and the wisdom of juries. Alix recounts, not for the first time, her poignant story of the adult illiterate who was driven to declare his illiteracy and seek help when he was called for jury service and could not read the oath.

The subject of Charles Headleand and his defection does not come up until they have finished with all these matters. But finally Liz, her feet tucked up under her on Esther's Turkish-carpet-covered couch, introduces the theme. Smoking a cigarette (which is not like her), she declares herself perplexed (which is not like her). Esther and Alix are not much perplexed, now they have accepted the new situation, but naturally do not wish to appear rude in their lack of astonishment. So they listen in silence as Liz confesses that she had had no suspicion, had really not foreseen this development at all. It is brave of her to admit this, they think; they glance at one another, wondering which of them will take the initiative of response. It is Alix. She leaps in boldly.

"But, Liz," she said, "you hardly ever spend any real *time* with Charles, you're both of you always working. And anyway, you said you wouldn't go to New York when he asked you, didn't you?"

"Well, that's one of the things I keep thinking about," said Liz, knocking a little ash carefully into the small green Venetian glass ashtray on the floor. "I can't remember now if he *did* ask me. Perhaps I just assumed we'd had a conversation that we never had at all."

"What did you think he said?" asked Esther neutrally, genuinely curious, handing round a blue and white bowl of dried apricots.

"I *thought* we'd had a conversation about whether or not I should go, and that I'd said I couldn't leave my job, particularly now I've got this new consultancy, and that I couldn't leave various people in mid-course, and that maybe in a year when Charles saw how things went in New York we'd reconsider. Anyway, I said, he might be back by then."

"That sounds perfectly plausible to me," said Alix.

"Yes," said Liz, "it's perfectly *plausible*. But did it happen? When I try to remember what Charles said, all I can remember is what *I* said. I don't think Charles did any talking at all. In fact, it wasn't a conversation, it was a monologue, with me telling him what I was planning to do. I did *all* the talking."

And they all three laughed, remembering other such non-conversations, and digressed for a while, recalling non-proposals of marriage, non-discussions of mortgages, non-agreements about which hotel to book for a holiday, before returning to the subject of Liz and Charles.

"In fact," continued Liz, after this digression, helping herself to a couple of apricots, "in fact, if I'd said I wanted to go with him, or made any sign of assuming that I would go with him, he'd have had to tell me then, wouldn't he, about Henrietta. It was me that made it possible for him not to say anything until he had to. And now I come to think of it, he did say something about selling the house. It seemed such a silly idea, I couldn't think why he'd even thought of it. We'd be mad to sell the house, I told him so. He seemed to agree. But perhaps he just didn't answer."

There was a slight pause. The room was small, warm, comfortable, intimate; a gas fire flickered, the lights were low, the red curtains were drawn against the night. They all thought of the high bright cream and white rooms of Harley Street.

"Whose house is it?" asked Alix, eventually. Liz sighed. She looked suddenly angry, exhausted, old.

"It's his, I suppose. I've never really thought about it much. I suppose it's his."

Alix and Esther glanced at one another. Liz sighed again. Esther opened another bottle of wine.

"We bought it," said Liz, eventually, "with Naomi's parents' money. And some that we borrowed. Charles borrowed money."

"But since then . . ." Alix prompted.

"Oh, since then, of course I've paid for things . . . yes, of course I have. Decorations, alterations, the roof, the boys' bathroom. That kind of thing."

"There aren't so many of you at home now," said Esther.

"It's a very big house," said Alix.

Another silence fell, disturbed only by the muffled comforting hum of the Black and Decker of the quiet man upstairs. Liz glared at her friends with some hostility, as they sat in judgement. Then she suddenly revived, sat up, pushed another cushion behind her back. "Selling the fucking house. That's what he was getting at," she said. "So he can buy another house for Henrietta. What a fucking cheek. What am I supposed to do? Move to fucking Kentish Town?"

Alix and Esther revived also. "Kentish Town is very *nice*," said Alix. "It's wonderful," said Esther, "in Kentish Town."

They all laughed.

"Kentish Town for *me*, I suppose," said Liz, "and they'll be buying a house—where, do you think? Henrietta lives in Kensington. I ask you. Kensington."

"This is Kensington," said Esther. "West Kensington."

"Ha," said Liz.

"Perhaps they'll settle in New York," suggested Alix.

"I can't picture Henrietta in New York. New Yorkers are meant to be dynamic, aren't they?" Liz lit another cigarette.

"I think it's her forehead that's *so* unsettling," said Alix, helpfully. And thus, for ten minutes or more, they settled amicably into abuse of Lady Henrietta, until Liz suddenly interrupted with "But if we sold the house, we wouldn't have a family house any more. There wouldn't be a home for the boys."

Esther and Alix looked at one another again.

"But," said Alix, "the boys aren't boys. They are grown up."

"And what about my consulting room? What about my patients? How can I move to Kentish Town?"

It was hard to tell whether or not, how much if at all, she was joking. Nor could they tell whether she was joking as she proceeded to outline further anxieties: about money, gossip columnists, pension schemes, life insurance or assurance (none of them was sure which was which), divorce settlements, sexual jealousy, alienation of children, shares in the marital home, the rightful ownership of the Albers pastels and the fake ancestor. When Alix pointed out, in an attempt at consolation, that Liz was in command of a good income and well able to keep herself in comfort, Liz snapped in response, quite irritably, "Yes, yes, I know I'm not going to starve, exactly. But that's not the point."

"Well, it's partly the point," said Alix, with what was, from her, considerable aggression. Liz glanced at Esther for support, but Esther was shrewdly staring at her new potted palm.

"Well," said Liz, after a short silence. "I know that neither of you ever *liked* Charles. You're probably both delighted."

"I wouldn't say that," said Esther. "I rather like Harley Street. I'd be sorry not to be invited to Harley Street any more. And I think the Albers and the ancestor are definitely yours. Charles would have thrown the ancestor out, if you hadn't stopped him. Definitely yours."

"Well," said Alix, robustly, "I *am* delighted. Yes, I am delighted. I think it's a very good thing, and I bet you'll think so too, in six months' time. Or less. And I think it's completely unnecessary for you to worry at all about money. In fact it would be ridiculous. That's what I think."

"Thank you," said Liz.

"And now we've disposed of *that*," said Esther, "may I ask both your advice—is that grammatical, I wonder? should I say the advice of both of you?—about something really important? I may? You see that palm that Claudio gave me? I'm very worried about it. They're tricky things, palms. Where do you

think I should stand it? How often should I water it? Liz,
you're better with plants than Alix, tell me about palms. I've
got to keep it alive. Claudio has already rung twice to see how
it's doing. Will it be all right where it is? Is it a desert palm,
or an oasis palm? What do you think? Do tell me what you both
think.''

On Friday evening, the first Friday of 1980, Henrietta Latchett
and Charles Headleand sat and stared at one another over their
charcuterie at Chez André in Walton Street. Henrietta sighed.
She raised a small forkful to her mouth, inserted it, chewed,
stared. She sighed again. Charles ate a larger forkful, more
vigorously, and stared back. He stared at her arched thin
eyebrows, at her dark eyes, at her pale throat, at her pearls. He
stared at the ribbon in her hair. He stared at her small, neat,
white nose. He stared at her small, even, biting, well-
maintained teeth, as they met in the marbled, swirled, veined,
green-peppercorn-studded meat. Somewhat to his own surprise, he was in the thrall of what seemed to be a violent sexual
passion. Fortunately, unfortunately, he had become sufficiently
introspective to be obliged to wonder at this development in his
physical and emotional life, and he stared at Henrietta not only
with longing but also with curiosity, unable to avoid reflecting
that his wife, Liz, might have been able to come up with an
explanation, had he been in a position to ask her for one. One
cannot live with a shrink for twenty years without asking
oneself a few questions, over the charcuterie.

But neither questions nor explanations could calm this fever.
It was a good fever. It would rescue him, it would rescue
Henrietta, it would transport them to the New World. Henrietta, he believed, sat there as enthralled as he, as she dabbed
a little mustard onto her forkful. Henrietta, thin as she was,
enjoyed her food. She did not consider eating a trivial
occupation. It was to be a highly fashionable occupation, in the
early 1980s, and Henrietta was always in the vanguard of
fashion.

In his pocket, Charles had a ring. He intended to present it
over the pudding. He did not know whether, in the circumstances, this was the fashionable thing to do or not, but the
banality, the romance, the innocence of the gesture had proved
irresistible to him. The male menopause, he had said to himself

briefly as he sat in a small back room with an elderly jeweller looking at stones. His first wife, Naomi, had received from him a pretty but inexpensive Victorian ring bought from Cameo Corner on the advice of a friend of his mother's: an appropriate gift from an ambitious but as yet poor younger son of a county court judge, to the only daughter of a Jewish banker. That ring was now safely hidden away in a little satin-lined blue velvet box, waiting for his daughter Sally, who could have it when she was twenty-one if anyone remembered to get it out for her.

Naomi was Sally's dead pre-stepmother. A curious relationship, Sally sometimes reflected, especially when annoyed with her own mother.

Liz had been betrothed by no ring. The seed pearls and sapphire which Edgar had given her she kept, but moved to her right hand. She married Charles with her old wedding ring. She and Charles had therefore never been engaged. They had been married, merely. A wild and heady time. The 1960s.

And now Charles was worn out by all that, he had come full circle, he wanted a proper wife who paid him attention, a wife who did not mock and boss and tease and vanish. He had grown frightened of Liz, over the years, of the Liz Headleand that he had helped to invent. She had become knowing, prescient. She had spoken sharply, foreknowingly, of his own thoughts, of the thoughts and actions of his colleagues; she had treated them and him with scant respect, as though his world were trivial, superficial. Her own had seemed to her solid, deep, serious; once too often she had made him feel that his was hollow, time-serving, transient, peopled by boys playing grown-up power games, while she attached herself to the timeless, the adult. She had excluded him from her knowingness, had indulged him with titbits, in passing. She had sapped his energy: he had felt it begin to wane.

Henrietta had restored him, had restored his vision of himself as a man of power, of action, a man who for the past decade had thrived on combat, confrontation, unpleasantness, on chopping out the dead wood of poor old Britain, on sacking mild older men and angry embattled younger ones. Now he could relax, he could reap the reward of past zeal. His new appointment was quasi-ambassadorial in dignity, and its potential (for it was not only a new, but a newly created appointment) was enormous: he would be in a position of inside knowledge, of influence, of suggestion, of patronage. Vast financial interests would sue for his approval, the new technology would clamour for his attention, he would negotiate between nations. And he would continue to oversee the recording, the selling, the creation of news.

One of the problems with Liz was that she had no idea what any of this meant. Her ignorance when it came to satellites, cables, teletexts, videos, home computers, home information services, was, she claimed proudly, lamentable. Yet her very ignorance was unnerving. Invent me a dream print-out computer, she would say, and he would wonder, for an instant, if this might be done. But what are you going to *do* in New York, she would ask, and he would find himself rambling slightly in his reply. Ah, those were the days, when you were making programmes for *Focus on Britain*, she would sometimes, nostalgically, dangerously declare, in an odd shared late-night moment in front of the box: recalling his pioneering, campaigning, radical days, the days when he battled heroically with the IBA for the right to show a film of naked old ladies in geriatric hospitals, to show doctors defending the legalization of marijuana, to show IRA terrorists and refugee black Rhodesian politicians infringing the rules of decency of utterance.

Well, all that was over, over forever since the revelations of New Year's Eve. No more quarrelling with Liz about the ethics of public and private broadcasting, no more ill-informed unnerving jokes about the tedium of news about news, no more cracks about the likely effect of breakfast television on the early-rising lifestyle of psychoanalysts. The battle was over, though who had won it, he could not say. His children were grown, his wife could have her freedom, her independence, and he could start a new life, with Henrietta Latchett. Henrietta would entertain him and entertain for him. (Liz, obviously, seemed never to have considered that a man in Charles's new position would need a wife.) Charles admired Henrietta's social style greatly. She understood the art of conversation, she did not leap or grasp obsessively or take too great, too sudden, too idiosyncratic an interest in a subject, she understood the importance of a bright, smooth, easy, transitional manner, she soothed and obscurely flattered, she impressed the powerful.

Charles had noticed that Liz and Henrietta tended to bring out the worst in one another. They diminished one another.

It must be admitted that Charles had had enough of Liz's eccentricities. As she grew into middle age, he had noted in her stubbornnesses, oddities, resistances that perturbed him, and he sometimes found himself asking who she was. Well, who was she? Where did she come from? These were questions that had not troubled him when he had first encountered her: she had been simply Liz Lintot, an aspiring doctor of sorts, ex-wife of the entirely respectable well-authenticated Edgar Lintot, ex-belle of Cambridge, ex-Battersby Grammar School. He knew that she'd had an odd, an unfortunate childhood, but had never thought much about it. His own hadn't been much fun either. The longer perspectives had not interested him. But now, looking at her, looking at Sally and Stella, he sometimes wondered. Who were they? Liz's mother, of course, was barmy. Mad, quite mad. Why hadn't he found that at all worrying, all those years ago? Had he really believed that one could make oneself, make one's own life, ignore genetics, ignore history, make a fresh start?

If one asked who Henrietta Latchett was and where she came from, there were highly satisfactory if complex and lengthy answers. Her entries in reference books were dense with cross-references, dense with a tangled web of titles and a maze of mysteriously transforming family names. Earls, barons, marquesses, dukes, viscounts, baronets mingled in her ancestry, providing trip wires for the unwary. Lady Henrietta was herself the daughter of a marquess; she had married the younger son of an earl, thereby creating confusion as to whether she should properly be addressed on envelopes as The Hon. Mrs. Peter Latchett, The Lady Henrietta Latchett, or by some other nicety of designation. Peter Latchett had vanished from the scene long ago, which had somehow made it easier for people to get it right. He had been a racing man, a drinking man, an old-fashioned Trollope-style younger son, or so Charles had been led to believe.

It would not be slandering Charles to say that he was greatly interested in this aspect of the configuration of qualities that was Henrietta. Charles Headleand, who had been president of a left-wing political discussion group at Cambridge, who had triumphantly won at the Cambridge Union the motion "This house believes that the abolition of private education is necessary for the nation's survival" in 1953, who had reeled out of his National Service with his head full of the brotherhood of man and the saving of mass culture, who had married the gentle, cultured, generous, sweet-voiced (albeit wealthy) Naomi, who had subsequently married the ill-born, ill-bred, brilliant Liz Ablewhite, who had made himself famous through the late 1950s and 1960s with his punchy social-conscience documentaries, who had pursued his triumphs through managerial and executive posts through the 1970s, who now was preparing himself to conquer the great democratic meritocracy of New York, would sometimes comfort himself for a few moments in his glassy Hockneyesque office by glancing at the pages of *Debrett*. Did he himself detect a paradox in this? Did it ever occur to him that in some respects Lady Henrietta closely resembled the dead wood to which, as a younger man, he had taken the axe? Did it occur to him that the post he had accepted, with all its dignities, all its trappings, was precisely the kind of post that was designed to arrest the activities of the kind of young man that he himself had been?

Lady Henrietta went down very well with Americans, and, moreover, she herself liked Americans and liked America. She loved New York. She said she thought New York was very amusing.

Lady Henrietta neatly laid her knife and fork together on her plate, as she had been taught to do thirty years before by a dragon of a nanny, who had terrorized Henrietta and her sister almost out of their wits. Her feelings about England were mixed. Her feelings about leaving it were mixed. Her feelings about Charles were mixed. But he had asked her to marry him, and marry him she would. There was risk in it, but she did not dislike risk. She sipped her wine. Whatever Charles Headleand did to her, he could not turn out worse than The Hon. Peter Latchett. And if he did turn out badly, she could always leave him. Meanwhile, she would do her best to keep him. Most of her education had been devoted to the art of getting and keeping a man. She resented this. And resented the fact that she had failed so early with The Hon. Peter Latchett. She would like to make a success of things with Charles. So thought Lady Henrietta, amorously, as she watched her white octagonal plate disappear, watched a pale blue hexagonal plate materialize before her, on which reposed a small piece of pink fish in a flat green sorrel sea.

"Pretty," said Henrietta, of the fish.

"Yes," said Charles.

And they proceeded to discuss the culinary possibilities of New York and the odd eating habits of Americans. Lady Henrietta did not cook, herself. But she was good at telling other people how to do it. When alone, Lady Henrietta would boil an egg or eat a piece of cheese or forget to eat at all. She felt self-conscious, eating alone. She liked company. Charles had led her to believe that there would be company in New York, some of it of a sort familiar to her from previous forays—the cultured international exhibition visitors and opera enthusiasts, the wealthy dilettantes, the party goers and party givers of her own set—and that the less familiar types would prove, at worst, amusing. Henrietta had a considerable capacity for amusement, and was herself, by her own set, considered witty. As she and Charles spoke of restaurants and receptions in New York, of diet crazes and drinking patterns, of contrasting the styles of entertainment practised in Buckingham Palace, in 10 Downing Street, in the British Embassy in Paris, and in the White House (to which, one might remind oneself, the Reagans had not yet brought their New Look), Henrietta's mind wandered pleasantly from food to dress, from plates to fabric, from wine glasses to jewellery, pausing to reflect idly on Liz Headleand's strange, apparently uncharacteristic (vulgar?) obsession with cut glass, moving on to construct a dark green (yes, dark green, with perhaps a little touch of blue?) formal evening dress: the skirt thus, the neckline thus, with a blue underskirt and perhaps a slightly lower waist, a waist resting just below the actual waist . . . yes, she would speak to Angela, she would have a day with Angela, planning her wardrobe. For, contrary to Liz Headleand's speculations, most of Lady Henrietta's clothes were not French, they did not even come from an English fashion house; they were designed and "run up" by a clever young woman called Angela Bryant from Dorking. Angela and Henrietta considered themselves the best of friends, and would laugh and gossip a great deal during Henrietta's fittings. Angela would be startled, delighted, amused by the news of Henrietta's impending departure, of her eventually impending marriage: news which, Charles had this evening implied, need no longer, could no longer be kept a semi-secret. Liz, Charles had said, knew all about everything and thought it was all absolutely splendid. Absolutely splendid. No problems there at all, of course not, Charles had said, stoutly. Hearing this, Henrietta had remembered with some misgivings that she had offered to meet Liz one day for lunch. For some reason she did not look forward to this occasion. Or not nearly as much as she looked forward to startling, delighting, and amusing the nimble-fingered, inventive, good-natured, light-hearted, undemanding, ill-paid Angela. Angela, thought Henrietta happily, as she pushed a flake or two of fish around the sorrel sauce, really is very very cheap. A treasure.

Yes, a dark wintery evergreen green, with a touch of blue. Of
tender blue. Of love-in-the-mist, of forget-me-not blue. A
vision of her garden in Gloucestershire swam into her mind.
Love-in-the-mist, forget-me-not blue. A mist of tears trembled
behind her eyes. She ate her fish.

Liz was late back that Friday night from Esther's. She parked
the car in the mews garage and walked round to her front door,
and stood there for a moment in the street. An almost full moon
hung over Regent's Park. The familiar façades walked away
towards the soft rising mound of green. Town houses, with that
strange visionary little female gleam of grass at the end. The
Post Office Tower rose amidst scudding clouds. Dutch gables,
Adam pediments, Queen Anne windows, Art Nouveau cor-
nices, blue plaques to dead statesmen and poets, brass plates to
living consultants and royal institutions. This was her London,
she felt at home here, its layers reassured her, confirmed her.
How would she be if transplanted, when transplanted? She was
shocked by the strength of her attachment to the house. Surely
it was middle-aged, timid, wrong, ridiculous, neurotic, to cling
so to bricks and mortar, even to so handsome a pile of bricks
and mortar? Esther and Alix were right, of course; it was a big
house, an extravagant house, for a dispersing family. She
looked up. The house was dark except for the window of
Sally's room, which glowed yellow, and the hallway. Light
streamed through the handsome semicircle with its repoussé
wrought-iron pattern, and full at her feet on the pavement. She
had never deserved it. She had reached too high, travelled too
far, from Abercorn Avenue and the house in which her
mother had walled herself up: a semi-detached house, a
twenties house, a frozen house, a house held in a time warp,
stuffed with her dead father's suits and shoes, stuffed with
ancient magazines and medicine bottles. A pupa, a chrysalis,
it had been to her and to Shirley, but to her mother a tomb.
Her mother would never emerge again. I should not cling to
my house, said Liz to herself, but she shivered as she stood
there in the cold night. What if I do not survive this? she
asked herself, under the lopsided, waning moon. She was
afraid. And as she stood, semi-paralysed, transfixed, as the
furies circled closer, smelling their destined prey, a taxi drew
up at the door.

It was Charles. She stood and waited for him to open the door. He did not seem surprised to find her standing there, irresolute. With no more than a murmured greeting, they went indoors together, and would have gone perhaps silently to their separate rooms, had there not been a call from the kitchen region: it was Aaron, who emerged in a black dressing gown, and seemed in his turn extremely surprised to see them standing there together in the hallway, divesting themselves of hats, scarves, overcoats. "Hi," he said, somewhat at a loss, "I didn't think—I didn't realize—I've got messages, for both of you, as it happens."

"At this time of night?" said Charles. Liz, for her part, felt oddly furtive, felt compelled to explain that she had not been out for the evening with Charles, had merely been to Esther's, had merely been spending an evening with Alix and Esther, had arrived home with her own husband coincidentally. Charles offered no such explanation, listened to her floundering self-incriminations, and then commented, She's been to one of her witches' covens. A women's evening. Yes, said Liz, sticking pins. That's how we spend our time. Sticking pins until the blood runs.

"I wrote them down," said Aaron. "The messages. I was just making a cup of tea. Would either of you like a cup?"

Meekly they followed him into the kitchen, read the messages he had taken down for them in the course of the evening: Ring Tuohy, Ring Bechoffer, Cancel Gaskell at 9:00. There was some discussion as to who had switched off the Answerphone and why. Aaron poured tea, they sat and drank it. So when is it to be, said Aaron. What, said Charles and Liz simultaneously. You know what I mean, said Aaron.

A silence ensued. "All in due course, son," said Charles, at the end of it. "Why not now?" said Aaron. "Why not what now?" said Liz. "Oh God," said Charles, glumly. "I know everything already," said Aaron, "so you might as well tell me."

"There are no hard feelings between your mother and me," said Charles. "I've always thought that a most unfortunate expression," said Liz. "She's not my mother," said Aaron.

All three of them laughed.

"Well, I don't know," said Liz. "I don't know why Charles doesn't move out, until he goes to New York. Wouldn't that be more orthodox, Charles?"

"I think I've lost my grip of orthodoxy. It's too late to be orthodox now," said Charles, not quite believing his own words.

"Has Henrietta got any children?" asked Aaron. "Are we about to acquire some new stepbrothers and stepsisters?"

His curiosity seemed genuine. Charles replied, neutrally, dispassionately: Henrietta had two children from her previous marriage, now aged twenty and twenty-two.

"Very suitable," said Aaron. "May we be introduced? Are they nice? Do they like you? Do you like them? Shall I marry one of them? Would I be allowed to marry one of them?"

"One of them is in Rhodesia," said Charles.

"I don't think that would be a legal obstacle," said Aaron. "Not like that chap who wanted to marry his mother-in-law. He had to get a special dispensation from the House of Lords."

"I must go to bed," said Charles, but did not move. "So must I," said Liz. And did not move. Liz looked from the one to the other. Aaron, of all Charles's five children, least resembled him, resembled him physically not at all, had inherited the pale skin and dark curly hair of his mother, her slightness, her delicacy, her long fingers, her expressive features; had been for some six months, at seventeen, of a great but ephemeral beauty; and was now, in his early twenties, in the process of becoming something different, something not yet clear, not yet fully manifested, but with little relation to the solid, square, commanding presence of his father—a commanding presence which both Jonathan and Alan had, in variant versions, inherited, which Sally had cultivated bizarrely in a baroque feminist manner, and which Stella, the absent Stella, threatened to bring to an almost alarmingly weighty fulfilment. (Stella, at seventeen, weighed eleven stone and had been captain of her school's hockey and netball teams.) Aaron had no command in him. he was jester, artist, dreamer, fool. He sat there in his black dressing gown, holding a mug of tea. "Or maybe," said Aaron, "maybe, now, I could marry Liz? Would that be permitted?"

"A very interesting point," said Liz, quickly, into the strange tremor that followed his words, as all three again laughed; all three of them conscious, though none could then have voiced it (for Aaron had spoken without premeditation), of a shaking, a shifting, a resettling in the relations, in the pattern, in the configuration that held the three of them. A shifting that moved an unknown twenty-two-year-old in Rhodesia into a new connection, that replaced Aaron and Liz at different angles to one another, that obliged Aaron to consider his father at yet one more remove. Beneath the surface, plates shifted, and familiar solid continents stretched and cracked, buckled and heaved. Charles was responsible for this movement; he sat there, guilty. It is not of my doing, thought Liz, invoking the memory of Aaron as a small child throwing crumbs for sparrows in the rose garden of Regent's Park. Twenty-four-year-old Aaron looked at her darkly over his mug of tea. "A very interesting point," said Liz, brightly, quickly, disliking the silence, the laughter, the triangle of them as they sat there: "very interesting," she continued, disastrously, her mind moving, unable to help her mind's movement. "I've often wondered about *Phèdre* and all the fuss there is about incest in *Phèdre;* after all, it's not as though there's any blood relationship between Phèdre and Hippolytus, is there? Ray Spenser wrote a very odd paper on Phèdre and the Minotaur and Hippolytus's horse . . . ," and on she went, disastrously, dangerously, as Aaron's eyes darkened and widened at her until, through sheer persistence, she emerged in the innocent safety of the other side of knowledge, and laughed, and made Aaron laugh, and they were safe again despite Charles's guilt, Charles's treachery, Charles's monstrous defection. Even Charles the monster laughed, and Liz got to her feet, and declared that this time she really was going to bed; it was far too late to be talking of incest and tables of consanguinity and such foolish matters. Aaron rose, and put his arms around her, and kissed her on her forehead, as was his way; Charles patted her vaguely, in what had lately become his way, and, like a normal family, like a normal, affectionate family, they mumbled good night to one another and went to their separate rooms. Liz, lying in bed, for twenty minutes pursued the offered clue, the false trail, the cancelled plot of illicit passion, suppressed illicit passion: Phèdre/Hippolytus, Oedipus/Jocasta (not thinking, oddly, of Gertrude/Hamlet, who had been uppermost in Aaron's mind): and knew that it would not be so, because Aaron had bravely voiced it, that she and her stepsons at least would continue to try to stand towards one another in the clear light of their own selves, though the earth might shift beneath their feet. Aaron was a brave boy, a brave and wise boy. Her admiration for him was great. He had spoken the unspeakable and survived. He was her baby, her little boy, she had rocked him in her arms, had bandaged his knees, had cajoled him from roof tops. Thinking of Aaron, she fell asleep.

*   *   *

Shifting terrain. Sometimes, over the next few months, the next year, Liz wondered whether it would ever settle again. The ironies of her position (or lack of position) did not escape her: she had observed enough of this kind of thing in others to find her own response unsurprising, but her lack of surprise proved not in itself wholly therapeutic. After all, everybody knows that the loss of a partner, be it by bereavement or by infidelity, is one of the worst traumas of modern life, but the knowledge does not bring peace of mind.

It would be wrong to suggest that Liz Headleand in any way revealed, professionally or in public or social life, any sense of misgiving, of uncertainty, of disorientation. Her professional life she pursued with customary diligence. She had long accepted that she herself, like many therapists and analysts, like many working in the field of mental health, had originally been motivated by her own needs, her own problems. The wounded healer. The fact that she had herself received another, recent, unexpected wound ought not to diminish her professional competence; might even (looking on the bright side) augment it. This was the kind of thing she said to herself, as everything in her recoiled from letters from her solicitor, phone calls from her solicitor, talk about money, talk about divorce. The recoil was inevitable, irrelevant, instinctive, to be discounted. This she said to herself. And continued to see her patients, to attend meetings, to sit on committees, never missing an appointment, rarely failing to give her full attention.

In public and social terms, those who did not know her well tended to think that she had taken on a new lease on life, that she looked better, brighter than before. She laughed more and had her hair cut, she bought a new coat. They assumed (as she intended them to assume) that all had gone according to plan. As news of the Charles-Henrietta liaison became official, Rumour on the whole supported the view that Liz had helped to engineer the relationship, and that her New Year's Eve party had been by way of celebration. Liz encouraged Rumour, when she could without dishonesty do so. Rumour reported that Liz and Henrietta were seen lunching together in that new restaurant in Marylebone High Street, drinking Perrier water and chatting civilly to one another of this and that. (Rumour's imagination boggled slightly at the content of their conversation, and Rumour had to admit to having been unable to overhear much.) Rumour reported that Charles, Liz, and Henrietta were all seen leaving a party together in the same car. Rumour reported (accurately) that Liz was making every effort to speed through the divorce, so that Charles and Henrietta could become legal as soon as possible. Rumour speculated that Liz was playing some deep game of her own; but was not very inventive when it came to suggesting its nature.

But Liz, as those who knew her well could see all too clearly, wasn't playing any kind of game. Even Charles recognized that she had in fact been taken totally by surprise by his new amour, and her children and stepchildren were in varying degrees disturbed and shocked by her (to them) evident vulnerability, by her at times evident distress. As none of them except Sally was living at home, they didn't have to do anything about it, and most of them didn't think about it very much, being too busy with their own lives. Sally, an emotional and embattled girl, took the strongest line, and refused to speak to her father; she consented to see him, once, before he flew off to New York, but gave him an uncomfortable evening of feminist diatribe as a parting gift. It must be said that Liz, although she disapproved intellectually of much of the content of Sally's attack, was weakly touched by its loyalty.

It might have been expected that in this crisis Liz Headleand would draw much support from her two oldest and closest women friends, Esther and Alix. Yet, as she rightly suspected, they observed its evolution with as much interest as sympathy, with a critical curiosity that was not entirely comfortable or comforting. This did not surprise her at all. She knew that despite their fondness for her, they were sure to find something almost satisfactory in watching her plunge and flounder and skitter off course—a plunging and floundering and skittering that their sharp, informed eyes could clearly detect, behind the confident public progress, the illusion of purpose, of direction. They knew quite well that Liz had lost purpose (momentarily, permanently, who could tell) and they were not wholly displeased. She had been too confident, too knowing, too rich; she had assumed privileges, had lived in her own charmed world, had despised those who had been less certain, less secure. Let her taste confusion. Had there not been something two-faced, double-valued, hypocritical, about her use of

Charles as a husband? Had she not exploited him when it suited her, ignored him when it suited her, used him arbitrarily, selfishly, as shield, as butt, as banker, as status symbol, as scapegoat, as excuse? And he had rebelled, at last, he had stood up and declared himself, had taken her manifesto of independence at its face value, and had walked away. No, they could not blame Charles, thought Esther and Alix, said Esther and Alix to one another, behind Liz's back, occasionally to her face. Job's comforters. So much for feminist solidarity. Esther, when Liz rang her as she did from time to time to complain about Charles's solicitor's letters or her own solicitor's fees, or about the stupidity of the law, or the malice of her friends and enemies, would reply enigmatically, tangentially, and would divert the conversation as quickly as possible to the health of her potted palm. Esther's interest in her potted palm, in the spring of 1980, was obsessive. She would talk of little else. She would listen to Liz impatiently for ten minutes or so, and then begin to describe her palm's symptoms. A brittleness of the extremities of the upper leaves, a slight paleness of the lower ones, an irregular drinking pattern: such things Esther described in exhaustive detail. Liz was much intrigued by this tactic, but not wholly satisfied. She knew that it was not intended that she should be satisfied.

She might have expected more obvious sympathy from the more obviously tender-hearted Alix, but did not get it. Alix's response to Liz's new situation was complex, and she questioned herself about it, deciding that it was probably determined at least in part by her envy of Liz and Charles's wealth. She herself had had a hard time, had chosen, perhaps, a hard time, and was still not exactly affluent: she still had to count the change, to stand at bus stops in the rain, to worry about the mortgage, the gas bill. And, moreover, and more importantly, from her various part-time careers she knew those and knew of those who had much, much less, those to whom a mortgage would be a luxury. So it was not surprising that she should occasionally have widened her eyes at some of Liz Headleand's extravagances, assumptions. For Liz Headleand, after all, was only a reincarnation of Liz Ablewhite of Abercorn Avenue, daughter of a madwoman and a missing engineer, and she ought, therefore, to remember; she ought to be tactful and considerate of the carefulnesses, the economies, of others. And Liz had not always been tactful, had not always been considerate. She had sometimes appeared to believe that with a little effort, a little will power, a little of the spirit of self-help, any woman could acquire a house in Harley Street, a top executive for a husband, a dozen children, and a brilliant career. It would do her good to be reminded of what life could be like without these props. Expose thyself to feel what wretches feel.

Though as a matter of fact, as Alix knew quite well, Liz was constantly, daily, professionally exposed to what wretches feel. It was her job. It was just a question of what kind of wretchedness one took most seriously. It was a matter that they had frequently discussed. Liz maintained that psychiatric problems observed no class or economic frontiers, that most forms of disturbance manifest themselves equally among the rich and the poor, that the dynamics of family abuse, the incidence of senile dementia or Down's syndrome, the distribution of drug addiction or schizophrenia were largely unaffected by income, by environment. Alix maintained that this was rubbish. Both of them were quite well informed on the subject and read widely, pooling their findings over the years, each tending to find what each, separately, sought, rejoicing when each discovered a paper, a statistic, an article in a learned journal, an intelligent colleague to support her own view. It was a useful, a stimulating, a continuing, a rarely acrimonious interchange. And yet, Alix said to herself, it remained a fact that Liz Headleand occupied a house in Harley Street worth a million pounds, and that inevitably she tended to see patients both from the public and private sector who in some way corresponded to that simple geographical and economic proposition. Liz very rarely saw the poor, the dull, and the subnormal.

Whereas Alix Bowen saw quite a lot of them.

If you're talking about *suffering*, Liz had been known to say when the subject was broached, the rich suffer as much as the poor. In my terms, in the terms of my trade. They suffer from paranoia, from hypochondria, from endogenous depression, from frigidity, from hallucinations, from claustrophobia. When their children die or their wives are unfaithful, they suffer; when they are filled with the fear of death, they suffer. Mythology, literature are full of stories of the equalizing power of suffering, of the reductive power of loss and death and fear. The king willing to exchange all earthly riches for a living child, for an hour of life, for freedom from pain.

And yet, and yet, Alix would stubbornly insist. You choose the glamorous illnesses. As did Freud.

Some of your murderers are quite glamorous, Liz would reply.

The point was sometimes taken, sometimes not.

And now Liz herself was suffering, and finding her glamour transformed into humiliation, if not in the public eye, then in her own. And it was true that all her riches, all her past investments, appeared not to avail her now; indeed, it appeared that some of them were not as solid as they had seemed, and might prove, like her marriage, illusory. The threat of a little house in Kentish Town continued to hover, although on the sale of the house Charles appeared willing to suspend decision for a year or two. But who was to pay for it? If Liz was to keep it, who was to pay its outgoings? What, in these rather unusual circumstances, were Liz's rights?

Alix, when consulted on this point by Liz, was particularly useless. She didn't even know what she ought to think. She in turn consulted Brian, who spoke up for Liz better than she could herself. "Twenty years," he said. "Twenty years, she stuck it out with him, she brought up his children, she had two children with him, and she says she paid the grocery bills. Of course he ought to make her a decent settlement. What if she falls ill? What if she can't work?"

"I suppose she pays her National Insurance contributions like everybody else," said Alix.

"You're a hard one," said Brian.

"No I'm not," said Alix. "I just don't know how it works, that's all. Why we all expect so much. And I expect, too. Oh yes I do," she insisted, as he shook his head. "I expect. And I get. So do you. On a different scale, but we expect."

"It's natural."

"But is it? Is it?" She knew he shared her doubts.

"Think of Nicholas," she said, in the shorthand of marriage. Her son Nicholas, aged twenty-two, was unemployed. An art school drop-out. He did not seem to wish to work. He drew the dole. He lived in a council flat with a couple of friends, also on the dole. Nicholas was charming, talkative, sunny of nature. He painted both pictures and houses. He did not seem to want a "proper" job.

"I may be out of work soon myself," said Brian. "If they make many more cuts. Then you can support me."

"Thank you," said Alix. She shook her head, fretting, frowning over her knitting.

"But what worries me most," she pursued, "is that maybe,

perhaps, they might be right?" (By "they" in such a sentence, of late, as 1980 moved onwards, Alix had tended to mean the Tory party.) "I don't mean about the Health Service, or Garfield, or Adult Education, or the Open University, but about social security. People getting used to not working."

"They've no intention of reducing unemployment," said Brian. "None at all. Nicholas is working for the nation by being unemployed. It suits them very well."

"I don't follow it," said Alix.

"Who does?" said Brian.

"I suppose," said Alix, "Liz may begin to feel better now Charles and Henrietta have actually cleared off. It was rather awful when they were hanging around with everyone being so polite and civilized. Gruesome, really."

Brian cleared his throat. Delicately, he observed, "Liz seems . . . unattached, herself, at the moment?"

Alix made a dismissive, small, snorting sound. "Unattached, yes. Not so long ago she was singing the praises of the unattached life. Sexual equilibrium, and all that. That was before Charles said he was on the way out. Just shows how deep it went."

"We could . . . ask her round to dinner?"

"You mean with a *man*? Liz knows dozens of men."

"Does she?"

"Dozens," Alix repeated, more faintly. Then, brightening, mocking, "And anyway, what do women need with men? All that's gone out of fashion."

"Still," said Brian. "We could ask her."

Alix reflected. "I don't think we *know* any men. As such."

Brian waited long enough for it to appear that he might have changed the subject.

"We haven't seen Stephen for a long time," he said, speculatively.

Alix put down her knitting and stared. Took off her glasses, and stared. Slowly, she smiled. Brian smiled back, more broadly.

"I thought Stephen was away? I thought he was in America?"

"He's back."

"But Liz must have met Stephen?"

"Yes, but that was a long time ago. They could always meet again."

"Will you ring him?"

"Why don't you ring him? He'd like you to ring him."

"Would he?" She picked up her knitting again. "Would he really?"

"You know he would."

Alix sighed, nodded, agreed. She would ring Stephen that very evening, if Brian thought she should. She thought it might be true that Stephen would like it if she made the phone call. For years, she had been cautious with Stephen, one of the most evasive, the most disappearing, though at times the most sociable of men; she had feared, diffidently, to interrupt his long, intimate, and mutually formative friendship with Brian, had kept out of their way, had left them time together, had absented herself from their conversations, had made herself scarce. Stephen and Brian had, she knew, altered each other's lives incalculably, and the nature of their friendship had to her a fine exclusive quality that she did not wish to penetrate or to dilute. At times, over the years of their marriage, Brian had half-jokingly suggested that they might invite this woman, that woman, to meet Stephen, in many ways a highly eligible bachelor, and she had done so, each time a little surprised that Brian should view Stephen in such mundane, such normative terms, but also pleased, each time, to find a partner for one or another of their single women friends—for Stephen was unfailingly polite, more than polite, pleasant, attentive, morale-raising, entertaining, a good companion, in need a loyal friend. But his relations with women had been odd. Brittle, inconclusive. He appeared to favour either very good-looking stupid women or disastrously neurotic, self destructive, hard-drinking, exhibitionist women. Sometimes he was seen with a woman who united—usually horribly—these qualities. But none of his affairs—if this is what they were, and Alix was not sure—lasted long. And meanwhile he remained, to Alix and Brian and to others, a good companion, a loyal friend, an eminently reasonable, civilized kind of chap, mildly distinguished, wholly presentable. No harm could come from asking him to dinner with Liz. So Alix reasoned with herself, as she counted her rows of dove grey purl.

Liz Headleand did not tell her mother that she was, once more, to be divorced. She did not see the point. She had succeeded in avoiding going to Northam for two years, on one pretext or another, and had managed to justify herself to herself, after a manner. She was, after all, very busy. She spoke to her mother on the telephone, but not often. The truth was, as she quite well knew, that she could not bear to see her mother. She hoped her mother would die, soon. She tried to put her out of her mind, and almost succeeded.

She told her sister, Shirley, in March, but told Shirley not to tell their mother. "Charles and I have decided to get divorced," she said, casually, in the middle of one of their rare conversations. "So I hear," said Shirley, in reply. Shirley was not very interested in Liz's life. She was far too worried about her own.

But as she put the telephone down from this interchange, Liz had a moment of apprehension, of half recognition of something that she did not wish to know, something she needed to know. She beckoned it, bravely, but it averted its face. It was to do with her mother. What was it? It had gone. Her mother, Shirley had told her, was getting deafer, and needed a hearing aid to listen to the radio. Rita Ablewhite listened to the radio day and night, though what she thought she was hearing who could tell.

"And these voices," Liz asked of the patient sitting before her, "what do they sound like? Is it a man's voice or a woman's voice? Or both?"

Silence. Liz scribbled on her pad, auditory hallucinations, bifocal glasses, poor teeth (NB—needs to see a dentist), says he can't drink milk or eat cheese but offers no reason, do the voices tell him this? Very insistent about it. Broad face, pleasant. Looks Middle European to me but says he's Welsh. Grey hair. Roll-neck sweater, jacket. Off-duty look.

"Sometimes," the patient tentatively volunteers, at last, leaning forward confidentially, speaking in a low, soft voice, "they are music." And he smiles, as though imparting something precious.

"What kind of music?"

"Music I heard as a child."

"Pleasant music?"

Silence. Liz scribbles again. Schizophrenia, onset aged forty, he says.

"At other times," continues the patient, "they speak Welsh."

"You were brought up in a Welsh-speaking family?"

He shakes his head. "No, no, I don't speak Welsh."

"But it is Welsh they speak?"

"Oh yes. And what worries me is this." He leans forward, emphatic. "The advice they give me, I have to do it, but it is bad. Bad things. That is what worries me."

"What sort of bad things?"

He smiles, mysteriously, and will not say. Silence.

"Is that why you went to see your doctor, because of the bad things?"

Silence. She writes on her pad, refer to Heber?

"Do you do what they say, the voices? Even when you think it is bad?"

A pause. "The voices are good. It is me that is bad."

"What makes you say that?"

"They do. They make me say that."

She scribbles, ascertain religious background?

"Tell me again about the music," she asks. And so they go on.

"You see," says the patient, a long-term patient, "it was all in the bus ticket. It was written there, in the bus ticket."

"What did it say?"

The patient looks suddenly coy, tugs at her fringe in a habitual, not unendearing mannerism, smiles, and says, "I don't know if I should tell you."

"Oh, don't be silly," says Liz, who has no pad out before her this time, who is merely listening.

"Well, I always read the numbers on bus tickets, and on this one it said 6969." She pauses, dramatically. Liz allows herself to smile. The patient laughs.

"I took it as an omen," she says.

"Of course," says Liz.

"What do you mean, of course?" says the patient.

"Haven't we agreed, time and again," says Liz, "that we're all superstitious? All of us?"

"Yes," says the patient. "But I'm *really* superstitious."

"And what did the omen mean?" asks Liz. And the patient proceeds to recount, in vivid detail, her latest sexual adventure, which had taken place, she claimed, in a bathroom in a hotel in Warwickshire. The number seven is also woven into this period of narrative, with considerable ingenuity. The young woman enjoys her own story. When she is with Liz Headleand, she is quite happy. For an hour.

"I don't know, I don't know what to do." She has her arms round herself, a middle-aged woman, is holding herself tight and rocking herself slightly, backwards and forwards, backwards and forwards. "I don't know, I don't know what to do. It is legal now, I know it's legal."

"Yes," says Liz. "Yes, it is."

"But how would I do it? How would I set about it?"

Liz is silent.

"And maybe it's better not? Better not to try? Or is that cowardly? What do *you* think? Dr. Headleand, what do *you* think?"

"You mean, you might not like what you might discover?"

The woman sits upright, to attention.

"I *know* I might not like it. I probably wouldn't like it, would I? How could I like it? How could it be good?"

"Then why do you think of trying it at all?"

"I've told you about that. The uncertainty. The fear of worse."

She looks at Liz, sharply. "I know what you're thinking. You think it may *be* worse. May be the worst. Incest. Rape. Are those things the worst?"

"They're not uncommon. But then there are other reasons. Good reasons. Reasonable reasons. Some of these stories have perfectly good endings."

"What do *you* mean by good?" Again, sharply.

"Endings in reconciliation. Forgiveness. Friendship. I would call that good, I think. Would you call that good?"

"I don't know, I don't know, I don't know." She begins to rock again.

"I do know people," says Liz, tentatively, "who have found out what you call the worst, and who have been quite able to accept it. For what that's worth."

"Truly? Truly?"

"Yes, truly." Liz hesitates, decides to proceed. She likes this woman, respects her, wishes to share her thoughts with her.

"Yes," she says. "For example, I know of a case in which a man of about your age—a little older, perhaps—became anxious, as you have, about the identity of his natural parents. Unlike you, he didn't know he'd been adopted until he was quite old. Until he married, in fact. His adoptive parents didn't tell him until he got married. He didn't worry about it for some time, but then his third child was discovered, in his teens, to have a heart lesion. And he took it into his head that this was his fault, that it was a hereditary disorder. He blamed himself. And, like you, he became obsessed by the idea of tracing his real parents. This was nearly ten years ago, just after the law was changed. Everybody discouraged him, but he persisted. And discovered what you call the worst."

"Yes?"

"Incest. Father and daughter. The daughter had subsequently committed suicide, after giving birth."

"And he took this well, you say?"

"Yes. It was established that there had been no family history of heart lesion or heart abnormality of any kind."

"So he was worried only about his own culpability?"

"So it would appear."

"And what happened to the child with the heart lesion?"

"That is not part of the case history. But as it happens, as you happen to ask, I can tell you that he was all right, when last heard of. It wasn't very serious."

"Sometimes I think," says Mrs. Hood, "that it's just because my own children have grown up now, have left home. That I've started to worry. Suddenly I have time. I worry."

"Time?" Mrs. Hood works full-time as a personnel manager with a large multinational electrical company. She visits Liz at 8:30 in the morning, before her day's work begins. Her two children are now at university. She is divorced.

"Well, you know what I mean. More time."

Liz smiles. She knows what Mrs. Hood means.

"Worry fills the vacuum?"

"Yes, it slips in. Leave it five idle minutes, and it slips in. Just when you think you've earned an evening off in front of the television."

"It's not uncommon for people of your age to adopt this particular worry," says Liz, a little vaguely, then suddenly jumps to attention, interested, surprised, amused, noticing her own curious turn of phrase. "The adopted adopt worry. They start to ask questions."

"When it's too late," says Mrs. Hood.

"Too late for what?" asks Liz.

Mrs. Hood smiles, shakes her head. She is more relaxed now, has stopped rocking.

"Too late not to have children oneself."

"Would there have been a question of that?"

"No, not really."

"You wanted children very badly, you say."

"I always had this picture of myself, as a little mother. I used to play at mothers and babies. Used to dream about what a wonderful mother I'd be. Patient, understanding. I had these fantasies. Even when I was tiny. I had these dolls. I played for hours."

"You planned to be a different kind of mother from your adoptive mother?"

"She was quick-tempered, my mother. Unpredictable. Moody. Sometimes she'd let you do things, sometimes she wouldn't. My real mother, I used to tell myself, wouldn't have been like that at all. She'd have been smooth. Even. She'd never have been cross. She'd always have known that I hadn't meant any harm."

"And did you never mean any harm?"

"I don't think I did. I honestly don't think I did. I tried all the time to please. I just wanted to please. I couldn't understand why she didn't understand it was an accident. When I broke something, or lost something."

"You never annoyed her on purpose?"

"Not knowingly. Not that I can remember."

"And your own children? Did they ever annoy you on purpose?"

"Of course they did. Children do, don't they?"

Silence. They look at one another, knowingly.

"And your adoptive mother is still much the same?"

"Much the same." Mrs. Hood's arms go round her tightly again, she begins to rock again, a look of deeply pained perplexity creases her face. "Much the same. Sometimes she knows me, sometimes she doesn't. When I saw her on Saturday, she didn't know me. She kept asking for someone called Monica. I don't know anyone called Monica. The nurses say she's getting more confused. I don't think she wants to see me."

"If she doesn't recognize you, how can she want not to see you?"

"If she doesn't recognize me, who am I?"
Liz does not answer. She does not know.

It's not that I don't find them as interesting as I always did,
thinks Liz, as she eats her lunch of cottage cheese, anticipating
a better meal that evening with Alix and Brian. I do. And I
don't think I say the wrong things. I don't think I mislead. I
don't think the quality of my attention has altered. In other
words, I am as serviceable as I ever was. But how can I be,
when I know that I do not understand my own problems, when
I know what I do not know, when I have been obliged to admit
that I do not stand on solid ground, when my own patterns are
obscure to me?

The wounded healer. But that is another concept: that is
the concept of the healer whose knowledge of the malady
springs from a fellow sickness, from a diagnosed fellow
sickness.

Is there, perhaps, an analogy with the faithless priest? Liz,
a child of the north of England and daughter of an irreligious
house, does not know much about Catholicism, but has read
her Graham Greene, and dimly recalls the notion that even the
unworthy vessel, the doubting vessel, can minister the true
sacrament. Her rational self accepts this as rational: it is the
nature of the healing, not the spirit of the healer, that is of value
both to rational and to religious man. The right words may be
said by the wrong, the unworthy priest. And it is not as though
I had lost my faith in the healing process. That is not it. It is
more subtle than that, this nagging, this anxiety, this sense of
falseness, of faithlessness. Is it merely a temporary, an
irrelevant loss of self-esteem, a minor personal neurosis, not
worthy to be dignified by adult attention, a neurosis like
anxiety about hair loss or a double chin or receding gums? She
suspects that this is how Alix and Esther see her current
uncertainty, and in part she admires their robust dismissal,
their refusal to take too seriously her panics, her complaints,
her dismays.

But nevertheless, something continues to nag, something
irresolute, unresolved, undiagnosed. Something suppurates,
something stinks in her own nostrils, if not in those of others.
A spiritual body odour. It is offensive to her, but she cannot

locate its source. Is it merely fastidiousness that wishes to trace it and remove it? She does not know. She truly does not know. She even thinks of returning to her one-time analyst in St. John's Wood, but does not do so. She knows it would be a useless exercise. There is nothing that Karl can now tell her. She has outgrown Karl. She is too astute for Karl, she can deceive Karl, she can read the tenor of Karl's questions before he has even himself formulated them, she can dodge him and run ahead of him into never-ending open space, she is faster by far than he.

So what does it matter what she does, out here in this grassy space, alone? On this high, solitary upland? Who cares? What harm does she do, up here? Who cares? She contaminates no one, she endangers no person.

Her mind returns to Mrs. Hood. The case of Mrs. Hood interests her, for obvious reasons. Mrs. Hood, as far as Liz can tell, never fantasized about her real father. Had no interest in her real father, until she was adult, and then her interest was only academic, it seemed. Mrs. Hood admits that she had always imagined herself to be the offspring of a woman alone. Her real mother had preoccupied her, haunted her, exercised her imagination, woven herself into her most infantile dreams. With Liz herself, it had been otherwise. The real mother had been there, solidly absent, a constant and insoluble distress, a damaged being, a victim, a mystery. Too painful, too inexplicable to contemplate. So Liz, as a child, had contemplated her missing father instead. She could not remember him at all, although she must have been nearly four when he vanished. She had been free to invent. She had invented wonders. Wealth, gold braid, uniforms, power, magnificence. A commander. When the war was over, he would return gloriously, he would rescue his daughter Elizabeth (but probably not Shirley) and remove her to a fitting palace, which, in her imagination, somewhat resembled the Alhambra Cinema on Jubilee Road. Marble and red carpet with a minaret. Her mother would at this point die, conveniently. Maybe her mother would be revealed, after her convenient death, to have been a princess in disguise, under a spell, bewitched. Or maybe she would be revealed not to have been Liz's mother at all, but a serving maid, charged with the care of the royal baby by a wicked thief. Anyway, she would die, and Elizabeth would be free. Lady Elizabeth, Princess Elizabeth, her adoring subjects would cry, as they reached out to touch her hem and be healed.

She played variations of this drama to herself until she was quite old, long after more realistic escape routes had begun more profitably to occupy her waking, working mind. She had learned that such fantasies were normal, part of a normal pattern, and had long since ceased to find them embarrassing.

And yet, and yet. During the terrible transformations of puberty, she had sat and brooded on her father. Shaming fantasies. Sexual fantasies. She had masturbated while brooding on her father, not knowing what she was doing, but knowing it was wrong. She set herself penances, but they did not help. A dark cluster gathered, inexorably, in her spirit. Increasingly masochistic grew its manifestations, its yearnings. Steel knitting needles featured. She dreamed of tortures, imprisonments, knives, daggers, dark towers. Wounds, blows, penetrations. Even now, she does not like to look back on them. They continue to shame, these fantasies.

Her mother being mad, and madly fastidious, there was nobody to warn her about the onset of adult life, of bodily changes. She knew about menstruation from school friends, from advertisements in magazines, from labels on discreet packets of sanitary towels read sideways in the chemist's. But nobody thought to warn her of the changes that precede menstruation, and she had thought herself uniquely diseased. She convinced herself at the age of eleven, twelve, that she was suffering from venereal disease. She had only the dimmest notions of what this was, notions gleaned from small-type-faced notices on the back doors of public lavatories and from consulting the dictionary and *Pears Encyclopedia*, but she knew that it was shameful, too shameful ever to mention to another human being. And she believed it had afflicted her, as a vengeance for her wicked imaginings (though how she managed to make quite such an accurate connection between such imaginings and such a disease was, in later years, to puzzle her, for her imaginings had been of an extraordinary anatomical naïveté). Miserably she had stared at the stains in her bottle green school regulation knickers. She would try to wash them, surreptitiously, before putting them in the laundry basket for her mother to inspect. She would crouch drying them before the bar of an electric fire, guiltily, dreading that Shirley would catch her at it, braving the strange, disturbing, wet, woolly, scorching sexual smell. Her daughter's growing, her daughter's threatening, burgeoning flesh.

Guilt, furtiveness, shame, concealment. Liz had experienced more of these in her girlhood than might, she later discovered, be considered normal. She had known early that sex was wicked, that the changes in her own body augured delinquency, that the satisfying of its urges would bring disaster. She could never discover the roots of her knowledge and was disappointed (lastingly) in Karl her analyst because he could suggest no acceptable explanation: he continued, apparently, to believe that Liz had merely been struggling against a strong parental prohibition against masturbation in early infancy. Liz knew there was more to it than that. She could not recall any mention of masturbation, ever (and however patiently Karl explained to her the irrelevance of her own conscious memories, they continued to interest her), and sometimes wished she had indeed suffered from the violence of a convent upbringing, from a dose of hell-fire threats, rather than from the blank, dark, backward nothingness of her own unknowing, from the sinister connections of her own guilt. A broken command from a parent, from a teacher, from a priest, would have been simplicity itself compared with the self-torment of conscious but inexplicable sin she had at times endured.

She had abandoned her fantasies and her self-abuse and with them her self-torment in her early teens, had forced herself to "give them up," as she put it to herself, and then devoted all her energy to success at school, to escape through university, an outlet that had received her mother's formal approval. All her sexual yearning was perversely poured into the state examination system, and the transference was so successful that by the time Liz got to Cambridge she had forced herself to forget the dark brooding, had become a daylight creature full of superficial vanity and worldly, skin-deep cravings. Banished was her father's image and its potent demands for pain, for sacrifice, for abasement: instead she herself received tribute, more innocent tribute, invitations, billets-doux, kisses, flowers, longings, declarations. The surface of her sparkled, attracted. The surface of her attracted Edgar Lintot, and, superficially, they married, and quarrelled, and parted, while the dark depths of both lay dormant, unstirred, impenetrable.

But Charles had stirred them. Liz, sitting there with her cottage cheese, made herself remember. Charles had called to the forbidden in her, demons had answered, from the place

where they had been waiting. His mixture of brutality and
desire had matched something in herself. He was cruel but
enslaved. He came to her as a man acquainted with grief, a
widower expected to run wild, an excessive man seeking
comfort in dissolution and promiscuity: a romantic figure. She
had fallen in love with it. Love? Well, she had thought it was
love, but lust might have been a more fitting word for whatever
it was that bound them together, in those early days—were lust
not a word that suggests simplicity and brevity rather than
obsession. Their lust had certainly not been brief, simple, or
easily satisfied. It fed on his mild sadism, her mild desire for
punishment, a desire that in no way reflected their social
relations. The first time that he said to her, in the taxi, on the
way back to her flat, that he would punish her in bed for
speaking to another man at the party they had just attended, she
was so overcome with sexual longing that she felt her body
blaze, and he, hearing her catch her breath and feeling her
loosen her knees, thought that he had found the key to her
forever, and had told her so, that night in bed in language and
in action that had roused in her an intensity, a violence, that
had seemed to purge and to purify all things. And so it had
continued: if not forever, for the best part of a decade. Rituals,
repetitions. The demons had become the kindly ones, the
terrors of the darkness of her body became physical delight,
pleasure, rapture. She and Charles connived with one another
in the satisfaction of the body, they understood one another
well. It had seemed a harnessing of perversion, a permitted
exploration of the psyche and the flesh, an odyssey of the
1960s. Marriage and children merely brought to their liaison an
added piquancy. In bed, in long drives in the car, in respectable
restaurants, in corners in parties, in darkened studios watching
rushes of Charles's early socially conscious documentaries,
they manifested their shadow selves, their sexual selves, and in
the daylight their fortified solid beings conducted negotiations
in another style on quite other matters: they made money, ran
a house, quarrelled with camera men and the IBA, bore and
brought up children, sacked staff, took on staff, entertained
friends, quarrelled with colleagues.

The seventies had been less euphoric: infidelities, small
betrayals, small conflicts. But beneath that, Liz had assumed,
an abiding loyalty, and abiding unity: above and beneath all, an
abiding sense of the profound importance of their mutual
self-knowledge and exploration, a sense that no other person in

life could ever know such things of the other, that no other relationship could truly supersede or overshadow what they had been to one another. Had she now to learn to disbelieve the meaning, the very existence, of their mutual past? This she still could not quite credit; this was, she suspected, her stumbling block. She could not believe that Charles had replaced her in his imagination, his sexual imagination, with Henrietta, and replaced her so seriously that he wished to marry Henrietta. How could he? She could not bring herself to believe it, and her lack of belief proved her either mad or foolish. For it was so. So this was what her patients had been suffering when they had spoken of sexual jealousy. Not the mild irritation or passing rage that had taken hold of her when Charles had had that ridiculous association with Nicola Stowell, or of Charles when she had started to sleep with Jules, but this, the real thing, the thing itself: a negation, a denial, an undoing of past self, of past knowledge, of past joys, of past certainties, a complete and utter unmaking of the fabric of one's true self.

Well, no, thought Liz, scraping clean the cottage cheese carton with a teaspoon and lighting a cigarette: not quite so, not quite as bad as that. The self still goes on, eating its lunch, seeing its patients, looking forward to having dinner with Alix and Brian. It is only the sexual self that has been undone, and the sexual self is only a part of the whole. Or is it? Is it? Well, that is the question, admits Liz to herself. It is to this question, I suppose, that I must now re-address myself, she tells herself.

Charles had always enjoyed hurting people, and Liz had enjoyed being hurt. Within limits agreed between them. A bruise, a bite, a threat now and then. But Charles had never in the old days overstepped the mark; Liz herself had set the marks. By a cry, a moan, a gesture, a murmur, a hint. Was it part of the same instinct in him that had now caused him to cause her this real pain? And if so could she forgive it? Or was he even now engaged in some serious and elaborate pain-pleasure contract with Henrietta, and so deeply engaged that he had forgotten Liz's identity, forgotten her claims on him? She could not tell.

Charles had always enjoyed dismissing people. It had been one of the features of his rise to power in the 1970s. When others quailed, Headleand would step in: with relish he would challenge the old, the weak, the woolly. He had cleared the stables not of filth and corruption but of nice woolly ageing men in their fifties, polite, gentlemanly, incompetent men. He had done it in the name of progress once, in the name of productivity now, but his own impulse had remained the same: the prospect of a confrontation or a dismissal, be it of a fellow director or of a hundred or two employees, had stiffened his sinews and made his spirits rise. And now he had given his own middle-aged wife the sack (an appalling but apparently current phrase, which Liz had heard, though mercifully not applied to herself, from one of her younger patients). The possibility occurred to her, for the first time, that he had actually enjoyed it, that the dreadful scene of New Year's Eve had been stage-managed by him as a rejuvenating rite, as a fifty-year-old's assertion of potency, of renewal.

The possibility did not appeal to her. It was so unpleasant that she wondered that she had not thought of it before.

Nor had she thought before of any possible connection between Charles's recent behaviour and that of her father, though she had long recognized that Charles had replaced the fantastic, punishing father of her childhood. But in real life, what, after all, had her real father *done*? What had he done to her mother? Had he died on her, or dismissed her before dying on her? Had he perhaps gone off with another woman? Was that the explanation of her mother's withdrawal from the world? She fingered her locket in which, it was alleged, the image of her father was imprisoned. But was it even him? Neither she nor Shirley (who carried an identical image in an identical locket) knew whether or not it was their father who gazed at them, solemn, unsmiling, clean-shaven, heavy browed, undistinguished, indistinguishable, from his small oval frame. No other images of him had adorned the house in Abercorn Avenue, an absence that had led the irreverent Shirley to declare defiantly late one night in the kitchen that she didn't believe that the photo in the locket was him at all, it was just any old photo, and that she and Liz had never had a father at all but had been born of a virgin birth. Liz had been shocked but amused by this suggestion, and had tried hard to recall a real shadow of a real father from her infant years—could she or could she not remember sitting on a man's knee, the smell of tobacco, the sound of a man's voice? She was not sure. She could not be sure.

And yet she, Doctor Elizabeth Headleand, was considered an expert in these matters. She wrote papers on fostering and adoption, on the psychiatric problems of the adopted, the orphaned, the stepmothered; she had appeared as an expert witness in court, had given respected evidence to the committee which had recommended the changes in law that made possible the disclosure of the identity of parents of adopted children. Physician, heal thyself. Physician, know thyself.

It will by now be evident that Liz Headland is concealing something from herself, and that it is for this reason that she sits there perplexed before an empty cottage cheese carton, smoking a cigarette. It is evident to Liz Headland herself, as well as to the reader, that she is concealing something from herself. But what is it? Does she know what it is? Do you know what it is? Do I know what it is? Does anybody know what it is?

Liz Headland asked herself what it was that she knew but did not know, and, naturally, received no answer from herself. She straightened her back, stubbed out her cigarette, looked at her watch. Where to go from here? Where but onwards? Almost cheerfully, she assented to her own stubborn proposition, her own long-held proposition, that effort will be rewarded. So it had been before; so it might be again. A continuing contemplation of the unpleasant will generate enlightenment, information, knowledge; and knowledge will restore health and life. So it had been, so it would be. She would continue. She would turn back in order to leap forwards. She would dig up again her father's corpse, she would explore once more those dark labyrinthine strong-smelling chambers and passages. She would hold the string tightly as she made her way to meet the beast. She smiled at her own imagery. She had always preferred the dreadful to the dull. Or so she thought. But even as she sat there smiling with a straight back, she doubted her own courage. In her heart, she doubts herself. She wonders if she dares to dig. She is afraid.

Esther Breuer for her lunch ate some old beetroots that tasted slightly off, slightly wet, slightly musty and dank; garnished with some hard crumbs of violent Roquefort and a cold boiled potato. She covered all with olive oil from Lucca, very good-quality olive oil delivered by hand by a musical friend who was living in Tuscany and writing a book on Guido d'Arezzo. As she ate, she contemplated some colour photographs of details from Crivelli's *Virgin and Child* and his *Vision of the Blessed Gabriel* that she had newly acquired for a lecture on Crivelli which she was to deliver in Birmingham the following month. She could by now have delivered a lecture on Crivelli standing on her head with her eyes shut and her back to the screen, she sometimes claimed, but she liked to vary her address, for her own amusement. She had in the past devoted a great deal of attention to the amazing arrays of greengrocery—pears, apples, peaches, marrows—with which Crivelli liked to adorn his subjects, and thought that this time she would dwell more on the phallic and the uterine as represented by the gaily coloured little arrows that so happily and decoratively perforated the sultry, smiling, androgynous Saint Sebastian on the Virgin's left, and by the Virgin's appearance to Gabriel from a vaginal slit in the sky, wittily echoed by the saint's own red rocky womblike bolt hole. They would like that in Birmingham. Esther Breuer was in a good mood. She had received a letter that morning inviting her to Bologna to deliver her opinion on the authenticity of a painting possibly by Carlo Crivelli himself, possibly by his brother Vittore, newly acquired from a monastery on the Yugoslav-Albanian border. She liked the idea of a trip to Bologna. She wanted to revisit the Carracci frieze in the Palazzo Salem. Romulus and Remus brought up by the she-wolf. A good excuse to do various things at once, with her fare paid.

She mopped up the oil with a crust of bread. The new Crivelli was described as a Baptism, probably part of a polyptych, the figure of John much damaged, but the waters of the Jordan pleasantly stocked with a charming array of fishes and lilies, and in the bottom right-hand corner, a nest of mallard ducklings. She longed to see the little ducks. She would go in March or April, for a week.

Shirley Harper for her lunch ate a cold sausage, a piece of toast, a lump of New Zealand Cheddar, a spoonful of Branston pickle, and a large slice of lemon cake with lemon butter cream filling. She had not meant to eat the lemon cake, but justified herself by saying that it would be a pity to let it go stale. It was rather a good cake. Shirley still baked, occasionally, although nobody seemed much interested in her offerings, apart from Cliff, and he was putting on weight and ought not to accept them. She had taught herself to bake, from books. One of the most vivid, powerful, and romantic memories of her early

childhood was of watching the mother of a school friend
baking. She had called in, on her way home, knowing she
would be in trouble for lingering, but unable to resist, and there
had been June's mother in an apron and a white wooden
kitchen table covered in bowls and wire trays and jugs of water
and pastry cutters and jams and packets of raisins and sultanas.
June's mother wielded the rolling pin with floury hands and
little bits of crinkly pastry fell off the edge of the board. June
picked one up and ate one, offered one to Shirley. Shirley
looked at June's mother in terror and apprehension, but June's
mother smiled and said, "Go on, try a bit, not too much or it'll
give you indigestion," and she had nibbled at the soft, doughy,
salty, raw paste. They scraped out the cake bowl with a
wooden spoon, raw cake mixture, yellow, smooth, liquid.
They nibbled at a glacé cherry. The wickedness, the security.
A smell of cooking and warmth filled the kitchen from the
old-fashioned kitchen range. Jam tarts, rock buns, a lemon
cake, coconut fingers, cheese scones. Those were the days
when a housewife would bake for a week. Rationing days, still:
substitute ingredients, poor substitutes, to June's mother—
dried egg, turnip-extended jam, margarine—but to Shirley and
June, God's plenty.

Shirley was late home, and chastised, made to stand in a
corner, brooding on illicit dough. Later that night she whispered to Liz, in bed, "Why can't we have cakes?" Liz had
snapped, "Don't be silly." "But why?" Shirley persisted Liz
pondered, defeated. "Because of the war," she said, finally.
An answer, and no answer.

Rita Ablewhite did not bake partly because she could not
endure the sensation of flour on her fingers, in her nails. The
soft wet putty in her hands. She had tried to keep herself at one
remove from food. She fed her girls on dry goods, raw goods,
straight-from-the-tin goods. Amazing, thought Shirley sometimes, looking back, that we didn't get rickets, scurvy, vitamin
deficiencies.

Rita Ablewhite had lived for years on diet mixes and
biscuits, on raw packets of jelly and soup cubes. Growing
skeletal, stooping, shrivelled. In her old age, Shirley had
rebelled on her mother's behalf, had braved her mother's
wrath, had called in the doctor. Her mother had not seen a
doctor in twenty years. The doctor had been appalled, but
helpless. She was not certifiable, what could one do? There is
no law against living on the edge of sanity, against eating jelly

cubes, against wearing the same clothes for thirty years, against letting one's teeth rot. He had recommended Meals On Wheels. To Shirley's astonishment, her mother had accepted the suggestion. To her greater astonishment, she had begun to enjoy her food, had become quite choosy. She would complain that it had been mince two days running, that the chicken was tepid, that the carrots were over-cooked. She would tell Shirley she fancied a bit of fish for her supper. Shirley began to provide evening meals, not always, but sometimes. Her mother sometimes said thank you, even.

In fact, said Shirley to herself, as she firmly put the cake back in the cake tin, the point was that their mother wasn't half as barmy as she made out, had never been half as barmy as her daughters had come to believe her to be. Eccentric, yes, odd, certainly, but not demented, not dangerous, not quite. If there had been anyone around to take charge, to intervene, to advise? But there had been nobody. Only Miss Mynors, twittering, midget, mildly deformed, inexplicable Miss Mynors. Miss Mynors, dressmaker, who would come in every day for tea and nibble a biscuit. Not much of a refuge, Miss Mynors.

No, Rita Ablewhite had not been barmy. She had kept her daughters alive, she had fended off enquiries with considerable shrewdness, she had driven away intruders, and preserved her citadel. She had abided by the laws of the land, had sent her children off to school regularly, had attended to their vaccinations and immunizations, had nursed them through sicknesses, had fed them regulation cod liver oil and thick, sticky, strong government orange juice, had clothed them and taken them to have their hair cut. True, as soon as they could safely make excursions on their own—and possibly slightly earlier—they had been obliged to do so, for Rita did not like going out. But she had not been totally out of touch, she had known which was the correct school, had fed Liz's ambitions, had even made one or two surprising ventures into the annexation of the outside world. She had, for instance, paid for both girls to have elocution lessons. At the time, this had seemed odd, but not nearly as odd as it seemed in retrospect. True, the elocution teacher had been a friend of Miss Mynors's, but she had been a perfectly regular teacher, not a freak. A large, broad-faced, double-chinned, plain, soft-spoken, plummy-voiced suburban woman in a tweed suit, who wore a shiny shirt and a tie with a fox's head pin. Rita Ablewhite had announced that she did not want her daughters to sound like common Yorkshire schoolgirls. (Which is what, of course, they were, what Shirley herself most wanted to be, and the commoner the better.) They had to learn to speak correctly, to speak like the voices in the wireless to which Rita so tirelessly attended. Rita's own voice was identifiably Yorkshire.

Shirley and Liz had quite enjoyed the lessons, in their different ways. Shirley enjoyed the outing, simply as an outing: a different sitting room, different flowers on the carpet, different cushions on the settee, a different glass shade on the central lamp, a china horse on the mantelpiece, an embroidered fire screen with a lyre bird, a vase of Chinese lanterns. She had enjoyed examining Miss Featherstone's skull. Miss Featherstone had a skull called Horace, with unlocking sinus chambers fastened by little golden hooks. Shirley used to try to make her get it out every week, but she wouldn't. It was a rationed treat. Everything was rationed in those days. Shirley also enjoyed the tweedy, lavender smell of Miss Featherstone.

Liz liked the poetry. She liked to hear Miss Featherstone intoning poetry. The splendour falls on castle walls, Gobling Market, Don John of Austria, Edith Sitwell, A. E. Housman, even, daringly, a little Dylan Thomas. Liz learned to intone it herself, and would drone for hours to herself in bed, under the bedclothes. Oh, shut *up*, Shirley would shout, as she tried to concentrate on her Enid Blyton or her Richmal Crompton, or her smuggled copies of *The Girls' Crystal*, but Liz would go on and on for hours, incantatory, entranced, drugged, like a spirit voice.

Rita Ablewhite approved of reading. She read books herself. Dickens, Trollope, Charlotte Brontë, that sort of thing. The same books, again and again, although when the girls were old enough to go to Boots Library she would send them out on her behalf for new fodder. How had she acquired this habit? Like so much about her, it remained a mystery.

Sighing, Shirley wiped the imitation marble tiles, wiped the stainless-steel sink, hung up her dishcloth. She was bored. Underemployed, bored. She herself no longer read books. Books seemed irrelevant to her life. They portrayed other people, their lives, other worlds. They bored her. She wished she had not eaten the slice of cake. She opened the tin, to see how much was left, and found herself cutting another tiny slice. Appalled, she ate it.

*   *   *

Cliff Harper for his lunch had a large plate of roast pork, crackling, applesauce, mashed potato, roast potato, gravy, boiled cabbage, and bright green frozen peas, followed by treacle tart with cream and white coffee. He ate this at the local pub, which did lunches in an upstairs room. He considered this a light lunch, in comparison with the smarter one he would be obliged to buy for a client at the Post House Hotel the following day. He was on good terms with the waitress, who teased him and his partner, Jim, about the cream. Always the same jokes. "I don't suppose you'll be having cream, will you? Or perhaps just a little? Whoops, sorry, the jug slipped." She enjoyed a laugh, did Lilian.

There were still a fair number of people eating lunch, in the spring of 1980, in the Old Forge in Northam, on the Lower Valley Road. But business was slacker than it had been: For Sale notices were going up on long-familiar premises, on old-established businesses, and men were being laid off by the hundred. The steel strike wasn't doing anybody much good, and Northam, although not exclusively a steel city, experienced ripples of rumour and dismay as small businesses collapsed, suppliers failed, distributors went bankrupt around it. The knock-on effect, it was called. Demand had slumped; nothing much was moving. The old manufacturing neighbourhood had begun to take on a new kind of grimness: it had never been pretty, but it had possessed a certain dignity, to some a homely dignity, and the extraordinary jumble of architectural styles—nineteenth-century factories, tall chimneys, huge buttressed walls, small squeezed lingering eighteenth-century domestic dwellings and public houses, cheap post-war *ad hoc* factories and offices, railway bridges, gas cylinders, weed-blooming canal banks, the odd cosmetic 1970s face-lift—offered a variety, a visual and human richness, a weathered and seasoned history of the city's prosperous past and present. But now there was an ominous slowing of the pulse: the age of the buildings and the neighbourhood was beginning to tell, a forlorn gust blew coldly down the empty streets, rust ate quietly at machinery, brick dust sifted from crumbling ledges, dirty glass panes slowly splintered as window frames rotted. The poetry of neglect. Jokes were cracked, these days, in Northam, about the newly and expensively restored industrial hamlet and museum up the valley: why not turn the whole dump, the whole East End, into one blooming big museum and charge Japanese tourists to come and gawp? You could pay old men in overalls to stand around and dress the show. Take them out of the unemployment figures. Give them a sense of purpose. Back to the good old days.

Cliff Harper and Jim Bakewell, in this accelerating slump, found themselves in an anomalous, an unlikely, a potentially worrying position. Demand for their product was too high. They were doing too well. Wing mirrors were selling better than they had ever anticipated, owing partly to a rumour that legislation was being drawn up to make provision of an offside wing mirror on all vehicles compulsory. Driving instructors had taken to recommending them, Ministry of Transport inspectors recommended them, new cars were built with them as an obligatory rather than an optional feature. Cliff and Jim were not interested in the new car market: they assembled an Attach-It-Yourself model for older cars, to replace damaged mirrors on newer cars. The parts came from Taiwan, as did the parts of their other, less briskly selling line of knife-spoon-corkscrew-bottle-opener picnic kit. What to do? To discontinue picnic kits, to concentrate on wing mirrors, to take on new staff, to borrow money to expand, to rent new premises? Cliff was conservative, Jim expansionist in spirit, but the truth was that neither of them knew what to do, which way to move, which way to jump. They talked knowledgeably of the government's anti-state-regulation stance (an anti-compulsory-wing-mirror stance, presumably), of the increasing leisure-product market (a pro-picnic argument, presumably), of the laws regulating employment in small businesses, of the advis-ability of taking on a cheap youngster or two through YOPS; but they did not know what to do for the best, they could not read the future, they could not trust the future. They comforted themselves with treacle tart and cream.

Alix Bowen spent most of her lunch hour shopping for the dinner she was to present to Liz Headleand and Stephen Cox. It was one of what she called her Home Office Think Tank days, though it wasn't the Home Office itself that she worked in, but a corner of a dusty, gracious, apparently forgotten building in Nightingale Terrace off Pall Mall, a building under the shifting shades of demolition or refurbishment, within easy walk of the cheese and ham shop in Jermyn Street where camp young men and small old-fashioned old men were sometimes charming, sometimes rudely dismissive, according to a plan, a rhythm that Alix had never been able to predict. Today was a charming day and after she had effected her purchases they pressed on her a sample piece of an unfamiliar cheese called Vignotte. Weakly, she ate it and bought some, and bought herself a piece of pie to eat in her office. She then ran back through the March wind and was devouring the pie when her boss, Polly Piper, came in. Alix looked up and continued to devour her pie. "Hi, Poll," said Alix.

Polly sat down on the spare chair, and put her feet on the desk amid the heaped files.

"Hi," she said.

"If you want some coffee," said Alix, "you could put the kettle on."

Polly Piper did not move.

"Where did you get that pie?" she asked, hungrily.

"Paxton and Whitfield. Jolly good. Have a corner?"

Alix parted with a few small crumbs.

"I've been looking at that report from Kendall, Illinois. Reading between the lines, I think they've had a lot of trouble there."

"Hmm."

"You wouldn't like to write to the governor, Alix, and find out what's really going on?"

"Wouldn't it come better from you?"

"I always put people's backs up. You write so politely."

"I'll draft it and you sign it. I think it would come better from you."

"No, I think not."

Polly Piper glared authoritatively at Alix, who said, ungraciously, "Oh, OK. If you insist. What else?"

And Polly proceeded to outline what else, in her strange, abrupt, elliptical manner, while admiring her own boots, which lay neatly crossed on Alix's blotting pad. They were high heeled, highly polished, burgundy red, with gold buckles. She spoke of a survey issuing from Leicester University on the correlation between accidents and pre-menstrual tension. She spoke of the correspondence between the defence offered in crimes of infanticide in the courts and the defence now beginning to surface in the cases of disturbance due to pre-menstrual tension. She asked Alix what she thought of the judge's summing up in the case of the housekeeper who had shot her widower employer while allegedly suffering from pre-menstrual tension. Two years younger than Alix, she had read Moral Sciences at Cambridge and devoted herself to Wittgenstein: she had then worked for an advertising agency, writing copy on anything that came her way, but with a marked flair for selling women's products: had then become Public Relations Officer, then a chief executive, in a firm manufacturing tampons. Thence she had been drawn to the Home Office, where she now headed a research unit into the care and control of women offenders. The unit consisted largely if not wholly of Alix. Alix did not know what to make of the concept of pre-menstrual tension. She had never knowingly suffered from it in her life. Did this mean that it did not exist, that it was a ghostly excuse, a medieval demon waiting to be cast out not by pills but by common sense? Or that she herself was merely lucky? She did not know. She and Polly Piper would talk for hours of these matters. Polly Piper did suffer from premenstrual tension, but then, she belonged to a slightly, significantly, younger generation of women for whom the rights rather than the opportunities of women were in sharper focus. Alix, old-fashioned, had been hopelessly, conventionally punctual and conscientious throughout her not very distinguished career, never staying off sick, never taking a day off when Nicholas had been ill, attempting to prove single-handed that women were as reliable, more reliable, than men. Polly, erratic, high-powered, high-mannered, had taken another line, and was now Alix's boss. Polly had long, dark, curling, greying hair, which she would shake like a mane when moved, and a handsome hawk-like nose, and a flashing, frequently contemptuous eye. Men were frightened of Polly, in a titillated sort of way that had not hindered her promotion. She and Alix got on, by and large, very well.

Alix was, almost despite herself, interested in the premenstrual tension business. She had discussed it with her class at Garfield, had read them some Sylvia Plath poems and some Peter Redgrove and Penelope Shuttle. Moons and tides, sanity and lunacy. She was also anxious to promote a campaign to remove purchase tax from sanitary towels. Polly had become predictably excited by this proposal and had thought of standing for Parliament on the issue. Both Alix and Polly agreed that the poor representation of women in the House of

Commons in Britain in the last decades of the twentieth century was a deplorable manifestation of—well, of what? This too they would discuss.

Alix, on the bus on the way home with her loaded shopping bag, worried about whether to make onion or spinach sauce with the gammon, and read her horoscope in the *Evening Standard* to help her make up her mind. It informed her that she would have to abandon her present romantic intentions, but that these would shortly be replaced by new and better prospects. Which was more romantic, onion or spinach? It was not clear. She leafed through to the "Londoner's Diary" and saw there a picture of Lady Henrietta Latchett and a young Royal at a charity ball at the Dorchester. Tickets had cost £50 a head. Champagne and imported delicacies had featured, dancing to the free services of The Wanderers had occurred, all in aid of research into a not-so-rare illness, research which in Alix's view was already quite well funded by the government. Millions a year were spent on research into this not-so-rare illness. The problem was not lack of money, but lack of discoveries, lack of progress. The not-so-rare illness, for all the money it absorbed, refused, like death, to go away. It fed on money. And there was Lady Henrietta, patron, with a young Royal. Alix had read somewhere the week before that a sum equal to half the defence budget is contributed annually to charities in Britain. What an extraordinary statistic, if true. She did not believe it. But what an odd system, just the same. She peered at Lady Henrietta's grey, diminutive, pinched, grainy features, at the jewels around her neck, at her low-necked gown. What an odd country. Did Lady Henrietta feel the illusion of virtue when attending such functions? Alix thought of her friend Liz Headleand, and was quite indignant for a few minutes on her behalf as the bus ground to a halt in the rush hour on Wandsworth bridge; but perhaps it was Liz Headleand's own fault, for mixing in such circles? Spinach sauce, perhaps, would be more entertaining. Brian would have to go to the off-licence for the tonic, for if the bus stuck here much longer she certainly wouldn't have time to go herself.

Charles Headleand in New York lunched (GMT 6 p.m.) on iced water, a salt beef sandwich on rye with dill pickle, and the telephone. He rang Bud Castellano in Los Angeles, Ricky

Dupont in Detroit, Sir William Salmon in Washington, Dickie Fisher in Bogotá (where his reliable secretary reliably informed him it was also GMT 6 p.m.), and then he dismissed his secretary to fetch him a cup of coffee and rang Henrietta Latchett in London, hoping to catch her before she went out to whichever party she had chosen to grace that evening. She was in the bath, she told him, getting ready to go to the Venables'. He commiserated. And how was the ball the night before, he asked her. Too too too, she said. Really too. She fluted, to amuse. What did *He* talk about? enquired Charles. Reindeer and elk, said Henrietta. He's the wildlife one, you know. Well, they have to take up something, poor things, said Charles. Moose, fluted Henrietta. He spoke of moose. Henrietta turned on the hot tap, and held the telephone receiver intimately for a moment to the sound of running water. I'll speak to you tomorrow, I'll see you next week, she said. She forgot to ask him how he was or what he was doing, but he didn't notice. She lay in her hot bath. Charles rang Bill Ryan in Toronto.

"Delicious," said Stephen Cox, holding out his plate for a second helping of gammon and onion sauce. Alix smiled at him benignly. Stephen, himself an excellent cook, always ate up and asked for more, which always pleased her. The onion sauce had turned out rather well. So had the conversation. Liz, occasionally overbearing in company, had been mild, attentive, responsive. She had arrived in mild mood, early, bearing a belated birthday present for Sam and a small plant in a pot for Alix. The present for Sam was a square perspex box with a complicated silver tubular maze inside it. "I think it's an executive toy," said Liz, sitting down with Sam on the settee to play with it, "but we mustn't let that put us off; it's quite nice, isn't it?" Sam agreed that it was nice. They sat together intently, as Sam shook it about to discover its secrets: Alix, chopping parsley, watching them, was pleased. Liz always took trouble with Sam, as she had in earlier years with Nicholas: she had once confessed to Alix that she did not find other people's children easy, envied the warmth of those who could open their arms confidently to all children, was still retrospectively surprised by the ease with which she had taken to her own three stepsons. "I suppose it's because I had to," she had once said: "I had to be intimate. And once I was over that, it was simple. They belonged to me, I had to open my arms, there was no choice. But it's odd that I knew how to, isn't it?'' Alix, who had put her own passion for Nicholas down to biology, had agreed that it was odd. She doubted if she herself could have taken to a stranger's children so readily. It was odd that Liz, who had never received, as far as one could tell, a motherly kiss or hug in her life, should have achieved such kissing and hugging with her stepsons, with her daughters. Alix liked Liz's children, though she found them easier now they were older. And she liked to see Sam and Liz sitting together, puzzling.

The pot plant was small and green and mossy and covered in tiny orange-red berries. "I hope it won't be a bore," said Liz, when offering it, "I hope you won't let it dominate your life." And they had proceeded to discuss, for a while, Esther's ludicrous obsession with her potted palm. "She talks of nothing else," said Liz, "it's bizarre, she ticked me off the other evening when I was speaking to her on the phone for failing to ask after it." And they both laughed, for they did not think Esther bizarre at all, or even eccentric. "And how *was* it?" asked Alix. "Turning a bit grey and stiff at its lower extremities, she said. I recommended soaking it, like an azalea, but she wouldn't have that, she spoke of the desert. So I said was she over-watering it, and she said how would she ever know?" "Oh dear, what a problem," said Alix. They were both in fact quite interested in Esther's palm. "Anyway," said Liz, "if this little thing dies, I won't blame you." "I like it very much," said Alix. "It's a very pretty little plant." "I thought it was rather you," said Liz, "but now I'm beginning to wish I'd got one for myself too. I got it in the garage on the way here. Funny, the things they sell in garages these days, isn't it?"

Idle chatter; soothing, reassuring. Small things. When Stephen arrived, they continued to talk idly, for a while, of plants and eccentricities: Stephen described a peculiar array of knitted pot plants which an aunt of his had created—you mean *knitted*? Yes, I do mean knitted, green leaves, white edged purple flowers, sort of knitted begonias in little pots with real earth, quite realistic from a couple of yards away—and Brian contributed a plastic cyclamen which for some reason had been given pride of place in his father's flat, although his father had green fingers and had surrounded it with some perfectly good real plants. It must have been a present, they concluded. Like the ominous palm, the gift of that sinister wizard Claudio Volpe.

Over dinner they moved on: Liz listened mildly, attentively, as Stephen gave an account of his recent visit to America, where he had been delivering a lecture: he recalled other lecture tours, speaking of pink buses with ears and tails in Dallas, of thick snow and meals of sunflower seeds in Vermont, of English muffins in Philadelphia, of mystic matrons in Albuquerque. Stephen's narrative style was hesitant, oblique, slightly stammering, whimsically sharp: as a young man, as Brian could well recall, he had stammered atrociously, paralysingly, disablingly, but he had learned to turn his impediment to advantage, had become an accomplished raconteur in person as well as on the page. Now he embarked upon an anecdote about his return flight from Boston, sitting next to a young American academic who was attending a conference in Monte Carlo on intertextuality in the works of James Joyce. They had fallen into conversation because both were reading a novel by David Lodge, a coincidence that in itself amounted to a form of intertextuality. This young man had also written a play which nobody would stage. Was it about intertextuality, Stephen had politely enquired, high above the clouds. No, the young man had replied (excited by a gin and tonic), it was about his mother. She was—had been—an Irish-American soprano. And it was about his father, an Irish peasant who practised as a hypnotist. O'Neill and Du Maurier were mentioned, in deference to intertextuality. Stephen had been enthralled. He had not revealed that he was himself a published writer, had affected ignorant, innocent sympathy, had nodded and smiled and prompted further confessions.

Brian listened, now, to his friend's familiar voice, which had tempted from Brian himself many a confession, in years gone by, and pondered on Stephen's success as a writer, his own relative failure as a writer, and the dilemma of an itinerant academic from New England torn between a longing for tenure and an excessive, inconvenient, unaccommodated love for his mother. Inassimilable material, perhaps? Like his own?

Brian and Stephen had first met when they were both eighteen, more than twenty years ago, while doing their National Service. The lads had taken the piss out of Stephen, in those first weeks of basic training, for his cultured voice, for the impediment in that cultured voice. Brian had taken Stephen's part. There was something affable, easy, determined

about Brian that compelled respect; he was also six feet, two
inches tall, and well built with it. The lads had laid off when
Brian was around. A born mediator. Blessed are the p-p-peace-
makers, Stephen had stammered at him one night over a pint,
the wooden table between them aswill with beer, the air thick
from the smoke of countless cigarettes, the beer mats sodden.
They had talked of many things, over the class barrier.
Stephen's father was a country doctor and Stephen had
attended, unhappily, a minor public school. Brought up in the
heart of rural England, in the West Country, in the heart of the
Tory shires. A sensitive, delicate child, a fourth son of a third
son, he suffered from hay fever, did not like riding, was afraid
of bullocks, was devoted to his Jack Russell, and greatly
enjoyed cricket though he did not play. A country child, an
outsider, a solitary.

Brian's father had worked all his life at Pitts and Harley,
hammering circular saws. His father's father had been a
furnaceman, and his father before him. Before that, nobody
knew where the Bowens had been, and nobody asked. Brian
had been brought up in the heart of urban England, in industrial
Yorkshire. He had attended the local school, where he neither
shone nor offended. When he was little, he wanted to be a
policeman. A town child, an insider, one of the boys. Or so it
had seemed to Stephen, during those first weeks.

But things had turned out to be not quite what they seemed.
Stephen, although delicate, was stoically unappalled by the
rigours of army life, which could not rival, he declared, the
incomparable physical and mental misery of boarding school.
He perversely praised the food, about which it was customary
to complain: bangers and tinned tomatoes were a treat, corned
beef fritters a delicacy, after the stinking fish pie of Moxley
Hall, he said. He praised the bedding—at least we've got
enough blankets; I couldn't sleep for the cold all winter at
school, he would say. He admired the uniform, which he
claimed to find much more becoming than the damn-fool
blazers and boaters which had attracted such unwelcome
attention from the local Teddy boys. The arbitrary nature of the
discipline and the incomprehensibility of the rules made him
feel quite at home, he maintained. Ideologically, he was
committed to preferring the army to Moxley Hall: he had
already decided not to apply for a commission, so he had to
like it. He had spent his last year at school reading about the
Spanish Civil War, and nourishing dreams of comradely

communion. He had read Auden, Spender, T. E. Lawrence. His head was full of notions. And Brian embodied those notions well enough. Some of the other lads were a bit of a trial (in particular that puerile little Geordie whose idea of fun was to plant beer mugs laced with washing-up liquid and worse substances on unsuspecting drunks), but Brian offered hope.

Brian, conversely, found the army something of a shock. His family were solid, respectable, law-abiding folk, non-conformist, mildly prudish, domestic. The black farce, foul language, hard drinking, skiving, practical jokes, and occasional malicious stupidity of his fellow conscripts offended him, and unlike Stephen he did not regard them as a challenge to his manhood: he was, more simply, offended. He had never slept away from home before, had never slept on a bed without sheets, was not accustomed to the lack of privacy, the incessant obscenity; he was dismayed by the nastier habits of his comrades, by their physical proximity, their smells and farts and belches.

Brian had already served an apprenticeship at Pitts and Harley, was assured of a job at the end of his two years. Stephen had a place at Oxford, where he was to read History. (It had not occurred to Stephen not to accept this place. It had not occurred to Brian not to return to Pitts and Harley.)

Brian, at twelve, at thirteen, had also known what it was to be tormented. For a time, he had been short and fat. Bunter Bowen, they had called him. But then he had grown taller and was teased no longer.

It was some time before Stephen discovered what he took to be a clue to Brian's protective nature, to his odd gentleness. It emerged that Brian had a sister. Well, he had two sisters, one of them a lively creature three years younger than himself, Barbara, who was subsequently to emigrate to Australia. The other, Kathie, was two years older than Brian, and from the age of sixteen had suffered from multiple sclerosis, which confined her to a wheelchair. Brian had looked after her. He would bear her in his arms from room to room of their semi-detached on the Coalbright Estate, would arrange her gently on the couch in front of the fire, would take her up and down the stairs to bed, would fetch and carry for her, would wheel her round the neighbourhood. Slowly Kathie faded, as Brian attended. Her eyes dimmed and Brian would read *Woman's Own* to her, would find her items in the Northam

Star, would tune in the radio for her, would read to her from Mills & Boon novels. She was particularly fond of doctor and nurse romances. He peeled her oranges and cut up her toast. Now that he was away for two years, how would she manage? How would his mother manage? Although Kathie was as light as a bird, his mother was too small to lift her easily. Should he have applied for exemption from his National Service on compassionate grounds? Would it have been granted? Brian fretted over this, but did not, at this stage, speak of this matter to Stephen. It was revealed, retrospectively, years later, when Stephen visited the Bowens: revealed as Brian tucked a plaid rug round his sister's thin knees, and squeezed her thin white hand. There was more intimacy, more tenderness in those gestures than Stephen had been offered in the whole of his boyhood: or so it seemed to Stephen.

As it happened, fate conspired to consolidate the tentative friendship of Brian Bowen and Stephen Cox. At the end of their basic training, as each awaited his first posting, a hitch appeared in their processing. Brian, who had been expecting to move on with the rest to some unknown destination—Egypt, Aldershot, Cyprus, Caterham—was told that he had scored mysteriously well on his IQ test and was to hang around waiting for important decisions from above. Did they think he was guilty of cheating, or of treason, or both, he wondered? Stephen was told he had a suspected shadow on the lung. The rest of the intake disappeared from Staffordshire overnight, never to be seen again. Brian and Stephen were left in limbo, waiting for something to happen. For a full fortnight they killed time together. Alone in their bunks, which were due for repainting or demolition (no one knew which), they lingered. The other bunks were empty. New conscripts arrived, nervous, naïve, pale faced, but they were allotted to another building, where they moved, beyond a wire mesh fence, like unknown soldiers from another world, undergoing at a remove the strange rituals that Brian and Stephen now knew so well. Brian and Stephen had the old space all to themselves. A physical leper and an intellectual leper—misfits. Nobody knew what to do with them. A shadow on the brain, a shadow on the lung. They enjoyed their isolation. They hoped to prolong it by marching purposefully, unquestioned, through the gates, then sliding off unobtrusively into the countryside, where they lay in the deep grass and tall cow parsley, beneath the dark red of a hawthorn, talking, smoking. A white warm milky light lay over the Midlands. They wondered if the summer might not last forever. A pastoral eternity.

Stephen confided to Brian that he wanted to be a writer. He lay on his back and stared at the blue sky. He felt exalted. Stephen spoke of the Spanish Civil War and George Orwell. He even persuaded Brian to make his way through some of *Homage to Catalonia*. The sun warmed them as they lay. They worried that they were becoming improbably brown, that their idleness would betray itself through suntan, that they would be put on a charge. But nobody noticed them. A romantic time, an idyllic time, a time of intense physical well-being. Soldiers in the grass. Diffidently, they pledged friendship.

(Alix, listening to stories of this period, a period which, despite its intermittent evocation, she could in no way visualize to herself, would speculate about sex, of course; then she would wonder if Brian ever speculated thus about herself, Liz, and Esther?)

After a fortnight, Brian and Stephen were transferred, and suddenly, inexplicably, to the Intelligence Corps Depot at Sutton Champfleur in Dorset. Nothing, it emerged, was wrong with Stephen's lung. The shadow was a shadow of a shadow, a negative smudge. Brian's grey smoky whisp of detected intelligence proved more substantial. It had caught the infra-red eye of the notorious Cohen-Brill, then engaged on a bizarre piece of research into correlations between educational background, geographical background, and the alphabet. In vain did Brian protest, when he arrived at Sutton Champfleur, that he did not have the relevant GCE certificates to become an Education Officer. His papers declared that he did. There's been a mistake, said Brian, patiently, repeatedly, over another pleasantly wasted month, during which he and Stephen managed to visit Thomas Hardy's birthplace, T. E. Lawrence's deathplace, and various tearooms. The southern landscapes, smooth, green, chalky, flinty, high, ancient, unfamiliar, butterfly haunted, astonished Brian's eye of millstone grit. When it was at last recognized that Brian's view of his own education was correct, he was ordered to rectify this. He was enrolled for various courses in various academic and non-academic subjects. He acquired O levels, he studied Vehicle Maintenance, he was cajoled into attending an evening class at Blandford Forum, taught by a retired economist of great distinction, where he studied Current Affairs, along with a handful of public school boys from a nearby sixth form, some teachers, a nun, and a market gardener. The army was Brian's sixth form, his introduction to university.

Stephen also proved unsuitable material for his intended destiny as Education Sergeant, despite his impressive paper qualifications. His stammer was too pronounced, he could not speak in public at all, he was unfitted to convey even the most elementary information. He was made librarian, then told he ought to enrol for the language course in Bodmin to learn Russian. Stephen resisted, on principle, but his resistance was eventually worn down, and off he went, a detected intellectual, to join a group of aspiring students and new graduates, middle class like himself, ex-public school, ex-grammar school. He had tried to avoid this classification, and had failed. (He was often to comment, in later life, on the oddity of a system which was so paranoid that it banned Karl Marx and Reed's *Ten Days That Shook the World* from the Sutton Champfleur library, which obliged Stephen to bind his George Orwell in brown paper, and then sent him off to learn, of all things, Russian.) Stephen in Bodmin held all the more strongly to his friendship with Brian, to whom he wrote long, oblique, tortuous, sentimental letters. These letters did not offend Brian, who replied, though more tersely.

By the time Brian left the army, he too planned to be a writer, encouraged by Stephen, by the mad Cohen-Brill, by the distinguished economist, and by an impassioned reading of *Jude the Obscure*. Stephen disliked Hardy, thought him melodramatic, crude, excessive, and wrote quite a strong letter to Brian about Hardy's shortcomings. Brian replied boldly. At this point, Brian knew that he was thinking for himself. Brian fell in love with English literature, which he now teaches, and teaches much better than Stephen could ever have done.

But both, eventually, became writers, according to plan. Brian resisted Cohen-Brill's suggestion that he should join the regular army, a suggestion repeated over various pints and eventually over a slap-up dinner at the Dorchester Arms; we need men like you, Cohen-Brill said with the utmost sincerity, his empurpled, intelligent, manic face glaring over the roast lamb and mint sauce. Brian, filled with sorrow and admiration for this lonely man to whom he owed so much, declined as gracefully as he knew how, and went home to Northam and his sister Kathie and his job at Pitts and Harley. But he continued to attend evening classes and university extension classes, eventually enrolled for a full-time course, and in 1965 acquired a degree in English literature. In the same year, Kathie died. Brian left Northam and got a teaching job on Tyneside. He published a novel about factory life in the north-east, another about a footballer who contracted polio. They met with a muted but respectful reception, and were sometimes quoted as examples of the regional working-class novel, along with the better-known works of Sillitoe, Storey, Braine, and Barstow. He was himself far from satisfied with them, for his critical faculties had by this time estranged themselves from his creative impulses, but he did not worry about this much. In 1968 (just before the Open University received its charter) Brian moved south, where he met and married Alix. He had now more or less abandoned the hope of writing the great chronicle of working-class life that haunts his imagination. He knows he cannot do it. But it haunts him, it will not let him go. He loves it. It does not sour him, this familiar failure. He is, broadly, he would say, a happy man. And an excellent teacher. He and Alix are happy. By and large. They have resolved themselves. It seems.

Stephen's progress was more erratic. After Oxford, he went to live in Paris, to his father's disappointment, where he earned a meagre living teaching English and writing subtitles for a film company, while trying to write his novel. He had an affair with a married woman. He finished his novel but nobody would publish it. He wrote another. Nobody would publish this one either. He watched the radical surge of the 1960s, then came home; he settled in London, in a bedsit above a dry cleaner's in Stoke Newington, where he nearly died of toxic fumes. He wrote a thriller and published it under a pseudonym. (He told nobody of this but Brian.) In 1969 he published his first serious work, a deeply eccentric novel of (it was immediately pronounced) distinction and originality, set, analogically, in Paris at the time of the Commune. It was much noticed and won a prize, and Stephen became sought after, both in England and in America. He was invited to give lectures, to take up residences, to grace universities with his presence. He published other novels, equally eccentric, equally successful. He was able to move away from the dry cleaning. His father and brothers are proud of him, but his mother wishes he would settle down. Now that he is in his mid-forties, this seems less than likely. But he does not seem unhappy. Neither happy, nor unhappy.

For Stephen, persistence has paid off. He has managed to justify, to afford, to occupy his oblique position, his anomalous role. It is more than, at various points, he had hoped for. Now he sits at table with his friends Alix and Brian Bowen, and their friend Liz Headleand, rolling himself a thin cigarette with thin fingers, over the remains of an apple crumble, his head tilted quizzically to one side as he listens to Liz's account of her apprehensions about her autumn trip to Japan. They are still talking about travel and mobility. The eighties will be the global decade, everyone says, says Alix, but if this is so, why don't Brian and I ever go anywhere? I spend all my time driving from Wandsworth to Wanley, or sitting on the bus between Wandsworth and Whitehall. That's mobile, but it's not global, is it? Whereas you, Stephen, you flit about like a bat.

One doesn't learn much, from the kind of visits I make, says Stephen mildly.

Then why go? asks Liz.

I suppose because one learns more than nothing, says Stephen. Just a little more than nothing.

They talk, inevitably, of Jane Austen and the country village. Of knowledge through width, or depth. Of South Londoners who never cross the river. Of Cobbett's own restlessness, and of his descriptions of a couple who had never moved beyond a five-mile radius from their cottage. Brian leaps up, tries to find the quotation in his copy of *Rural Rides,* fails. They speak of Kissinger and Lord Carrington, of global diplomacy. Stephen tells them a story about his old tutor, Sir William Hestercombe, at Oxford, a historian whose hobby is collecting honorary degrees. He'll go anywhere, says Stephen, incredible stamina, and he must be getting on for eighty. America, Canada, Australia, Israel, New Zealand, Ceylon, he thinks nothing of it. He's got a whole heap of honorary degrees lying in a corner in his study, like cricket bats or hockey sticks, ready for some mysterious game of carpet French cricket. Red tubes, blue tubes, green tubes, those mock-leather things with gilt lettering on. Maybe they're real leather? He'll only accept those that come in nice round tubes, he says, and with a free airfare. I noticed in *The Times* the other day that he'd just got back with another one from Argentina. Have you ever seen his entry in *Who's Who*? It's getting beyond a joke.''

''I see from your new entry in *Who's Who* that you've listed sitting in Russell Square as your hobby,'' said Brian. ''What prompted that?''

Stephen smiles, gently, and explains. Alix watches him. He

has a delicate mouth, with a thin, fine, curved upper lip. Alix thinks of Charles Headleand and his big teeth and hard jaw. She looks across at Brian, whose face is so familiar to her now that it merely seems to be humanity itself, the archetypal human face, the natural face. Brian's hair is thick, grey, and curly. Stephen's is white, soft, and straight. Suddenly she remembers her first husband, Sebastian, for a moment. Sebastian lives, for a moment. Had he lived, would his golden hair have faded, receded? She ceases to listen to the conversation. Her son Nicholas's hair is receding. The knowledge of this fills her with distress. He is so beautiful, so young, how can he be submitted, already, to the processes of age? For herself she cares not at all, she laughs to see her face wrinkle, she prides herself on being without vanity; but for Nicholas she grieves, grieves more than she could say. Or is it for herself that she is grieving?

She shakes herself, returns to the conversation. It has changed tack completely, but completely, and Liz, who had been growing somnolent, is suddenly sitting forward with an expression of intense animation, as Stephen declares, "Yes, anything beginning with a B or a P, those were always my worst consonants. But never in French. Or in Russian. Or when singing."

"Fascinating," says Liz, "fascinating. Has anyone ever offered any explanation for it?"

"For what? For the selectivity?"

"For the selectivity *or* for the origins."

"I think a lot of people are selective. Most. Most people have their own worst consonants. And find foreign languages easier. Do people stammer in all languages?"

"In Japanese, for example? I've no idea."

"Somebody must know."

"I can ask when I'm there."

"Do, do ask." Stephen hesitates, pursues.

"I think the consonants were something to do with embarrassment. Embarrassing words always seemed to begin with P or B. Bum, balls, bollocks, bugger, prick, penis, piss."

Stephen recites the list, enunciating politely, delicately, carefully.

"Bosom, breast, belly," says Liz, and laughs.

"*Very* selective," says Stephen. "Of course, the other words, the Lady Chatterley words, I didn't learn till I was much older, past the formative stage. I had a very sheltered childhood.''

''What *was* the formative stage?''

''My mother says I began to stammer when I fell off a pony when I was three. I fell on my head. So it is alleged.''

''And got up stammering?''

''So she says. Not a very likely story, I imagine.'' He begins to roll another cigarette. ''But it is true that I'm afraid of horses. There could be a connection?''

''Were you afraid of your father?''

''I can't remember. How would I know?''

''And when did you get over it? Did you really *never* stammer in French?''

''Only very occasionally. And then only if it was a word I'd been working up to for a long time. Like asking for a ticket to Passy, or Palais-Royale, or Pigalle. If it came out suddenly, I could do it. It was the nervous apprehension that made it happen. So I'd pretend to myself that I was going to say something quite different, and then at the last moment I'd change my mind and say Passy, or Palais-Royale, or P-P-P-Pigalle. Like a horse with blinkers.''

''How do you mean, a horse with blinkers?''

''I was afraid of refusing, like a horse at a fence. So I wouldn't let myself see the fence. Till the last moment.''

''Fascinating. But you *were* the horse? Do you see your psyche as a horse?''

And on they went, engaged, rapid, backwards and forwards, Liz quoting papers, asking questions, promising to look up statistics, suggesting parallels, her mind whizzing and whirring, humming and singing, the machine running fast, smooth, efficient, functioning perfectly, sweeping up notions, quick, quick, excited, gathering momentum, cruising; and undetectable, that smell of burning rubber, or is it still there, hanging, haunting, burning rubber, the wrong engine note? Stephen is less rapid, more enigmatic, more tentative, but he too gathers speed under Liz's acceleration, and Alix sits back and listens to them run along together: they speak of Freud and Little Hans and fear of horses, they speak of Plato's metaphor of the harnessed horses of the self. It is going so well, this modest supper party, that Alix is simultaneously exhilarated, exhausted, jealous, delighted. It is one in the morning, it is time for bed, but they still gallop along, in step, Liz and Stephen. Well, it is done, they will have to arrange the next outing themselves, thinks Alix. She wonders if Brian is annoyed. She has never quite known what Brian thinks of Liz. Maybe there will be no more outings. Stephen is elusive, he vanishes, frequently. He is faithful only to Brian in, perhaps, the world.

National Service was said to offer young men an opportunity of meeting other men from other walks of life. And indeed, it did so. (Women were not offered this enforced opportunity.) Most reminiscences about National Service include a tribute to the educational benefits of mixing with others. Few maintained their friendships over the years, as Brian and Stephen did; in fact few made what could even be called friendships. But some did, some did. And young men did learn something of the realities of other classes, other ranks. Some look back with a real nostalgia to this mixing. Some do not like the divisions that constitute what is called society, do not like the fear and mutual suspicion that reinforce these divisions, the arrogant assumptions of privilege, the grumbling quiescence or reductive, aggressive envy of want, the constant maintenance of distinctions. Some would like to get to know their fellow men. They are too frightened to attempt to do so. What are they afraid of? Of the hatred on that other, alien face? Or the hatred reflected from their own? Or of fear, fear itself?

The only other form of service which brings people—men and women alike in this instance—into such enforced proximity is jury service. It is commonplace to hear middle-class people declare that they enjoy their jury service because it gives them an insight into how other people think and live. As though there were no other way of discovering these things. They enjoy the brief illusion of community, the sense of joint purpose.

Alix Bowen is a sentimentalist about class, it has been alleged. This is why she found herself teaching working-class children in Newham, and prisoners in Garfield; why she talks to drinking men on park benches; why she married Brian Bowen. And Alix herself would be the first to admit to herself—although she can never quite find the words to explain it—that Brian's attraction for her was massively, deeply connected with his class origins. Brian, for her, represented—well, what? Not exactly the working classes, for Brian, by the time she met him, was a published novelist and a teacher in an

Adult Education College: hardly a representative working man.
Yet he brought with him—well, what? A sense of not being
afraid. Brian was neither suspicious, nor afraid. Lying in your
arms, Alix said once, not very seriously, to Brian, I am in the
process of healing the wounds in my own body and in the body
politic.

Brian laughed, as she meant him to; but she meant it.

The first time Brian put his arms around Alix one night after
a plate of spaghetti bolognese at the Trattoria Primavera, she
was aware not so much of sexual attraction as of a deep
suffusion of warmth which filled, without any particular erotic
effect, her entire body. It was an extraordinary, an unprecedented sensation, flowing from him to her and through her,
through the centre of herself, through the small of her back and
her shoulders and her chest, and spreading, glowing, to the
more differentiated, less serious edges and surfaces and extremities. It filled her and consumed her, she felt that she was
thawing at last, after years, after a lifetime of separation, of
chill. Making love with Brian seemed to have a basic,
reassuring, comforting continuity, a timeless, all-inclusive
warmth which made nonsense of such modern notions as
arousal, excitement, orgasm. The weight of him anchored her.
She had observed, from a distance, across the canteen, across
the staff room, in corridors, his delicacy, his easy familiarity,
his sense of being at home in his own body, his comfortable
communications with the bodies of others. He radiated presence, immediacy. He touched people easily—took old ladies
by the elbow gently on stairs or at corners, put his arm in
comfort or congratulation or communion round the shoulders
of friends of either sex, touched the back of her hand as they
talked, for emphasis or in appreciation, long before they
thought of becoming lovers. People loved Brian, warmed to
Brian. Or did she imagine that, because she loved him? No, it
was not imagination, it was so. He was alive in his body, and
that was a rare thing.

And she connected this living self with his past, with his
sister Kathie of course, but also with his familiarity with
objects, with his knowledge of the tension of circular saws. At
one point, as she watched Brian repotting a geranium, it
occurred to her that it was not so much a question of what was
remarkable about Brian: it was more a question of what had
gone wrong with everybody else. His grace seemed natural,
normal. But in fact was rare. Brian was the normal man, but

there was only one of him. As she watched him one evening as he replaced the vandalized car aerial with a bent coat hanger, she knew that Brian was in tune with messages, could pick up sounds from the air, as well as through the earth. Fanciful, fanciful. When she saw him in the company of big straight dull heavy self-important British meat-faced men in striped dark suits—as she did, occasionally, at meetings, even socially—she would stare at his open-necked shirt, his open smile, his throat, his hands, and wonder how they could not envy him. Perhaps they did. Coats on coat hangers, stiffly packed and padded, to shut out the messages. Did they hate him, because he smiled?

Fear had become normal, clumsiness of various sorts had become normal. Men wore dark suits and ties and were solemn inside them, or they shouted on picket lines. None of them made love, much, to their wives, the faces of their wives as well as the enquiries of sociological research suggested. Women were afraid to stand at bus stops after dark, to catch the last tube home, to walk down an underpass. Girls formed themselves into gangs and terrorized other girls with coshes made of billiard balls stuffed in the ends of old socks. Men talked about cars and video machines and cameras and the money supply and the base lending rate. Women talked of biological washing powders and the price of beef and television commercials and operations on the gall bladder and the Royal Family.

And Brian, who was so good with his hands, taught classes in English literature to middle-class housewives, because that was the nature of Adult Education. He also tried to write the great pedestrian realistic working-class novel of the 1970s and 1980s, but he had moved to London, married a middle-class wife, and acquired too good an education to write what he wanted, as he wanted.

Alix, lying in bed after her middle-class dinner party, her successful dinner party—warm, wakeful, herself safe from the storms of fear, wrapped up, protected, listening to Brian's even breathing, feeling the warmth of his sleeping arm around her breasts—Alix, lying there, thought of all these things. All of them. She put them one beside another, like building blocks. National Service, Jury Service, Men, Women, Manual Work, Fear, Picket Lines, the Royal Family, Social Class, Adult Education. Patiently she lined them up. Unlike Liz, she was patient. They made no sense, these blocks, they did not make a building, but she would continue, patiently, persistently, to line them up and to look at them. To rearrange them. She would compel them; or if she failed to compel them, it would not be through want of effort.

Liz, in bed that night, had forgotten Stephen, had leaped on from thoughts of Stephen, had left him far behind, as she thought of her mother, lying there in Abercorn Avenue, blocked not by a stammer in speech alone, but in the centre of herself, in all things. A fall from a horse, a sexual misadventure; a dead husband, a faithless husband. Trauma. Shock. Permanent shock. What had happened to her father? Where was her father, who was her father? Had he left her mother and vanished, as she sometimes suspected? Her mother claimed that he was dead. But maybe he was not dead. Maybe he was still alive. Maybe he had merely left her mother, as Charles was leaving her. The possible parallel appalled her. She had not consciously made it before. How could she not have done, she asked herself. She got up and made herself a cup of tea. Unable to sleep, thinking of Charles and her father, and abandoned wives. *Abbandonata, abbandonata*. Music plays in her head, women lament in Palladian palaces. She lies in bed, she switches on her radio cassette to drown their cries. She is listening to Sibelius's fifth symphony. She has taken to playing it, as though she could thereby invoke Naomi's help from the past. Benevolent ghost. A kind of madness.

She knows that she should track down her absent father. Thus she had decided, at lunch time, over her cottage cheese. Her position is false, false, false. Essentially false. She knows that she dares not. She knows that she will not. She stares at this knowledge, and is deeply, deeply, in the small hours, afraid.

A few families in a country village. A few families in a small, densely populated, parochial, insecure country. Mothers, fathers, aunts, stepchildren, cousins. Where does the story begin and where does it end? Even Charles Headleand has an aunt, though you would not think it to look at him across a board-room table, across an editorial desk, to watch him address a meeting. He is ashamed of his aunt. She is a sub-postmistress in a small village in Norfolk. She is a woman of the greatest, the most unselfconscious eccentricity. She runs the village shop. He would not like Lady Henrietta to meet his aunt. His aunt, however, expects to meet Lady Henrietta. I wonder what Jane Austen would say. Alix Bowen would find the existence of Charles's aunt interesting, but she does not know it. Liz Headleand has not thought her worth mentioning. Meanwhile, in another part of the country, Nicholas Manning, Alix Bowen's son, has taken to visiting his grandmother Deborah, his father's now widowed mother in Sussex. He likes the house, he likes the life there. Alix finds this connection disquieting, but is not quite sure why.

On a more public level 1980 continues. The steel strike continues, a bitter prelude to the miners' strike that will follow. Class rhetoric flourishes. Long-cherished notions of progress are inspected, exposed, left out to die in the cold. Survival of the fittest seems to be the new-old doctrine. Unemployment rises steadily, but the Tory party is not yet often reminded of its election poster which portrayed a long dole queue with the slogan "Labour isn't working." People have short memories, many of them are carried along with the new tide. They are fit. The less fit get less and less fit, and are washed up on the shore. Some of the fit, it is true, begin to get a little breathless, at times. Cliff Harper, for example, is in trouble. Cliff Harper's business flourishes, in theory at least, but the steel strike hits his haulage contractors, his supplies, his distributors, and the loyalty of some of his workforce: the edges begin to crumble. Tory voter, small businessman, entrepreneur, he looks for help but none is forthcoming. He continues to praise the government and to deride the left-wing Council which takes Meals On Wheels to his mother-in-law. He believes in the glamour, the logic, of the hard line. He is a desperately worried man. His children are costing him a fortune at their private schools. Occasionally, in moments of gloom, it occurs to Cliff that he may not, after all, be one of the fit. He is not as young as he was.

Doubts also creep up on Charles Headleand from time to time. He too is not as young as he was, and New York is a fast city, a breathless city. He has noticed an unpleasant tendency to breathlessness. Luckily there are not many stairs in New York. He has taken up jogging, and jogs around the Upper West Side at seven in the morning. Diet, luckily, is a fashionable topic, and he cuts out (well, almost cuts out) butter, salt, milk, eggs, fat; he is told to eat raw fish. Raw fish is fashionable. He thinks he is enjoying his work, his new importance, his power, his eminence; he enjoys the deference accorded to him.

He is the ambassador of a large section of Independent Broadcasting, he is a public person, he has a vast salary, a vast and luxurious apartment, he negotiates from a semi-governmental position, the future is partly in his hands: he is a spy for his country, keeping track of cable television, satellites, video equipment, teletext systems, the ever-increasing dissemination of images, of news, of horrors. He is here to read the writing on the wall, the writing that flickers on the screen. He is here to nudge on the debate, the power struggle between public service and independent broadcasting, to monitor the collapse of empires. Well, that is how he sees it, for he has little doubt but that the empires will collapse, and that the old BBC and IBA will, in twenty years, have vanished. Which shall he do, support the old régime, as he is paid to do, or tell the truth about the future and thereby precipitate collapse? A moral dilemma.

Sometimes he wonders what on earth he *is* doing. Negotiations, conventions, congresses, committees; policy decisions, diplomatic manoeuvres, budget forecasts, legal investigations, public enquiries. Once he made films. Once, in the late fifties, in the early sixties, he made films. He sometimes allows himself to remember those days; but not often, for he despises nostalgia. But occasionally, despite himself, as he lies in the bath or jogs in Central Park, he recalls the old days of *Focus on Britain*. He was assistant producer, then producer; he made of it what he wanted. A weekly programme; a good pattern to the week; an end product to celebrate. They would go off for a Chinese meal, all the crew, colleagues together; they would sit happily, triumphantly, and order huge platters of crudely spiced pork and chicken and duck and abalone and crab claws and greasy translucent bean sprouts and fried rice and prawn crackers and soft and crispy noodles. Ben Feather always insisted on having a fried egg on top of his. Drenched in soy sauce, thoroughly anglicized, cheap, delicious, washed down with lager or gin and tonic. They would eat and eat and talk and talk, on Friday nights, when the programme was safely finished, safely in the can. They would discuss what went wrong, which contributors had lied or muffed it, which had spoken out boldly: which shots had worked, which might have worked with more time, more money: they would laugh and talk and crack jokes and plan future programmes. They were young and keen and full of ideas; Charles had ideas, and he received ideas: he was one of a team. And he kept some of the team when he went on to make his series on education, the series that decisively established him: it was shown in 1965, by a brilliant mixture of guesswork and timing, just as the Labour Government issued its Circular 10/65, designed to end selection at eleven-plus and introduce comprehensive education. Charles's programme became a talking point, it was quoted in Parliament, in academic studies, at educational gatherings throughout Europe. A series that demonstrated, eloquently, movingly, the evils that flow from a divisive class system, from early selection, from Britain's unfortunate heritage of public schools and philistinism. *The Radiant Way* was its ironic title, taken from the primer from which Charles had learned at the age of four to read at his mother's knee. The nation wept as little Olive Peters, twelve years old in Barrow, revealed her humble expectations from life; as Johnny Maher, son of a driving instructor, seventeen years old in Liverpool, discovered he'd got a State Scholarship; as twenty-four-year-old Barry Furbank, from a London children's home, was shown eagerly clocking in for night school after a long day working on the buses. The nation smiled as the camera elicited words, accents, attitudes of extraordinary, outmoded quaintness and patronage from Oxford dons, from headmasters and pupils of public schools, from prep school boys in short trousers; then frowned thoughtfully as the camera showed these attitudes to be entrenched within the educational structure itself, and within the very fabric of British society. It was great television: Charles let his people speak for themselves, they condemned themselves in their own words from their own mouths, they won sympathy by the way they stood at a bus stop or fed their rabbits or bought a copy of *Exchange and Mart* at the corner shop: or so, at least, it seemed to the British public, which was still innocent in its response to the television documentary. Charles reinforced his programme's impact by commissioning campaigning articles in conjunction with *The Times Educational Supplement*, by arranging discussions on BBC television's *Late Night Line Up* with eminent educationalists and sociologists, by persuading the independent television company for which he worked to publish back-up material with charts and statistics. Charles put everything he had into this series, he pulled together everything and everyone he knew: he filmed one of Alix Manning's Further Education students from Newham, an Asian girl who spoke of the arranged marriage of her sister as she herself tried to learn to use an electric sewing machine: he filmed Ben Feather's nephew at a village primary school in Norfolk: he filmed his own sister's son trotting off to prep school in Sevenoaks in blazer and cap (regretting that the peculiarly unfortunate shade of dusty pink would not emerge from his black and white images): he filmed a niece of his dead wife, Naomi, as she sat her Cambridge entrance: he filmed the by now very elderly but still distinguished economist who had once taught Brian Bowen in Blandford Forum, teaching the very same evening class (the same nun still attending) and floating, subtly, charmingly, almost unnoticeably, the notion of an Open University. (Neither he nor Alix had at this stage met Brian Bowen, so Charles could not film him although he would have been highly suitable material.) He filmed his wife Liz's sister Shirley's little boys and tried to use them to comment on attitudes to pre-school education, but for some reason the sequence didn't work and he never used it: the little brats simply wouldn't look innocent enough, unspoiled enough, as they played half-heartedly with their wholesome toys, and Shirley, although a strong advocate of nursery schooling (so strong that she and a group of other mothers had founded their own playgroup), refused to cooperate by letting the crew bribe the kids with sweeties. The infants sulked, hotly, under the cameras. The truth and not the truth. Liz had laughed as Charles repeated this defeat, and said that it was Charles's fault for being unable to understand the social niceties of Shirley and Cliff Harper's circle. She had refused to lend their own children to the enterprise, and Charles had conceded that it would not be proper to use them. But in every other way she had backed him: she had admired the films greatly, had talked about them ceaselessly, had encouraged and suggested and cross-questioned with exemplary loyalty. Heady days. They had all enjoyed it. They had believed in it, all of them. Team work. Ben Feather, Dirk Davis, Lindsay Potter, Sally Hewett, Peter Canning. They had won awards. Charles had made speeches. And over the chop suey and the sweet and sour they had put the nation to rights: Charles Headleand, Ben Feather, Dirk Davis, Lindsay Potter . . .

The Brave New World, it would be, and the new populist

and popular medium of television would help to bring it into being. The team itself, with its mixed skills, its mixed social origins, its camaraderie, its common purpose, was a microcosm of what would come about: a forward-looking, forward-moving, dynamic society, full of opportunity, co-operative, classless. The Chinese meal was a classless meal: it brought no echoes of the *ancien régime*. All over Britain, from Berwick to Broadstairs, from Peterhead to Penzance, Chinese meals were consumed, with or without fried eggs on top. Sound technician sat down with producer, graduate with van driver, artist with engineer. The nation would demand better and better schools, better welfare, better houses, better hospitals, more maternity leave, more nursery school, more theatres, more swimming pools, more paternity leave, and everything would get better and better all the time. Charles had believed in this vision; he, like Brian and Stephen, had done his National Service, had seen how the rest of the nation lived, had determined even at that period (although never for a moment thinking of not becoming an officer) that he would speak to it all, to the whole undivided nation, as journalist, as broadcaster. (Television hardly existed in those early days.) The army had radicalized Charles more than Stephen. Stephen had joined it as a radical, and left it as a loner, but Charles—healthy, vigorous, comradely, ambitious—had joined it as a minor public school boy of vaguely right-wing views and left it much changed. And it gave him pleasure to sit down with sound technician and lighting man, with van driver and make-up girl: it gave him pleasure to invite them all round to his Harley Street home and sit up late as Liz yawned and laughed and poured glasses of cheap wine and produced, occasionally plates full of spaghetti, occasionally crying babes. A family. And the films they made were the expression of this spirit, this informality, this comradely enterprise. They made films. They could look at what they had made, and feel satisfaction.

And what had happened to all that? Union rules had happened to it. Overtime, over-manning, disputes, strikes, dissension. As the classless society moved forward, film crew members were no longer satisfied with Chinese meals: they would not sit down for less than a plateful of the best smoked salmon followed by a tournedos. They were no longer content to wait for the right light, for the right shot. They became vain and temperamental, coy and hard to please. They considered themselves an élite; they developed appropriate tastes, appro-

priate demands. True, Ben Feather continued to prefer chop
suey with a fried egg, but he was outvoted, outmoded. One of
the new-old régime.

The going overnight bed-and-breakfast hotel rate for a
member of a BBC film crew in 1985 is, one gathers, £33.47
per night. Take it or leave it.

Charles watched this process with very, very slowly accu-
mulating rage. What the hell's the point of comparing what
they earn with what I earn, or what the Director General of the
BBC earns, or what the fucking Prime Minister earns, he
would splutter, late at night, at Liz. And what the hell's the
point of *not* working another five minutes? *I* work, why can't
they work? I'd rather mend the fucking fuse myself, Charles
would roar, than lose a whole two hours of work. Don't they
care?

They had cared, once: what had gone wrong, Charles
wanted to know, that they cared no longer, that they were
interested *only* in money, in overtime, in differentials, in
negotiating structures, in anything but film? What treachery,
what disloyalty, what corruption, what materialism, what
vandalism of the good cause, what reactionary, backward-
looking, old-fashioned ill-tempered greed. Liz watched the
process of Charles's disillusion less with rage than with
interest, with a detached curiosity (for she could not believe
that he cared as he did, in fact, care: had herself always been
more cynical, more suspicious, of comrades and colleagues
and employees: had harboured fewer illusions about the esteem
in which she herself was held or not held): she did not think
Charles vulnerable, was surprised and rather touched to find
him so, in these power struggles of the late sixties and early
seventies, as the television unions flexed their muscles, as
teachers and nurses and other nice people watched and worried
and learned how to strike. It was a distant comedy, to Liz;
merely one of many varied and largely displaced manifestations
of human aspiration and conflict. It did not touch her to the
quick.

But Charles it touched, and blood flowed. On a Friday night
in November 1972 it flowed, at the end of a day of disaster,
when fifty men had come out on strike because a technician had
driven a van from one end of a car park to the other to unload
some equipment at Charles's request: work had stopped on
several programmes, recriminations had buzzed furiously
round high and low places, settlements were offered and

rejected and re-negotiated and finally accepted, and Charles had raged, stormed, and handed in his resignation. Never again would he submit to such wilful sabotage, such deliberate provocation, such shameful capitulation, he declared, and slammed his working papers boldly down on his executive director's desk and walked out into the night. Out there in the night, in another car park, a certain exchange took place between Charles Headleand, as he made his way towards his BMW, and his one-time colleague Dirk Davis, who appeared to be (but was not) lying in wait. It resulted in a bloody nose: Charles, protecting his two capped front teeth, hit out more violently than he had intended, more accurately than he had known he knew how, and Dirk Davis had gone down against the BMW with a frightening crunch. Remorse had instantly entered the breasts of both parties, fortunately, and they had tenderly brushed one another down, each admitting a measure of guilt, leaning breathless against the gleaming dark blue bonnet, testing teeth, dabbing at noses, spitting in the dirt, as far away the rockets of Bonfire Night rose into the clear, dark, crisp, leaf-scented air. "Fuck it," said Dirk, mopping blood from nose and split upper lip onto his beige check cashmere scarf, "fuck the whole fucking lot of you, fuck the whole fucking mad country, you fucking near broke my fucking nose." "You should learn to keep your fucking mouth shut," said Charles, morosely, reassured that his caps were still in place, but disturbed by the muffled banging in his rib cage and the sour prickling of his skin. And both stood, for a moment, silent, on the uneven rubble of a makeshift car park in East Acton: a moment of truce and dismay, of intimacy and disarray. And above them slowly arose a great distant display of softly exploding quiet bruises of green flowers, silver stars, red stripes of flame, great arcs of golden rain. They gazed, subdued. "I told the kids I'd be back to light the bonfire," said Dirk glumly. "Too fucking late now." "Too late," echoed Charles. "Too late, too late." A smell of gunpowder floated in the night air. Acrid, final, pure. There were no witnesses. "Where's your car?" asked Charles. Dirk nodded towards it; it stood meekly, waiting, embarrassed, mute. Tacitly, no word spoken, Charles and Dirk agreed that no more should be said; that each would forget the incident; that each would drive off into the darkness. They would forever avoid one another, forever avoid another such personal confrontation, would fight on with different weapons, different warriors. They would not speak again; they would never again mingle blood or earth or eat salt together or look one another in the eye.

Charles never made another film. He never completed the film on which he had been working that night. He persisted in proffering his resignation, went off, formed an independent programme-making production company (the parent company of Global Information Network), busied himself simultaneously with television politics; but within eighteen months was back with his old consortium, at a greatly increased salary, as executive director. He rose steadily, aggressively, through the hierarchy until there was nowhere left in the UK for him to go, and now he is in New York. He very rarely thinks, now, of his one-time ambition to speak to the whole nation, in a language the whole nation would understand: the language of film. He accepts that he was wrong to dream that this was possible or desirable. There is open war, now, and he considers that he did not declare it. But he sometimes remembers, sadly, subversively, the Chinese meal, the fried egg: he sometimes even wonders what happened to Ben Feather, to Dirk Davis, to Lindsay Potter . . .

And occasionally, as he jogs to the mocking rhythm of Widdecombe Fair, he thinks that the 1980s have come a little late for him: five years younger than the Prime Minister he may be, but is that young enough? An uneasiness grips him. His life is expensive. His salary is high, but his life is expensive. Henrietta is an expensive woman, and much of her money seems to be tied up with her children. He has five children of his own. Obscurely, unfairly, guiltily, he blames Liz. He tells his solicitor to tell Liz to sell the house. Liz, through her solicitor, refuses, or at least temporizes. Sometimes he telephones Liz directly at odd hours of day and night, for they are still on speaking terms, but she refuses to speak seriously, saying merely that she hasn't yet found a suitable little home in Kentish Town and is too busy to look, and anyway isn't it a bit short-sighted of him even to think of selling such a valuable property? She even has the cheek to mention capital gains tax. Charles is fairly sure that Liz doesn't know what capital gains tax is, but nevertheless he is a little shaken to find that she has even thought of it, and wonders who is advising her, apart from her solicitor. It can't possibly be Esther or Alix, he correctly supposes: has she perhaps a lover? A mercenary lover? Liz herself is by no means indifferent to wealth: her attitude to it is a little eccentric, a little high-handed, but it is not an attitude of indifference. A mercenary lover. A perfectly serious possibility, he supposes. Liz is not likely to remain unmarried long. He jogs on, despondently, determined that the lover shall never take up residence in Harley Street.

Liz, for her part, intends to be reasonable about the house, intends to be reasonable about Henrietta, intends to behave like a rational, adult, independent woman, but finds that this is not as easy as she had hoped. She finds herself responding pettily, irritably, emotionally. She does not succumb: she has observed and cross-questioned too many extreme cases to allow herself to succumb. She detects the symptoms early, checks them, controls them, but they continue to recur, in a mild but persistent form, and she as mildly and persistently continues to dismiss them. This is quite hard work, and absorbs some of the energy which is usually directed towards her professional commitments. She has managed, by reasoning with herself, to suppress the attacks of financial anxiety that threatened her when Charles originally came up with the notion of divorce: she knows that in her case it is unnecessary, a mere reflex tic, a vestigial fear, a displaced fear. (Nevertheless she cannot help sounding ill-tempered when Charles mentions her income, or the selling of the house.) She knows that, by a mixture of instinct and management and luck, she is extremely well placed to face the 1980s—better than Charles with his vast salary, for she is five years younger than Charles, and considerably fitter and in a less cutthroat line of operation. (Charles is worried: she, his wife of twenty years, can smell worry across the Atlantic.) She is so well placed that she almost suspects herself of an exceptional cunning, of having foreknown that she would find herself here, without Charles, in 1980, with her own life still to consolidate. The new government, although she did not vote for it and frequently criticizes it, suits her well, much better than it suits Cliff Harper, her brother-in-law, who did vote for it. She is not threatened by cuts in public spending, by the decline of the National Health Service, by the new and growing emphasis on privatization: her income is derived from a judicious blend of public and private practice. She believes in the National Health Service, in public welfare, of course (is she not a close friend of Alix Bowen's?), but she also recognizes, as Alix does not, that the private sector must encourage experiment, excellence, variation of treatment; naturally, some of her most interesting patients are from the private sector. The son of a cabinet minister, the adopted daughter of a millionaire, the (presumed) grandson of a philandering painter. She does not feel that she is betraying the public cause when she treats these patients. She believes she is offering therapy to those in need. Which, of course, she is. It is difficult to convey this in Alix Bowen's terms but Liz Headleand is, at least in her own terms, an honest woman.

And this is why she is obliged, at this odd, transitional stage of her life, to recall memories that she would rather sweep under the carpet. Professionally, temperamentally, she knows it is bad for her to sweep things under the carpet. And therefore, having reassured herself that she has herself no acute financial anxieties, she is obliged to recall certain details of her childhood: the threadbare, thrifty, dimly lit, pinched, highly polished home of her childhood. It had not been comfortable, the house in Abercorn Avenue. It had been dark, and cold: low-watt electric bulbs had to be extinguished each time one left a room, a corridor; nothing could be left lit or burning. Bedrooms were unheated; there was one electric bar fire in the dining room which Shirley and Liz would carry secretly upstairs in bitter weather. They would sleep in socks, in jerseys, wrapped up in dressing gowns. Nothing in the house seemed to have any softness, any warmth in it: the bedcovers were shiny, the cushions were shiny, the lavatory paper (which was strictly rationed, to so many sheets a day) was both coarse and shiny. Everything was rationed, except the water from the tap. Rita Ablewhite had not thought of that.

Rita Ablewhite liked a high gloss. One of the bizarre duties of Liz's childhood consisted of polishing her dead father's shoes. They stood on a shoe rack, in the kitchen, and once a week they had to be polished. There was a putting-on brush, and a taking-off brush, and a duster. A ritual. Liz disliked it intensely. Shirley would not do it. Shirley refused. But Liz, who was playing a waiting game, continued to polish the shoes until she was fifteen, sixteen. And it was at this age—fifteen, sixteen—that it began to occur to Liz Ablewhite that maybe her mother had once been in service? She never dared to ask, but such a history would certainly explain some of her mother's odd domestic behaviour, her strange, below-stairs behaviour, so out of place in a three-bedroomed, bay-windowed, 1920-built suburban semi-detached house.

It would have explained, for example, the cleaning of the silver. There was only one piece of silver in Abercorn Avenue (apart from a few teaspoons and one gravy ladle): it was a mysterious round object which sat in the front room on a small side table. It stood about six inches high, had two silver circular handles like loop earrings which could be rotated in their holders, and two detachable rims, one a flat silver disk, the other a grooved and slotted barricade, an inch high, which sat inside the flat disk. The round base of this object was of cracked and elderly wood. On one of its silver sides it bore a device, an engraving, in the form of a mailed fist: on the other a monogram which Liz, over the years, gradually deciphered as an interlinked S, H, and O. There was also a hallmark of four digits, displaying a tiny anchor, a tiny lion, a letter Z, and an illegible squiggle which might once have been an arrow. The function of the object was by no means clear to Liz and Shirley Ablewhite, but then it did not occur to them that it might have a function: it was clearly a symbol rather than a domestic utensil. Late Victorian? Edwardian? These were questions that only raised themselves retrospectively. But silver it was, solid silver, for so, Rita Ablewhite informed them, the hallmark proclaimed. It had to be taken to pieces and polished, with a pink soapy paste, then washed in hot soapy water, then dried on a special dark yellow cloth. Liz enjoyed the silver more than the shoes. It was more rewarding. It came up well. But what was it? Whence had it come? How had it made its way to Abercorn Avenue? These were mysteries that found no answer; they posed questions that could not even be asked.

Rita Ablewhite hoarded everything; but then, so did most people in those days. Paper bags, rubber bands, silver foil, jam jars, the humble paraphernalia of depression and war. Hoarding was not then neurotic, obsessional, eccentric.

Well, nobody in her right mind would want to go back to that. Cold, darkness, and the smell of boot polish. No, let the lights of Harley Street blaze, let the central heating waste its beneficence on empty rooms, let bottles be hurled into the bottle bank, let the garbage men collect the affluent rubbish of an affluent house. Aristocratic largesse; *fin-de-siècle* waste; warmth, life, light. Projects of thrift do not attract Liz Headleand, as they attract, in different ways, her friends Alix and Esther. She does not wish to turn back, to cut back, to live in a reduced style as a divorced woman, although she has in her time bracingly recommended this course to others. She wishes to keep the lights on. She feels justified in this, up to a point.

And it is not only the comfort that she needs, though that is part of it. She is afraid that if she takes a step back, all her worldly riches will crumble, like Cinderella's at midnight, and that she will find herself once more polishing the boots. Well, of course she is afraid of this, we are all afraid of this, if we have any imagination. But she is more afraid of this than most. She knows she is not the true princess, but only a fake princess, a scullery maid dressed up by a Cambridge scholarship and her own wits, and rescued by a dubious prince. Henrietta Latchett is the true princess. Blue blood flows in her veins. It is embarrassing to have to admit this, but Liz Headleand, who knows she should know better, has taken to trying to work out Henrietta Latchett's pedigree from *Who's Who*.

Charles Headleand, as we have seen, also spends some little time at this pursuit, but he uses *Debrett*, of which he happens to have a copy in the office for other purposes. Liz does not have a *Debrett* and would not know how to use it if she had. *Who's Who* is not entirely helpful, for it records achievement, not mere existence. Charles himself is in it (and Liz is not quite looking forward to that "marr. diss. 1980" which will make its way into his biography), but Henrietta Latchett is not. Nor are any other Latchetts, for none of them has ever done anything of either influence or interest. But various of Henrietta's relatives have been more forthcoming, more public-spirited, and they provide points of reference, connections, bits of plot. Liz weaves her way from Air Commodores to Deputy Acting High Commissioners, from Presidents of Learned Associations to Governors of Merchant Banks, from Directors of Trusts to Members of the Royal Aeronautical Society. An uncle has written a monograph; a distant cousin has won the Nobel Prize for Chemistry. And back, beyond each of them, beyond each name, stretches a long line of precedent. Of the named and the known. She traces the family name, Oxenholme, and its delicate interweaving with the Hestercombes and Stocklinches. *Debrett*, were she to sink so low, would tell her more. Her own name, in Charles's entry, stands bleakly: m., 2nd, Elizabeth Ablewhite, MB, B.Chir., MA, FRCP. When Charles divorces her, will she be excised? She checks precedents. They seem irregular. Maybe it depends on Charles? The possibility of this irritates her. In fact, Liz, though not a pompous woman, has sometimes considered that she is worthy of a *Who's Who* entry in her own right; if she had published more, surely she would by now be registered? After all, she has sat on public enquiries, has contributed to her profession, is held in high esteem by her colleagues . . .

It is ridiculous, Liz knows it is ridiculous, but she feels that Charles's abandoning of her for a more ancient lineage threatens her solidity, her survival. He has withdrawn his approval, and she has become nobody. People will laugh at her behind her back, they will not want to come to her parties any more, they will all want to go and have dinner with Charles and Henrietta. She voices these absurd thoughts to Esther and Alix, and they all laugh; but the thoughts are not entirely dispersed by the laughter. Liz is, on one level, amused, dispassionately interested, by these comic vagaries of her middle-aged psyche. Who would have thought it? How odd people are. What odd things they worry about. What irrelevancies exercise them. So, to herself, thinks Liz Headleand, as she firmly congratulates herself on her sound financial position, her impregnable social position—for surely, surely, people will still want to come and have dinner with her; or would, if she ever had time to invite them? Surely?

Alix, Brian, and Esther are less immune to the spirit of 1980, to the policies of the new government, for which none of them voted. It does not suit them as it suits Liz. Alix's research unit is precisely the kind of outfit that could be disposed of without any trouble or outcry, a mini-quango of questionable purpose and absolutely no productivity: she and Polly Piper, who find their work intellectually interesting as well as remunerative and believe it is socially useful, hope that they are so cheap, so insignificant, that nobody will notice they are there at all. Garfield, more seriously, is also at risk. It is expensive to run, with a high staff ratio. Luckily, not many people outside the Home Office know much about Garfield, but if they did, they would certainly consider its régime too liberal, its buildings too comfortable, its faith in psychiatry and psychotherapy absurd. (An accusation not levelled by sons of cabinet ministers against Liz Headleand.) It would be easy to whip up public feeling against Garfield. It would be a prime target in any law-and-order, longer-deterrent-sentence, short-sharp-shock campaign. Women prisoners have traditionally been treated differently from male offenders, but Alix can see the possibility of a backlash of anti-feminism, a new harshness, a new "equality"

on the horizon. Garfield, the pride of the prison service, the
showplace, may not survive. It faces cuts in staffing, in
medical expenses, in laundry bills, in catering. The warden has
always maintained his faith in the civilizing influence of
tablecloths and reasonably leisurely meals. Tablecloths do
more to rehabilitate than drugs, or mailbags, Eric Glover, the
warden, has been heard to declare. The tablecloths at Garfield
are red-and-white check, blue-and-white check. Alix, who
rarely gets round to using a tablecloth in her own home, who
tends to serve meals on a bare unpolished ancient Habitat table,
marked by saucepan rings, imbedded *Guardian* print, and
much wear, has faith in the tablecloths at Garfield. But they
will vanish, within the next two years, she suspects. And she
herself may vanish with them, for the civilizing effect of
classes in English language and literature is also open to
dispute. A luxury. It occurs to Alix that if she loses her various
part-time jobs, she will be eligible for next to nothing in the
way of redundancy payment, having worked, as women do, so
episodically, in so piecemeal if persistent a manner. And
where, at her age, would she find another job?

Brian's Adult Education College also suffers cuts. It is
forced to amalgamate with various other South London institutions. Brian's boss asks Brian if he would like to run courses
in Commercial English for foreign business students. Brian
says he would not know how to. He likes to teach D. H.
Lawrence and Blake, Bunyan, and George Eliot. He starts as
a sideline to teach a course for the Open University. The New
Right continues to complain that the Open University is
wasting taxpayers' money on Marxist propaganda.

Meanwhile, Pitts and Harley, where Brian once hammered
circular saws, is picketed by striking BSC workers. There are
ugly scenes on the picket line, as most Pitts and Harley men
continue to go to work. Brian and his father support the
strikers: verbally, of course. In two years' time, Pitts and
Harley, like the tablecloths of Garfield, will be no more. A
hundred and twenty years of manufacture will come to an end.
Six hundred men will lose their jobs. Eddie Duckworth,
manager, and president of the Chamber of Commerce, will sell
his house. His wife, who was always a little unbalanced, will
commit suicide.

Esther Breuer's connection with market forces has always
been tenuous, but even she is a little affected by the magnetic
shift. The series of public lectures in one of our public galleries

which she had intermittently graced with her erudition is discontinued. As she was only paid £12.50 a lecture this ought not to make much of a hole in her budget, but as her budget is rather small, it does. Her course at the Feldmann Institute is also threatened. English students are failing to get grants. Luckily there seems to be a supply of wealthy young foreigners who like to while away a year or two studying art history. For the moment, they fill up places. As Esther has no social conscience at all, in her own view, she is quite happy to teach Americans and Jews and Arabs, Japanese and Italians, Germans and Persians. Many of them are very bright, very sophisticated, very well connected. They like Esther. They consider her smart.

Her Workers Educational Association evening class on the Italian quattrocento is axed. Its members, mostly middle-aged or retired, who had been looking forward to an Italian holiday, are annoyed; they protest, they offer to pay more. They are told it does not work like that. They are given a speech (not by Esther) about the allocation of resources. Esther feels sorry for them. As she says to Alix one evening, what could be milder, more harmless, more inoffensive, than the study of Italian art? She cannot see why harmless leisure activities, in a society of increasingly high levels of unemployment, should not be more encouraged. But she does not worry about it very much. There are plenty of other people to worry about it for her. She is more curious, as she tells Alix, about her own response to the articles that now frequently appear in the press mocking the abstruseness of higher education and the subjects selected for research. Whenever *The Spectator* or the *Guardian* (says Esther, with studied political neutrality, knowing that Alix out of deep fairness will disqualify any too evidently biased comment) picks out any particular topic—or they may even invent them, for all I know—such as "Lesbianism in Lesotho," or "The Voting Habits of Publicans in the 1920s," I always think it sounds particularly fascinating and immediately want to know all about it. I mean, after all, what is knowledge but a sum of its parts? Why not know about lesbianism in Lesotho or the politics of publicans? Who knows where they may lead?

It's all to do with money, says Alix, vaguely. It seems there isn't enough to go round and we ought to be training people to make microchips.

We're bound to get it wrong, and have far too many people making microchips and not enough people making wire netting, says Esther, and proceeds to describe to Alix her new project; she plans to set up an exhibition, preferably at the Hayward Gallery, of scarecrows. I don't think it's ever been done, says Esther. International scarecrows. The scarecrow in art and mythology. All I need is an anthropologist, to go round the world collecting scarecrows. I'm sure I could get a grant from the GLC, or do you think it's a bit too folk-arty for them? Not quite urban enough? The global scarecrow. What do you think?

Alix thinks it is a great idea, and offers as her contribution the opening passages of *Jude the Obscure,* where, as far as she can remember, Jude is employed by a local farmer to scare the crows from his corn, but is sorry for the poor birds and encourages them to eat. A bit literary, says Esther dismissively. This is an exhibition, not an anthology.

In the summer of 1985, a Midlands farmer who lives not far from the army camp where Brian and Stephen first met will offer unemployed school-leavers a wage of £50 a week and free self-catering lodging to scare the birds from his fields of cherries. I feel sorry for youngsters today, with no hope of a job; they could have a bit of fun on the farm, he says. Human Scarecrows, the headline in a progressive paper will read.

Meanwhile, and very much meanwhile, monetarist theories did not prevent Esther from going to Bologna to look at the possible Crivelli. Red Bologna. Red politics, red arcades. Esther travelled by train. She preferred to travel by train. Aeroplanes were more expensive and less enjoyable. A journey by train was full of adventure, of calm; of tension, of tranquillity; from the moment of departure from Victoria Station to the moment of arrival at Bologna Station (which some months later in this year will be the scene of a particularly successful terrorist bomb explosion, which will kill eighty-five). Esther, however, had a peaceful journey, and a peaceful arrival. She read her books (*La Chartreuse de Parme,* which she had begun several times but never managed to finish; E. H. Carr's *What Is History?,* pressed upon her by Alix as the result of a dispute about terminology; and Pett Petrie's latest novel, *Ziggurat*). She studied her periodicals (the recently founded *London Review of Books, The Spectator,* and *Clique*); did the *Times* crossword; and wrote various lists of things she would like to see in Bologna. She also gazed out of the window and enjoyed her recollections of previous journeys, as they mingled with the spring hedges and oast houses of Kent, the grey sea, the pursuing gulls, the smoky bar, anarchic stewards and

drunken school parties of Sealink, the oak trees and mistletoe
of northern France, the disputed couchettes of middle France,
the glimpsed nocturnal Alpine snows, and the glorious emerging morning of the falling, spreading, tumbling spill of the
south. There they still were, the vineyards and the oxen, the
steep descending slopes, and then the plain. Reassured, she
drank some coffee from a plastic cup. At the age of seventeen,
she had first made this journey, at the same time of year, or
perhaps a little later; she had been on her way to Perugia, her
head full of expectations, but of she knew not what, for she had
never knowingly been abroad (although born in Berlin), and
Berlin and Bologna, Venice and Vienna, Munich and Mar-
seilles were then but names to her. She was acquainted only
with rainy Manchester, with a smart girls' boarding school in
Shropshire, with the Cheshire homes of friends, with London
(a little), and, yet more fleetingly, the Oxford and Cambridge
of her interviews. Italy had been a revelation, a deliverance, a
new birth.

She had stopped, then, in Florence, where her parents had
arranged for her to spend the night, before catching the
morning train to Perugia. She had been timid but reckless,
exhilarated by freedom, unable to believe that she could go
where she wished: that she was, at last, unobserved. She was
booked into a small, safe, respectable hotel on the banks of the
Arno, with a view of the Ponte Vecchio. She had left her
luggage at the hotel, and had taken to the streets. She had
wandered, past façades and windows, past shops selling
marbled paper and tooled leather purses. She drank a small
green drink in one bar and a small red drink in another bar. She
had a conversation with a nun and was followed by a soldier.
She sat on a bridge and watched the river. She walked through
narrow streets, and saw a woman from an upper window lean
over an array of geraniums and drying stockings and call,
"Mario! Mario! Ho buttato giù la pasta! Mario!" and knew
that she was listening to the tongue of angels. She ended the
evening sitting in a café in the Piazza della Signoria with an
American student from Iowa who said that he also was on his
way to Perugia, though his way was not as direct as her own.
He was reading a novel by Dostoevsky and wrote out for her
from memory a short poem by William Carlos Williams, of
whom she had never heard. These seemed good credentials,
though Esther was past caution. They drank a bottle of wine
and ate a pizza. She had never eaten or even seen a pizza. They

gazed at people, at the fountain, at Giambologna's statue of
Cosimo I, at Michelangelo's *David*, at the Loggia, at the
pigeons, at a man selling little painted mechanical flying birds.
The American, who was gaunt and livid of aspect, with a long
thin melancholy quixotic face, bought her a little bird. (She has
it still.) The American persuaded her to accompany him back
to his *pensione*, where he attempted to seduce her, but she told
him, primly summoning her meandering resources, that she
was only seventeen and therefore legally beneath the age of
consent. He received this information solemnly with some
relief, and desisted. Nevertheless in the morning, after collecting her suitcase from her small hotel overlooking the Arno, she
agreed to alter her plans and to hitchhike with him to Siena and
Arezzo.

And so she made her acquaintance with Tuscany, with
Umbria. And now was on her way to Bologna, which she had
first visited in the company of her middle-aged American art
historian, who had in Perugia displaced the innocent student in
the inner circle of her affections.

Bologna is famed for its food, which had pleased the
American art historian, who (unlike Esther) took food seriously. The American art historian had talked to her of
mannerism and the baroque, attempting to distract her from the
obviousness of the over-postcarded, over-fashionable trecento
and quattrocento, from what he called the schoolgirl and
schoolmistress raptures aroused by Botticelli and Giotto, Piero
della Francesca and Fra Lippo Lippi. Esther, at seventeen, had
been torn between a desire to please him by cultivating a taste
for swirling gloomy grandeur, for unlikely colour schemes and
over-sophisticated elongations, and a desire to point out that at
seventeen she had a right to enjoy, for a while, her first
meetings with the obvious.

She had compromised, in the long run, with Crivelli, an
unfashionable artist of the quattrocento, little admired by
schoolgirls and schoolmistresses, and sometimes wonders
whether this is the fault or the credit of the American art
historian.

The American art historian was called—and indeed is
called—Hubert Swann. Hubert Swann, like the American
student from Iowa, made only the most half-hearted attempt to
seduce Esther. It was somehow obvious that this was not what
Esther was for. Hubert readily settled for a platonic passion,
which has now lasted for more than a quarter of a century. In

1969, when their relationship had settled into what each rightly took to be its lasting form, they went together to Urbino on what they admitted, a little guiltily, could only be described as a holiday; they visited together the Palazzo Ducale, wandering from room to room, past paintings and hangings and marble fireplaces, past spiral staircases, gilt-touched cherubs and inlaid marquetry squirrels and mandolins, gazing at framed views of green hills, and discoursing elegantly and allusively of their enduring affection for one another, and of Castiglione and Isabella d'Este. No reference was made by either to wilder nights endured or enjoyed in other cities, in other company. Esther knew nothing of Hubert Swann's other life; he knew nothing of Esther's affairs. A satisfactory arrangement. An innocent relationship.

Esther sits on the train as it nears Bologna station, thinking of bygone days, wondering what became of the young man who gave her the painted bird, reflecting on the numbers of American vagrants which now infest the Ponte Vecchio and Florence railway station with their rucksacks and their trannies and their syringes, wondering if Bologna is also thus infested; recalling Alix's views on tourism and the paradox of its diminishing returns when too many people have the money and/or the education and the wish to travel (you can't blame the people, says Alix, why shouldn't they sit in Florence station in a sleeping bag if they want to?); thinking of her middle-aged and elderly students and their wish to have nice holidays; thinking of Hubert Swann in Urbino, of Harold Acton at La Pietà; thinking of her satanic anthropologist Claudio, who is perhaps a little less manageable than Hubert Swann, and wondering what Claudio's sister and her apartment will be like, and whether she was wise to accept an invitation to sleep there. She has never met Claudio's sister, and was flattered to receive a card from her, but worried also by the possibility that this might mean that Claudio might wish to make himself, at last, in some other way, "real" to her—whatever, in relation to a person as outré as Claudio, the word "real" might mean. "You will like her," Claudio had threatened. What could that imply?

A mile from the station, just as Esther has her thoughts and expectations marshalled, the train grinds to a halt, by a bank of irises and a cabin called Jollybox. It sits, a mile from the station, for an hour and a half. Esther conjures up the red arcades. Bolognese red. She compares this colour with Tuscan pink, with what she calls Bloomsbury pink. She wonders what she would do if she were to go blind. Would she bother to learn braille? Would she be able to remember colour? Was there a real blind man who said that the colour red was like the sound of trumpets, or was he merely a philosophical figment? She thinks of the red earth of Somerset, where she will go to stay shortly for a weekend with her friends Peggy and Humphrey, painter and blacksmith. It is the most beautiful place in England. It is as beautiful as Italy. Peggy and Humphrey are trying to persuade Esther to take a cottage on the estate. At times she almost thinks she might seriously be about to consider the suggestion.

London has become difficult. Not impossible, but difficult. Even Esther, who likes urban life, is becoming slightly distressed by the visual impact of some stretches of Ladbroke Grove, by the apartment blocks of the Harrow Road, by the strange surreal landscape under the arches of the Motorway. Her niece Ursula, who has a taste for the *louche*, likes it immensely, strikes up terrible friendships in public houses and on street corners, sits drinking cans of beer with impossible people in condemned and boarded cottages in the middle of rubble wastes. The Apocalypse Hotel is her favoured rendezvous. Esther, who once liked the *louche* herself, feels a little old for that kind of thing. She could sublet her rented flat for a while to Ursula, and try a few months in Somerset on the estate. Would she be bored, in the countryside? Would she miss Alix and Liz? She could live on next to nothing, in the countryside, Peggy and Humphrey assure her. She could write the book for which she was advanced some £250 five years ago. She could live rent-free, in a cottage standing empty; she could keep at bay the nettles and the ivy.

She knows the cottage has grave disadvantages, and knows that Peggy and Humphrey think she does not care about that kind of thing. Comfort, warmth. She is not sure whether she cares or not. The Ladbroke Grove flat is quite damp, at times.

The cottage is very beautiful. Why does nobody else want to live in it? Because most people want to buy, and it is not and never will be for sale. So say Peggy and Humphrey, who do not own their own, larger house, in which they have lived solidly for twenty years. It is something to do with property and capitalism. We are artists, vagrants, grasshoppers, say Peggy and Humphrey, aproned, calmed, settled; come and join us in the deep insecurity of nature.

Ladbroke Grove, the wrong end, is really remarkably ugly, by any normal urban standards. Somerset is remarkably beautiful. Bologna also. Beautiful, ugly. Dangerous, safe. I wonder, ponders Esther, is it from Alix that I have caught this extraordinary notion, so alien surely to me myself, that there is something *immoral* about living in a beautiful place? If so, Alix has a lot to answer for. And yet it is true, thinks Esther, that I think Liz is mad, to want to hang on to that vast house in Harley Street. In that, Alix and I are of one accord.

Artists, vagrants, grasshoppers. Esther reflects on the reasons why she is so little attracted to the notion of owning property, when she is so interested in the visual aspects of the material world, so attached to the details of her own immediate environment. Maybe it is merely a continental aberration, a Viennese inheritance, an unsettled, refugee spirit, an un-English spirit. Alix and Brian, good socialists though they try to be, own or at least are paying a mortgage on their house in Wandsworth. It is, of course, a fairly horrible house, which mitigates in their favour, morally.

The train lurches forward. She rearranges her baggage.

Later, over dinner, in Claudio's sister's apartment, she only intermittently remembers these thoughts. Claudio's sister's apartment is of a dusty, antique, grand, gilt, high-ceilinged, baroque grandeur; it is a corner of a baroque palace, overlooking the Via Santo Stefano. A canary hops and sings in a high white wicker cage. Statues stand on marble tables. Claudio's sister is wearing a severely cut grey flannel skirt with a grey English woollen twin set; the effect is exotic. She is an archaeologist. She studies the Etruscans. They speak of Perugia, of Volterra, as they loop up their *pasta al pesto*. Claudio's sister is excavating, intermittently, a dig in Tuscany, on a high little hillside crowned by an ancient wood. Esther enquires about the lichens. They talk of pigmentation, of the possible Crivelli, of dating techniques, of restoration, of government grants. Claudio's sister is a civil servant, paid by the state. The bird sings. They drink *grappa*, after their meal, and Elena puts her feet up on the rickety chaise longue and smokes a cigarette. She has a low, hoarse, husky voice, a seductive voice. Her skin is dark, her slightly prominent, slightly irregular teeth are white, firm, precise, she has a necklace of red glass beads around her neck. She and Esther have not met before. They like one another very much. They speak, briefly, familiarly, of Claudio and his eccentricities. Elena laughs a guttural laugh, raises her glass, and gazes at the light of the red-shaded lamp, reflectively, through the pale, pale gold of her *grappa*. She sighs ominously. She invites Esther to visit her Etruscan dig, to see the toad that lives in the tomb, the old Etruscan toad. Elena asks how things are in England. Esther says, which England?

Esther finds herself perplexed, the next day, by the alleged Crivelli. She stares at it for hour after hour, intermittently consulting her notes from London, her own Crivelli catalogue, Pritajoli's *Proposta*. She ponders the story of the painting's discovery. It is implausible; but so are all such stories. It was found, she is told, by an eccentric Marxist monk from Bologna on a walking tour in Dalmatia. He spotted it in the woodshed of a small derelict monastery, while sheltering from the rain and chatting about the cultivation of broad beans to an aged farmer. It was leaning against a pile of firewood and some broken furniture. He had surreptitiously rescued it, and slipped it under his habit, and brought it home to Bologna.

Now the monk-thief has vanished into silence. Esther is not allowed to cross-question him. The monk is not allowed to speak to women. Or so she is told.

It is all very fishy. She suspects the hand of Claudio Volpe, for no good reason. Claudio is Bologna-born, though now attached to the University of Turin: he may well have wished to magic a Crivelli into his home city, to please Esther, to please the citizens. But even Claudio could not have forged this quattrocento little panel. It is surely authentically of its period? Perhaps it is, as Esther had hoped before she saw it, part of the lost but documented Zara polyptych, known variously as the *Madonna della Pesca* or the *Madonna del Pesce*, an old textual crux. Esther had so longed for the more surprising fish. But all she has before her here, at the most, at the least, is one of the panels from the predella. St. John the Baptist, 37 centimetres by 11. An elongated San Giovanni Battista, standing on a flat spiked cracked rock, with a thin blue film of baptismal water washing over his bony ankles. Sitting on the rock is a duck, by a dry twig nest. John is wearing one of those decorative reversible hair shirts with which Crivelli liked to clothe the wilderness saint; the outer skin, delicately girdled, reveals soft curling wisps of hair from within, suggesting more delicacy than penance, more refinement than martyrdom, more style than asceticism. But a hint of the werewolf, nevertheless: he could turn inside out in a trice, this locust-eating prophet.

The treatment is Crivelli, the subject Crivelli, the signature

Crivelli. OPUS KAROLI CRIVELLI VENETI. No date. If the Yugoslav period, then from 1460s? She suspects the signature. There is something wrong with the signature. It looks somehow superimposed, post-dated. If there had been no signature, she would have been less suspicious.

Carlo Crivelli's brother Vittore had also painted in Dalmatia.

Esther is perplexed, but entirely absorbed. Time passes without reckoning. She would like to think that this is a true work by Carlo, her friend and ally, her doctorate-bestower, for that would justify her (very modest) expenses for this visit, but if it is by another hand, well, that is equally interesting. And if it is an immensely subtle forgery, a *jeu d'esprit* from a mad monk, well, she supposes, that is even *more* interesting, although not quite in her own line of interest.

Maybe the facts will never be established. What is history? *What Is History?* She is haunted by Ranke's now apparently scorned ideal, to tell things "*wie es eigentlich gewesen.*" To tell things as they really were.

If the Crivelli authentication were to run and run, Esther could be the beneficiary of many free trips to Bologna. But Esther's mind does not work in this way. Esther is a scholar. If there is such a thing. Esther wonders if there is such a thing, as she walks back towards Elena, tempted, through the mild spring evening light.

Shirley Harper's youngest child and only daughter, Celia, sits in her bedroom at her desk and breathes heavily over her homework. She is thirteen, the baby of the family, the child born to fill the gaping time that Shirley knew would approach when the boys grew up; not consciously planned, of course, for consciously Shirley was angry to find herself pregnant yet again, after a gap of seven years. She has made Celia aware of her anger, rather than of her delight.

Celia's homework is a project on the Brigantes, the association of tribes which dominated northern Britain at the time of the Roman invasion. She has drawn a map of Iron Age hill forts; there is one just north of Northam, to the right of the Motorway to Leeds. Now she is drawing a cross-section of a typical fort, copied from a book she found in the public library which she competitively hoped nobody else has discovered. She is using red, blue, green, and brown pencils, nicely sharpened. She is engrossed. Her mouth is open, for she has trouble with her sinuses; the doctor says it is caused by a deviated septum but nobody knows what that means. It is inoperable, he says.

Celia attends an expensive, conventional, highly regarded private day school in a northern suburb of Northam. Most of the city's professional families who do not opt for boarding school send their daughters there. It is said to have high academic standards. Celia is happy there and enjoys her work, perhaps rather more than she should: she is in danger of becoming teacher's pet. Teacher is Miss Grigson, a bright young woman with an interest in local history which she has successfully communicated to some of her nice, polite, well-mannered, uniformed flock. Miss Grigson is a romantic. She is engaged to be married and will sometimes, eccentrically, interrupt a class on igneous rocks or the structure of the flowering plant to speak of a May Ball she attended with her fiancé, or of her fiancé's dislike of aubergines.

Celia Harper is devoted to Miss Grigson, and her imagination has been captured by the Brigantes. She takes Miss Grigson's point that most schoolchildren know about Boadicea, very few about Cartimandua, Queen of the Brigantes, and that therefore to know about Cartimandua is special. Cartimandua, says Miss Grigson, appears to have been something of a rotter, but there may have been reasons. Why did Cartimandua betray Caractacus to the Romans? Miss Grigson's eyes flash as she speculates. Was it because of a private dispute with her consort, Venutius? Miss Grigson is no feminist; she lives too far north for that. She is simply the sort of woman who always takes the woman's side. She is a romantic, she wishes to exonerate Cartimandua from the reproaches of history. She plans to take her form, Form 4B, on an outing in the summer term to visit Ian Kettle's dig in North Yorkshire. Celia is excited by the prospect. She colours in her cross-section. She murmurs to herself:

> My name is Cartimandua, Queen of Queens,
> Look on my works, ye mighty, and despair.

Shirley, sorting the sheets on the landing by the airing cupboard, hears this murmuring, stops sorting, listens. Celia can remember only these two lines, so she intones them again and again, with varying emphases, as she colours. Shirley listens. What does this chant recall to her? Of course, it recalls her sister, Liz, under the bedclothes, thirty years ago. Shirley shivers, begins to fold, diverts her irritation to the non-folding qualities of fitted bottom sheets. Every improvement creates a new problem, she reflects. But Liz chants on, in the back of her mind. Is there something odd, formidable, about Celia's concentration? Why should one feel uneasy about such a model schoolgirl? She knows that Cliff worries about her too, takes every opportunity to encourage her to go out to play, to have friends to tea, to join in the game of rounders on Blackridge Green. She and Cliff are guilty, responsible. They chose for their daughter this education, these enthusiasms, they sometimes think. The boys are not academic, they rebel, they are tiresome in a conventional way with hairstyles and drink, a way that Cliff understands, although he complains, conventionally. But Celia: she is another matter. She is only a girl, so it is not so important, Shirley can see Cliff thinking; but it is a worry. This intensity perturbs him. On an impulse, Shirley strides towards her daughter's door, flings it open, presenting a dark green towel. Celia looks round, startled, sees it is only her mother, puts on a blank, deceitful, expressionless face, expecting reproach. Her mother looks around for something to reproach her with, stalling slightly by offering the clean towel, then says, "And what's that heap of clothes doing on the floor?" She points at a pile of socks, pants, shorts, aertex shirts.

"I was just going to take them to the laundry basket," says Celia, without a pretence at plausibility.

"So I see," says Shirley. The lines she has to utter tire Shirley. She has built round herself this wall of words, of lies, of actions. A fortress. "I've just put another load in the washing machine, they'll have to wait till next time."

"Yes," says Celia, patiently.

"What are you working on?" asks Shirley, relenting.

"My ancient history project," says Celia, protectively, reluctantly. She does not want to talk about it with her mother. Her mother, unlike Miss Grigson, has no interest in such matters.

"Very nice," says Shirley, flatly, looking at her daughter's closed face, her neat brown bunches, her freckled nose, her braced teeth. A very promising pupil, all her teachers say. Promising for what? Shirley bends down and picks up a bus ticket and a piece of KitKat wrapper off the floor. "This place is a pigsty," she murmurs, almost politely. "Now you put your clothes away before you come downstairs," she says, and backs out. Celia is breathing hard over her project before Shirley even shuts the door.

Shirley goes down to the kitchen. She puts the kettle on, for something to do. She wipes a Formica surface. Cliff tells her she should have domestic help, more domestic help than that provided by Mrs. Rathbone, who comes twice a week, but Shirley resists. She is afraid of domestic help and anyway what would she do with the extra time? Some of her so-called friends have domestic help and fill in their time with coffee mornings, good works, discussion groups, even a little part-time real work. Shirley wishes she could work but Cliff would not like it, and anyway she is good for nothing, trained for nothing. She thinks of her sister, Liz, and her frenetic, over-active social life, her stepchildren and her children, her vanishing husbands. She thinks of Celia, intent up there, sucking her pencil, in her nice bright room with its old nursery frieze of Noah's ark still marching round the walls, with its snowflake mobile. She thinks of her mother. She has usually assumed that Liz's manifest intellectual superiority must have been inherited from the unknown father, for she believes in heredity, in genetics, but of late she has begun to regard her mother in a new light. That strange, cracked, singleminded persistence, that fanatical bleakness, is it perhaps a sign of intelligence gone wrong?

And Celia, perhaps, has inherited this? Liz's daughters, Sally and Stella, do not seem to suffer from morbid intensity. They dissipate their energies in a hundred directions, they are always out and about, rushing and restless. London life. The street life of the 1970s, the 1980s, with its affectation of working-class manners and speech, its toughness, its colour. Celia leads a protected, quiet, refined life, in Northam. A provincial life, a middle-class life, an old-fashioned life. Shirley makes a cup of instant coffee that she does not want, that she would in fact rather not drink.

Cliff tells her she should go to London, take a week off, go and stay with Liz and do some shopping, go to the theatre, catch up with things. He cannot go because he cannot leave the business, does not like to leave the business. Cliff knows she is bored, underemployed, mildly depressed, that her mother gets on her nerves, that she needs a change. He is generous with his suggestions; the more worried he is about money, the more defiantly expensive his suggestions become. Shirley says she will go, perhaps in the autumn, not yet. She does not know if she wants to stay with Liz. She does not like her role as country mouse. But she thinks it wrong to lose touch with Liz, can see the probability of losing touch with Liz altogether, of their becoming strangers. Does she feel this because she sees her own boys growing away, estranging themselves from her, finding her and Cliff tedious? Cliff is quite a heavy father, and they resent it. If he is not careful, they will vanish.

Dully, she turns these things over. London, Regent's Park, Harrods, Shaftesbury Avenue, Bond Street, the National Theatre. What excuse shall she offer to her mother? Her mother claimed to have been to London in 1937 for the Coronation but frankly Shirley cannot imagine this. She cannot imagine her mother anywhere other than in Abercorn Avenue, though she has been known to venture as far as the shops on the corner of Victoria Street and once or twice, astonishingly, to Silcocks department store in the city centre. Perhaps I'd better go to London, *make* myself go to London, Shirley decides. I don't want to get too like Ma.

She crosses to the sink, pours away half her unwanted cup of instant coffee, washes the cup, washes a foil milk-bottle top, puts her foot on the pedal bin, opens it, drops in the foil top, gazes absently for a moment at an empty egg box, an empty tomato tin, the scrapings of last night's spaghetti, some apple peel, some kitchen roll, a browning lettuce leaf, a cigarette carton, a tonic bottle. She wishes they would not throw tonic bottles in the pedal bin: she likes to take them to the newly provided Bottle Bank. She thinks of rescuing it, but does not. I don't want to get too like Ma, she repeats to herself: but even as she rehearses these words, a strange perverse, numbing respect for her mother seeps through her: how she has persisted, her mother, in being what she is, how stubbornly she has refused to divert herself with trivia, how bleakly and boldly she has stared over the years into the heart of nothingness. For it is trivial, it is all trivial, coffee mornings, eating, drinking, the National Theatre, shopping outings, reading books, embroidery, evening classes, country walks, wiping surfaces, emptying wastepaper baskets, Bond Street, Regent's Park, saving bottles for the Bottle Bank, gardening, telephone calls, listening to the radio, Terry Wogan, going to the hairdresser, chatting to the window cleaner, giving small donations to Oxfam, throwing away silver foil, collecting silver foil, cleaning the bath. It is nothing, all of it nothing. Sex and small children had provided a brief purpose, the energy they generated had made sense of the world for a while, had forged a pattern, a community: clinics, playgrounds, parks, nursery groups, mothers waiting at the school gate—and now, nothing. An idle flutter of garbage over an empty pavement. Coldness, nothingness grips Shirley as she stands in her kitchen. She knows herself to be biologically dead. Her spirit shudders: she has seen a vision, of waste matter, of meaningless after-life, of refuse, of decay. An egg box and a tin can in a blue and white plastic pedal bin. So might one stand forever. She lifts her foot. The lid drops.

Liz regretted her acceptance of Ivan Warner's invitation to lunch. Lunching was usually a mistake; seeing Ivan was almost invariably a mistake. Ivan always had lunch: it was his job. Liz had no wish whatsoever to see Ivan, or to eat lunch. Nevertheless, here she found herself, at one o'clock on a weekday in Soho in late spring, settling herself onto a comfortable upholstered banquette, shaking out a large thick well-ironed dark pink damask napkin, smiling politely, professing herself delighted to see Ivan, and allowing herself to order a Campari and soda. It arrived, clinking, misted, in a long-stemmed tulip glass, with a slice of orange. How had it happened? How had he managed it? She gazed at his unattractive, malevolent, highly coloured, smug face with curiosity. It was almost as though Ivan had some power of blackmail over her, over all those he held in thrall: but what could the secret be, when she could think of nothing dishonourable that he could know of her, when she knew so many dishonourable things of him? And why was it that she felt, in his company, a sense of illicit, uncomfortable pleasure, a sense of slightly corrupt collusion? Was the very fact of her presence, here, in this restaurant, a shared crime; did he know her distaste, her reluctance; was it because of her distaste, her reluctance, that he continued to press her, continued to seek her out? Or could it be that she actually *wanted* to be cross-questioned by Ivan Warner about her divorce proceedings, about how Charles was getting on in New York, about Henrietta Latchett, about the children's response to Charles's move? She had observed in some of her patients a guilty pleasure in surrender of secrets; was Ivan Warner her analyst, her therapist, her confessor? Thoughtfully, she sipped her cold bitter drink: thoughtfully, she smiled at Ivan. She had not seen him for months. Not since the New Year's Eve party. There was a lot of gossip to make good.

Ivan raised his own frosty glass of gin, tonic, and lemon wedge, and saluted her. "Cheers," he said. Liz smiled coldly. "Basilisk," said Ivan. "Cheshire cat," said Ivan. She smiled more warmly. The waiter hovered, and Ivan waved him away, which caused Liz to glance surreptitiously at her watch; she had to be back by 3:30, she could tell already that he would try to make her late. A battle of wills. "Well?" said Ivan. "Well?" said Liz.

Ivan proceeded to interrogate her about her own plans, her own affairs, her own thoughts of remarriage, picking up a theme which he had attempted to explore at the party itself; she had assumed then, in panic, that he had introduced it through malice, but now, in the calm of luncheon, nibbling a stick of raw celery, she thought perhaps that he was genuinely interested, genuinely curious, genuinely trying to wheedle information from her. After all, how could he know that she had nothing to divulge? Gallantly Ivan offered suggestions to people her supposed private life: he brought up once again, for example, Gabriel Denham, an old enemy of Charles's. A good-looking man, Liz conceded, though a bit gone to seed; and no fool either—had Ivan seen his series on Pakistan? They discussed Gabriel, his first wife, Phillippa (now an Orange Person, according to Ivan), his second wife, Jessica, his affair with his secretary. A bit of a falling off there, they concluded. They moved on to Anthony Keating (too mad for me, said Liz, picking at her *salade tiède*, admiring the dull green-red tints of the fashionable leaves—by which she meant that she liked Anthony Keating and did not wish to discuss him with Ivan). Humphrey Potter, then? Or Jules Griffin? No? Liz smiled appreciatively. What about Otto Werner? But Otto Werner, Liz said, has a *wife*. Whatever do you mean by that? asked Ivan. He has a proper *wife*, repeated Liz, forbiddingly, reprovingly. But surely, Ivan insisted, there must be somebody. No, said Liz. Nobody at all. I have lost all interest, said Liz, in the pleasures of the flesh. She sipped the white burgundy, sampled the sweetbreads. They were excellent. Excellent, she nodded at Ivan, giving credit where it was due. How dull, said Ivan. No, it is peaceful, said Liz; and as she spoke, suddenly recalled that she had that morning received from Stephen Cox a copy of an article he had mentioned to her that evening, some weeks ago, at Alix's, and with it a note saying that he had wanted to telephone her but dared not as she was always so busy. Could she let him know if she would like to go out to dinner some time, and talk about Japan? He had promised her contacts in Japan.

She did not mention Stephen Cox to Ivan, but attempted to change the subject by mentioning Japan. Ivan was not interested in Japan, as he had never been there. He was interested only in Home Affairs. He quickly manoeuvred the conversation back to the domestic front: how was Charles, how did she, Liz, get on with Henrietta, when was the marriage to be, had Liz ever met Peter Latchett? Liz latched on to Peter Latchett, a relatively harmless topic: no, she had not met him, what was he like? Ivan offered a thumbnail sketch. Bad blood, the Latchetts: drinking, gambling, feckless. Not that Henrietta's blood was that much better; lucky she was too old to have children, or poor Charles might find himself saddled with a few little delinquents. Had she not heard of the skeletons in Henrietta's cupboard? Had she never heard the story of the old marquess, the grandfather? Ivan rattled on, assured of his audience. Madness, violence, crime—as in all the best family trees. There was even a candidate for the role of Jack the Ripper. But if you look at any family, Liz mildly protested, you find the same horrors. Not in your family or mine, my dear, said Ivan, pouring her another glass of wine, ignoring her feeble gesture of protest; good middle-class stock, we are, not interbred degenerates. Look at your wonderful children, said Ivan.

But Ivan's mind was wandering again—he was not interested in Liz's wonderful children, they were not newsworthy, they were ordinary, hard-working, sober young people—and he bounced back again after the briefest courtesy discussion of them to the topic that had been fascinating the whole of London, smart and un-smart, lunching and non-lunching: the new horror committed by the Horror of Harrow Road, who had claimed another victim. Everybody claimed to be horrified, everybody was delighted: except, presumably, the victim herself, who had been found, said Ivan (wiping his lips delicately on the dark pink napkin), sitting in a waste lot in the driver's seat of a wheel-less Notting Hill Carnival float, headless, neatly wearing a safety belt with her head by her side on the passenger's seat. Ivan recounted to Liz more details, which the press had not thought fit to release. She accused him of making them up. He bridled, and swore that he had not, and she had to admit that they were convincingly circumstantial: so either they are true, Ivan, she said, genially, or you must be the Horror of Harrow Road yourself, in fact or in imagination. She called for coffee, and said she must be on her way.

Ivan would not relinquish the Horror so readily. He wanted (perhaps genuinely?) to know her views: were the attacks racist as well as sexist, was it an accident that most of the victims had been black, what was the significance, psychologically, of the severed-head motif, was the attacker mad, and what did Liz mean by mad? Liz responded at first vaguely by saying that perhaps after all Esther Breuer ought to give up walking along the Harrow Road by herself late at night, but then attached herself more generously to the subject of madness and psychopathology in general and to the history of the McNaghten Rules in particular. Liz and her ex-husband, Edgar Lintot, share the view, as Liz now explained to Ivan, that not much is gained by the use of the word mad to describe deviations from the norm as wide as that of Virginia Woolf, her unfortunate cousin F. K. Stephen (also, oddly, a candidate for the role of Jack the Ripper), and the supposed Horror of Harrow Road, but that does not mean that the rejection of the term implies that the Jack the Rippers of this world are not suffering from diminished responsibility by reason of insanity: insane they are, responsible they are not, and let us forget the emotive word madness in this context. But, argued Ivan, did that mean that she and Edgar thought *all* murderers were insane and of diminished responsibility? Liz prevaricated slightly, for in fact she and Edgar are, in a sense, of this opinion, but in a sense that would need careful presentation to a layman, and she did not wish to see herself quoted in the press on the topic: but Ivan, to do him justice where one could, was not a man for hanging and flogging, for interminable prison sentences and short sharp shocks, and the severed-head business had suggested to him as strongly as it had to Liz and Edgar that the Horror of Harrow Road was probably not quite in his right mind. "Not that that makes it any nicer for the corpse," said Ivan, as Liz glanced again, this time ostentatiously, at her watch. "Ivan, I must go," she said. "I've got a consultation at three-thirty, and I can't be late." He rose to his feet, escorted her to the door, saw her onto the shabby, sunlit, sex-postered street. "It's been a delight to see you, Liz," he said, "as ever"—taking her hand, squeezing it, reaching up slightly to kiss her cheek—"it's a pity we didn't have more time, I wanted to ask you where you're going to live when you've got rid of that great gloomy house of yours. Such a dark, depressing, lumpen-bourgeois street, I've always thought, haven't you? You must be so glad to be able to get away at last—do keep in touch, let me know what's happening, won't you? You know I like to be in the know." And she walked briskly off, blinking, in the bright light, furious, amused, outraged: his timing, one had to admit, was inspired.

Esther Breuer stared meditatively at a postcard from the National Portrait Gallery, portraying the diarist John Evelyn with his long thin white hand resting elegantly, caressingly, upon a yellow-brown skull. She was in the process of composing a palindromic message to send to Claudio, who was attending a conference in Grenoble. Esther highly prized the art of the postcard, the new epistolary genre of the twentieth century, and had a fine collection of items, many of them from Claudio himself, who could pun in several languages, not all of them decipherable by Esther.

Esther was feeling unaccountably depressed. She had been haunted all day by an appalling dream, a dream so bad that she thought she might ring Liz up that evening and tell her about it. She thought it was indirectly connected with Crivelli and John the Baptist: in her pursuit of materials related to the possible Crivelli panel (which she was inclined to consider authentic) she had had cause to look through various collections of portrayals of John the Baptist— preaching, baptizing, denouncing, and headless. One severed head led to another, and she had spent hours musing over Judith and Holofernes, over Perseus and Medusa, over David and Goliath, over Caravaggio and Artemisia Gentileschi and Giordano. So it was not perhaps surprising that she had dreamed that she was walking along the canal bank where it passed under Ladbroke Grove, at the Harrow Road end of the canal—a walk she often took, particularly at this pleasant time of year—and there had seen, on the towpath, a severed head. It had spoken to her. It had asked her, civilly, menacingly, obsequiously, imperiously—oh, in an extraordinarily chilling, real, memorable mixture of tones—to take it up, to care for it. It was the head of a young man, a bearded young man, and it sat on the towpath on the dry flat yellowish severed stalk of its neck, and spoke. But I cannot, she had protested; then, feebly, apologizing, I would be afraid to hurt you. But the head would not relinquish her so easily. I will teach you, he had said, softly, reasonably, remorselessly. It is easy: I will teach you. Pick me up. I cannot, I cannot, you must understand, I am a little afraid, afraid of causing you pain, said Esther: terrified, unwilling to show her panic and fear and revulsion: and the head had raised itself on a bloody shoulder, a torn ragged bloody arm, and moved towards her, and in terror she had woken, shaking with fear, cold with sweat, her own arm (caught at a strange angle under her pillow) prickling and tense. Well, she had calmed herself: well. Too many John the Baptists on platters, too many horror comics of the seicento and the settecento. Pins and needles in her arm, and perhaps half a vague memory of that legless man who sat begging at the door of the Girolamini in Naples, who sold her a postcard of Reni's Baptist? That implausible trunk of a man, grinning in his wheelchair? But the dream would not go away with reason; it haunted, it spoke, it opened its lips at her. And she began to connect it with Claudio: reluctantly, reluctantly. Esther, it must be said, loved Claudio, and she knew that Claudio was a dead man. His Satanism, which she had once thought an elegant affectation, a literary joke, was, she had learned too late, a true sickness, a disease of the spirit. She never spoke of these things to anyone, ever, for she and Claudio had an understanding, of a dark, shared seclusion: an erotic, a satanic understanding. In her it was love, in him it was sickness. Or so she now thought. And this severed head that spoke to her from the pavement, saying pick me up, pick me up, care for me, was it not the sick, mad head of Claudio? She could not, she could not. She could not endure the physical intimacy, the daily intimacy, the perverted intimacy. She loved, but she could not save. How could he speak to her thus? She had strayed too far into darkness with Claudio. She longed for the voice of daylight, of reason, of the fresh air. And why now, why this dream now? Was it because of Claudio's sister Elena, who had said to Esther, suddenly, in the daylight of the bright Bolognese morning, over coffee and bread and butter: Esther, I am worried about Claudio, I am a little worried about Claudio, I am so glad to have met you at last, to know that you are there . . . and her dark eyes had fixed themselves upon Esther's, wide with appeal. And Esther had known herself helpless. She had dropped her eyes, had looked down at the innocent crumbs on her green and gold rimmed plate.

Why should she collude with Claudio, why should she send him a skull and a palindrome? She looked down now at poor long-dead John Evelyn. Because it is too late, that is why. Too late, too late, too late. She had colluded for too long, she had entered his dusty, airless, candlelit world forever. She loved him. She loves him.

But in the evening, she rang Liz. They chatted for a while, Liz confessing, guiltily, to her lunch with Ivan, Esther proffering some misleading rigmarole about her potted palm and its response to Greengro Crystals; and then Esther said, "I had this dream, last night, about a severed head."

"Well," said Liz, to Esther's astonishment, "I'm not at all surprised. And I hope that that teaches you not to walk alone so late in such insalubrious districts. It is 1980, you know."

"What *do* you mean?" asked Esther.

"Well, you know, severed heads are quite topical," said Liz, thinking that Esther was merely being evasive again, "not to say topographical, from your point of view."

"What *do* you mean?" repeated Esther, without any evasiveness at all, with a directness that Liz had not heard from her for some time. And thus Liz was obliged to recount to Esther the story of the Horror of Harrow Road, a story which in Liz's view Esther knew quite well: indeed she was sure they had often discussed it. Esther was obliged to listen, apparently dumbfounded. "But you *must* have known," said Liz, again and again, at the end of Esther's rebuttal, "how can you *not* have known?"

"I don't read the popular press," said Esther.

"It was in *The Times*," said Liz.

"I don't read *The Times*," said Esther. "I don't read the newspaper at all. I listen to the radio. Selectively."

"Then you must," said Liz, "have glimpsed subliminally the headline of last night's *Standard*. On a placard. Under the arches, at Ladbroke Grove Station. Or at Latimer Road. On your way home from the Warburg, or the Courtauld, or the Feldmann, or wherever you spent your scholarly day . . ."

A small silence followed.

"And what did the *Standard* headline say?" asked Esther, cautiously.

"HARROW HORROR'S HEADLESS HOAX," said Liz, and was relieved to hear Esther laugh.

"I wonder if they consult Roget? Or is there a new headline

dictionary?'' asked Esther, reverting to the potted-palm tactic, which for once Liz was glad to hear: it seemed in this context a sign of normality. But Esther quickly lapsed into fact. "Did it really say that, or have you made it up?'' she fairly earnestly enquired.

"I *think* it said that. And if it didn't, I could certainly apply for a job on the *Standard*, don't you think?''

"I suppose I *may* have seen it. I don't remember seeing it, but I *may* have seen it.'' And, again cautiously, "And how long have these—these alleged decapitations been taking place?'' Her ignorance was, Liz could tell, unfeigned, and therefore Liz proceeded to enlighten her: recounting the gruesome story, or as much of it as she could recollect—the eight (or possibly nine?) victims over the past eighteen months, all in the Harrow Road area, all of them female, most of them black, and the last three ostentatiously decapitated. One found in the service lift of the Bellenden flats, one on the canal bank, one in Kensal Green Cemetery, one in a derelict house under the Motorway arch, one in a dumped car . . . a dismal catalogue, which Liz attempted to lighten in the telling for Esther's sake, but she could hear Esther's silence intensifying, and at the end of it Esther merely echoed, a little faintly, "One on the canal bank, you say? I often walk on the canal bank.''

"Well, for God's sake stop,'' said Liz. "I was telling Ivan only today at lunchtime that I'd tell you to stop. And warn that niece of yours, won't you?''

"Ursula's not here, she's gone to Ireland for her holidays. Term's just over.''

"Well, at least you don't have to worry about *her*. But, Esther, seriously, you're not seriously telling me that you didn't know all this? How can you *not* have done?''

"Easily, it seems,'' said Esther, who was wondering whether or not to tell Liz more of her dream, or whether it would somehow be bad luck to evoke it now. "We don't talk about that kind of thing in art history. Well, I suppose I knew there'd been some murders, but there are always murders, aren't there? I've never found such things very interesting. I never read about them.''

"Well, you're quite right, of course, but perhaps you've been a bit *too* right this time. Your dream was a subconscious warning, a subliminal warning.''

"Do you think so?'' Esther decided to divulge details, after all, but without mentioning the Claudio element of her own interpretation. Liz in turn was satisfactorily astonished. "On the towpath?" she repeated. "On the canal bank?" Liz couldn't remember whether the towpath victim had been a headless one or not: but anyway, Esther pointed out, her severed head had been the head of a bearded young man. John the Baptist, in fact. "Well, I think that's very very *interesting*," said Liz, several times over, with much emphasis. Esther was quite cheered by her enthusiastic response. They fixed a date for supper the following week and Esther agreed to try to get hold of Alix to join them at Liz's. "And by the way," said Liz, casually, "I've decided that perhaps it would be best if Charles and I sold the house. So you can come armed with your recommendations. Of desirable residences off the Harrow Road."

And they both laughed, reassured.

Alix Bowen was out when Esther rang her to invite her to Liz's for supper. It was Alix's Garfield night, as Brian politely reminded Esther. Brian found it slightly puzzling that Esther and Liz seemed quite incapable of remembering which night— which more or less regular, weekly night—Alix worked at Garfield, but it did not seem to puzzle either of them or to offend Alix, so he supposed it was none of his business. He said he would pass the message on, exchanged a little mild gossip, and returned to marking a pile of essays on *Hard Times*, his mind wandering from the texts before him to the hard times of Northam in 1980, and the hard line being taken by British Steel Corp. and the unions. He supposed he was well out of it, but it was uncomfortable, sitting on the sidelines while other men marched and picketed. His friend Otto Werner now tended to blame the unions, for intransigence, for unrealistic demands, for failing to understand the true and inevitable economic shift away from the manufacturing industries, for exacerbating the conflict, but Brian argued that Otto himself failed to understand the government's intentions, which were neither realistic nor benevolent; they want conflict as much as the unions, he would argue. It was a stalemate argument. Brian had himself had an unpleasant confrontation that morning with the boss of his own college, who had summoned Brian to his office to report that next term Brian would be required to teach an extra hour on a Thursday evening, a request (demand?) that Brian would find inconvenient to meet, as Thursdays were Alix's Garfield days, his baby-sitting-with-Sam days. You can cancel your lunchtime class on Wednesday, Dr. Streeter had offered. Brian had explained that that was not the point, he didn't mind the extra hour, it was the timing of it that was tricky. He said he would go away and think about it. But he feared he would give in. He was too affable, was Brian. He needed a firm negotiator to stand up for his rights. He sighed, and returned his attention to the world of Gradgrind and Bounderby. What a crude job Dickens had made of Stephen Blackpool, his student Rosemary Lawson was claiming: the blameless, gullible, implausible artisan. Brian nodded, as he read her argument, and placed a red tick of approval in the margin, not noticing that the argument she had reproduced (though with subtly different illustrations) was his own.

Alix, in Garfield, was teaching a couple of poems by Blake, worrying about what would happen when Brian (inevitably) capitulated and agreed to teach on Thursday evenings (when would Sam be old enough to sit on his own? thirteen? fourteen?), reminding herself that she must send her ex-mother-in-law, Deborah, a birthday card, and trying to keep her students off the subject of the new Harrow Road murder. It was a bad evening, and everyone was in a bad temper. It had begun badly, with a long, unprovoked, abusive, psychotic diatribe from Sandra Parker about conditions in Holloway, where she'd been (she alleged) locked into a cell for hours on end, for weeks on end, without a word of explanation, with no plug for the washbowl, with bugs in the mattress and vomit on the blankets, drugged up to the eyeballs with Valium: "I'd be there now," said Sandra, staring angrily from her square, scrubbed, plain red face, "if I hadn't gone on hunger strike and tried to kill myself, that put the wind up them, that did, and I complained to my solicitor, I wrote a letter to my solicitor, but they wouldn't post it, they wouldn't let me communicate with my solicitor, it's an offence, that's what I told them, not to post that letter to my solicitor . . ." On and on she went: this is meant to be an English class, Alix repeated, patiently, mildly, until Sandra wore herself out into mumbling: dangerous to interrupt Sandra too abruptly, she was only just on the borders of reasonable behaviour at the best of times, it was good to let her rage a little; but it annoyed the others, who were getting restless, whispering, yawning, on the verge of revolt. With a sudden, well-timed flourish, Alix rose from her chair and distributed her Xerox copies of "A Poison Tree" and "The Clod and the Pebble," and called on Toni Hutchinson to read the first aloud. They listened: Blake was at least a change from Sandra Parker.

> I was angry with my friend:
> I told my wrath, my wrath did end.
> I was angry with my foe:
> I told it not, my wrath did grow.
>
> And I water'd it in fears,
> Night and morning with my tears;
> And I sunned it with smiles,
> And with soft deceitful wiles.
>
> And it grew both day and night,
> Till it bore an apple bright . . .

Alix had found Blake, on many previous occasions, a useful poet for generating exchange of ideas, for getting people harmlessly to tell a little wrath; she wondered whether or not to point out the connection between Sandra's outburst and the poem they were reading, whether they would discover it for themselves, whether it would be dangerous to stir up Sandra again. Sandra had lapsed into a sullen, heaving silence: her lips moved in private invective. Alix asked the class what they thought the apple was. Nobody answered. She asked Miriam Jarry to read "The Clod and the Pebble": "Love seeketh only self to please, To bind another to its delight"—and asked them what they thought of that. Did it mean the same as the other poem? What was the clod, what was the pebble, did it matter? Were both views of love right, or only one? Stubbornly, cloddishly, they sat silent, punishing her, punishing Sandra, punishing one another. Frustrated, impatient, Alix asked Sandra if she thought there was any connection between what Blake was saying about anger and her own feelings about describing the way she'd been treated in Holloway? Sandra was miles away, locked in her inner prison, munching and mumbling over the angry apple of discord, she was not listening, but newcomer Marilyn spoke up: "Yes," she said, "but the poem says it all a damn sight quicker, don't it? It don't go on and on, do it? That Sandra, she never stops, all night long, on and on and on, she's a real pain, they ought to give her something . . ." And Alix, jumping on to this small raft, managed to steer towards five quiet minutes of sensible discussion about diction, about short words and long words, about words that they themselves might call poetic and words they wouldn't expect to find in a poem. But the atmosphere was too bad for this happy calm to prevail: the conversation was rapidly transformed into an exchange of bad language and unmentionable phrases (Alix valiantly attempting to fish from her memory soothing examples of poetic usage of four-letter words, and coming up with Philip Larkin's classic "They fuck you up, your Mum and Dad," which gave momentary respite), and then plunged, inevitably, inexorably, as she had always feared it must, into the subject of the latest Harrow Road murder, brought in rather ingeniously by Jilly Fox, who wanted to know whether it was Blake who had said that it was better to murder an infant in its cradle than to nurse unsatisfied desires, and if so, whether Blake would have thought that this also applied to the perverted desires of the Harrow Road murderer? Alix, while admiring the intellectual sophistication of this intervention, could have kicked Jilly, for there in that very class there was, as Jilly quite well knew, a mother who had murdered her own not-quite-infant toddler, a woman deeply unpopular with the rest of the class. Luckily nobody seemed to make any connection (odd how some of them never suspected poetry could mean anything about anything real, and just as well in this context), but the subject of murder proved, as Jilly had quite well known it would, irresistible, and it put paid to any serious literary discussion for the rest of the evening. Anxieties broke forth, great flares of passion exploded, insults were exchanged, horror stories were narrated, appalling prejudices aired. Violence filled the air: anti-man, anti-woman, anti-prostitute, anti-police, anti-press, and, most dangerously, anti-black violence. What would Blake indeed have said of this unleashing? Taunts of voodoo, of savagery, were hurled, contemptibly, at the class's two black members, Miriam and Tessa: at Miriam because she alleged that the killer was obviously a mad white racist, at Tessa because she dared say nothing at all. Hubbub reigned, as Miriam sat in her corner yelling, "Pigs! Pigs! Stinking fucking stupid ignorant pigs!" in a loud, persistent monotone, as Tessa cowered and clutched at her crumpled Xerox, as Sandra Parker in her private nightmare began to sob, as an unidentified voice cried, "You should hear her, all night long she's at it, all fucking night long—"

"Oh, for God's sake, shut *up*," shouted Alix, above the noise, angrily banging on her desk with her fist, "shut *up*, or I'll go and get Dr. Glover—"; a fairly empty threat, by this stage, but luckily they seemed to have shouted themselves out, their wrath began to subside, the tide of fury ebbed. "Sandra," said Alix, "you'd better go to the cloakroom and get yourself a drink of water. Tessa, could you help Sandra?"—and the storm was over. Only five minutes to go, to the end of the so-called class. Alix gazed at her students, as they sat slumped in their chairs. She read them "Tiger! Tiger!" to fill in the time. She could see that Jilly Fox had buried her head in her hands, that Toni Hutchinson of the blonde braids was whispering ostentatiously, intimately, to newcomer Marilyn. Schoolgirl passions? Well, not really. Jilly Fox looked up at the end of the poem, and wearily, mockingly, like a schoolgirl, raised her hand. "Yes, Jilly?" said Alix, forbiddingly, coolly. "Why do you only read us the songs of experience?" said Jilly. "Why don't you try us with the songs of innocence?"

"Because they are too subtle for you," said Alix, tartly, after giving the matter a little thought. Jilly smiled, sourly. The hour was over. Alix collected her papers, shut her books, stacked her briefcase. Jilly was waiting for her, at the door. "What do you mean, too subtle?" she asked, as Alix set off down the corridor. "Oh, I don't mean anything," said Alix. "I was just trying to think of something to say that would shut you up. You shouldn't come to that class, you know, Jilly, it's far too elementary for you. It's not fair on the others. It's not fair on me. You should be getting on with the Open University stuff."

"I like your class," said Jilly, stubbornly.

"Well, try to keep the temperature down next week, or I'll make you all read *Cranford*. Or do punctuation exercises."

Jilly laughed. She padded along the corridor by Alix's side.

"Alix," she said, as Alix reached the Pass Door, and paused, key in hand.

"Yes?"

"I'm going to murder Toni Hutchinson. I'm going to cut off her head with an electric carving knife."

"Oh, Jilly, Jilly," said Alix, helplessly. Moved, helpless. She put her hand on Jilly's arm. They stood there, immobile, for a moment or two. Jilly shrugged her thin shoulders, twitched at her long cardigan, stared crossly back at Alix.

"Alix," said Jilly. "Do you ever ask yourself about yourself? And why you come here?"

"Of course," said Alix.

"And what's the answer?"

"I don't know. It's not what you think, I don't think." She hesitated. "I think it's because I feel—at home, here. After all, I was brought up in an institution."

Jilly gestured, hopelessly. "I don't like institutions," she said. "And I haven't got an electric carving knife. And if I had, I bet it wouldn't go through that thick neck."

"Each man kills the thing he loves," said Alix. " 'The Ballad of Reading Gaol.' "

"A quotation for every occasion," said Jilly.

"Well, that's my job," said Alix. "I spent three whole years studying English literature, so it's a good thing something stuck. Jilly, I've got to go, let me go."

Jilly stood aside. "Sorry," she said ironically, without apology.

"I'll see you next week," said Alix.

"Yes, oh, yes," said Jilly. "You'll see me next week. I'll be here." And she stood and watched, mockingly, accusingly, appreciatively, as Alix let herself out and relocked the door from the other side.

Alix, walking to the car, getting in the car, driving home through the light summer evening, down the pink ornamental cherry avenues of suburban respectability, worried, pointlessly, pointlessly, about Jilly, about her own intimacy with Jilly, about her own slightly dangerous, slightly irregular sympathy with Jilly: based on what? On (well, perhaps) a shared class background? Middle-class girls, from nice middle-class homes: innocence and experience. Jilly Fox, teacher's pet. Was it wrong, was it unprofessional, to speak subversively in a corridor to Jilly Fox? Jilly Fox had said, one evening in class, that she loved crime. Just like that, she had said it. Normal life doesn't attract me, said Jilly. It's dull. Alix had shut her up quickly (they were not meant to discuss such matters), had reprimanded her later in private, had told her she was irresponsible, intelligent enough to know better, that she would be expelled from the group if she didn't observe the rules; and Jilly had stared at Alix with a sultry, intimate colluding intensity. Alix understood Jilly. She understood what it was that Jilly found dull. Bourgeois life. Dull, dull, dull. Jilly had broken out of it by violence, by crime, by extremity;

she had by a short cut, by a short circuit, attempted thus to join the human race. She had found herself a new society in which (as she had just very aptly pointed out) Alix had chosen to join her, of her own free will.

Jilly's father was a prosperous solicitor. Jilly hated him, and when Alix would permit her, would speak of him with extreme rancour: prim, priggish, pompous, snobbish, tedious, hypocritical, devious, sexually abnormal or subnormal—an impossible man. I have made him suffer, Jilly would say, with bitter satisfaction. I have got through to him, I have made him pay.

Yes, Alix could understand this. She knew that Jilly knew she understood, and that somewhere here, for some reason she could not understand, danger lay.

"Esther?"

"Alix?"

"Hello, how *are* you?"

"Fine, and *you*?"

"Fine. I'm seeing you at Liz's, tomorrow, is that right?"

"Well, yes, but that's why I am ringing. Liz asked me to ring to warn you."

"To warn me?"

"Well, sort of to warn you, though she did say that she didn't quite mean it like that . . . but she thought you ought to know that she's got her sister Shirley staying with her. She didn't want just to spring Shirley on you. She couldn't remember whether you'd ever met Shirley."

"Have you met Shirley?"

"Oh, yes, I've met Shirley."

"And have I?"

"I don't know. How would I know?"

"I don't *think* I have. I don't seem to recall her. What's she like?"

"Oh, sort of—well, I don't know really. She's not much like Liz. Well, she's quite like Liz, in *some* ways."

"That's *very* helpful."

"Anyway, you'll see for yourself. Tomorrow."

"Why is she staying with Liz?"

"Because she invited herself, I gather. Liz didn't seem best pleased but she said it was such an unusual occurrence that she had to go along with it. Apparently she's been ill, in hospital, or something. She's come to convalesce."

"To convalesce? At *Liz's*?"

"Well, to perk herself up, or something." A pause. "Brian knows her. Brian knows her husband. Brian says she's very nice."

"Brian says everyone is very nice." Another pause, as Alix relays this comment to Brian. Alix says: "Brian says to say that he doesn't think Dr. Streeter is very nice. Or Mrs. Thatcher. Or Mr. McGregor."

"Of those, I only count Dr. Streeter," says Esther. "Brian doesn't *know* Mrs. Thatcher and Mr. McGregor. He might quite well decide he liked them if he did."

Another pause. "Brian says, fair enough, but unlikely," says Alix.

"Well," says Esther, "I shall look forward to meeting Shirley. What does she do?"

"I don't think she does anything," says Alix. "She's a housewife, mother of two. Or is it three?"

"I see," says Esther.

"I say, Est, did you know that Liz and Charles are actually going to sell that house? I thought she was set against it, but she's changed her mind. She suddenly seems to have decided it's a gloomy monstrosity. Isn't that odd?"

"Well, it is a *bit* gloomy," says Esther, carefully.

"Good God," says Alix, dumbfounded. "What *do* you mean? Explain, explain."

Shirley sat back in the pale-yellow armchair and watched Liz, Alix, and Esther. A summer evening light fell slanting on the polished inlaid coffee table, lending it a strange, watery, reflective sheen: a gold-sprigged white cup swam prettily on the veined wood, next to a posy of daisies in a tiny cut-glass vase. Liz, Esther, and Alix were talking, with much animation and many an apparent non sequitur, about London districts, property prices, houses, the police, no-go areas, rape, violence, murder, robbery, Tennyson and Arthur Hallam, Leslie Stephen and Virginia Woolf. Shirley listened. There was, perhaps, a thread linking this rambling, discursive, allusive, exclusive, jumbled topographical discourse: the sale of the Harley Street house itself, in which they were now sitting. Shirley had little to contribute to this discussion, so sat quietly, observing; it was obvious to her that the house should be sold, but then, people do not always, even often, obey the obvious, and she could tell that both Alix and Esther were a little surprised by the turn of events.

She had in fact met Esther before, more than once, though she could see that Esther had forgotten their meetings. She remembered Esther quite well, as Esther was visually rather memorable, rather distinctive, and had not changed much over the years. There she still was, small, neat, olive-skinned, with her hair cut short and dark and straight like a Chinese doll; still neatly dressed, this evening, in a timeless smart fashionless combination of dark green velvet trousers with a pale duck-egg blue shirt: tidy, neat, ageless, contained—with perhaps just the slightest hint of a wizening, of a wrinkling, of a preservation to come? But really, remarkably little changed from the undergraduate Shirley had first glimpsed over twenty years ago in Cambridge, from the graduate she had once secretly heard lecture at the National Gallery, from the Esther to whom she had spoken at some length some five or six years ago, at one of Liz's boys' birthday parties. She was not surprised that Esther had forgotten these encounters.

Alix, in contrast, had remembered Shirley well. In Shirley's eyes, Alix had changed more than Esther: her brown hair was fuzzily streaked with grey, she now wore glasses (which she would impatiently remove from time to time to peer fiercely from face to face, as though indignantly unable to believe that she could not see properly without them), she was dressed more stylishly (if more ethnically) to Shirley's eye than she had been in the old days, and looked somehow more adult, more imposing than Shirley had ever thought she would; though as relentlessly pleasant as ever, her docility, her air of anxious humility, had vanished. And Liz—well, there was Liz, also looking older, a little stouter, more solid in her chair, her face fuller, her neck fuller, her voice as loud, her opinions forceful as ever, her hair dyed? highlighted? And looking, Shirley thought, not quite well, transitional somehow, as though she hadn't decided quite what to look like for the next ten years, the next twenty years? Though it was Shirley herself who was in theory not well, Shirley who was here in London to recover from a D and C, the necessity for the D and C caused (according to the gynaecologist at the Royal Infirmary) by spending too many years on the pill. Sterilize me, then, Shirley had demanded, and the gynaecologist had done so, and now Shirley was, in theory, recovering from this shock to her emotional and reproductive system. Though in fact she was not here for anything of the sort: she was here to force Liz to confront the problem of their mother. And knew, already, after five days in London, after a couple of suppers, after a night at a Tom Stoppard play, after an exhibition at the Royal Academy, after walking in the early evening with Liz beneath the deep, honey-scented red of the horse chestnuts in Regent's Park, that she had failed. Liz had refused to listen, had stolidly, solidly, professionally, refused to allow the subject to be raised. Liz would do nothing, nothing at all. Looking at her, as she sat there in her own elegant drawing room, in her rather less than elegant Indian wrap-round skirt and cotton slogan-printed T-shirt (had Liz started to dress a little oddly, with the years?), Shirley thought: my God, she's beginning to *look* like our mother. God help her, that's what she's beginning to look like.

Shirley, Alix noted, was extremely well dressed. She was thin, pale, carefully made-up, and very smart. Her maroon shoes matched her maroon handbag. Her suit was well tailored, fashionable, of the year. Her silk shirt was tied at the throat with one of those complicated bows that Alix instantly noted as a tribute to high chic and considerable manual dexterity: she had once made the mistake of purchasing a shirt with a similar kind of adornment at the neck, and had never managed to make it look like anything but a ragged, bunched, shapeless mess. In fact, Alix had noted, peering closely, putting on her glasses to peer more closely, the detail of Shirley's outfit was remarkable: the buttons and button holes, the handkerchief in the pocket, the well-chosen costume jewellery (well, Alix supposed that that was costume jewellery, for if it wasn't, what was?—she'd never been quite clear), the beautiful little golden cuff-links protruding from the shirt cuffs. Elegant, that's what Shirley was: this was no doubt her going-away outfit, her newly purchased-for-London outfit, Alix recognized that, but nevertheless to Alix it bespoke a habitual confidence, a knowingness, a town-smartness. Alix knew she wouldn't know how to look like that if she tried, couldn't look like that even if dressed in the same (or similar) garments; it wasn't in her range. The cuffs and cuff-links particularly astonished her: so clean, so impractical! At home, Alix seemed to have to roll up her sleeves every five minutes, and even here, at Liz's, where the

washing up went in the dishwasher, she noted that she had
rolled back the full sleeves of her monsoon shirt in a business-
like manner, in order not to trail them in her dinner, in order to
be at the ready for any domestic emergency that might arise.

And Alix had forgotten that Shirley was so handsome: her
post-operation pallor, lightly heightened with rouge, became
her, and she had kept her figure well. She wondered about Cliff
Harper's business: presumably he was making a fortune? She
could never remember what it was his firm made. Shirley
didn't look happy, but unhappiness suited her. Happiness is
turning me into a slob, thought Alix, idly: then dismissed the
thought, an ill-luck thought, and returned her attention to Liz
and Esther on the subject of St. John's Wood. Liz rather
favoured St. John's Wood, and was describing the house of her
own analyst of bygone years: a very secret, secluded town
house, almost a Chekhovian house, with a garden with
benches, and high dark green painted wooden fences round it,
and large trees, and shutters—rather like a house in a painting
but I'm not sure what painting, a psychiatric sort of painting,
or is that just association? Munch? suggested Esther. It was a
good house, said Liz. Why not buy it? said Alix. It's not for
sale, said Liz. It might be, if you made an offer, said Alix.
How odd that would be; it would be sinister, surely, to live in
one's ex-analyst's house? said Liz. It is a house with secrets,
but good secrets, said Liz. She seemed quite pleased by the
idea of looking for a new house. That St. John's Wood garden
looks as though it ought to have owls, said Liz. Do you
remember the Cambridge owls?

And suddenly, belatedly, as they launched into Cambridge
memories, they realized how rude they were being to Shirley.
Just as suddenly, they recovered themselves, in a collective
leap: suddenly they began to discuss summer holidays—a
universal, a banal, a relatively safe topic: Shirley spoke of
plans to go to Spain, Alix and Brian were borrowing a cottage
in Dovedale, Esther was torn between Somerset and Tuscany,
Liz said she didn't know what she was doing because she
didn't know how many if any of the young people wanted to do
anything—but that she herself rather fancied France, if any of
them would come with her. And on they comfortably rambled,
exchanging anecdotes of past holiday joys and disasters, until
Esther and Alix said they had to go. Alix insisted on driving
Esther home: no more walking late at night until they catch the
Horror, she and Liz reiterated. All right, all right, said Esther:

who had noted on several occasions that the more she protested her love of walking, the more paradoxically certain she was of securing a lift to her own front door.

Liz hoped that at this juncture Shirley would go to bed. But Shirley was still there, when she returned from the front door, still sitting almost attentively in her large armchair. Unavoidable. Liz yawned, suggestively. The London version of Shirley looked very odd, in Liz's view: why ever was she wearing that department store suit and that strange shirt with a watch-strap pattern, and a big bow? It was hardly appropriate for an evening with old friends, thought Liz. Was she wearing it to keep her distance, to mark herself off? And if so, why? Liz yawned again. She noted that Shirley was wearing, as well as several chunky cheap gold necklaces, the thin silver locket, twin to her own, that was alleged to contain a photograph of their father. She wondered if she, like Liz herself, wore it most of the time. It was rather disquieting to see it there—like an echo, a commentary, a mocking reflection. Seeing Shirley here, like this, in such intimate estrangement, was unpleasant; Liz was not enjoying Shirley's visit, and was ashamed of herself for her lack of enjoyment, her lack of ease. She had no idea what Shirley thought about, these days, and she thought she did not want to know. The gulf between them had widened with the years: too late, now, to bother to try to cross it. But Shirley spoke.

"I forgot to speak to Alix about Brian's aunt," she said. Unaccountably.

"Brian's aunt?"

"Yes, Brian's aunt. Brian's mother's sister. Brian's aunt Yvonne. Dora's very worried about her."

"Who is Dora?"

"Dora's my sister-in-law. Steve's wife. Cliff's brother Steve's wife. She's Brian's aunt's niece. By marriage, that is. Not a proper niece."

"Good Lord. What a kinship network." Liz spoke without enthusiasm, warily, distrusting the conversation's tendency. "I always forget you're sort of related to Brian. It seems such an odd thing to have happened."

"It's not all *that* odd. It's us that's odd. Having no relations at all. Or none that we know of."

"Tell me about Brian's aunt," said Liz, quickly.

"Aunt Yvonne? Oh, it's just that she's in a bad way, and no one quite knows what to do about her. Or to be more honest what they can face doing about her. I meant just to mention it to Alix. Though I don't suppose there's anything Brian can do either.''

"What kind of bad way?"

"Old age. Ill health. The usual sort of thing." Shirley spoke flatly. "Bad feet, bad dentures, noises in her head, solitude. Going mad, if you ask me." More conversationally, Shirley continued, "As a matter of fact, it *is* rather awful, at Auntie Yvonne's. I've only been twice, and I was shocked. It's filthy. She never washes anything. Bedclothes, tea towels, her own clothes, it all stinks. And she took her shoes and stockings off to show me her feet, and I've never seen anything like it. You couldn't imagine. Terrible. Her toenails. Her corns.''

"Can't the social services help?"

"She doesn't get on with the social services. She's suspicious. She really wants to go and live with Dora, Dora says. But of course Dora can't have her.''

"And there's nobody else?"

"Not really. Well, there's Brian. And Alix.''

Silence fell. Liz felt her energy, her stone-walling intimacy-blocking energy flag: it was late and she was crumbling, and she knew that Shirley knew. It's not, thought Liz plaintively, as though I've led an idle life; I take on a lot, I work hard, I have to be up at seven in the morning, I cooked that supper she's just eaten. Self-pity filled Liz; she felt it seeping in; horrified, amused; people are dreadful, thought Liz (meaning herself), quite, quite dreadful. She was ashamed of herself; but determined not to relent.

"Luckily," said Shirley, in a clear, high voice, a public voice, a voice that betrayed, perhaps, a certain fear, "luckily, our mother seems not to want to live with anyone. She still maintains that she prefers to live alone. Not that I ever ask her. But she says it, just the same.''

"That's what she always said," said Liz.

"Maybe she means it," said Shirley.

"I'm sure she means it," said Liz, doubtfully.

The room was vibrant with conflict, with pain. Liz realized that she was cornered: there was, for once, no question she could ask, no direction she could give to the conversation, no guide, no lead, no hint. Anything she said could be used in evidence against her. She must wait on Shirley; Shirley had won.

"You haven't seen her, I think, for some time?" asked

Shirley, almost compassionately, as though regretful of the vulgarity of the query.

"Not for a year or two, I'm afraid," said Liz. Both knew, precisely, how long: three years it was, since Liz had been in Northam, three years and a month. "But I spoke to her last week," said Liz, bravely.

"Yes," said Shirley. "So she said."

Another long silence. Liz suffered. She felt wretched. She accepted Shirley's position. Of course it was wrong, it was unfair, it was a scandal—that Shirley should do all, she herself nothing: that Shirley should cook and run errands and suffer criticism while Liz remained the favourite, the exempt, the righteous. Anybody could see that it was unfair. Liz knew that her very posture conveyed guilt: she tried to straighten herself in her low chair.

"I don't know what's going to happen to her," said Shirley. "She can hardly get up the stairs by herself now, you know."

"No, I didn't know," whispered Liz, humbly. "She never mentions anything like that to me."

"She's got very heavy," said Shirley.

"*Heavy?*" asked Liz, in genuine surprise.

"She's put on a lot of weight in the last few years. You'd be amazed. You'd hardly know her if you saw her. That's partly what I wanted to ask you, you know, I mean, is it common, to put on weight like that, at her age? What can it mean?"

"Heavy?" repeated Liz, bewildered; noticing, however, that the balance had tipped slightly, that Shirley had had pity, had asked a question, had ceased, bleakly, to reproach. "Really heavy? She was always such a stick."

"Well, she's not now. She must weigh twelve stone. Not that one could ever get her near a pair of scales."

"*Twelve stone?*"

"I thought you'd be amazed. I thought I ought to tell you."

"Whatever can have caused it?"

"That's what I wanted to ask you." Shirley paused, dramatically, then pursued, "But in my view, it's eating."

Both sisters laughed.

"But you know what I mean," said Shirley. "*Why* is she eating?"

"Because you're feeding her?" suggested Liz, momentarily throwing away all sense of advantage, all battling for position, in a desire to pursue the truth, in curiosity for truth.

Shirley considered. "Yes," she agreed. "I'm feeding her,

and Meals On Wheels are feeding her. But *why is she eating what we give her?* It's odd, isn't it? After all those years of Complan and jelly cubes and Oxo?''

"A second childhood, perhaps," said Liz.

"It seems a bit like that, at times. She's like a great fat baby waiting for its next spoonful.''

"God," said Liz, "do you remember those dreadful dreadful suppers? Stale bread and fish paste. Do you remember?''

"Bread and dripping. Bread and marge. And do you remember that wonderful treat we used to make ourselves, of bread and marge and sugar and a bit of cocoa powder?''

"What do you feed her on now?''

"Chicken. Fish. Casserole. Shepherd's pie. Sometimes a chop. You know, proper meals. She's got quite fussy. Complains if it's not quite right. It *is* odd, isn't it? I thought old people ate less and less, not more and more?''

"Well, she's never been exactly normal, has she?'' Liz began to laugh, a little wildly, at her own understatement. "She's never been much of a guide to normal behaviour, has she? I suppose we should have expected some oddity like this, but I must say you've taken me by surprise. Twelve stone? I can hardly believe it. Does she still fit in her clothes?''

"Hardly. They're bulging. But she doesn't seem to notice, she just lets them gape, and puts on another layer.'' Shirley too began to laugh, also a little wildly. "She's an amazing sight, you ought to come up and have a look at her, just out of curiosity. A freak, that's what she is, a freak.'' Shirley hiccupped, and blew her nose on her immaculate handkerchief, and wiped away a tear.

"You know,'' said Liz, who had rallied, who had remembered, at last, the position that she believed herself to occupy, "there's no *need* for you to take her meals. There's no *need* for you to see her at all. You have a right to cut yourself off. She has no right to coerce you. You must do it only because *you choose* to do it. *If* you choose to do it.''

"It doesn't seem to be a question of rights any more,'' said Shirley. "It's just a question of what I do. I don't know why I do it. I know I don't have to, yet I do have to. I don't know how you manage to keep your distance. I feel sucked back into it, all the time.''

"It's because you live so near,'' said Liz. "You should have moved. It's not natural, to stay put. All one's life.''

"You say it's not natural,'' said Shirley, "but a lot of people think it *is* natural. Have you forgotten what people are like, in Northam? Probably you have. But believe me, it's normal to stay put, it's natural to stay put. It's you and Brian and Alix that are the exceptions, you know. And anyway, I *have* moved. From Abercorn Avenue to Greystone Edge. Upward social mobility, I think it's called."

"You're not telling me Abercorn Avenue is in *any way* normal," said Liz. "Or ever was. Well," she said, striking a more discursive tone, "no, perhaps that's not quite true, perhaps there was a very short patch of time, in the 1930s, when it was normal. When our mother behaved like other people and ate what other people ate and wore what other people wore and had chairs like other people's chairs and opinions like other people's opinions. I sometimes think that. But I don't know, I can't know, because I wasn't old enough to make comparisons. But since then—since 1939, anyway—it's been utterly utterly abnormal. Frozen. Fossilized. Stuck. Don't you think?"

"I don't know," said Shirley. "How would I know? I don't think about it, I just get on with it. And to tell you the truth, thinking of abnormality, I'm not *so* sure that our mother is all that much *more* abnormal than everyone else. You should meet Brian's Auntie Yvonne. She used to work on the trams. She's barmy. And Cliff's mother is pretty mad too, now I think about it. But I don't know why I'm telling you about it, you're meant to specialize in madness, aren't you? You see mad people all day long."

"Yes," said Liz, unthinkingly, incautiously, "but they're a different class of mad people." Luckily Alix Bowen was not there to pick her up on this, but Liz, who had been well trained by Alix, picked it up herself, in silence, and stored it away for future reference. Shirley did not notice the terminology, and returned, after another comment or two on the high proportion of elderly in Northam and the inevitably rising rates, to their mother's eating habits and growing weight problem, and to the even more unsavoury and perplexing matter of the way in which she now appeared to wish to discuss her own bowel movements and body fluids with Shirley in the most embarrassing and uncalled-for detail.

"I really do draw the line," said Shirley, "at having to gaze at her knickers: I mean, what next?" And indeed, indeed, what next. Liz, before they finally went off to bed, repeated her view that Shirley need not feel obligation, had brought the sense of obligation upon herself, and could chuck the whole business without a word of reproach from Liz at any moment: Shirley again pointed out that this was not practical advice, in the situation that in fact existed, and that while she, for her part, did not reproach Liz for keeping her distance, she did wish she would telephone her mother slightly more regularly, and would much appreciate it if Liz could find her way to finding her way up north to visit before too long.

"After all, you are a doctor," said Shirley, slightly aggressively, as they paused together on their way up the stairs, on the half-landing, beneath the portrait of the fake ancestor. "You ought to be able to make a professional diagnosis."

"It's notoriously difficult to diagnose illnesses within one's own family," said Liz, defensively, but promised, nevertheless, that sometime soon, when she had a free moment, she would make her way north and brave her mother, her gross mother, swelling and ageing in her traumatic den.

But it was three and a half years before Liz Headleand found a free moment to make her way to Northam. The time did not pass idly: she managed to visit, in these three and a half years, Japan, the Dordogne, New York, Brussels, Hull, Stuttgart, Inverness, and Newcastle-upon-Tyne, to name but a few of the places that solicited her presence or attracted her attention. All of them somewhat farther away than Northam, some of them considerably farther. She also, in these years, was party to the sale of the house in Harley Street, became the independent purchaser of a house in St. John's Wood, exchanged correspondence and had dinner several times with Stephen Cox, broke her ankle while sledging with her stepson Aaron on Parliament Hill, attended the wedding of Charles Headleand and Henrietta Latchett, gave up smoking, contributed a paper to a book on the extended family, resigned from one committee and joined another, lunched with Ivan Warner, took up smoking, spent a number of evenings with Esther and Alix, contributed to their old college's Building Fund by Deed of Covenant, was more than rationally pleased when her daughter Stella obtained a place to read Modern Languages at this college, wrote a letter to *The Times* (prompted by Alix) about conditions in the psychiatric wing of a well-known women's prison, and acquired, perhaps most improbably, a small tabby kitten, which was to prove a conversational rival to Esther's potted palm and which was, in Liz's view, much more fun.

The potted palm hung on, through these years. It did not look very well, but it hung on, turning crisply, fiercely beige at its sharp extremities, but preserving its deep green inner upward heart, its growing core.

These were the years of inner city riots, of race riots in Brixton and Toxteth, of rising unemployment and riotless gloom: these were the years of a small war in the Falklands (rather a lot of people dead), and of the Falklands Factor in politics: these were the years when a new political party boldly declared that it would attempt to find a way out of the impasse of class conflict: these were the years when strange, tattered, vulture-like grey and black false plastic creatures began to perch and cluster in the trees of Britain: these were the years when cast-away fast-food cartons of indeterminate texture and substance proliferated in the streets and front gardens and underpasses and hedgerows of Britain. Some began to claim that the toxic ingredients contained in the fast food were driving the nation mad: others blamed the consequent litter. A slightly more serious epidemic called AIDS gripped the nation with panic, paranoia, and *timor mortis*. Television, like grey vultures, fast food, and AIDS, also spread inexorably. A fourth television channel opened, with a powerful and eloquent drama bravely portraying Britain (at least in the recollection of some) as a mental hospital peopled by malevolent dwarves, ravening pigeons, shit-strewn corpses, geriatric patients, inadequate warders, and innocent lunatics. Television at breakfast time was launched, with a cast of frogs and rats and astrologers and acrobats and pretty, litigious, wide-eyed, bright-complexioned front women.

Alix Bowen has still not managed to see any television at breakfast time, ever, or so she says. She simply cannot believe that there is such a thing. Once, greatly daring, with a sense of cultural empires crashing, of millennial confrontation, she approached the television set in the front room while tidying away the glasses and coffee cups of the night before; 8:15 it was, by her watch and by the oven clock in the kitchen. Dared she push the button? Would she thereby have crossed a Rubicon? Would she slump, instantly gaga, and never get to work again? She pushed the button, and there, to her amazement, to her horror, bouncing about on a big comfy highly coloured settee, wearing a highly coloured, mother-knitted, robin-emblazoned pullover, was her irrepressible old friend from Cambridge, bald Pett Petrie, talking about birds; she only let him get out a couple of words—"Wimbledon Common" said Pett, harmlessly, as Alix switched him off—but it was too late, her innocence was destroyed, she had thenceforth to believe the implausible, to accept that all over Britain people were watching television at *eight-fifteen* a.m. and that people like Pett, normal, civilized, cultured, harmless people, were prepared to get up in the small hours to appear on it. When she recounted this alarming experiment to Liz, Liz responded with various anecdotes about Pett Petrie, and about a patient of hers who had done herself an injury trying to follow the *Janice Jackson Work-Out Seven A.M. Special*—and then suddenly went serious and said that the latest news from Charles was that he was thinking of giving up his New York post and setting up his own production company again, and what did that, could that, signify? Was he resigning, or was he being pushed? Would he come home and, if he did, what would that mean to Liz?

During these years, war continued to rage between Iraq and Iran, but the West did not pay much attention. (Kate Armstrong's one-time lodger, Mujid, was injured by a shell, but not seriously.) Every week seemed to carry a headline which read, "FIGHTING BREAKS OUT AGAIN IN BEIRUT." Famine swept the Sahel. Aeroplanes crashed from the skies. Superpowers smouldered. Soldiers in Afghanistan killed guerrillas in Afghanistan, and guerrillas in Afghanistan killed soldiers in Afghanistan. An ageing film star became President of the United States of America and his wife bought a lot of new clothes. The heir to the throne of England married a kindergarten assistant and she bought a lot of new clothes. Much attention was paid to these new clothes by the media of the Western World, to the derision, bewilderment, envy, curiosity, or ignorance of various non-Western nations. It was stated on a fairly level-headed BBC radio programme that the wife of the President of the United States "must be an important person, because she had her picture on the front cover of *Time* magazine."

Meanwhile, on the home front, the new political party, which is called the Social Democratic party, forged an alliance with the Liberal party and spent a great deal of time studying opinion polls. It also attracted the support of a good many of the characters in, and potential readers of, this novel, who had been alienated by the New Right but perhaps even more by the

New-Old Left. A plague on both your houses, they said, and tried to build their own, amidst the cries of hypocrisy and treachery that filled the democratically elected playground of the House of Commons, cries which now, perhaps unwisely, reached the ears of the listening electors through the medium of BBC radio.

Otto Werner, one-time tutor of Alan Headleand, and old friend of Brian Bowen, was a founder member of the new political party. Alan Headleand, who was still doing research and teaching in Manchester, was shocked by this declaration of intent on Otto's part, for was it not from Otto that he had imbibed much of his own left-of-centre political theory? But the shock was intellectual only, and proved in fact the source of much interesting political discussion. Otto sent Alan photocopies of articles from the *Economist*, the *Financial Times*, the *Alliance*, the *Social Democrat*: even, occasionally, from *The Times*. Alan retaliated with bits out of *New Society*, the *New Statesman*, the *New Socialist*, the *Aylesbury Anarchist*, and the neo-Cobbetian, reformist, anti-EEC, agricultural curiosity *Red Rag to a Bull*.

They both read the *Guardian*, so they didn't bother to plunder the *Guardian*.

They would decipher one another's scribbled notes, then get on the phone to one another for further elucidation: Otto went up to Manchester once or twice to lecture and sat up for hours in Alan's shabby flat; Alan in London had lunch with Otto once or twice at the LSE. They talked and talked. The debate consolidated their mutual respect. Alan continued to think Otto a traitor, but not, at least, a dishonest traitor, and anyway he pardoned him on grounds of age: Otto continued to think Alan a self-deceiver, but not, at least, a cynical or self-serving self-deceiver, and anyway he pardoned him on grounds of age.

With Brian Bowen, the difference of opinion was not so comfortable. Otto knew Brian too well to expect Brian to share his own modest hopes for the future and sensed that Brian would find Otto's commitment distressing. Otto therefore tried to keep away from the subject of politics when he met Brian, but of course it was impossible. Politics could not be avoided. Brian was, and for many years had been, a rather inert member of the Labour party; he would rouse himself at election time and do a little canvassing and fund-raising. Alix (whose parents, it was to be said, had, like Otto, joined the SDP) occupied a similar position, though more doubtfully. Brian was distressed by some of the vote-losing tactics of the militant left, but he thought the militant left was ideologically correct, and therefore he had to give it his support. Brian wanted to see socialism in his lifetime. So did Alix. So they said, and they thought they meant it. Otto's new discovery of the middle ground disturbed and distressed them both: it distressed them more than the unlovable excesses of the government, which were so easy to deplore. Nobody in their right mind, Brian, Alix, and Otto all agreed, could listen to the Prime Minister saying Rejoice over the death of hundreds without wincing, could hear a Secretary of State for Employment tell people to get on their bikes without groaning: yes, they were agreed on that. But when it came to the employment figures, to public spending, to the unions, to postal ballots, to the steel strike, to the decline of the manufacturing industries, to privatization, it was another matter.

Otto felt at a disadvantage when arguing with Brian. As Otto was far more interested in ideas than in personalities, in theory than in psychological history, in large thoughts than in local thoughts, he could not really place the reasons for his own sense of disadvantage, though they were obvious enough to Alix, as, from time to time, she witnessed or joined in their discussions over supper and a glass of wine. To Alix, it was clear that Otto felt uncomfortable in the face of Brian's firsthand (if outdated) knowledge of some of their subjects of debate. Otto's personal history was of rigorous, undiluted intellectual discipline: an academic from his school days on, he had never worked outside an institution, and was not entirely sure (as his wife, Caroline, remarked) of many of the common facts of daily life. Classically, he could hardly boil an egg, and frequently forgot where he had parked his car: he could rarely remember the age of his children, and was often to be observed wearing odd socks, a matter to which he attached little importance. There was something in Brian's easy handling of a carving knife that subdued Otto. Otto was keen on the new technology: he loved computer games, word processors, calculating machines. Brian, on the other hand, was not at ease with these things. The old order changeth, yielding place to new. Was Brian the old order? Did Otto feel *guilt*, as he discussed with Brian the closure of Brian's old firm, Pitts and Harley, with the loss of six hundred jobs? If he did, he felt it unknowingly, Alix suspected; but some unease there was between them.

And Alix, for her part, did not like to think of Brian as belonging to the old order. She preferred to think of him as a symbol of the new, the classless society of which she had dreamed. But was it so? Could it be so? Grey-haired, Brian was now, and suffering, in winter, from arthritis: too old for the new dawn. Was he not rather a refugee, an ageing refugee, escaped just in time from the crumbling streets of Northam? The Coalbright council estate, where Brian had spent his childhood, was in a sad way now: its inter-war-built, patterned ribbons of semis were shabby, its little front gardens a little neglected, its corner shops oddly forlorn in their attempts to turn themselves into MiniMarkets and Self-service Super-Savastores. Uncertain, old-fashioned, quietly decaying, like old Mrs. Orme, who had once been Brian's family's next-door neighbour: she still hung on there in her council house on the old estate, creaky, slow of step, too old now to bake the fairy cakes with which she had once treated Kathie, Brian, and Barbara (and now, alone, widowed, what, she asked herself and others, was the point of baking?), living, Brian and Alix suspected, on sliced white bread and bits of cheese and biscuits and fierce cups of tea. A relic of a bygone age, her house as clean as she could keep it, but she could not see very well or move very fast, and the cosiness that Brian remembered from childhood, would attempt to evoke in descriptions to Alix— sitting at her kitchen table, being allowed to play with the nest of painted eggs from the mantelpiece, helping to cut up bits of glacé cherry for the buns, buttering a pikelet, looking at a collection of Brooke Bond cards of Birds from Many Lands or Famous Aviators, admiring with reverence the matchstick models of a Mississippi paddle steamer and an old hay wain made by her grandfather, timing an egg with the hand-painted egg-timer with its softly running, everlastingly renewed sand— all this warmth, all this cosiness had faded, had dwindled into a lapsed evening melancholy, a cooling, an irreversible, dim decline. The sand had run low, and Mrs. Orme no longer had time for such amusements, now that all of time stretched before her. When they called on her for their yearly visit, Brian and Alix would take her pikelets from the market, and toast them, and butter them, and sit and listen to her reminiscences of the crowded past: of the Blitz; of Kathie ("eh, a lovely girl, your Kathie"); of her long-dead dog Lucky; of her nieces and nephews; of the pantomimes at the Lyceum; of the decline of fish and chips; of diphtheria epidemics; tedious, repetitive, mournful, nostalgic; occasionally spiteful as she remembered old grudges, more often sentimental: and Alix, bored despite herself, bored despite her good intentions, bored despite the fact that she listened to Mrs. Orme for only one afternoon a year, would watch Brian's face as he listened, intent, puzzled, courteous, responsive, and could see that he was trying to capture from Mrs. Orme the essence of the past, the distillation of childhood, the images of a way of life that was fading forever. Precious, priceless, a delicate, tenuous, flickering, fading coal. Brian would ask to look at the egg-timer, and Mrs. Orme would laugh as Brian turned it over in its little wooden stand: "I can't think why he sets such store by it," she would say to Alix, "I never use it now."

I never use it now. Other images floated back to Brian, were presented at times even a little desperately, for Mrs. Orme and Alix: a round wooden ball, a monkey on a stick. She didn't know where they'd gone, she hadn't seen them in donkey's years, she said; children didn't care for such things nowadays, they were all wanting computer games. Triumphantly, in the spring visit of 1982, she discovered in the back of a drawer of the sitting-room what-not the white wooden cotton reel on which Kathie had learned to do French knitting; it had four little tacks hammered into it, and a little tail of mysterious useless woven red wool tubing still projecting from its hollow middle . . . I used to think it magic, said Brian, gazing awestruck at this relic, but you wouldn't teach me how, you said boys didn't do knitting. I never, said Mrs. Orme, I never did, I'm sure of that. Oh yes you did, said Brian, and they quarrelled amiably. I must have been having you on, said Mrs. Orme. Milk bottle tops, round, perforated, waxy cardboard milk bottle tops had featured in other pursuits: Brian had helped to make woolly bobbles for baby Barbara's pram, unravelling the wool from moth-eaten old jerseys, rewinding it into crinkly, jimpy balls, threading it round and round the cardboard disk, then cutting the edges—and hey presto, a fluffy pompom, a many-coloured fluffy pompom.

The amusements of the poor. Matchsticks, cotton reels, milk bottle tops, cigarette cards, unravelled wool, patchwork, scrap rugs. A way of life, a culture. It did not immediately occur to Brian or even to Alix that these objects represented poverty, so rich were their associations, so common a bond had the war forged in their childhood between working and middle class— for Alix too had unwound jerseys, pegged rugs—but driving south one year, down the M1 in the middle lane at a steady soporific seventy in the early 1980s, with Sam asleep in the back, Alix, to keep Brian awake as he drove, entertained him with conversation about these objects, about the nature of toys and artifacts, about wood and plastic and Plasticine and Play-Doh: and as she spoke, she saw, perhaps for the first time, how pitifully sparse by modern standards had been Mrs. Orme's collection, how rich in its sparseness, how eloquent.

"Yes," said Brian, "I feel that if I stare at these things hard enough—I don't know, I feel that history will speak from its cradle and tell me where I came from. You know what I mean?" The Mississippi steamer, the hay wain, the eclecticism, the oddity, the eccentricity, the china horses with their real little brasses and their real carts with real bits of leather tack and bridle that stand in front-room windows up north, commemorating Arcadia in the industrial back street. A deep, deep yearning, up and down the ribboned semi-detached estates, up and down the older terraces, and surviving, who knows, on the lofty, unseen unvisited fourteenth-floor windowsill of the new, already derelict high-rise walkways in the sky. "Oh, yes," said Brian, as they spoke of these things, as they passed Watford Gap driving south to Wandsworth, "yes, that's my life, you know, that's the imagery of my life, I knew nothing other."

Sentimentality? To visit an old woman left largely friendless, to stare at rubbed knobs of wood looking for time past?

Otto Werner had never worshipped an old wooden cotton reel; he was not entranced by the past. He was a refugee. He believed in the future. He believed that the British Labour movement in general, the manufacturing north more specifically, and Brian Bowen his old friend in person were all in danger of worshipping an old wooden cotton reel. Some called it class solidarity. Otto could not see the charm of it at all. Otto once, after standing over Brian in Brian's Wandsworth study, watching Brian typing out a letter of recommendation for a mature student, had taken it upon himself to comment on Brian's typewriter, an old, heavy, battered manual machine, which Brian attacked with four fingers, which had developed various idiosyncrasies, and which made a loud, thumping, stuttering, machine-gun rattle that shook the room and, according to Alix, the room below. "Brian," said Otto, "that machine is prehistoric, I've never heard such a din, why on earth don't you get yourself an electric typewriter, if you won't consider a word processor?"

"What do you mean, *din*?" said Brian, turning round indignantly, placing his big hands gently, defensively over his keyboard: "it makes a lovely noise, a lovely, *companionable* noise, I wouldn't *dream* of getting a quiet machine, I wouldn't know I was working, would I?"

Downstairs, over a whisky, Otto had continued to tease Brian, inviting his wife Caroline's and Alix's collusion: "It sounds like heavy industry," said Otto, "it's absurd, don't you think so, Alix?"

"Oh, I don't know," said Alix, "I've got used to it, I quite like to hear him at it."

"It sounds like someone drilling the road," said Otto.

"Writing *is* like drilling the road," said Brian. "And I like to know I'm doing it."

Well, one could read a lot into that, thought Alix, later, and quite rightly; for it was there to be read. Brian, grey haired, bending benignly over his battleship-grey semi-portable, semi-immovable machine, hammering, with the inherited rattle of machinery soothing his exiled heart: Otto, quick of movement, quick of mind, restless, sitting before his glowing screen, pressing the soft silent smooth gentle effortless keys, watching the play of digits, the flitting of illuminated messages in synthetic green and luminous white, accompanied by a quiet, incomprehensible electronic, south-of-Watford hum. At the mercy of cleaning ladies and electric plugs, or roving children and distant power cuts, but modern, for all that, modern; as Brian hammered away at the past.

Alienation. Well, we are all alienated; some of us don't think about it much, but Alix and Brian Bowen did, and Otto Werner did, and Alan Headland did, in their different ways, and within themselves they confronted confrontation. They noted the words Class War Now as they appeared sporadically in large white letters on low suburban walls or high railway bridges, they noticed them as they lurked less aggressively, more insidiously, more archaically, in the subtext of the tabloid press, in the subtext of the increasingly right-wing respectable press. They observed that the establishment, through ignorance, through stupidity, or for its own ends, continued blandly to attempt to deny the persistence of the class system, continued to pretend that things were getting better all the time, instead of worse and worse.

"Of course class dominates people's thinking," said Otto, "this is the most class-divided society in Europe, we all know that, it's just a question of deciding to go forward from here, because if we don't, we're done for. But how?"

"Your proposals," said Brian to Otto, speaking of the new political party which Otto supported, "your proposals," he said (a little pompously, but with feeling), "would bring about the permanent disenfranchisement of the working class."

"Rubbish," said Otto, "they will bring about the transformation, the integration of the working class: it's seeing the working class in this old-fashioned way that's holding us all up." Otto came up with some ingenious arguments about the changing base of the working class, but Brian did not accept them. He stuck to his old cotton reel. In a way, Alix admired him for this, and phrases like "the permanent disenfranchisement of the working class" continued to work on her emotional loyalty, to bring tears to her eyes: but at the same time she noticed in herself, over these years, as she listened to demagogues on the radio and watched newsreels of workers confronting pickets and pickets confronting police and journalists egging on both sides of any dispute—well, she felt, as we have said, a certain unease, a sense that Otto might be right in his analysis, and Brian—well, wrong? Were there not, on the left as well as the right, these days, these years, some deeply dishonest people? She did not like to think these thoughts, even in the privacy of her own heart; she felt an uncomfortable, unhealthy, but at times exhilarating excitement as she heard Otto and Brian argue these issues. She and Otto's wife, Caroline, would occasionally cross sides, Caroline (who was in fact apolitical, little concerned) taking Brian's part, Alix taking Otto's; and sometimes Alix fancied that Otto was looking to her for more than nominal support. He seemed to think that she knew what he was talking about; and the truth was that she did.

As Brian and Alix worried irrelevantly over these important matters, and grew grey, Alix's golden boy Nicholas grew more and more irrelevantly golden. He paid no attention to politics; he lived outside the system, painting his paintings, going to films, sitting around with his friends, earning money intermittently, signing on intermittently, smoking marijuana, drinking beer or cheap wine, and eating pizza out of huge square cardboard boxes. He was happy. He had no reason to be, but he was. He was in his mid-twenties, older already than his father had been when he died, and his hairline, to Alix's great relief, had stopped receding. Nicholas was relieved too, for he condescended to worry about going bald. It was the only anxiety he admitted. He claimed to have defeated incipient baldness by a homeopathic medicine bought from the Indian chemist on the corner, but when cross-questioned about this by Alix admitted he'd only used it twice and then forgotten to continue the treatment.

"It must be will power, Mum," he then claimed—a commodity of which Alix had once assumed he had little. She was now beginning to wonder. For there was something oddly persistent in his way of life, in his application to his own work, something very unlike his father. True, he had dropped out of art school after a couple of terms, and refused to consider any other form of higher education, but now, some years later, he was still painting. In the spring of 1980 he acquired a girlfriend who painted: they kept one another at it.

The girlfriend was also golden. She was called Ilse, and her family came from some Middle European country, though she had been born in England: and she was a little taller and a little older than Nicholas. She wore her coarse silvery-golden hair sometimes harshly, spikily loose, sometimes in pigtails, and she dressed with a hint of folklore: embroidered blouses, coloured skirts, wooden necklaces, bright scarves. She had an extra finger on her left hand, and claimed to be a white witch. She was larger than life: bold, emphatic, widely gesturing. The first time that Nicholas brought her to supper in Wandsworth, Alix had been a little alarmed by her, a little put out by the ease with which she charmed young Sam, a little awed by her large, loud laugh, her throwing back of her head, her swooping, husky voice, her rapid eating of large mounds of food: on guard against jealousy, Alix had repeated invitations, had attempted to befriend her and domesticate her, and Ilse and Nicholas had accepted eagerly, had come round quite frequently to gobble up plates full of shepherd's pie and fish pie and pot roast and cassoulet, to drink tumblers of cheap wine. Alix assumed they were hard up, that they appreciated a free meal, for it was not at all clear to her what they lived on: Nicholas had moved out of his squat, and he and Ilse now shared a flat in a condemned building in Stockwell. Alix assumed they were glad to be asked out of it, and was surprised when, one evening, Ilse formally invited Alix, Brian, and Sam to pay a return visit.

"Come to supper," Ilse said, leaning forward eagerly on her elbows across the table, nodding emphatically, smiling broadly: "Do come, do come." Alix glanced at Nicholas, but he nodded support: "Do come," he echoed.

So Alix and Brian and Sam Bowen, one evening in 1982, called upon Nicholas Manning and Ilse Nemorova, with, on Alix's part, some foreboding. What would it be like, would it be warm, would it be habitable, would the food be edible, would there *be* any food? She envisaged bare floorboards, torn curtains, cracked windows, mattresses on the floor: inner-city, cracking, creaking, peeling squalor. And the exterior of the house where they lived was not promising: it stood alone, at the end of a dingy little terrace cul-de-sac, with boarded windows, awaiting demolition, a detached house, once better than its neighbours (the doctor's, the rectory?), but now in terminal decay: tall, oddly shaped, eerie in the gusty late autumn night, its upper windows bright, its lower windows dark and forbidding.

"Help," said Alix bravely, and bravely rang the bell. Down came Nicholas like an angel, and let them up, past the derelict ground floor, up uncarpeted stairs, to paradise.

"Good Lord!" said Alix, staring around her, gaping, amazed. "How beautiful, how absolutely beautiful!" The two angels smiled proudly, as they took coats and scarves and gloves. "Ilse," said Alix, "how have you done all this? Brian, isn't it wonderful? Wonderful?"

And wonderful it was, like a fairy story, a Bohemian fairy story. The little room was illuminated by candles, by a paraffin lamp, by crackling packing-case twigs in a real fire in a real Victorian grate; its walls were painted a dark midnight blue, its floor was painted a deep red with a dark blue and green patterned border, wooden painted chairs stood at a table covered with a white embroidered cloth and painted bowls and plates, huge cushions lay in heaps in a corner, there were two comfortable chairs covered (Alix recognized the material) with the old velveteen curtains her own mother had brought down from Leeds years ago, and which she'd never got round to hanging.

"Sit, sit," said Nicholas, and Alix and Brian sat in the comfortable chairs, while the angels hovered, with glasses of firelight-glinting red wine, with olives on a white plate, with nuts on a blue plate.

"I must just *gaze*," said Alix, boldly, as she sipped,

speechless, and stared around her: at the paintings hanging on
the walls, at the painted dresser with its rows of plates, at the
plants on a cane table, at a wooden sculpture, at dyed dried
flowers and grasses, at a heaped bowl of gourds and onions and
peppers, at a smiling pumpkin head with a glowing inner
candle. A wooden loom stood in a corner, with a stool before
it: a cloth of red and gold was in progress.

"But how do you do all this?" repeated Alix, and Ilse
smiled, and said: "Of course, we do it all ourselves, we make
these things ourselves. By magic, in the dark, dark night."
And she laughed, and clapped her hands and went into the
kitchen through the archway to stir the soup, as Nicholas
continued the story: the furniture was junk, some of it they'd
picked up off skips, they painted it themselves, they painted
everything, they were really into painting wood: they picked up
firewood from the skips, from the waste ground, from the
empty houses in the half-demolished street: they sold painted
plates and chairs to a man in Peckham: they scavenged, they
scrounged, they transformed: and upstairs, in the roof space,
they had their studio; they could go up to see it after supper if
they chose. And Alix, listening to this, remembered that Ilse
and Nicholas had mentioned such things before, but that she
had not listened, convinced as she had been that they were
speaking of the scruffiest, the most incompetent making-do and
getting-by; how could she so have misjudged them? Her heart
overflowed with penitence, with admiration; twenty times nicer
it was than her own home, she told them, as they nodded and
smiled happily, as they ladled out barley soup, followed by
stuffed cabbage leaves: twenty times more delicious than my
own cooking! she cried. No, not at all, they protested: and Ilse
said, glowing, her hair flaring in bright sparks and points in the
candlelight, "but we have only just got this ready for you, we
have worked for months on this—" And Alix could see that
this was so, the labour involved was immense, that this island
of colour and light had been salvaged from the darkness by
long hours, great pains, great ingenuity. It moved her almost
unbearably, the beauty of it, the warmth of it, in the surrounding night. She did not dare to ask what tenure they had, was
relieved when Brian raised the subject, was semi-relieved to
hear that the house could not be demolished as its yet
untraceable owner lived in Sarawak and the agency that had
previously let it was happy for Ilse and Nicholas to stay on
pending interminable enquiries.

"We're a freak, we're an anomaly; that suits us fine," said Nicholas.

"But your investment here, you could lose it at any time," said Brian, worried, stepfatherly.

"We can always begin again," said Ilse, dismissing fear with a toss of her head and a munch of beetroot salad, "we can always move on."

"There's a brave gypsy," said Brian, admiringly; and the illicit firelight flickered in the hearth, sending a thin flag of dissident smoke into the Smokeless Zone of South West Nine where Nicholas Manning and Ilse Nemorova camped, comfortable in the heart of urban desolation.

Sam Bowen thought the house was great, but drew the line at beetroot salad. He hated beetroot. He recommended that Ilse and Nicholas should get a kitten and informed them that Liz Headleand's tabby was expecting. A kitten would go really nicely by that fire, said Sam, who had himself long and ineffectually been pleading for a springer spaniel. Out of the mouths of schoolchildren, thought Alix, for it was clear to her that Nicholas and Ilse ought to have not a kitten but a baby: a baby in a little painted wooden cradle, a baby with golden hair. She wondered if they had ever thought of it themselves. They seemed prepared to consider one of Liz's cat's unborn kittens. They also told her, to her surprise, that they were going to spend the weekend with Nicholas's grandmother Deborah, who was not well— information which aroused in her a pang of jealousy, and also of sorrow, for she herself had not kept adequately in touch with Deborah, and felt a certain guilt.

After supper, they went up to the studio under the roof. It was too dark to see the paintings properly, and too cold to linger. By torchlight they inspected Ilse's work (small, icon-like, jewelled landscapes, rich miniatures) and Nicholas's (much larger, cooler, more spacious, more abstract, with suggestions of figures in geometrical distant perspectives; very different from his early phase of sub-Bonnard domestic interiors), but they could not see them very well, and could think of little to say, being illiterate in the vocabulary of the visual arts. "Very nice," they murmured, politely banal, Alix conscious that they might be works either of considerable commercial or considerable artistic potential, or of none at all, for all that she knew, for all that she could tell. She had learned little, from her brief marriage with Art, from her long friendship with Esther Breuer, art historian; and indeed the thought of Esther crossed her mind, as she made her way carefully down the unlit lower stairs to the front door, for Esther had often crisply, emphatically, not wholly credibly, disclaimed any interest in or knowledge of art of any period later than the late Renaissance, yet Esther would surely have responded as strongly as herself to that bright, glowing, candlelit, coloured interior, that jewelled nest? Had it not, perhaps, a touch of Esther's own style—less sombre, more cheerful, more naïve, more peasant-like, but a touch nevertheless? Domestic art, easel art—she thought of these contrasts, and of Virginia Woolf and Vanessa Bell, as she descended the stairs: her own house was shabby, she did not care how she lived, it was comfortable but shabby, she did not work at it, she had no concept of it: and Nicholas had this grace, this gift, this heritage, this Ilse. On the cold pavement they stood and looked upwards, at the lighted windows in the dark, windy, high-clouded moonlit night, in the wasteland.

"An ark," said Brian, "floating above the rubble."

"Ah," said Ilse, "we shall unhitch it one day, we shall weigh anchor, we shall sail off into the storm," and she turned to Alix, her huge loose-stitched red shawl flapping, her very hair vibrant, and folded Alix in her arms. Alix returned the embrace: a great warmth filled her, a deep emotion. They stood together, the two women, on the pavement, in one another's arms. Nicholas the angel serenely smiled.

"Wonderful," said Alix, "a wonderful evening."

"Wonderful," echoed Brian.

"Very nice," said Sam, "and remember the kitten." Dark silver-edged clouds scudded and swirled in revelatory swags and swathes past the silver moon: a night of splendour, as the Beautiful People waved goodbye.

Brian squeezed Alix's hand as they settled in the car. "They're all right," he said.

"Yes," said Alix, and they drove back through the dismal small cramped mean terraces, on to the main six-lane through-road, along a bit of Motorway, under a tunnel and over a tunnel, under the harsh, ugly yellow light of the neon lamps, and along more back streets to their own home, in front of which stood, in what they considered their own parking space, a dumped car.

"I wish somebody would move that thing," said Brian, patiently, without irritation, as he had said a dozen times in the past fortnight.

"I'll ring up the Council," said Alix, as she had said a dozen times. But they both knew she wouldn't: she was too depressed by her own foreknowledge that during these years, one more supposed victim of the Horror of Harrow Road was discovered, in the autumn of 1980, in a dumped van in a little road linking the Harrow Road and Kilburn Lane: an unpretentious, shabby little street called Fifth Avenue. The victim was white, female, and headless. The head was never discovered, and the identity of the murderer, like that of Jack the Ripper, was not established. Prisons grew more and more crowded as judges and magistrates declined to listen to arguments in favour of shorter sentences and continued to impose the longest sentences in Europe, as government ministers failed to respond to not-very-popular, non-vote-catching pleas from within and without the Home Office for more spending on prison building. But the Horror did not swell the ranks of the imprisoned. There were cuts in some areas of prison spending, and the tablecloths of Garfield vanished, as Alix had known they would, while the central heating continued inexorably to overheat its inmates despite frequent requests for a lowering of the temperature. Alix hung on to her job, although there were murmurs about cutting the educational services; Hannah and Eric Glover would shortly be retiring, a prospect which Alix viewed with apprehension. Jilly Fox was, at last, about to be released, a prospect which Jilly Fox viewed with apprehension.

As the Harrow Road murders receded slightly in folk memory, Esther Breuer resumed her patrolling of the streets of West and North-West London, reflecting as she did so from time to time on the pastoral beauties of Somerset and the hill towns of Tuscany, and wondering why she stayed where she was. Was it for her friends, or from habit, or from some more mysterious compulsion? She sat in the bar of the Metropole Hotel, sipping a Strega, watching the curiously aimless international clientele, trying to remember what the décor had been like before it had had this strange pale green plastic wickerwork chintzy-cushioned face-lift, noting that the tender blue hydrangeas were of plausible plastic, but that the drooping tiger lily, with its backward-curving spotted petals and its powdery stamen, was real: she walked beneath the great strutting legs and curved segmented underbelly of the Westway, where a little herd of horses stood sadly in a dry ring of sand, like an abandoned circus: she wandered over waste grass near Wormwood Scrubs and found a woman's glove and a pair of shoes: she gazed at the bizarre, paint-dripping, surreal façade of the condemned house that called itself the Apocalypse Hotel: she bought prawns from the barrow, and peered through corrugated iron walls at building sites. Once she saw, swinging high from a crane above a yard of scrap vehicles, a hanged man: a lifesize dummy, in workman's green overalls, dangling against the sky. Alsatians roamed, cats scavenged, buddleias grew from abandoned rooftops. She walked past the Car Breaker Art Gallery, past a house that described itself as Interesting Books, past the Embassy Café. Once a small boy in a van drove past her, crazily, red-bristle-haired, white-faced, hardly able to reach the wheel, but driving; he scraped along a row of parked vehicles, ripping from them expensive trim, dinting and bashing and banging, and disappeared around the corrugated-iron corner of dead-end Bard Road in a clatter of midget fury. Giant graffiti marched and sprawled, machinery rusted, padlocked gates labelled Reception and Welcome led to nowhere, and in the midst of it a man sold lawnmowers from a tin hut, and a couple of girls were to be seen playing tennis in the rain.

Esther sat by the canal, reading Dante's Purgatory, and thinking of Hugh Capet, who became king of France: *Figlio fu' io d'un beccaio di Parigi.* Son was I of a butcher of Paris. A good man, the father of evil. From good sprang forth evil. She sat in Kensal Green Cemetery and read Zola's *La Bête humaine.* She dreamed, twice more, of the severed head. *Io fui radice della mala pianta.* I was the root of the evil tree. North Pole Road. Little Wormwood Scrubs. Droop Street. Warlock Road. Fifth Avenue, Sixth Avenue. She discovered a new café on the corner of Lykewake Gardens and Mortuary Road down by the gas station, wittily entitled the New Caprice, where she would sit with a cup of tea and a cheese sandwich, perched on a high uncomfortable stool at a narrow, smeared, Formica ledge, watching the world go by, in the company of one or two old men, persistent regulars, and a shifting company of builders and roadworkers from nearby acres of demolition. One day they would rebuild, she supposed, but when? There was a lot to flatten first. Through the glass she stared at shabby grey old women with prams full of shopping or rubbish, and stylish young black men, with huge transistors, wearing dashing woollen hats, and at the occasional pony and cart with a pale raw-nosed lank-haired driver and a load of scrap. A landscape of nightmare, an extreme, end-of-the-world, dream-like parody of urban nemesis.

One Sunday in the late spring of 1983 she tempted Liz out for an afternoon walk: they lunched together in Esther's flat, on prawns and crab sticks from the barrow, with brown bread and butter and a little mayonnaise, then they set off down the towpath by the canal, on the far side from the green cemetery. Weeds grew tall from cracks between bricks and slabs of concrete: obelisks reared to their right, a gasometer loomed before them. Old men and young boys took dogs for walks, but nobody, unusually, was fishing, and after a while they could see why: the green still water was full of dead fishes, thousands of small dead fishes, belly-upward in the sun. They stopped, gazed, pondered: a chemical disaster, they concluded, pollution, an overflowing factory, a catastrophe upstream? Maybe it's a sign of the end of the world, said Liz, staring at the poor innocent fish in the hot afternoon; this is where the apocalypse would announce itself. That's what I've always thought, said Esther. Perhaps that's why I stay here. To be in on the act. *Il trionfo della morta*. The final scene.

They wandered on, chatting idly, then paused as they saw in the far distance approaching them a strange, a disturbing group of walkers: two men, and between them, struggling, and (they could dimly hear) moaning, a youngish woman. She stumbled and protested, one man gripped each arm. Liz and Esther slowed their already slow pace; the towpath was narrow, they were directly in line, they would have to pass within feet; intervention was, it would seem, forced upon them. The woman's legs were buckling and wandering, splayed at angles, ungainly as she tried to free herself. "Christ," said Esther. There was nobody else within yards. The three advanced. Esther and Liz hesitated, then moved forward, and as the trinity of figures came into focus, so the little narrative of their lives composed itself—a father, a brother, taking for a walk, kindly, familiarly, a mentally, a physically handicapped young woman, who was struggling against their benevolence, wanting to walk freely, wanting to turn back, wanting she knew not what, wanting to kneel by the water and scoop up dead fishes. As they passed Liz and Esther she lunged yet again for the water, mumbling about the fishes; and the two patient men held her and soothed her as they would a frightened horse, calming her: Come along now, Nelly, they said, there, there, Nelly, carefully does it, Nelly. Her arms were everywhere, every now and then she gave at the knees and sank in a heap of sullen protest; firmly, not very gently, they would drag her up again and drag her on. The men looked exhausted: their faces were red and streaming with sweat. They did not look at Liz and Esther as they passed, and went their painful, struggling, desperate way.

Liz and Esther walked on. "We should have said good afternoon," said Liz.

"Yes, we should," said Esther.

"She probably sits in all week, with the mother," said Liz, sighing. "This is mother's afternoon off."

Sombre, subdued, they wandered on, reaching after a while the source of the poisoned water: an ancient dirty dark brick hospital, from which belched terrible steam and a white, dangerous seeping flood. They sat on a bench, and asked one another whether they should report it.

"Alix would," said Esther.

"No, she wouldn't," said Liz. "Alix has given up hope of ever getting anyone to do anything. She thinks it's all hopeless. Alix told me that she herself threw a crisp packet out of the car window on the way to Wanley the other night. Littering the A10. The lovely, scenic A10. She said she thought it would never come to that."

They spoke of Alix and Brian, of Nicholas and Ilse; Nicholas and Ilse were well, they had acquired a tabby kitten from Liz and a gallery was to exhibit some of their work in the autumn in a new Arts Council–sponsored show, but Alix and Brian, they thought, were not so well. Brian's Adult Education College was to close. It was to be amalgamated with another institution, and Brian was not sure whether he would be kept on, or whether he would be offered redundancy payment. He had become militant, and spoke of taking a more active interest in politics. "A disastrous idea, at his age," said Liz, "and disastrous in this political climate, wouldn't you agree?" Esther agreed. The Falklands business had unsettled Brian: he had become violently, irrationally anti-Government, in Alix's view, was obsessed with thinking the worst of it and the best of any militant opposition. A patient, reasonable, gentle man, gone a little wild. And Alix, as a result of this and other things, was depressed.

They rose from their bench, and wandered on.

"Men are a strange lot," said Esther, meditatively; "they are so inflexible. So extreme. They have to take sides. Now me, I don't know what I think, on almost any public issue you may happen to name. But men have to have an opinion. I only have opinions on things I know something about. Men aren't like that at all. They have opinions. And speaking of men, Liz, how is your errant ex-husband, dear Charles? I have always thought of Charles as an archetypal man. I rather miss Charles.''

"Charles?" said Liz. "Yes, Charles. Well, to tell you the truth, I don't think things are going too well for Charles, and I don't know whether to be pleased or sorry. I think there's been some monumental cock-up. Some sort of almighty boob. I think he's fallen out with the company over something to do with cable television, whatever that is, and that he's about to be given the chop. Last time I spoke to him he was raving on about dish receivers, whatever they are, the weak-kneed lily-livered IBA, and the dim-witted governors and the dirty dealings of various directors and the Monopolies Commission and American law and English law and getting a barrister's opinion. All of which made me think he was about to quit, either voluntarily or because they've had enough of him. And I think he's probably had enough of New York. He's never forgiven the Americans for what he called their two-faced attitude to the Falklands. Charles thought the Falklands was Britain's finest hour.''

"So will he come home?"

"I think so." She paused, stopped, stared at the water. Upstream there were no dead fish, but a pleasant healthy life-supporting life-concealing green scum. "I wonder if London is big enough for Henrietta, Charles, and me," said Liz.

"What news of Henrietta?"

"None, directly. I never speak to her. I hear gossip, sometimes. It filters through."

They began to stroll back, retracing their steps.

"I heard some gossip about Henrietta the other day," said Esther.

"Really? Do tell," said Liz, lightly, attempting to disguise even to Esther her disproportionate, unhealthy interest in the subject, an interest which she did her best to control; it slightly surprised her that it should linger on, after all these years.

"I met this chap called Oxenholme," said Esther. "He claimed to be some kind of cousin of hers. Youngish chap. Some kind of lord, or viscount, or something like that."

Liz did not wish to reveal her intimate, her excessive knowledge of the Oxenholme lineage, so merely prompted, "Yes?"

"Robert. Robert Oxenholme. That was his name."

"And why did he come up with Lady Henrietta?"

"Because we were standing in front of a portrait of her as a girl. 'Oh look,' he said, 'there's Hetty, do you know her, everyone knows Hetty.' I said I did."

"Where was this portrait?"

"At the Caspar exhibition at the National Portrait Gallery. Funny, when you think about it. I first saw Henrietta and Charles together at the National Portrait Gallery. At some other exhibition. I can't remember what. Years ago, now."

"And what did he have to say about Henrietta?"

"Nothing much. That he used to play tennis with her. That her mother committed suicide. That kind of thing. Just gossip. It must have been one of Caspar's last portraits. She was sitting on a window seat, against a red velvet curtain, holding a rag doll. It wasn't very good. We agreed it wasn't very good. Tired stuff. There was a much better one of her father, done in the twenties. Very savage. A dreadful man, but a genius, the viscount said. I can't remember what he said he was a genius *at*."

"And what did the viscount himself do?"

Esther began to laugh. "Oh, Lord," she said, "it really is too absurd. He told me all about it. He's some kind of Arts Sponsorship Coordination Executive. Or something like that."

"Whatever does that mean?"

"It means he goes round persuading industry to sponsor the arts. The Knight of Arts and Industry. He spends his entire life persuading other people to part with their money. To Covent Garden, and the Hayward, and the Royal Shakespeare Company, and literary prizes, and things like that. He told me that he knew of an Italian bank that would be only too delighted to sponsor my unwritten masterpiece on Crivelli. He said that in Italy all art books are sponsored by banks."

"You liked him," said Liz, accusingly.

"I thought he was absurd, and it was absurd. But yes, I liked him. He is rather good-looking. He has curly hair."

They passed an old man sitting on a bollard, with a small mongrel dog. The dead fish floated eerily.

"Absurd," said Esther. "Tax incentives, he spoke of. But

he knew quite a lot about Crivelli." The still, hot air mocked. "He wrote a book on Signorelli," said Esther.

KILL THE MOZART, declared a large scrawled notice on the canal bridge.

"Is that advertising? Or sponsorship? Or GLC popularist anti-élitism? Or what?" asked Liz, as they paused to stare at it. They had not noticed it, walking the other way.

"The use of the definite article intrigues," said Esther, as they progressed. They were approaching the scene of Esther's dream-severed head, of (as she had surreptitiously, with some shame, established) the real, live, actual, dead, historical corpse of 1979. Esther Breuer was attempting to summon up the courage to ask her friend Liz Headleand about the latest problems with Claudio, whose death-in-life was strongly suggested to her by this locale; it was to ask Liz about Claudio that she had suggested this lunch, this walk. She found it difficult to speak. She prevaricated, meandered, played for time.

"The word monomania," she said, suddenly (so wrapped up in her own thought-sequence that she did not notice Liz's guilty start of recognition), "—the word monomania, is it still used? Whence does it date?" And they discussed, circuitously, fashions in psychiatric language, changes in meaning in psychiatric terminology. Liz guessed that the term monomania was certainly pre-Freudian, perhaps late nineteenth century, then recalled that it had been used by Dickens apropos of Mr. Dick's King Charles's Head in *David Copperfield*—therefore mid-nineteenth century or earlier? They spoke of obsessional neuroses in art and life, of Freud's view that the Gorgon's head represented the castrating vision of the female genitals; they spoke of the eighteenth-century concept of the "Ruling Passion," of Jonsonian humours, of the extraordinarily persistent popular after-life of astrology and horoscopes in a post-superstitious, post-Christian era; they spoke of Freemasons and Rosicrucians; and eventually, at last, as they climbed up the steps from the canal bank onto the pavement of the wrong end of Ladbroke Grove, Esther spoke of Claudio. Casually, lightly, pleasantly.

"Did you by any chance see that bit in *The Times* about Claudio?" So casual, so light, so pleasant was her tone that Liz froze in her tracks. "No, what?" she said, stopping halfway up the steps, her hand on the rail.

"It was so *silly*," said Esther, deprecating, "such a nonsense. The Montano di Salvo lecture. In the Institute. Quite the wrong time and the wrong place. For what"—her voice wavered, queried—"can only have been a *joke*? Of a sort? A sort of joke?"

"Tell, tell," said Liz: and Esther, as they walked back to the flat, told. She told well: an interesting little narrative. Claudio, she reminded Liz, had for some years been working on medieval superstition and heresy in a small mountainous region of the Greek-Bulgarian border, and had indeed recently published a book on the subject which (although not yet translated into English) had been noticed in the English academic press: yes, Liz at this point interjected, she remembered a lengthy article in the *London Review of Books* which Alix had drawn to her attention, and which she had herself attempted to penetrate, but had found to be of a brilliant obscurity, of a deep and dazzling intellectual darkness, and had reeled back exhausted: impossible to tell, from the review, on the simplest level, whether Claudio was merely describing the miraculous shamanistic powers which his medieval witches (descendants of the Bessi of antiquity, in Claudio's claim) believed themselves to possess, or whether he himself shared that belief in those powers, or whether (at this remote, intellectual, near-thousand-year remove) there was any difference between these two positions.

"Yes, precisely," said Esther, "precisely so. It's not," she hastened to add, loyally, defensively, "that the book itself is *muddled*, you know, it's very scholarly and very elegantly written—but it's *difficult*, and readers tend to get themselves lost in the arguments . . . Anyway," pursued Esther, unlocking her front door, putting on the kettle (this was the period when she favoured rosehip tea), "anyway, Claudio had been invited to give the Montano di Salvo lecture at the Institute (an honour, even for one as much honoured as Claudio) and it had been suggested, of course, that he should speak on his witches."

"Wasn't there something about the Mary Magdalen and the Holy Grail and the Sang Real?" interjected Liz, at this point.

"Certainly *not*," said Esther, sharply. "You're thinking of that ridiculous book published by Cape about the Rosicrucians, or was it the Cathars, and President Kennedy, or was it General de Gaulle—no, no, Liz, this is all serious scholarly stuff, not popular rubbish. Or so it was until Claudio delivered his lecture at the Institute."

"And what happened at the Institute?"

"I only have it from the newspapers, the Italian newspapers," said Esther, "and from speaking to Claudio's sister Elena, on the phone."

It had been thus, it appeared. Picture the lecture hall of the distinguished, ancient, and honourable Institute in the heart of Rome: its high, painted Renaissance ceiling, its marble columns, its little gilt chairs, its chandeliers. Picture the gathered audience, in sober evening suits, wearing discreet ribbons and decorations in button holes; fine, ascetic, wrinkled faces; plump expansive attentive faces; the ageing aristocrats of the academic world. Picture the expectant hush (for Claudio was known as a lecturer of panache, of provocation); picture his arrival upon the platform, a dark gown over his dark suit, a suggestion of billow and flourish of dramatic, even theatrical suspense. Claudio, although small of stature and bespectacled, was a man with stage presence. He had listened to his own praises, smiling secretly at the titles of his own works, at the lists of his own achievements: had risen from his golden chair and strolled to the lectern: had arranged his papers upon the lectern: had taken a sip of water from the provided glass, had refilled the glass from the provided carafe: had adjusted the microphone with professional expertise: and had embarked upon his theme.

For some twenty minutes he spoke carefully, precisely, soberly, of sources and documents, of learned controversies and misapprehensions of yesteryear, of the achievements of his fellow scholars, of the unexplored nature of his own small chosen plot, of his unexpected discoveries, discoveries so unexpected that he had chosen not to publish them, for fear of calling into question his own credibility as anthropologist, as historian: But here, honoured colleagues, he had proceeded, here in the sanctum, as it were, of our own mystery, here, to you, tonight, I can reveal to you some of the—odder, less explicable revelations of these last five years. All, at this stage, reported Elena, were on the edge of their seats, breathlessly attentive as Claudio conspiratorially lowered his voice.

"And what then, what then?" asked Liz.

Well, then Claudio had proceeded to describe, in a first-person, informal, circumstantial narrative style, his own adventures into the supernatural. He had been driving, he claimed, alone, through southern Bulgaria, not far from the Greek frontier (where he had been staying with friends at the

University of Salonica); it was one of those sentimental
excursions at the end of a long research project, he assured his
listeners, one of those mildly relaxing journeys which one
takes through terrain overfamiliar through study, in order to
learn again the smell of the mountain air, the shapes of the
hills, the darknesses of the forests, in order to summon up that
small ghost called inspiration that brings to life our documents
and transcriptions, our months in libraries and years at our own
desks . . . in short, he had been travelling in search of a little
local colour, through scenes where the descendants of ''his''
people still lived, and lived, moreover, in a primitive style little
changed by the turning of the great wheel of time (at this point,
Elena had begun to feel deeply uncomfortable, but could see
that the rest of the predominantly elderly audience was, like a
group of children, still unsuspecting), and, as he drove along
a remote lonely wooded mountain road at dusk, he had seen a
werewolf. (A *frisson* ran through the audience: perhaps Claudio's lecture style was after all a *little* too flamboyant for the
occasion? But it was effective, they conceded: they listened,
entranced.) The werewolf had been standing by the side of the
road—or perhaps crouching would be a better term—yes,
crouching, by a pile of logs. The upper body of a man, the
lower limbs of an animal. True, the man portion was excessively hairy, but human it certainly was: human features stared
from its wild matted bearded head. And an intelligent face: a
questioning face. Naturally, I stopped at once, said Claudio,
and cautiously lowered the car window to attempt to make
contact. I cannot tell you, said Claudio, how astonished I was
at the sight of this werewolf, for, as those of you who have read
my latest publication will know, werewolves were certainly not
a prominent feature of the heresies and superstitions of this
particular region. (At this, a certain change in atmosphere, a
slight shifting of bodies and clearing of throats, took place; but
it might, after all, be a fable, some speculated, a fable to throw
light on the nature of historical or anthropological research?
They listened on.)

''It was not, apparently, a parable. Claudio had communed
with the werewolf, in a kind of sign language and the odd word
of Greek, and had agreed to follow it to its village. It had loped
off along the road, pausing to make sure Claudio was following, and had turned off up a track through the woods. Its
intentions, Claudio was sure, were benevolent. He quelled his
own desire to stop to take its photograph—luckily he had his

camera with him (this aside caused a tremor of anguish to ripple through some members of the audience)—intent on maintaining the fragile bond of communion which had been established. Picture this strange sight, said Claudio, smiling malignly: the man-beast in the twilight, followed by the professor in his little orange Fiat 125. A good little car, for it brought me to the very edge of the compound where the werewolf lived.

"And what was in the compound? Claudio narrated. A group of villagers: ordinary, human, two-legged villagers, primitive, certainly, but recognizably human. They came from their huts to regard him. The werewolf crouched on the outer edge of the circle. A young girl stroked its matted arm. They offered him food and drink; diplomatically, he accepted. A handful of olives, a piece of flat unleavened bread, some bitter herbs, a tin mug of rough wine. When he had eaten, they indicated by signs and words of an unknown language that he should follow them to a hut which stood, slightly isolated, slightly raised, at the highest point of the clearing; he obeyed, and shortly found himself in the presence of two women, one elderly, one young, sitting side by side on a low bench by a somewhat smoky fire.

"Now, of course, said Claudio, my interest was truly aroused, for this combination of the younger and older woman is, you will recall, a most important feature of the magical life of the Perelikesi: and imagine my excitement when the younger woman (who, incidentally, was naked from the waist upwards, displaying one pair of breasts and two supernumerary sets of nipples) spoke to me in a language I could understand!

"At this juncture, Elena reported, a note was passed by one of the senior academicians to the professor who had performed the rite of introduction: the professor was seen to shake his head, no doubt indicating that he hadn't the guts to interrupt Claudio's ghost story, and that it would be wiser, less sensational, to let him have his say. The fifty minutes were nearly up; let him finish. All this was conveyed, wordlessly, to the entire gathering, by that passed note, that shaken head, and conveyed to Claudio also, who smiled sardonically at the interchange, and continued his tale. It was his claim that the younger woman had informed him, in a simple but by no means incomprehensible tongue, that she had divined his presence on the road, and had sent the wolf-man to attract his attention and shepherd him to her presence.

"From this moment onwards, the narrative interest rather dwindled. Claudio declared that he was well aware that he had only four minutes left of his allotted time, and that the last thing he wished to do was to bore his listeners by outstaying the welcome they had so generously extended. The rest of his visit, he had to confess, had proved both frustrating and disappointing. For, although he could understand some of the verbal communications of the younger woman, she appeared not to understand him at all: it was a one-way transmission. After some hours of tedious misunderstanding they had agreed to abandon their efforts at communion, and he had been taken to a sleeping hut, where he passed the night comfortably, disturbed only by vaguely hallucinatory half-waking dreams, induced no doubt by the strangeness of the situation and possibly by the chewing of the bitter herbs. In the morning, it was indicated to him that it was time for him to be on his way; he was fortunately able to win the consent of the two women to be photographed, but alas, the werewolf had vanished. As werewolves do. And may I conclude (said Claudio, seriously, respectfully) by remarking that I believe that my little adventure in the field—or perhaps I should say in the wood and the clearing—has indeed added a dimension of inwardness, of sympathy, to my study-bound explorations of structures of thought and mental powers, now deeply alien to us all?

"And then he had marched, billowing, from the platform, to muffled, bewildered, anxious, intermittent, hesitant applause."

"Good God," said Liz, "so that was that, was it? No question time?"

"No question time," confirmed Esther. "Claudio vanished, like the werewolf. Walked off the platform and vanished. Leaving everybody quite confused at first. Most of them decided it was some sort of deconstructive attack on diachronic methodology and after half an hour or so had persuaded themselves it had all been most interesting and stimulating and challenging and all that sort of thing. Elena said that it was wonderful to hear the rationalizations they managed to come up with. Of course, knowing he was her brother, they had to be polite in her earshot, and she probably didn't manage to overhear any of the more enraged comments. It all ended quite peacefully, as though it had been the most normal lecture ever given. Though of course that all altered somewhat when the press got onto Claudio in the morning and he gave them the photos of the lady with the nipples."

Liz laughed. So did Esther.

"Yes," continued Esther, "a real lady, and six real nipples. Well, two proper breasts, and then two lower pairs of flat nipples. The press loved them. Even *The Times* thought them worthy of comment."

"But," said Liz, "lots of people have vestigial nipples. It's quite common. It doesn't mean anything."

"Quite so," said Esther.

"And the real question," said Liz, nursing her second mug of rosehip tea, "is what Claudio thinks he's doing. What kind of game he thinks he's playing. Is that what it's about?" she asked delicately, gazing obliquely as she spoke at the potted palm, which still hung on, bristling darkly in its pot, against the red wall.

"Yes," said Esther, and proceeded to attempt to outline to Liz the oddity of Claudio's state of mind. Reality and imagination, the false werewolf and the real werewolf, the forged photograph, the forged historical document, the false interpretation. "Look," said Esther, "I don't know how to explain this. I know quite well that Claudio knows he hasn't seen a werewolf or spoken to a witch, but that so great is his power of—well, of what? of self-hallucination—that he can persuade himself that he *might* have done? No, not even that. He knows he hasn't. But"—and Esther glanced at Liz in anxiety, in embarrassment, for never in all their years of close friendship had she ever made such a confession—"the thing is, when I'm with Claudio, I find myself believing these things myself. It's as though I know I'd *better* believe them. That, when I'm with him, it's safer to believe them. Does that make any kind of sense at all?"

"Yes," said Liz, slowly. "You're speaking about some kind of *folie-à-deux*. A willed, mutual hallucination. Is that it?"

"Yes, I suppose it is," said Esther.

"The mind has powers that we know not of," said Liz. "And you are afraid to disturb Claudio's madness, because by disturbing it, you might drive him mad."

"Yes," said Esther. "I can keep him sane by collusion. I suppose that's it. But it's a terrible strain. And, frankly"—a certain robustness suddenly entered her voice—"I think this time he's gone too far. I've had enough. I've never been very good at the real world, I know that, but I do know the difference between a werewolf and a Bulgarian woodcutter. Or at least"—her voice weakening slightly—"I *think* I do."

"I liked the touch about the orange Fiat," said Liz.

"Yes, bloody good, wasn't it?"

The therapy session was over. Liz said she had to go home; she had someone coming to supper.

"Liz," said Esther, standing on the doorstep, in the late afternoon sun, "thank you for listening; you've saved my life."

Liz was expecting Stephen Cox to supper. He had been in Japan, had returned with anecdotes for which Liz, he assured her, would prove a suitable audience. Liz liked Stephen Cox. She trusted Stephen Cox. He was no trouble. He would never impose. One could risk a tête-à-tête with Stephen without fear of boredom or annoyance.

Their friendship had, over the last three years, mildly flourished. Alix Bowen, who had brought them together over dinner with gammon and spinach (or was it onion?) sauce, was mildly pleased. Had she planned or hoped for anything more than this mild friendship? Alix did not know.

Liz had admired Stephen's evasive style, his discretion, his impersonality. Stephen liked to communicate by post, not by telephone, as do most who are afflicted or have been afflicted by speech problems. After their dinner together at Alix's, he had written to her with a photocopy of a page of Schiller he had mentioned, about dreams, and a couple of addresses in Japan: she had responded with a booklet on stammering by Tim Newark which had been brought to her attention by a patient. Stephen had pursued the correspondence with a postcard from Dublin: she had responded with a postcard from Oxford. They had dined, to discuss her plans for her visit to Japan: she had sent a postcard from Japan. They had dined again, on her return. And so, over the years, intermittently, they had met and corresponded. A pleasant escort, Liz found him: and she needed, at times, an escort. Her fears that the break-up of her marriage with Charles might portend a life of solitary, uninvited, ostracized, divorced neglect had not of course been fulfilled, but neither had they been wholly without foundation. Some of their acquaintance did drop her: the Venables, for example, whom she had always disliked, seemed on Charles's departure to forget she existed, a fact which should have pleased her but, naturally, did not. Her life was by no means empty—she still saw most of her old friends, her real friends— but she was no longer part of a television-journalist-media social circuit of married couples, as she had been, and she no longer had the energy to give parties herself, deprived as she was of Charles's questionable support. Little suppers for Alix and Esther continued; anything much grander was beyond her, although she occasionally made an effort and invited a Pett Petrie or a Jules Griffin, for old times' sake. Stephen, in this situation, had proved a useful ally. He had even taken her to the theatre to see Hilda Stark play Hedda Gabler; a very amusing evening, they had both agreed. They had laughed heartily.

And now he was coming to supper, in what she still thought of as her new house in St. John's Wood, although she had already been in residence for nearly two years. She liked her new house, and looked back on the solid Harley Street mansion with a slight shiver of distaste. The new house was irregular, and airy, and odd, and it had a garden, unlike the Harley Street house, a garden to which she had curiously taken. It was a house of character: it had one of those Edwardian glass canopies from front door to street, and pretty little romantic leaded windows with bits of dark fine art-nouveau stained glass. It rambled, eccentrically, with strange shaped rooms, and alcoves. It had once been the home of an eminent zoologist. It had charm. Everyone agreed it had charm. Esther had given it the seal of her aesthetic approval: the glass canopy had particularly enraptured. Alix too had approved. Liz and Esther maintained that Alix approved because the house's undeniable attractions and the exclusivity of the neighbourhood were doubly modified, partly by a Family Planning Clinic next door, occupying what had once been an equally attractive private house, and partly by an extremely ugly block of luxury flats opposite, built in the 1960s from a horrible pinkish stone, and known vulgarly in the district as Menopause Mansions on account both of its colour and of the average age of its inhabitants. Thus surrounded, Esther and Liz claimed that Alix claimed, Liz could hardly put up her shutters and retire entirely into fool's paradise.

Alix, in fact, said nothing of the sort; she liked the house, of course, who wouldn't, but was principally surprised Liz managed to keep the garden in such good order. How ever did she find the time? Did she have secret gardeners in her pay?

Menopause Mansions. Liz, putting glasses and an ice bucket on a tray in the front room, in preparation for Stephen's arrival (or was it warm enough to have drinks in the garden? She hesitated), gazed across at this offending block, which reminded her occasionally that she had herself as yet suffered no hints of an approaching change of life. Since she had given up sex and contraception, her bodily existence had been of an exemplary calm and regularity. Odd to think of, almost impossible to remember, the tormenting anxieties of those earlier decades: whether one was or was not pregnant, whether one had thrush or trichomoniasis (Charles had passed on a very nasty dose of this and had made himself ill by insisting on drinking alcohol all the way through the prescribed ten days of pills), whether or not one was bleeding irregularly, whether the contraceptive pill was masking real illnesses, whether or not one's partner was losing interest, was too interested, was inadequate, was faithless. Tempestuous times. So much anxiety, about one's reproductive system. Abscesses, infections, lumps, sores, effusions, discharges.

"Surely," thought Liz (deciding they could after all have drinks in the garden, picking up the tray, opening the door with her foot), "surely it is time for some more little disturbances? Hot flushes, for example? This is an unnatural calm."

Her tabby cat followed her into the garden, and leaped with a muffled little cry, a small squeak of pleasure, onto the warm wood of the garden table, and began to weave backwards and forwards, rubbing herself against Liz's arm, against the ice bucket, and (rather unsuccessfully) against the unstable water jug. Silly, said Liz fondly. She was extremely attached to her cat, and much amused by her own attachment. She felt about the cat rather as she had once felt about her children—that they were without doubt the prettiest, the most intelligent, the most endearing children in the world, and that she was without doubt a fool to think them so, but a wise fool, wisely foolish. The strange little flicker of reflected, perpetuated emotion which hovered around the tabby cat like a striped halo amused her. It seemed a harmless, innocent indulgence, to be fond of one's cat. An affectation, but a harmless affectation. The cat purred, loudly, cheerfully, companionably. Liz sometimes dreamed that her cat could talk; after one such dream, in which the cat had said, when Liz expressed surprise at its new-found power, that it had always been able to talk, of course, but simply hadn't chosen to, Liz had woken herself up with her own laughter. Laughing, to herself, alone, in the dark.

She smiled, now, remembering this, and gently knocked the cat's nose out of the water jug. The colours of the garden deepened in the evening light; scents of rose and tobacco and honeysuckle mingled. The table and the garden chairs stood on a little paved terrace; beyond it stretched a small lawn, and, set in the lawn, unexpectedly perhaps, a small square pond, surrounded by bluish paving stones, flat bluish-yellowish-grey paving stones. The pond was divided into four small squares by two symmetrical paths of stone: one could walk into the middle of the pond and stand, as though in the middle of a chess board, at the crossroads of a watery game. The design, though of the greatest simplicity, was peculiarly pleasing; few guests resisted the temptation to walk into the middle of the water. Stephen Cox, upon arrival, made his way there almost at once, with a glass of deep yellow Portuguese wine in his hand, and stood gazing down into the shallows, where a few small silver fish swam. Liz, lying back with her feet up on one of the cane chairs, her cat on her knee, watched him. A blackbird sang, and a robin perched on an urn. Irises grew in the pond; the flat blades of their blue green leaves, the intimately shaded blues and greys and mauves of the spikes of flowers blended with the colours of the lichen-encrusted flat slabs of stone, suggesting antiquity, eternity, eternal harmony, a strange shivering fusion of light and shade and form. Stephen stood in the centre, and looked back at Liz, and smiled.

Returning to his chair, he reclined, and sipped his wine. "I prefer your pond to the ponds of Japan," he said. "I prefer your flat little bridges."

"But they were beautiful, those Japanese ponds, those little willow-pattern bridges," said Liz. "Didn't you think?"

And they embarked, as they had planned, upon their Japanese conversation: the difficulties, the enigmas, the linguistic obscurities, the disorientations, the cultural impregnability of Japan; the silk parcels, the screens, the wrappings-up, the slicings, the patternings; the delicacies, the crudities of Japan. Stephen had accustomed himself to the raw fish better than Liz, in her visit, had done, but he confessed that one night he had escaped his host's attention and slipped off into the night of Nara to purchase himself a hamburger and chips. He spoke also of an evening in a restaurant when he had politely and whimsically enquired (having eaten jelly fish, chrysanthemum leaves, strange microscopically thin sections of unknown forms of radish, sea urchin, tiny floating large-eyed spawn) about the edibility of the floral decoration on the table; to his alarm, one of his companions had reached forward with his chopsticks and had, whimsically, elegantly, fastidiously, without comment, extracted blossom after blossom and munched and crunched them up.

"But what *kind* of flowers were they?" asked Liz.

"Oh, quite a variety," said Stephen, "chrysanthemums, carnations, anemones . . . quite a selection."

"Nonsense," said Liz. "I don't believe a word of it." But, almost, she did. Liz herself had been almost at her wits' end in Japan, although she would not disclose this, even to Stephen; the memory of it alarmed her still, which is one of the reasons why she found it pleasant to speak of Japan to Stephen, domesticating a past terror. Indoors, they went, still speaking, to their iced soup and fish salad: they spoke of Yukio Mishima and his stammering hero (stammer for homosexuality?), of Somerset Maugham and his club-footed hero (club foot for stammer-plus-homosexuality?), and of other such transpositions, as they gazed through the dining-room window at the darkening sky and the by now deep, deep blue-purple shades of the little pond. The light play of reason and discourse, over the terrors of the unknowable, the unknown. So lightly spoke Stephen, so lucidly, so gently: a thin, clear, rational, feeling man. Or so he seemed, or so he wished to seem. A man with no harm in him, or a man who had as cunningly as a serpent evaded his own powers of doing ill: at the high price of loneliness. Liz sometimes wondered. Was he ever at his wits' end? Who could say?

Stephen described a strange encounter in a hotel in Osaka. Dining alone there, in the panoramic Western restaurant on the twentieth floor of an exceedingly luxurious, modern hotel, happy with his book and his well-done steak and his bottle of claret and night view of bright lights, glad to be alone for an evening, glad to be spared for a while the trial of smiling and the uncertainty of the significance of his smiling, his attention was suddenly snatched from the history of Lon Nol and the rise of Pol Pot by a mild commotion: an elderly American guest, risen to his feet in some agitation, was pointing at the floor and at the huge, cloth-skirted, central, colourful, help-yourself, abundant Swedish-style buffet table that ran down the center of the room, and Stephen was just in time to catch sight of the disappearing hindquarters of an enormous grey rat, whisking away under the tablecloth.

"A rat, a rat!" exclaimed the elderly American, not quite *à haute voix*—more in a muffled anguish of disbelieving protest: waiters had gathered, claiming not to comprehend, wisely not repeating the offending syllable, quietly, firmly, collectively forcing the gentleman back to his seat, where he collapsed, with his bottle of beer, muttering still to himself, "But I saw a rat, I saw a rat."

Stephen had gazed round the assembled diners, to see how they responded, to see if any others, like himself, had been well placed enough to see the rat (a *rat*? On the *twentieth* floor?). But wisely, they too were pretending to have seen nothing, to have noticed nothing—all, that is, save another solitary and elderly gentleman whom Stephen, to his quickly tempered astonishment, recognized as his one-time tutor from Oxford, the eighty-year-old historian, then plain Sir William Hestercombe, now Lord Filey of Foley. Lord Filey—red nosed, silver haired, elegantly dressed, diminutive—was watching the subsiding of the ripple of excitement with interest above the top of his half-reading glasses, his copy of Paul Hargreaves's flamboyantly entitled *The Resurgence of the Right* momentarily laid to rest on his empty plate. He had clearly already noted Stephen's presence: he saluted him with a modest wave, as soon as Stephen registered his identity. "I had the uneasy feeling," said Stephen, "that he'd been watching me all evening. Me and the rat." A moment of hesitation had followed: then Lord Filey had indicated, in dumb show, from some three tables away, that when Stephen had finished his steak, he would be welcome to join his ex-tutor over coffee. Stephen, humbly, had nodded his consent: and then, munching rather more rapidly than he would have wished, and washing down his claret more carelessly, he had reflected on the recent eccentricities of Lord Filey, which might well be about to let him in for an odd half hour. Lord Filey, he reminded Liz, who only dimly recalled the *furore*, had insisted during the Falklands War on returning his honorary degree to the Argentinian University of San Lázaro, and on returning it with maximum publicity, letters to the press, interviews, and varied diatribes against a startling range of offenders, including the Post Office, which had charged him £8.59 postage and refused to guarantee prompt delivery of his degree because of the hostilities. His diatribes had in turn made him the target of much violent abuse from fellow academics protesting on behalf of the international community of scholarship, the free exchange of ideas, the mutual respect and dignity of independent men of letters. Filey had responded with some scandalous tales about skulduggery and tenure rigging in the history department of San Lázaro; others had hit back with allegations about unsavoury proceedings in Filey's own old college in 1952. And so it had continued, to the amusement of some, to the distress of others, and to the momentary confusion of Stephen Cox as he sat savouring his last glass of claret, wondering how to approach the old boy, and whether it would be necessary to speak of the Falklands and Argentina. But the old boy had made it very easy: with a charming smile, removing his glasses, calling for coffee, he had waved Stephen to a seat, and had opened with the information that he was here in Osaka to collect an honorary degree from a small independent women's college—small fry, small fry, but a very handsome piece of packaging, and it keeps up the score after that small mistake with the Argentine, to which, if you please, we will *not* refer. So they did not refer. They spoke, briefly, of the rat: "A great whiskered chap, a real grandad," said Filey, with glee; of the hundreds of neatly uniformed, charming, diminutive, uniform girls who had lined up to watch his degree ceremony; of Yukio Mishima and Angus Wilson and Edmund Blunden; of raw fish and chrysanthemums; of Stephen's novel, newly translated into Japanese.

"And then," said Stephen, "I went back to my bedroom, and thought about the rat. Twenty floors up. And you know what those hotel bedrooms are like—so spotlessly clean, so hygienic, everything so well laundered, the towels, the toothpaste, the slippers, the kimono laid out—and a *rat?* In a way, I rather admired that rat."

"I think I'd have found a rat quite *friendly* in Japan," said Liz. "I've never felt so"—she rejected the word lonely—"so isolated in my life."

"And now," said Stephen, "you have a little cat. She's nicer than a rat, really."

The cat purred, proudly, when mentioned; she was sitting, as usual, on Liz's knee.

A little silence fell, as Stephen and Liz, separately and knowingly, considered the nature of solitude. Would anything be said? Probably not. And it was not, for at that moment the telephone rang: it was Stella, from Cambridge, wanting, for some reason, the address of Deirdre Kavanagh. Deirdre Kavanagh had, mercifully, vanished from Liz's life: she hoped Stella was not about to reintroduce her. Stephen had never met the colourful, red-haired pastry-making Deirdre; Liz described her, then was persuaded to move on to an account of the state of play with her various offspring and step-offspring. "So *many* of them it takes so *long,*" she deprecated, as she ran down the list. Jonathan, somewhat in his father's footsteps, working for Anglian Television, Aaron on the dole writing a play, Alan, academic and conscientious and political in Manchester, Sally running wild and witless for six months in India, Stella, semi-wild and semi-studious reading Modern Languages at Cambridge. Jonathan, she thought, might be getting married. She hoped so. A grandchild, she said, would be welcome. "I wouldn't like to think," she said, "that being brought up in so large a family had put any of them off having children of their own. But that, I suppose," she said, "is a most selfish thought."

Stephen said that Alix had said to him that she hoped Ilse and Nicholas would have a baby. "A baby?" said Liz, "what could *they* need a baby for? They've got one of my cat's kittens."

The cat purred fiercely, in agreement, and put up her paw to Liz's breast.

And Stephen went on to speak of Alix and Brian. Like Otto, Stephen was anxious about Brian. Brian, his oldest friend, seemed to have struck a bad patch.

"It's politics," said Liz.

"Yes," said Stephen. "In a word, politics. Did you hear he was on strike? That most of the staff at the college are on strike?"

"I thought the college was closing."

"It is. That's why they're on strike."

"That's grim," said Liz.

"Yes," said Stephen, "it is."

"What would you do, Stephen?" asked Liz, tilting her chair back, putting her knees precariously against the circular table, stroking the cat, putting her head quizzically on one side. "What would you do, if you were in charge of this wretched country? I always think you know the answer to these things. What would you do?"

"Ah, me," said Stephen, evasively, as though wondering who he was.

"Yes, you."

Stephen helped himself to a glass more of yellow wine, and began to roll himself a thin little cigarette.

"Me? Well, to begin with, I would abolish the Royal Family. And after that, all privileges, all titles, all honours, all degrees. I would take degree away, and give the other possibility a chance. I would establish equality of income, and see what happened. That's what I would do."

"Really?"

"What do you mean by *really*? I think my programme is at least as practical as Brian's. Or as Otto's. Or as the programme of the present government."

"What do you mean by practical?"

"More likely, if implemented, to have a beneficial effect on the community as a whole, and on the individuals that compose it. More likely to promote health, and wealth, and happiness."

"I think it's very sad that Brian should get the sack," said Liz. "He's a bloody good teacher, I bet."

"Of course he is," said Stephen.

"But your views are even more extreme than Brian's," said Liz.

"My views," said Stephen, "belong to another time scale, they are drawn on another graph altogether. Brian's tragedy is that he lives now, in this time, in these times. These times are not good for men like Brian, who mean well. I do not mean well. Not personally well. So it does not matter much, to me. And it does not matter much to you, for other reasons. But for Brian and, therefore, for Alix—if you may permit me to speak of Alix, who is your friend, not mine—for Brian and Alix, these are b-b-bad times."

"I think these are *mad* times," said Liz. "But here we sit, not at all mad, or at least I don't think we're mad, do you? And enjoy our supper. Or, at least, I enjoyed mine. Here we sit, and enjoy our supper. Is that wrong?"

"Brian and Alix think it is wrong," said Stephen, "but so great is the despair in my heart, and so great the hope in yours, my dear Elizabeth, that we do not."

"That's just phrase-making," said Liz, flattered.

"Yes," said Stephen. "It's called the dying art of conversation."

*   *   *

The darkest, longest night of the year, and the rain poured against the windscreen, violently, relentlessly; the old car was struggling, and not only against the rain. It had some internal problem; it grew more feeble at every incline, its power was dying in it. Alix, on her way home to Wandsworth from Sussex, feared she would not make it. She had no idea what was wrong with the car; it had been sickening for some days, but she had been unable to consult Brian, for he was in Northam with his dying father, and she did not like to trouble him. She had been visiting her ex-mother-in-law, Deborah Manning, who was also dying. And the car, with the year, was dying too. The windscreen wipers battled frantically, manically, against the driving sheets of wet; solid water swept darkly on the glass, and through the glass she could only dimly see approaching road works, striped cones, cones blown over the road in the high wet wind. A bad night to be out. In Alix's view it was St. Lucy's night, the twenty-first of December, and she recited to herself as much as she could remember of Donne's ode: " 'Tis the year's midnight, and it is the day's": and it was indeed almost midnight; it was 11:25. It had been a long day, a long short day. According to Harvey's *Oxford Companion to English Literature*, St. Lucy's Day was not the twenty-first, the shortest day, but December 13. Alix did not believe this, but she had been unable to find anyone to support her. She had asked her Garfield students if they had ever heard of St. Lucy's Day, and one of them, a lapsed Catholic, had claimed that it was celebrated on December 20. Alix's friend Lucy Hattersley, when consulted, had complicated the issue by talking about the winter solstice. Esther, who knew about iconography and saints, had failed to answer her telephone, and Alix had been unable to find her battered old edition of Donne, which might also have supplied the answer. If St. Lucy's Day really was the thirteenth, as Harvey claimed, was Donne under the impression that the thirteenth was the shortest day of the year when it wasn't? Or had the calendar changed? Or the solstice shifted?

With such speculations Alix Bowen attempted to cheer herself as the engine gamely laboured. She was near the end of the last stretch of Motorway, nearly into the safely, more brightly lit purlieus of Greater London. "Come on, poor car," she said aloud, as strange memories of dating classes at Cambridge drifted back into her consciousness; she had loved those dating games, she had looked forward to them, the thrill of an unknown poem on a piece of paper, and one had to guess when written, suggest if possible by whom. Like a television quiz: what would Dr. Leavis have made of the infiltration of television by his ex-students? Making games of that which is most serious. Some of her Garfield students (oddly, in Alix's view) enjoyed playing punctuation games: inserting commas, quotation marks, semicolons, capital letters into chunks of otherwise meaningless undifferentiated prose. "That which is most serious." A Shakespeare echo, but from which play? Alix hunted it through her mind, as the car climbed the last curve of the last overpass. And there, just before the summit, it pitifully choked and expired.

Alix's first emotion was pity. "Poor car, poor car," she said, aloud. How not to identify it with poor Deborah Manning, gallant and wasted, propped up on her window seat with many cushions, gazing across the dark, windswept, muddy tragic lawn at the moaning leafless trees; with poor Fred Bowen, on the fourteenth floor of the Royal Infirmary, his lungs full of water, struggling for breath, gazing across the steep hillsides of his expiring city? The pathetic fallacy. The quotation suddenly came to her: "Do not play in wench-like words with that which is most serious." *Cymbeline*, she suspected. Wench-like words. Did that dismiss all language, all poetry? Was Shakespeare, as she had always expected, in these late plays turning on his own art with a sardonic, elegiac, disenchanted wit?

The rain fell in torrents, noisily, beating against the roof and the bonnet. Alix sat and listened. It drummed, it danced. Thank God, she thought, that Sam decided to spend the night with his friend Willy Heoghor. He would have been worried.

She supposed she would begin to worry herself, eventually. But not yet. She had better things to worry about than sitting near the brow of a Motorway overpass in a clapped out old Renault 4 in the pouring rain. She began with the most recent, the most obvious, with Deborah Manning, in her Sussex farmhouse, dying of cancer, attended by her grandson, Nicholas, by her granddaughter-in-law, Ilse Nemorova, by the tabby cat, daughter of Liz Headleand's tabby cat. Nicholas and Ilse had moved in; their own home had been demolished. Its owner in Sarawak had been, at last, located, and the house, with all its flower-painted walls and floors, with all its bright little grates and beacon windows, had gone, had been flattened, had bowed and crumbled beneath the swinging soft heavy playful inexorable caress of a great metal ball swinging on the end of a crane. Gone were the painted gentians and poppies, gone was the dresser with its rows of plates, gone was the pumpkin lantern. Nicholas and Ilse had moved to Sussex, and now lived with Deborah. When Deborah died, they would inherit the house, the paintings, the estate. Alix had not expected this, had not known why she had not expected it. Deborah had confided the information herself, holding Alix's hand tightly with her bony wasted yellow fingers. "There is no one else," she had murmured, almost apologetically, watching acutely as Alix attempted to respond to the information with appropriate emotion.

And indeed, this was true. There was no one else. Deborah's husband, Sebastian's father, had died five years earlier. Sebastian had been the only child. "I left a few little legacies," Deborah whispered, "a painting or two, to my nieces and nephews. And something for Mrs. Clayton. But the rest is for Nicholas and Ilse."

At this, Alix had looked round at the paintings: those in that room alone were an inheritance. Even Alix, who knew nothing of such things, could recognize Ben Nicholson, Gwen John, Matthew Smith, Ivon Hitchin, David Jones, Rigby Saunders: and in the dining room hung a couple of rather gloomy Modiglianis, given by the artist to Sebastian's grandfather. They had not paid out big money, the Mannings: they had received gifts in kind, for small loans, or chickens. They had paid out little sums, to help friends. They had not invested: they had collaborated with their fellow artists, in early poverty, in comfortable middle age. "There has been no harm in it," Deborah seemed to wish to indicate as she clung to Alix's hand. "I didn't think, my dear," said Deborah, "that it would be right to leave you anything but a token. I knew you would not wish it, you have been so independent"—and here the tears flowed down her thin cheeks, to be brushed impatiently away. "I cry so easily now," said Deborah, "so easily; it's old age, it's ridiculous. I open the paper and read a sad story about a road accident involving a total stranger, and I cry."

Alix too by this time was crying: for Sebastian, for herself, for Deborah, for what? "I never wished to interfere," pursued Deborah, "but I would like to thank you for not keeping Nicholas from me. He has been a great joy to me, has Nicholas."

"Don't say that, don't say that," said Alix, by now weeping copiously, embarrassed, appalled, relieved, prickling, unable to apologise now, at this late moment, for her attempts to keep Nicholas away, her failed, half-hearted attempts. "But I must say it," said Deborah, "for it is true, whatever *you* think to be true. It is true. And it has all worked out well, for Nicholas. He has a real talent. He will not waste his talent, you know. At one point I feared . . ." and here she broke off, and gazed suddenly, abruptly, across the darkening lawn, at the cedar and the bare chestnut, at the end-of-year, end-of-her-life, sombre, damp, rain-gathering gloom. "Sebastian," she said: "Sebastian." She called to him across the garden. The wind moaned in the double glazing. On the walls, bare landscapes of eternal autumn glimmered, pale faces of pale girls stared sadly. Alix sobbed into her handkerchief. "It's so dark," said Deborah Manning, crossly, irritably. "I've always hated this time of year. The dark ditch of the year. And now it's going to be 1984. I suppose we'll get used to its being 1984? It seems improbable. Put on the lights, Alix, would you? Let's have a little indoor sunshine."

And Alix had switched on the lights, and the autumn landscapes and pale girls had faded, and the paintings of bright flowers and fruit had glowed, and Ilse came in with tea and cake on a tray and a clutch of late-delivered Christmas cards. Alix sat there, a guest, a visitor, sipping tea, as Nicholas lit the log fire, as Deborah opened the cards, exclaiming as she did so with pleasure, amusement, mock bewilderment: "Here is one from Horace Ewing Fast Plumbing Services," she announced proudly, displaying a fine stage coach crossing a snowy mountain, "and this one, I do believe, is from that disgraceful young charmer Robert Oxenholme. Well, well, I wonder what *he* wants? Is that the family crest, do you think? Or is it some kind of charity logo? Do tell me, Nicholas, is it true that at art school now one can spend *three whole years* learning how to design logos and holograms for bank cards?" She peered more closely at the card. "I *think* it's the family crest. An S, and H and an O. With a sprig of holly. That young man ought to be ashamed of himself. I saw him on television the other night, talking about the so-called policy of the so-called Arts Council. Disgraceful." She nibbled a piece of cake. "His book on Signorelli was said to be quite good," she said, "but I never read it."

"I don't know who he is," said Ilse, examining the crested card with mild curiosity.

"He's the son of that old monster Johnny Hestercombe.

They came to lunch with us a few years ago at Saint-Ballerin. Weren't you there, Alix? Do you remember them?''

"No," said Alix, "I wasn't there." How could she have been there, she reflected, as she picked up a crumb on the end of her finger: how could she have been there, when she had never been to Saint-Ballerin? And it occurred to her that Deborah did not remember that she had never been there, did not remember that she had been married to Sebastian for only a little over a year: that Deborah in her old age had jumbled time and memory, had extended that brief marriage over impossible meetings, had placed Alix herself in scenes, in landscapes, in houses she had never visited, a fabric of imaginary marriage, an imaginary daughter-in-law, a son who lived on and merged with later years; and why not, why not? She looked at Nicholas, as he knelt by the fire, and prodded it with tongs. "Damn," said Nicholas, as a log dislodged itself and fell into the hearth, scattering sparks. So this was his house, his hearth, his home.

The rain battered the windscreen. Alix was getting cold. Soon she would have to go for help; the rain showed no sign of stopping. Cars flowed past her, regardless.

And who was she to resent Nicholas's inheritance? She did not resent it, she told herself. Let him live comfortably, with his double glazing and his log fire and his Modiglianis and his Ilse and his tabby cat. He had done no wrong: he had loved his grandparents, that was all. They had proved themselves, Nicholas and Ilse, with their little house in Stockwell, with their exhibition at the Serpentine. They had passed the test. And now they looked after Deborah, affectionately, tenderly, gracefully: the angels in the house. What was wrong with that? They would ask her to stay, in the spring she would sit in the garden in a deck chair and gaze at the distant downs, as blackbirds sang. Tears rose again to her eyes. It had been a dreadful day, a day of terrible strain. "Shit," said Alix, growing angry, and switched on the engine, to see if it had recovered; nothing happened at all. Nothing. A dead, wet, depressing click. Then nothing.

"Shit," repeated Alix aloud. "I can't sit here all night." Whatever was she supposed to do? Flag down a passing motorist? Walk to a telephone? Nobody would come out to rescue her on a night like this. She groped in the glove compartment for the torch, and was rather surprised to find it there. She also discovered a bar of fruit-and-nut chocolate,

Brian's favourite. She started to eat it, although she had had a large dinner, at the long candlelit farmhouse table. Brian. His father was dying. His college was closing. He had an interview for a new job on January 18, at Gloseley Polytechnic in Leicestershire. He had applied for several jobs; this was the first interview that had come up, though others were to follow. Gloseley did not much attract Alix, but she kept her mouth shut, on her alarm at the thought of moving to this non-town in the middle of nowhere (27 percent unemployment, two steelworks closed recently the threats of a major coal strike making prospects even dimmer), and praised instead the adventurous educational policy of Leicestershire. Better that Brian should have a job anywhere than he should drift on to picket lines, aimlessly, with his new militant chums. Picket lines that had nothing to do with him, moreover. She could understand his rage at Dr. Streeter's shilly-shally feebleness over the Adult Education Institute: he had a right to protest about threats to his own job and those of his colleagues, for he understood the issues, the problems, and she knew enough herself to agree with his condemnation of Streeter's managerial talents. Streeter was a pompous ass, a self-important yet cowardly timeserver, who always bullied the weakest and allowed himself to be bullied by the powers above. He had let the college's resources run away into the sands: the best of his younger staff had left, and he had mishandled the loyal older members to the point of revolt. And they had revolted. It was all a dreadful mess. Brian was quite right, in principle: but what good would his principles do him, when it came, at his age, to looking for a new post? How would his reference from Streeter read, by now? Gloseley. Well, Alix supposed she could live in Gloseley. But would she herself ever find a job there?

She still clung on to her one day a week at Garfield, to her three days a week with Polly Piper, in the building in Nightingale Terrace off Pall Mall. But the Glovers, her friends Eric and Hannah, had left Garfield, had resigned, had retired early, and there was a new warden, who viewed Alix and English studies and indeed education altogether with suspicion. She seemed to favour a more punitive régime, which she claimed had been forced upon her by government austerity. Alix did not like Miss Higden. She was not as obviously useless as Streeter; one did not immediately ask oneself how she got the job. Indeed, she impressed one as a capable woman and her curriculum vitae was daunting. But she was quite fond of shutting people up in solitary bedrooms, of locking doors on the art room and pottery room between classes, on locking the little kitchen between acknowledged tea and coffee times. She was fond of keys in locks, on principle. She liked to know where everybody was, all the time. She quarrelled with the consultant psychiatrists about treatment, which was none of her business, and she cut Alix's book allowance by two thirds. Alix was reduced to using the Home Office photocopier in Nightingale Terrace. The atmosphere was growing more and more sour, less and less therapeutic. If she were to move, with Brian, to Gloseley, Alix would not now, she thought, miss it very much. But would feel a sense of failure. Of lingering failure.

Jilly Fox had at last been released. She had tried to keep in touch with Alix, but Alix had discouraged her, for it was considered unethical, unprofessional, for staff to maintain personal relationships with ex-inmates outside the institution. The Glovers had often spoken about this to Alix, had discussed the problems such relationships created, had warned her against Jilly Fox in particular: but while they had upheld the spirit of the law, they had occasionally, as good Christians, disobeyed its letter, and indeed numbered amongst their personal friends an elderly woman, a one-time lavatory attendant, who had murdered her eighty-year-old mother and handicapped son in a fit of despair. She came to tea with them, on Sundays, once a fortnight: there was no harm in that, no harm in her. But there was harm in Jilly Fox. Growing, surging, desperate harm. Alix knew it, could feel it, could breathe it in the air. Jilly's last weeks at Garfield had been terrible. She had stalked the corridors, padding quietly in her flat sneakers, white of face and sharp of tongue, prophesying doom. Toni Hutchinson of the blonde braids had long been released; on the day of her disappearance, Jilly had attacked Marilyn, her replacement in Toni's affections, attacked her with nothing more dangerous than a bowl of soup and a flood of abuse, but attacked her, nevertheless, thereby earning herself (intentionally? unintentionally?) another month inside. But out, eventually, she had had to go; Eric and Hannah did not want to release her, but could no longer find any more excuses for keeping her, at the state's very considerable expense. She was not thought to be a danger to others: but a danger to herself she was, and would remain. Eric, Hannah, and Alix spoke of this. Jilly refused to go home to her parents; understandably, as all three agreed. She had, after all, very nearly succeeded in murdering her father, whom she did not forgive, and who did not forgive her.

"What she needs is some kind of halfway house," said Eric, chewing at his pipe. "But there is nowhere. Nowhere. And we can't keep her here. And that's that."

They knew there was nowhere. Nothing, for Jilly, between Garfield and the streets, which in 1983 were even more lurid with temptation than they had been when Jilly was convicted in 1979. Law and order had hardly prevailed, in these years: Jilly would wander out alone into Vanity Fair, into Sodom and Gomorrah, into Sin City, into the arms of pushers and parasites, pimps and pornographers. On paper, she would be cared for: social services would keep an eye on her, she would be helped to find accommodation, she would be encouraged to look for work. On paper. But in practice, there would be no work; in practice, she would within a week be thrown out by her landlady or throw herself out: in practice, she would give her social worker the slip and find other friends. Everybody knew this. Jilly knew it. She had said to Alix, at their last official meeting, "Alix, let me come and live with you, let me, I'll do anything for you, let me." And Alix had turned cold, and shaken her head, and said, "No, Jilly, no, you know I can't do that."

"I'll come in the night," said Jilly, "I'll come in the night and cut your head off with an electric carving knife, if you won't have me."

"Oh, Jilly," said Alix, "don't, don't do such things to yourself, take care of yourself. I beg you, take care of yourself, for my sake."

"I haven't the strength," said Jilly, "I don't care for myself. Why should I take care of myself?"

"For no reason that I can give you," said Alix.

"Goodbye," said Jilly Fox.

"Goodbye," said Alix.

And so they had parted. But within days of her release, Jilly was on the phone to Alix, pleading: she was standing in wait at the bus stop, pleading; she was sitting on Alix's front steps in Wandsworth, alternately pleading and threatening. Alix, desperate, had consulted Eric and Hannah, had consulted Liz Headleand: they had all given calm, calculated, professional advice. Never, never let her over your threshold, they had all said, the professionals. Never speak to her for more than two minutes..Ring for the social worker. Change your telephone number. Get Brian on to her. Change your route to Whitehall. Contact the police.

Irrelevant-seeming counsel, but Alix, dutifully, had tried to follow it. She had hardened her heart, had spoken no kind words. If you give in now, Liz said (and Alix knew this was true), she'll burden you forever, and there's no curing her. You know there's no curing her, she'll only turn on you when she finds you can't really help her. You will do no good to her, and a great deal of harm to yourself. You must save yourself.

So Alix had changed her telephone number, to the considerable inconvenience of the whole family, and to the deep suspicion of Dr. Streeter, who was convinced that Brian had changed the number because he had reason—good reason—to believe his phone was being tapped by the police. Alix had found herself for a while imprisoned at times in her own house, lying flat beneath the drawing-room window when she glimpsed Jilly in the street below, crouching beneath the panes of the glass front door as the doorbell rang and rang; once she dodged into the British Council car park in Spring Gardens when she saw Jilly stationed in a dark corner of Cockspur Court as she walked to the bus stop from work. Crouching there, hidden behind a red Triumph down at the seventh level, her heart beating fast with fear and humiliation and sorrow, she had witnessed strange sights, strange car park sights of the underground city: a dapper executive eating a hamburger from a square box with ravenous, with starving speed and a demented, hunted expression; a woman who removed her jersey, sniffed her armpits, sat there in her brassiere, applied deodorant, then reclothed herself in a blouse and jacket and calmly made up her face, smiling at herself obsequiously, seductively, in her driving mirror; a strange, furtive interchange over an open car trunk between a policeman and a young man with an orange sports bag and a squash racket; a weeping older woman with an angry younger man. Half an hour she had crouched, hidden away, waiting for Jilly to move, waiting for Jilly to give up and grow bored and go away. Hard, it was, the hardening of her heart, but eventually, after some weeks, it worked: Jilly stopped haunting her, gave up hope of her, moved elsewhere. Alix felt like a murderer. Where had Jilly gone? She had liked Jilly, had loved Jilly, had loved the desperate edge of her, the rocky hardness of her, the sullen recalcitrance of her. When she vanished, she missed her.

Jilly had written her a letter, for Christmas. Not a very soothing letter, not, in conventional terms at least, a very Christmas-spirited letter. "Dear Alix, dearest Alix, I forgive you," it read. "I would like you to know that I forgive you, for I shall not last long. You will think to hear the last news of me soon. But it will not be the last news, for I shall be with you forever. There is no death. There is death only of the body. This have I learned. I fly, I fly into the higher air, and I look down and see the small world turning. The upper reaches are thick with spirits. Perpetual life. The cry of the cockatrice is transformed into the music of the spheres. There is no evil: evil and good are one. At the extremities we meet. Crime is not; sin is not; evil is not; all is good, all is holy. The winter solstice is now, and forever, and never, for the light shines forever, in eternal glory, and we are consumed and not consumed in everlasting fire. Dear Alix, I no longer need your telephone number, for I speak to you magically, in my thoughts, whenever I wish. Goodbye, goodbye, and Happy Christmas."

This letter had been written in a perfectly normal hand on perfectly ordinary Basildon Bond paper. The postmark was W.10. There was no address, and the date Jilly had given was not the December date when it had clearly been written, but the date of Jilly's own birth: July 7, 1958. Alix did not show it to Eric and Hannah; she felt she had in this context showed them perhaps too much obedience, perhaps too much respect. She did not even think of showing it to the new warden, Miss Higden. It was none of Miss Higden's business, and never would be. But she did show it to Liz. Liz read it with curiosity, and said at once, "Drugs. Obviously. She's back on drugs. What was she on before?" Alix listed, as best she could, the drugs she believed Jilly had been taking before her committal. "Yes," said Liz, "yes that would figure. Easy enough to get hold of these days." Liz did not seem surprised. Alix supposed that she was not herself surprised. Nevertheless, she had said, from loyalty to the Jilly she had known, "But it's so sad, Jilly was such a—such a *reasonable* person. Such a rational person, really. And now this—this nonsense?"

"Well," said Liz, rather unexpectedly, "it's not *such* nonsense. And it's rather well written, really. It may not be the last of her at all."

"You mean she may get through it? Recover?"

"People do. It's very usual, when you come out like that, to

go on a binge, isn't it? Of drink, or drugs, or whatever you're
hooked on? I'm sure I would myself, wouldn't you?''

"And some people get over it?''

"Some, yes.'' Liz had peered at the letter again. "That bit
about the cockatrice is a bit odd, isn't it? What *is* a cockatrice?
Is it Biblical?''

And she had diverted the conversation from Jilly, expertly,
but had left Alix with a glimmer of hope. Alix prayed for Jilly,
now, at the winter solstice, as she sat in her car in the driving
rain. A leak had developed, water was dripping on the back
seat. Midnight. The year's turning. This is *ridiculous,* thought
Alix suddenly, I can't sit here; I must get to a phone. There are
phones on motorways. I'll ring the AA. Come on, get moving,
she said to herself, and ate another square of fruit and nut.

Walking was difficult, along the hard shoulder, in the harsh
orange fluorescent fallout, in the wet blare of the headlamps of
other, luckier, mobile motorists. No Good Samaritan paused
for Alix, and Alix, still brooding on her cruelty to Jilly, felt she
did not deserve one. She would get the help she and Brian had
paid for, from the AA. Luckily she had her Associate Member's Card with her; luckily she had Sam's yellow-hooded
cagoule to keep her dry. She hoped she was walking towards
the nearest telephone; she had been told (but maybe it was
folklore?) that Motorway telephones were never more than half
a mile apart. Rain bleared her glasses even though her head
was bent against the weather; she took them off and put them
in Sam's pocket, where she encountered the end of a tube of
mints, a no doubt filthy handkerchief, a crumpled, soft,
matted, decomposing piece of paper, and his Swiss Army
knife. The Swiss Army knife made her smile, reassured her.
He was a proper boy, Sam; a proper boy, as Nicholas had never
been. A boy with a father. Brian adored Sam; maybe they
should have had more children, but they had agreed, by
unspoken consent, to preserve an equilibrium, to rest there, not
to push their luck. Their luck. Well, yes they had been lucky,
so far, but the prospects for 1984 were perhaps appropriately
bleak. Brian had been asked to conduct a class, as part of his
interview at Glosely Poly, a class of unknown students, in
front, as it were, of an examining tribunal. An insult, at this
age, she felt on his behalf, although he did not say so himself.
At times, Alix could not bring herself to think about Brian.

Wherever was the telephone? She plodded on. A car slowed
down to inspect her, and she waved at it for help, but it drove

on: kerb crawling seemed an unlikely pastime on such a night as this, *think* of the discomfort, but one never knew, some people were desperate. Maybe she presented a mad, a formidable figure, as she walked alone through the darkness in a yellow cagoule, wisps of greyish hair escaping and blowing in the gale? Motorway rape was a relatively new phenomenon: women drivers forced off the road, kidnapped, abducted, raped, hijacked, dumped in distant fields or trussed in warehouses. Alix fingered the stubby smooth closed heavy knife. She refused to be afraid of her fellow citizens. She refused. Defiantly, she put up her thumb for the next passing car (which ignored or did not see her), but a moment later caught sight of the welcoming phone. She didn't, of course, know what to do with it when she reached it, never having been in such an emergency before; it didn't seem to have a proper dial. She looked for instructions but failed to spot them. Eventually she lifted the receiver, and after a while a comfortingly normal voice said: "Yes? Can I help you?" Alix explained. The policeman on the other end of the line told her to return to her vehicle and wait for the AA. "All right," said Alix, meekly. And off she went, back towards her car, for what must have been at least half a mile; emboldened, she thumbed every vehicle that passed, thinking she might at least get back into the relatively dry as quickly as possible. But nobody stopped. Nobody. She was mildly shocked. On such a night, mine enemy's dog, though he had bit me, should have stood that night against my fire, she quoted (misquoted?) to herself, as she made her way, more easily, with the wind behind her, to the waiting Renault.

And there, marooned, she sat. For a quarter of an hour, half an hour, three quarters of an hour.

The police had been unable to give her any idea of how long she would have to wait. One in the morning, a quarter past one. Her thoughts returned, inevitably, through boredom, to Jilly Fox. Jilly had spoken very eloquently of boredom and in the end Alix had been obliged to listen. It was boredom that had driven her to drugs and crime; and in her case, the crime had not been wholly in pursuit of the drugs, it had been embraced for its own sake. For thrills, for excitement, for a sense of being alive, for a momentary freedom from the tyranny of time. "All my childhood," Jilly had told Alix, "I sat with my eyes on the clock, waiting for things to be over. Waiting for time to pass. Bored? I thought I'd die. I thought I'd *die* of boredom. And I mean *die*. I thought I'd just stop breathing, at the dinner table, in front of telly, in school, prayers, in lessons. I used to play these games with myself—that I mustn't look at my watch or at the clock until I'd counted three hundred backwards, until my father had cleared his throat three times, until a cloud edged across the window pane, until the history teacher blew her nose—and then I'd look, and only a poxy five minutes would have passed. Five miserable minutes, out of a lifetime. And it just seemed *stupid*—wrong, stupid—to spend the rest of my life waiting for time to pass. Glad when every day was over. Sorry when I woke up every morning. Relieved whenever a minute passed without my counting it out, second by second. What was wrong with me? I don't know. When I was high, time flew. And it was even better, breaking into the chemist's, breaking into corner shops. The excitement. Planning what to go for. Hiding in the dark. Listening out. Hearing one's heart beat. You know what I mean?''

Garfield, Jilly had admitted, had eventually given the hours, the days, the weeks a meaning. The régime had parcelled time out, carved it up, made shares of it. Better than boarding school, because less full of lies, Jilly said.

One has to learn to parcel out one's own time. To make shapes of it for oneself, said Alix, piously.

Oh, I know the theory, said Jilly. But how? How? How? And why? Who cares? Why?

Half past one. The rain, at last, had abated. Where was Jilly now, on what bare floor, on what damp mattress, beneath what leaking roof?

Alix thought of Esther, who had made sense of time: or so it seems. The thought of Esther comforted her. The aesthetic principle. The organizing principle. Esther's interests were timeless, enduring. Solitary.

The axolotl, on the other hand, had missed out. It had got stuck. Sam had been studying the axolotl at school, in zoology. He had been captivated by its unusual morphology, its eccentricity, its harmlessness. He had done a project on the axolotl. He had always liked underwater creatures, had begged for a fish tank which he kept stocked with snails and caddis larvae, water daphnae, beetles; he was too compassionate to keep fish. It upset him to see them swim in circles. He wanted to live in a house in the country with a pond. He wanted a springer spaniel. There was a fair-sized pond in the grounds of Deborah's house in Sussex. When Deborah died, he would be able to go to stay with his half-brother, Nicholas, and study pond life in the summer. The teeming life of the menis cus, the darting minnows below, the crawlers of the deep. In Wandsworth, there was no space for a pond or a springer spaniel. In Gloseley, she doubted very much if there would be space for a pond or a springer spaniel, though perhaps housing would be cheaper, up in Leicestershire? The thought of Gloseley depressed her dreadfully. Its very name (though of course the poor place could not help its name) struck a chill to the heart, and its description in Robert Waller's *Almanac of British Politics* offered little comfort: a New Town in danger of becoming a Ghost Town, a Midlands anomaly, a manufacturing town flanked to the north and east by Tory foxhunters, to the south and west by nuclear missiles and army camps. Gloseley had been designated, in 1981, as one of the first Enterprise Zones in England: a dubious accolade. There were prospects of new jobs in frozen foods and potato crisps. And the most depressing aspect of the prospect of flat, barbed-wire, muddy Gloseley was that Brian would not get the job. It would go to a younger man. A younger man with safer references.

Brian, redundant, would have time to write his novel, the great chronicle novel of the northern working class. Brian would be forced, by redundancy, to confront the knowledge that time was not what he needed; Brian would turn sour. Already he had become unreasonable; later, he would, like everyone else, become sour.

Alix had suggested to Jilly Fox that she try to write. Jilly had looked at Alix with contempt and said, "What, me? Adding to the crap? How I was a gangster's moll? How I came off the hard stuff? How I tried to kill my father? That kind of shit? No thanks."

Jilly Fox, like Shakespeare, did not approve of playing, in wench-like words, with that which was most serious. Although, when constrained, when forced through lack of other options, she had enjoyed reading, in class, for Alix; had studied well, passed exams, had enthusiasm. She would never continue, of her own accord. She knew that. Alix knew that. Why?

I have failed Jilly, thought Alix; she pushed out of her mind, as too painful, too unbearable, too raw, the notion that she was now, even now, and more profoundly, in the process of failing Brian. She concentrated on Jilly Fox. She ate a mint. She was frozen.

The AA, when at last it arrived, did not fail Alix. It arrived in the form of a pick-up truck and a young man with a moustache. He clucked and hummed and muttered over the open bonnet, walked round and round the car several times, and delivered his verdict: it was the exhaust. It could not be fixed there and then: he would take the Renault to a garage in Croydon, and Alix home to her bed. "Lucky you'd got a Relay membership," he said. "Yes," said Alix, meekly, and meek she remained as he entertained her on the way to Wandsworth with various faintly sexist anecdotes about women drivers in distress; he was chivalry itself compared with her one-time driving instructor, who had made her drive round Leicester Square and Piccadilly Circus with her L-plates while he described what he would do to the layabouts, tramps, and addicts who huddled disconsolately there on steps and benches. "I'd dig a large *pit*," this man had declared, "and *shovel* them into it, and *douse* them with petrol, and set fire to the lot!" The AA man confined himself to stories about women summoning him to tune their car radios or to enquire why their engines had stopped when they had merely run out of petrol; some women, said the AA man, believe me, don't even know what a dip stick is. Amazing, murmured Alix politely. There was no fight in her, and anyway, what he said was no doubt, in its own terms, true.

He dropped her on her own doorstep. "You'll be all right, then?" he enquired, glancing up at the narrow dark building. "Oh, yes," she reassured him, thanking him effusively: if she had been young, wild, sexy, would she have asked him up? Did he sometimes get asked up? It was three in the morning. He drove off, waving goodbye: she switched on the hall light and locked the door behind her, and as she locked it, the telephone began to ring.

She hesitated. Brian, with news of his father? Sam, ill? Nicholas and Ilse, with news of Deborah? Any of them might have been ringing all evening, might have continued to ring, anxiously, finding her neither there nor in Sussex. She lifted the phone. "Hello," she said, ready with explanations. But it was, as she had half suspected, Jilly Fox.

"Alix?" said Jilly. "Alix, is that you?"

"Jilly," said Alix. "Is that you?" She was curiously relieved to hear her voice.

"I was ringing to wish you a Happy Christmas," said Jilly.

"What, at *this* hour?" said Alix, in her old schoolteacher voice.

"What time is it?"

"It's three in the morning," said Alix.

"And where've *you* been? I've been ringing for hours. For hours and hours and hours." Accusing.

"I've been sitting in the rain on the Motorway," said Alix. "I've just got in." She explained, briefly.

"Poor you," said Jilly. She didn't sound high, or mad, or desperate; she sounded like her old sharp self. "Alix," said Jilly, "let me come and see you. One last time. I've things to tell you."

"You know I can't," said Alix.

"One last time. Then I'll never bother you again. I promise. I solemnly promise. Please, Alix."

Alix temporized.

"I'll come and see you," she offered. "Tell me where you are."

"Will you? Will you really?" Jilly sounded pleased, innocently pleased. "Will you come soon?"

"I'll come after Christmas," said Alix. "I've got to go up north, tomorrow, to see my family. I'll see you when I get back. Tell me where to find you."

Jilly told. She was in a squat, Lykewake Gardens, off the Harrow Road. Alix could find her there, but should come in the afternoon; mornings are hopeless, said Jilly, and evenings are worse. They agreed on an afternoon: Monday, January 9th, 1984. "I'll be there," said Liz. Four o'clock. Prompt. Then, as an afterthought, asked where Jilly was calling from.

"From a friend's," said Jilly. "A lady friend's."

"And how did you get my new telephone number?" asked Alix.

A brief silence.

"From Otto Werner," said Jilly, and laughed.

"From Otto Werner?" echoed Alix. "But you don't know Otto Werner."

"No, I don't. But I know that you and your husband know him. You made me read an article by him once, remember? So I rang him. He's in the telephone book. I rang him. And he told me. Silly of him, wasn't it?"

"It was a bit silly of him," said Alix. "But it doesn't matter."

"Really not?"

"Really not."

And, brushing her teeth, clambering exhausted into bed, Alix thought that it didn't matter, much; she had to see Jilly, of course, one last time. I am in blood so far, to go back were as tedious as go o'er, she recited to herself, as she shut her eyes, expecting instant sleep.

But sleep did not come. She was too tired to sleep. And as she lay there, restless, tired, irritable, she submitted herself to a version of the following questionnaire, prompted, perhaps by the introduction, the off-guard, unexpected introduction of the name of Otto Werner, at the darkest hour of the longest darkest night of the year. Thus the questions presented themselves:

Q. Did she, Alix Bowen, in December 1983, consider that London was a more dangerous, more drug-infested place than it had been when Jilly Fox was convicted of various offences way back in 1979?

A. Yes, she did.

Q. Did she blame the Tory government for this deterioration in law and order?

A. No. Not really.

Q. Yes or no?

A. No.

Q. Did she believe the Labour government for which she had herself voted would have halted this process of deterioration?

A. No. Not really. No.

Q. Would she have given this answer five years earlier?

A. No.

Q. Would Brian expect that a Labour government would have halted this process of deterioration?

A. Yes.

Q. Did Brian believe that the Metropolitan Police was corrupt and racist, and that drug taking and violence were caused by inner-city decay and rising levels of unemployment?

A. Yes.

Q. Did Alix agree with this?

A. Yes. In part. Yes.

Q. But nevertheless Alix believed that a Labour government could do nothing to halt this process?

A. Yes.

Q. So Alix believed the process was inevitable, and that unemployment would continue to rise, violence to increase, drug taking to multiply?

A. Yes. Sort of. Yes.

Q. Did Brian believe this?

A. No.

Q. Did Brian believe that a radical left government could rescue Britain from the death throes of capitalism?

A. Yes.

Q. Did she?

A. No.

Q. Did Brian think a radical left government would be elected?

A. It depends what you mean by *think*.

Q. Answer yes or no.

A. Well, then, no.

Q. Does Brian say he believes a radical left government will be elected?

A. Yes.

Q. Is Brian lying?

A. Not really. Sort of. No.

Q. Do you think a radical left government will be elected?

A. No.

Q. Do you think that the militant group which Brian has joined is hindering the prospects of a Labour government of any complexion?

A. Yes.

Q. Is that its intention?

A. No.

Q. Do you think it possible that Brian's group and other such groups, that Arthur Scargill and the Liverpool Council and the left-wing polytechnic-trained intellectuals of Northam, are ensuring the continuance of right-wing rule, indeed the increasing popularity of right-wing rule, and are positively encouraging the growing inequality of the society they claim to wish to redeem?

A. Yes.

Q. Do you think, as some do think, that this is their intention?

A. No.

Q. So you think they are deluded?

A. Yes.

Q. And you think Brian is deluded?

A. Yes.

Q. Can you talk about this to Brian?

A. No.

Q. Why not?

A. I thought I was only allowed to answer yes or no. Could you please rephrase that question?

Q.? A.? Q.? A.? No.

Q.? A.? Q.? A.? I think you don't know how to phrase that question, because you haven't thought it through properly, because you don't know *how* to think it through. Is that correct?

A. Yes.

Q. Have you been trying to suggest that my answers to your questions put me in some kind of representative position of representative confusion?

A. Yes.

Q. You think there are millions more like me?

A. Yes. Well, hundreds of thousands, let us say.

Q. You think I ought to make up my mind?

A. Not necessarily.

Q. Yes or no, remember.

A. No, then. No.

Q. Is that because making up one's mind involves internalizing lies?

A. Yes.

Q. Could you have conceived, ten years ago, of my occupying this position? This lack of position?

A. No.

Q. What has happened?

A. Q. A. Q. Could you rephrase that question, please?

A. Q. A. Q. A. Q. . . . Yes, no, yes, no, yes, no. The dialogue of self and self. On and on and on and on. Self and self, self and self. Alix and Brian can no longer speak, as once they did.

Q. One last question. Do you, Alix Bowen, still call yourself a socialist?

A. Yes.

I'd be very interested, in that case, to hear your definition of the term socialism. So would Brian, I'm sure.

Well, you'll have to wait.

Wait for what?

I'll work it out. In the end. You wait.

And meanwhile, you're prepared to go on living falsely, in a false position, on undefined premises?

Yes. Well, sort of. Yes.

In the morning, Brian rang. His father had died in the night. They talked, muddled, sad, of the funeral, of Christmas, of the car stuck in Croydon, of arrangements. She put the phone down, and it rang again instantly. Nicholas, to ask why she had been home so late, they had tried to ring her to tell her not to worry when she discovered she'd forgotten her reading glasses; they'd found them in the bathroom. We gave up ringing at midnight; we were worried, he said. She told him of Brian's father's death. They spoke of Christmas, of altered plans. She put the phone down, and it rang again, instantly; and this time it was Otto Werner, a worried Otto Werner.

"Alix," he said, "I've been so worried, I'm afraid I've been a dreadful fool, you're going to be so cross with me, and quite right too—I've been a dreadful fool, I gave your new phone number to a woman who rang up last night, and then I realized I've probably given it to *exactly* the wrong person, the one person you're trying to avoid? She said she was your sister, but then I thought later, surely you'd have *given* your new number to your sister? Do tell me it wasn't that woman from Garfield. Did she ring?"

Poor Otto, he sounded very guilty. He *was* guilty.

"It doesn't matter," said Alix. "It doesn't matter at all. It's probably all for the best."

"I just wasn't *thinking*," said Otto, at this confirmation of his crime.

She reassured him. She told him of Brian's father's death. She told him about her night on the hard shoulder. Poor Alix, said Otto, with feeling, it's going to be one of those Christmases, I can tell. And I was also ringing to invite you to a 1984 Twelfth Night party, but it seems a little tactless, in the circumstances, perhaps?

Alix said that on the contrary, they might want above all things to go to a Twelfth Night party. She took down details: Friday 6th, 8 p.m. onwards. Otto kept on apologising for asking them, she kept on assuring him that they might well turn up. It would be good for Brian, she said, but I suppose it depends on the funeral arrangements. Do try to come, urged

Otto. And, as an afterthought: it's such a long time since you saw Caroline. Caroline would so much like to see you both.

"We'll do our best," said Alix. "Give my love to Caroline."

"And hers to you," said Otto, vaguely. "And hers to you."

Liz Headleand was also invited to Otto and Caroline Werner's Twelfth Night party, and accepted with alacrity. She said she needed the prospect of a party: "I've had a horrid week," she told Otto over the phone, "I hate Christmas, such a hassle and all the family get so cross, and Charles will be in England and wants to come to Christmas dinner with the boys, can you imagine, and then on top of all that we've had this disaster with a patient, he'd got this thing about having AIDS—he used to think he'd got cancer, but then he decided it was AIDS. We thought nothing of it, and went on with group therapy as usual, and now it turns out he really *has* got AIDS and all the group are furious with us, and have lost faith in our diagnostic powers completely, and I must say I can't blame them, but how could we have known? He was a classic depressive hypochondriac, poor chap, and now he's got this dreadful dreadful illness. God knows where he picked it up. The whole Institute is in a state of depressive hypochondria now. We all think we've got it."

"Oh dear, never mind," said Otto, who had not been listening. "We'll look forward to seeing you on the twelfth."

"You don't mean the twelfth," said Liz, "you mean the sixth, don't you? That's what you said the first time round. Twelfth Night is the sixth."

"Oh God," said Otto, "how confusing," and without saying goodbye, absent-mindedly rang off, thinking not of Liz but of Alix Bowen and his own gullibility and culpability. Otto Werner found himself thinking quite often of Alix Bowen these days. More than he used to. He had no idea why. Transferred worry about Brian, perhaps? The last thing he would ever have wanted to do was to make trouble for Alix. She had enough trouble, he feared, with Brian, these days.

Liz put the phone down, wondering how many people Otto had managed to ask for the wrong night and returned to the decoration of the Christmas tree. In theory, Sally and Aaron were helping her, but they had dodged off into the kitchen to eat a toasted sandwich before departing for their respective

nights of entertainment. Aaron was off to the theatre to see an
Alan Ayckbourn, Sally to a party in Kentish Town. Liz
adjusted a streamer of tinsel, and clipped on a silver bird. The
tree was gold and silver, this year; no other colours permitted.
Liz hadn't been intending to get a tree, but Sally and Stella had
insisted. And there it was. Beautiful, said Aaron, re-entering
the room with a mouthful of toast, even better than Harley
Street, don't you think?

Aaron was in good form, these days. His play was to be put
on in the new year, at one of the more established fringe
theatres. It was, he informed Liz, a transvestite drama entitled
Squeaking Cleopatra, with a double time scheme, set partly
backstage at the first performance of Shakespeare's tragedy in
1607, and partly backstage at a 1984 production of the same
play at one of our large London-based subsidized companies.
It's political drama, said Aaron, about the Arts Council. That's
what he said, but Liz and Sally thought he was joking. Neither
of them had been allowed to read the script.

The tree glittered, frostily. I must dash, said Aaron, I'll see
you on Christmas Eve. Enjoy the play, said Liz. Aaron was
living in a flat in Highbury, with a couple of friends. It had all
worked out well. And Sally too was well; back from India,
unemployed, but well, and honourably looking for work. She
had an interview with a publisher the next week. But how
would she react to Charles? Liz fretted, as she draped the little
white lights. Of all the children, Sally had taken Charles's
remarriage worst: she had refused to see him, to speak to him
on the phone, to answer his letters, she had even, ominously,
refused to bank his conciliatory cheques. She had accused Liz
of being feeble, female, slavish, eager to please, in her
acceptance of Charles's defection, Charles's renewed demands. "You just want everyone to love you, Mum," she
accused Liz, "you just want everyone to think you're wonderful. You should stand up for yourself."

"But I do," said Liz. "In my own way. I just don't like
quarrelling, that's all."

"No," said Sally, darkly. "You prefer to manipulate.
Old-fashioned stuff. Underhand stuff."

"That's right," said Liz.

And would Sally, now, think the manipulation had paid off?
Now that Charles was creeping back to London and begging
for his Christmas dinner? Would she think that this was what
Liz had wanted? *Was* it what Liz had wanted? And whatever

had happened to Henrietta? Liz hummed ''In the deep Mid-winter'' tunelessly to herself, as she dressed the tree, and thought of all the houses, all over London, all over Britain, where families forced themselves to congregate, to quarrel, to fight, to feud, to smile, to weep, to complain, to overeat, to jostle and gather and litter and lay waste. As children, she and Shirley had hated Christmas, for it had marked them out for the lepers that they were: outcasts, treeless, without kin, without comfort, without presents, without past. She preferred the densely populated world she had created, with all its problems. She was not afraid of Charles, she told herself: no, not at all, not at all afraid. But her hand trembled slightly as she reached to adjust the topmost star; she had achieved calm, after four years of battle, and was he on his way to disturb her yet again?

Esther Breuer had decided to spend Christmas in Bologna, with Claudio's sister Elena, rather than in Manchester, with her parents and her brother's family, or alone, in Ladbroke Grove. Claudio was in New York, on a sabbatical with his wife. She had seen him only once, since the summer of the lecture of the werewolf: he had been to London for a week in October, and had spent all his free time with her. Hour after hour they had sat together in the red room as in the old days, talking, drinking, talking, talking. But Esther had deceived him, had played him false: she had not given herself, during these long sessions, she had remained detached, conscious, rational. And he had not noticed the difference. This had shocked her. Sitting, now, at Heathrow (for she had decided that, in 1983, at this time of year, at her age, she had to fly), she reflected that this was what had most shocked her—more than his yellow pallor, his shaking hands, loss of appetite, his evident ill health. He could not tell whether she was with him, accompanying him, in his ramblings, or not. Maybe he had never been able to tell, maybe she had herself been deluded into believing in their great, their unique, their disembodied mystic intimacy? How much easier it would have been, to fall once more under the spell, to believe, with Claudio, that black was white and white was black, to allow herself to be, as of old, seduced and hypnotized into half light, into his self-creating, self-perpetuating, self-validating terms and shades. But she had forced herself to withhold herself (remembering Liz by the

canal bank, remembering the severed head): had sat, treacher-
ously, faithlessly, emptily, coldly, by his side, faking odd
murmurs of response when his monologue halted. She had
withdrawn belief, had withdrawn love, and he was falling ill
from her refusal, but he knew it not.

She would speak of these things to Elena, her new friend,
her new ally.

Her potted palm, astonishingly, survived. Claudio had
commented upon its perseverence. It is a long time dying, he
had said.

On the way to catch the tube to Heathrow, Esther had passed
Jilly Fox on the street, but without knowing it, for although she
knew the story of Jilly Fox, almost to the latest instalment, she
had never seen her. Jilly Fox was staring at a *Standard* placard
which read HORROR LATEST: ESCAPED VICTIM DESCRIBES
ATTACKER. Esther too paused briefly to stare, before hurrying
on. She did not buy a copy.

And now she sat at crowded Heathrow, on the afternoon of
December 23, waiting for her flight to be called, and reading
her selected travel literature: she was just beginning to make a
little headway with an offprint of "Some Florentine Moneyers
and Reflections on the Organization of Italian Mints in the
Fourteenth and Fifteenth Centuries" from the *Numismatic
Chronicle* when she sensed that somebody was trying to attract
her attention, looked up, and saw, standing over her, elegant,
lightly suited, smiling enquiry and greeting, Stephen Cox.

"Esther," he said, in his slightly husky, polite, hesitant
drawl. "Are you making a b-bid for freedom as well? Leaving
Christmas behind?"

"That's the plan," said Esther, moving along the padded
bench to make room for him. "And where are you off to?" she
asked.

He was off to Istanbul, he said. His flight was delayed. So
is mine, said Esther. They chatted, exchanging news. They did
not know one another well, but were pleased, for a short time,
to meet: lone travellers, escaping England, family, festivities.
Because they did not know one another well, they spoke of
mutual friends: of Alix, of Brian, of Liz Headleand. Stephen
had not heard of Brian's father's death, but knew more than
Esther of Charles Headleand's arrival: Charles had already had
a row with his son Jonathan, but had at least temporarily
placated Sally, according to Liz: and it appeared that the
dreaded Henrietta had departed, ambiguously, indecisively, to

spend Christmas in Zambia with her daughter, who was married to a farmer there and about to produce a baby. Gossip, they exchanged, in the Eurolounge, until Stephen was called to Gate 36. A Happy Christmas, a Happy New Year, a Happy 1984, they politely wished one another. I prophesy it will be a grim year, said Stephen, but not quite in the way Orwell predicted. And it will be all right for you and for me, if we continue to keep out of the way.

And, smiling, he backed away, and faded, like a mirage, from her sight.

Esther had expected, indeed hoped, to spend the rest of her journey in silence with her *Numismatic Chronicle* and Cellini's autobiography, but this was not to be. She found herself placed in a window seat, next to a tallish, young-middle-aged man, whom she vaguely and indifferently noted to be strikingly handsome, in a raffish, casual, seedy sort of way: the handsomeness penetrated her screen of Florentine moneyers, though he was making no effort to project it, nor she to receive it. Indeed, he seemed to be admirably intent, at first, on minding his own business, a little subdued, perhaps, by having hit his head rather smartly on the luggage rack while trying to get out of the turbulent way of a large fur-coated woman with two large teenage sons and a great deal of oddly shaped Harrods-wrapped hand baggage. He had crumpled into his too-small seat and sat there meekly, staring at nothing much, reaching for his *Executive High-Fly Business Magazine*, returning it to its pocket with a rustle of boredom, then shutting his eyes, all in the best manner of an habituated, weary, over-travelled man of the world. But as the plane took off, Esther thought she detected in him a slight jerk of alarm, of unnatural tension: it subsided, and he shut his eyes once more, but she felt tension building in him once more after twenty minutes or so, as she heard the rattle of the drinks trolley approach. She was rather looking forward to a stiff, festive drink, and was turning over pleasurably in her mind the possibilities: a vodka martini? a couple of whiskies? a whisky and a quarter of champagne?— for it was, after all, Christmas—when she noticed that her neighbour was grabbing the arm of his seat very tightly, and breathing in short, shallow gasps. Was he about to pull out a hand grenade? she inevitably, in 1983, wondered. Was he an international terrorist? Was he an Italian Neo-Fascist, an Italian Marxist, a member of the PLO? He did not look Italian: he looked more Nordic. She didn't think he was English: she had glimpsed a foreign-looking passport in his inner pocket as he reached for his cigarettes. He was smoking now, somewhat frantically: maybe he was merely trying, unsuccessfully, to give up nicotine, and suffering from withdrawal symptoms?

The drinks trolley jangled and clattered its slow, tantalizing way towards them. Esther had settled on a vodka martini and a small white wine, and was about to place her order with the stewardess when her neighbour ungallantly, forcefully, intercepted her request and demanded a couple of whiskies. The stewardess obliged, instantly: for he was a very handsome man. Esther waited, and received in turn, or rather out of turn, her dinky little paper disk, her mini-packet of nuts, her beaker of crushed ice, her little bottles: she arranged them in front of her as though for a doll's tea party. She herself had relaxed, completely, having diagnosed the complaint of her unchosen companion. He was a drinking man, and he needed his Scotch. He poured out one of his little bottles and knocked it back in one, undiluted (he had, in an almost unnoticeably foreign accent, expressed great displeasure at the thought of ice); then he poured out the second and sat back, as Esther assumed, a happier man. But she had got it slightly, though only slightly, wrong: for after a few minutes, he suddenly leaped to his feet, waving his arms, and shouting in an unknown tongue. He hit his head again on the luggage rack, but managed to stay on his feet, flailing, crying out.

Passengers and crew reacted with instant panic and consternation. Some ducked and covered their heads; the stewardess fell on the gangway behind her trolley, screaming; a woman shouted that she had been shot. As it slowly became clear that no one had been shot, and that the man was not armed, people began to collect themselves, ashamed of their display of instant terror; a steward began to approach, as the man, hooked onto the luggage rack by one long arm, orated. Esther had by now worked it all out. Her new friend was not mad, or crazed, or violent, he was not demanding hostages or requesting to be flown to Tripoli; he was simply very very drunk. His quiescent behaviour at the beginning of the flight had been the careful calm of a man who knows he has already had too much: the irresistible miniature whisky had taken him over the top, into another realm.

As it happened, Esther was thoroughly familiar with this realm, and well used to conversing with its inhabitants, though not, perhaps, in the language which he was currently employing. She tugged at his sleeve, as he swayed above her, as the gold-braided, nervous-camp steward descended upon them, and whispered, "Hey, sit down, come on, sit down, you're going to knock my drink over if you go on like that, and I've been looking forward to it for hours."

He gazed down, took in her presence, took in her little tea party, switched currents, smiled, bent at the knees, sat. The steward was at his elbow. "Now then, sir," he said, ingratiatingly, "now then."

The man was tugging at the top of his second bottle. Esther thought it would be much better to let him have it: experience hinted to her that the next phase might be maudlin, conversational, quiet, rather than noisy. Calmly, she poured out her own little drink. The steward, crouching on his haunches in the aisle, watched her small ceremony. "You with this gentleman, madam?" he asked. Esther hesitated, prevaricated, sipped from her beaker.

"Well, no, not really," she said, "but we've been getting to know one another. Haven't we?"

She laid what she hoped was a soothing hand upon the man's arm, as he managed to unscrew his second bottle, and to pour its contents, with an impressively steady hand, into his beaker. The man nodded, mumbled. "We're quite all right, thank you," she said, firmly, and followed this statement up with various nods, winks, and facial contortions by which she intended to indicate to the steward that she thought everything was under control, and more likely to stay so if the steward absented himself. The steward responded by a similar barrage of nods and winks, and by pointing discreetly to the service button. He rose to his feet, said, "We'll be back for your dinner order soon, madam—that is, sir and madam," and backed away.

Interesting, thought Esther, as she took another sip. Not really much one can do to calm people down inconspicuously at this height above sea level, in this cramped space. Did they have straitjackets on aeroplanes? she wondered. The man was drinking his whisky, slowly, meditatively, as though nothing had happened. Carefully, gingerly, she reached under the tray for the *Numismatic Chronicle*. The sight of this innocent publication aroused him, however, as she had half feared it might, and he put down his glass and turned his attention full upon her.

Civilly, gallantly, courteously, in his near-perfect English,

his too attentively articulated English, he enquired her destination. As she was flying to Bologna, and had taken some
trouble to find the only airline with a direct flight to Bologna
that week, she felt she should answer truthfully. "Bologna,"
she said, with a lightly censorious intonation, which might
have implied, "of course, you fool."

He picked up the subtext at once, with all the free-playing
instinct and subtlety of a person liberated by alcohol from
time-wasting niceties. "You needn't have been going to
Bologna at all," he said. "I, for instance, am not going to
Bologna. I am going to Ferrara. But as there is no airport in
Ferrara, I was obliged to catch this flight to Bologna. I could,
of course, have travelled from Venice, as there are direct
flights to Venice, in fact there are more regular direct flights to
Venice than to Bologna, so it took me some time to work out
that it was wiser to travel via Bologna, so I think it was not at
all necessary for you to imply that I ought to have known you
were travelling to Bologna."

"I could have been going to Ferrara, you mean," said
Esther, curiously delighted by this turn of conversation; and
she continued delighted, through another quarter of an hour's
discussion of airports, flight schedules, duty-free allowances,
and such matters. He was, he said, a Dutchman. He showed
her his passport: she inspected it, as he seemed eager for her to
do so, and noted that he appeared to be something to do with
antiques, and lived in Amsterdam. She showed him hers. They
conversed a little of art, unwisely perhaps, for when she enquired whether or not he was familiar with Jacopo della Quer-
çia's *Madonna* in the Museo del Duomo in Ferrara (as his
previous observations on the Sienese school had led her to
believe he might well have been) he suddenly turned violently
against poor della Quercia, whose very name seemed to inspire
him with a barely controllable rage, for he repeated it some
twenty or thirty times, in varying experimental pronunciations,
in a diatribe interrupted only by the arrival of a meal—tea?
supper? dinner? at that time of day, who could say?—and by the
solicitous enquiries of the steward as to whether sir and madam
were enjoying their flight. Yes, said Esther, firmly, but her
friend (whose name, she had learned, was Leo Steen) disastrously struggled to his feet again, folding up his plastic dinner
in its folding table, and waving his arms. "Oh, do sit down,"
said Esther, sharply, "that's quite enough of that, you'll send us
all plummeting down into the Alps if you go on like this."

The word Alps worked like a charm. He sat down at once, muttering to himself some rubbish about the Zillertaler Alpe and the Julijske Alpe, and about a journey he'd once made through them many years ago with a woman in spring, and about trains and boats and cars, about a wonderful instant passion on a night ferry, and about the inferiority of air travel. "Yes, yes, of course," said Esther, hungrily gobbling up her unidentifiable stew, her portion of salad, her roll, her biscuits and Bel Paese (but drawing the line at the trifle); yes, she agreed, trains and boats were much pleasanter; but there were fewer and fewer of them; one was obliged to travel by air, air travel was boring, unromantic, frightening, tedious, all at once; yes, they agreed, yes. The steward brought him a replacement, pacifying meal but, like a true drinker, he wouldn't touch it, so Esther unobtrusively stole his cheese. She was ravenously hungry: she hadn't got round to eating at all earlier in the day. The North Sea, he was saying, The Hague, Felixstowe, Harwich, the Hook. Yes, yes, said Esther. It was music to her ears, for some reason, this conversation, of which (she knew the signs) he would, the next day, remember not one word. The next day, it would be as though this conversation had never been. He was telling her about his mistress, who was married to an art dealer. Yes, yes, said Esther.

After the plane had landed, she was somewhat dismayed when the usual announcement telling everybody to stay in their seats until the Seat Belts sign had been switched off was followed by the arrival of the steward and another, larger, fiercer, heavier man in uniform, who indicated to her new friend that he should arise and follow them. The cowards, the bullies, they wouldn't take him on in mid-air, she said to herself, as Leo stumbled away up the aisle to the exit, having muttered a farewell, and pledged undying devotion and a fervent desire to meet her again on the return flight. Should she protest? What could she do? She would at least enquire after him, she resolved, as she made her way through the aircraft door, but the steward was already waiting for her, with explanations, with official thanks from the airline. "Averted an unpleasant incident," "most grateful for her intervention," "very tactfully handled," the steward and a new, unexplained sidekick from the ground staff said, as Esther stood in a drafty caterpillar-corridor ten feet above ground, clutching her canvas bag. When Esther, feeling herself getting truculent, feeling her calm fray at the edges, asked what they had done with her companion, they assured her that he would be dealt with by the authorities. Whatever for? said Esther; he didn't hurt anybody, did he? And they, sensing they had given the wrong answer, immediately began to assure her that they meant he would *not* be dealt with by the authorities, that there would be no further proceedings, that they had merely allowed him off the plane first for the convenience of other passengers and his own safety, and that he would already be on his way to his desired destination. Esther stared at them with displeasure. "You're a two-faced lot, aren't you?" she said, as nastily as she dared, and picked up her canvas bag and marched away, firmly, before they arrested her too for connivance and collaboration and abetting disorder in the skies.

Christmas Day in St. John's Wood. A fearsome scene. Wrapping paper strewed the carpet, wastepaper baskets over-flowed, black bags bulged, dirty glasses and plates stood on bookshelves and desks and mantelpieces and stairs, and the washing-up machine ground its way through load after load to no visible effect. The domestic infrastructure could not support its extra burden and Liz, accustomed moreover to three days a week of well-paid skilled domestic help from an energetic young Polish woman, was overwhelmed by the mess, by the indifference of others to that mess. All the younger Headleands were assembled: Jonathan from Bury St. Edmunds, with his girlfriend: Aaron from Highbury: Alan from Manchester; Sally and Stella, both of whom still officially lived at home with Liz. They sprawled on settees and bickered in corridors. And there was Charles, traitor Charles, sitting snoring in an armchair, full of turkey and brandy butter and Christmas pudding. Enjoy the peace while it lasts, Liz told herself, as she took cover in a corner behind *The Times*, as the dark evening thickened. She stroked her cat, also full of turkey, for comfort. The cat sneezed and coughed. Soon, at six, she would ring Alix, up in Leeds; poor Alix, her Christmas ruined by Brian's father's funeral, or rather with Brian's inability to organize a funeral. It hung over them, and Brian's father lay in the hospital morgue. For years, now, she and Alix had spoken to one another, on Christmas Day at six; it was a tradition. They had not missed in how many years—fifteen, sixteen? They had reassured one another that there was a world elsewhere, away from the hearth, away from the conflicts of family life.

Esther, the deserter, was eating pasta and prosciutto in Bologna. Wise Esther.

Conflict had sprung up this year where least expected: not between Sally and Charles, who seemed to have buried the hatchet over an amber necklace and a g. and t. (Sally's new designation, initially adopted to annoy Charles, perhaps, but signally failing to do so, and by now a conspiratorial mutual joke), but between Jonathan and Alan, between Jonathan and Charles, a three-cornered conflict, an Oedipal/fraternal triangle. Jonathan and Charles had always got on well before; now they provoked one another deliberately, and Alan, usually aloof, had involved himself in the fray. It was to do with television; and Liz, glancing at her watch, felt her spirits sink as the door opened, as Charles woke with a start, as Jonathan burst in with a fresh pile of video cassettes.

They were back on it again: television talk. "Now look, Dad," thirty-year-old Jonathan was saying, crouching on the floor and twiddling with the video control, "look, just look at this sequence," and he began to play yet again a piece of his own recent film about life at an expensive, sporty, minor public school. Liz yawned, resentfully. How silly they both were, squabbling jealously, childishly, the pair of them; and all because Jonathan's programme had been well received, had won an award, had been a *succès d'estime*. It was a direct challenge to his father: he had first shown Charles the film immediately on Charles's arrival, three evenings earlier, and Charles had gone straight back to his hotel room and devoted an hour on the telephone to rustling up some old copies of his own classic on education in the sixties, *The Radiant Way*, and had played them, relentlessly, competitively, mournfully, angrily, nostalgically, on Christmas Eve. Now here they were on Christmas Day, still at it. Alan, slouched on the settee, opened his eyes and shouted at Jonathan, "Turn that bloody thing off, Jon, I'm not sitting through that crap again." "Shut up, son," said Charles, leaning forward, belching, his attention gripped, despite himself, by Jonathan's camera technique. And on they went, round and round again, the same old insults, the same old arguments. Alan hated the film because it showed a crowd of upper-middle-class twits making fools of themselves for the entertainment of the nation, egged on, in his view, by

Jonathan. Jonathan would then claim his film was social satire, or at least that Alan ought so to perceive it. Alan would retort that Jonathan's own position was neither objective nor satiric, but simply vacuous, timeserving, frivolous. What's wrong with frivolity, Aaron would interject, to keep them all at it, to the irritation of both; your film's got no moral centre, look at the difference from *The Radiant Way*. That was a committed film, Alan would argue. Yes, and look where Charles stands now, Jonathan would respond, look where commitment gets you. What's wrong with where I stand, Charles would retort. And on they would go, hopping round and round the same old treadmill, each shifted by the others from his natural position, Alan forced to occupy the role of snarling Thersites, Aaron the role of Oscar Wilde, and Charles—most oddly of all—finally forced into the role of peacemaker, as his sons went for one another and for him. It was all Jonathan's fault, Liz suspected, for making so naked a bid for power, so naïve and threatening a claim to his father's respect, and yet of them all Jonathan appeared the smoothest, the most controlled, the least engaged in the dispute. She remembered them as small children, rolling, fighting, on the floor. And now Jonathan has a handsome salary, a self-possessed girlfriend called Xanthe (Liz does not like her much, she talks too much about food, but she hopes Jonathan has settled at last), and parked outside stands his smart new car, a competitive red GTI convertible.

Liz was rather impressed by Alan's dismissal of Jonathan's successful film, which she would never have been able to formulate herself. So, she could see, was Sally, though Sally was trying not to be involved. Jonathan's film *was*, as Alan had said, curiously unfocused in intent if not in image, its mocking, tongue-in-cheek evocations of privilege and prejudice curiously flattering to viewer and subject. For Amusement Only, it seemed to say. And yet, and yet—it was smooth, acute, revealing, and Jonathan was rightly enjoying his success. It was mean of Alan to try to spoil it, petty of him to envy it; did he not thereby invalidate the moral grounds of his own objections? Liz yawned again, as she watched a languid dinner-jacketed young seventeen-year-old speaking about the thrills of gate-crashing parties and stealing kegs of beer; and describing the delights of filling the evening bags of dull young women with Camembert when they weren't looking; claiming that he had slept with the matron of his previous school when he was only fifteen. "As a social document," Alan was beginning, once more, to argue, "that sequence is completely worthless. I'm sure Dad would agree you can tell the boy is lying, what's the point of filming that?" Jonathan said something about the revealing nature of people's fantasies, and tried to invoke Liz's support, but Alan was not to be deterred. "Fantasy," he reiterated, "fantasy, that's all we get fed these days, we can't tell the difference between fact and fiction, we watch *garbage,* night after night, we've all gone soft in the brain."

"And what are you doing about it, up there in Manchester, teaching political theory? You're just pandering to another kind of fantasy; the fantasy of social progress, the discredited dream of Utopia; better to show people as they are than to make them dream they can have what they can't have," said Jonathan.

"I don't think he *was* lying," said Stella, who had been placidly knitting throughout this, "I know lots and lots of people at Cambridge who are just like that."

"Well, that's *your* problem," said Alan, but not very viciously, because she was, after all, only his half-sister and his baby half-sister at that.

"No, it's not," said Sally disloyally, "there really *are* lots of people like that; it's just that you go through life ignoring them—you live in an even more self-selected world than Jonathan."

"Oh, my God," said Charles, clutching his head, "could you either stop arguing or turn down the volume or both? My God, it's hot in here."

And then the cat was sick.

"It's *hell* here," moaned Liz to Alix over the phone. "Pure *hell.* They never stop quarrelling and watching telly. Both at once."

"It's much the same up here," said Alix, but more glumly, with less spirit, from her parents' bungalow in Leeds.

*   *   *

Esther and Elena smiled at one another gently, quietly, over their Christmas *grappa*, in perfect harmony, in deep peace.

The Bowens' Renault stood in a garage at Croydon. Its fault had been diagnosed: some witty Wandsworth vandal had shoved a bird's nest up its exhaust.

It was still Christmas Day in St. John's Wood. Liz could hardly believe it had gone on so long. And unaccountably, improbably, after eating a vast lunch at two, everybody seemed by eight to want to eat again. Nothing much, just a snack, they all cried, and Liz was standing in the kitchen making smoked salmon sandwiches when the telephone rang. It was her sister, Shirley. "But I spoke to her this morning," Liz began, defensively, in response to Shirley's opening phrase, "It's mother." And then, in the ensuing silence, quickly replayed, reread that phrase, that intonation, and for one wild glorious moment hoped that her mother was dead. "What is it?" she asked, as Shirley said nothing. "Shirley?" And Shirley explained that their mother had had a stroke. She gave details. Quite a severe stroke, but not, said Shirley grimly, severe enough. She had been admitted to hospital.

"You'd better come up and see her," said Shirley. "Because I'm damned if I'm going to cope with this alone." Her voice was suddenly trembling with rage. "Five bloody years I've waited, and you haven't lifted a finger, you haven't come near, you haven't done a bloody thing," said Shirley. "Well, I've had enough. I won't go on, do you hear, I won't. You can come up here and take over. I can't go on. You are the most selfish woman on God's earth, Liz Ablewhite, and I hate you. I hate you. Do you hear? I hate you."

The Christmas spirit.

"Of course I'll come," said Liz. "Calm down, Shirley, you've had a horrible shock. I'll work out how to get there, and I'll ring you back. Are you at home?"

"Of course I'm at home. Where the hell else do you expect me to be? Wherever else *am* I? Ever, ever, ever?" shrieked Shirley.

"There, there," said Liz, and put down the phone. Mechanically, she went on cutting sandwiches, as tears of shock and indignation and self-justification and fatigue started to her eyes. Raised voices from the drawing room reached her; they were shouting about dish receivers, and the break-up of the fabric of society, above the soundtrack of an old American movie of gangsters in L.A.

The news of Rita Ablewhite's stroke was greeted, over the sandwiches, with an embarrassed silence. So something had happened, at last, in this non-story, this non-sequence of non-events. Nobody could find an appropriate response. Was Liz Headleand judged, at this moment, for her neglect of her mother, for her failure to answer earlier appeals? Did she judge herself? It was not clear. She gave them no lead. She passed round the sandwiches silently, and sighed, several times. Then she said, as the silence prolonged itself uncomfortably, "I spoke to her this morning. She sounded all right this morning. Much the same as ever, really."

The young people looked down at their plates.

"I sent her a Christmas card," volunteered Stella.

"Yes," said Liz. "Yes, she mentioned she'd got it. That was nice of you, Stella." She spoke dully, evenly. Rita Ablewhite's other grandchild and stepgrandchildren eyed one another covertly, guiltily: they had not sent cards, had not set eyes on the old woman for many years, could not imagine what had got into Stella.

"I'll have to go up to Northam, I suppose," said Liz. "I can't leave it all to Shirley." Without emotion, flatly. "What a nightmare," Liz said.

"I'll drive you up," said Charles. "In the morning. You can't do anything now. I'll take you up, in the morning."

"Really?" said Liz, without much change of tone, as though deeply unsurprised by this somewhat surprising offer. "That would be kind."

Charles's children and Liz's children looked at one another, as they sat slouched around the drawing room. Alan helped himself to another sandwich from the tray at his feet. "Hey, pass them over here," said Aaron, observing this. The sandwiches were passed. Coffee was poured. Sally looked at her watch. Jonathan eyed the television set. Liz stared into space. The Christmas tree sparkled. Charles yawned.

Jonathan cleared his throat. "Liz," he said, "would you mind *very* much if we just watched a few minutes of Martin's programme? It's on in a couple of minutes."

They all stared at Liz. "No, no, of course not," she said absently, "watch away, please do."

"It was a *lovely* day, Mummy," said Sally—anxiously, questioningly, ironically—as Jonathan crawled across the floor to switch on. It was the end of the Queen's speech, yet again.

"Oh, my *God*," said Alan. Jonathan switched channels, quickly. Aaron began to laugh. And they all began to laugh, heartlessly, companionably, as life flowed again, as their mother unfroze and smiled, and began herself to laugh.

"Yes, yes," said Liz, herself again, "a simply *lovely* day."

Driving northward, up the M1, on Boxing Day, Charles attempted to bring Liz up to date on the subject of dish receivers, birds, footprints, and NTVROs. His company had long been planning to develop their struggling subsidiary, the hubristically labelled Global International Network, into a truly global, international, satellite-transmitted and dish-received commercial news agency. The plans had gone wrong, because Charles in New York had backed the wrong kind of technology. Charles was in disgrace. He had erred paradoxically through insufficient patriotism: brainwashed by years of confident American sales talk, he had crucially underestimated a small British homegrown discovery, and had found himself outwitted. Charles explained some of this to Liz, as his mind roved over Anglo-American relations in general and his own discomfiture in particular. Was she listening, could she follow him? Who could tell? One could never tell, with Liz. When it suited her, she played the Little Woman, unable to follow a manual for tuning a car radio, yawning with boredom at the mention of anything electronic, even protesting (implausibly, surely) that she was not interested in The News. But on various occasions over the Christmas period he had heard her dropping some well-informed comments on information technology, videotex, and videodata, when discussing the philosophical implications of this brave new world with Jonathan and Alan. There she sat, listening or not listening. Charles's voice described a landscape covered in watching white bowls, turned like sunflowers, moonflowers, to the speaking sky. Why, he wondered, was he driving her all this way? To get away from those huge, threatening, amazing overgrown children in London? As revenge on Henrietta? As an act of kindness? He did not know. The visionary white uplifted faces watched, beseeching, as the dirty grey featureless landscape unrolled: exits and entrances. The miners would strike, in the new year. The Old Country. English drivers! thought Charles in the fast lane, slamming on the brakes of his hired Ford Sierra to frighten the bastard on his tail. The most aggressive in the world. He had forgotten, after years of courteous America, how bloody the English were.

Liz sat silent, distant, unaware. She was trying to reconstruct what might prove to have been her last conversation with her mother: her last opportunity to ask questions, receive answers. What had they talked about on Christmas morning? Nothing, as usual. "How are you, Mother?" "Not too badly, I don't complain." "Happy Christmas." "What's Happy about it?" "We're all here, all the family, we all send our love." "Stella sent me a card." "Oh, good. How's Shirley?" "Not too badly." "How's the weather up there?" "Raining." "It's been raining here, too, but it's a little brighter now." "How's Stella enjoying Cambridge?" "Very much, she says." "Has Sally got herself a job yet?" "No, not yet, but she's looking." "Did you hear about that accident at Pontefract? I heard about it on the radio." "No, tell me about it." And so on, and so on. They had discussed Radio 4's *Book at Bedtime* (a Surtees novel, which Rita Ablewhite had not liked, and which Liz had not heard, though she pretended she had) and the intellectual aspirations of Celia Harper (in which her grandmother took considerable interest, to Liz unaccountably) and then, duty done, they had said goodbye. A long goodbye, as it might prove. And the greatest enigma of all, to Liz, remained the knowledge that this conversation (one of many thousands), if reported, if tape-recorded and played back, would have betrayed, even to her own, expert, deviance-detecting ear, no trace of abnormality, of eccentricity: motes and beams, motes and beams. What was the Latin name for those little floating particles that drift, transparently, amoeba-like, across the surface of the eyeball?

Charles, turning off the Motorway, following sign posts, muttered that the place had changed out of all recognition. Liz, too, found it changed, and could only with difficulty direct him to the Royal Infirmary. It's the one-way system, she said, as they circled for the third time round the same stretch of inner

ring road. In the hospital car park, they parted; Charles to
investigate hotels, Liz to seek her mother.

"Cheer up, old thing, cheer up, sweetie," he said, on the
tarmac, patting her on the back, bracingly. "It'll all be over
soon. I'll be back in an hour."

"Thank you," she said faintly, and made her way to the
smoothly sliding automated portals.

But it might not be over soon, it seemed. Rita Ablewhite lay
semiconscious, and might so lie for months, for years. Liz
stared at the heap of flesh that was her mother. Shirley was
right, she had put on weight, mountainously. Four stone, over
the past six years. Monstrous. She did not seem to know Liz,
did not seem to know anything. Liz stood by the bedside and
stared. The flesh twitched. One side of the face was paralysed;
it sagged, lopsided. This is nothing to do with me, thought Liz,
and yet it is myself. Dry-eyed she stared. The hospital staff was
polite but obliquely censorious. Liz felt her own face twitch,
drily, as she answered their questions; her skin was dry and soft
with age at the sight of her mother. The hospital smell filled her
with nausea. Obscene Christmas decorations dangled in the
ward. Dusty fluff lay under the beds in little rolls and wisps.
Rita Ablewhite's hair was thin and white and wispy: her scalp
showed, freckled. Liz Ablewhite's scalp prickled. An old
woman behind a screen further down the ward moaned and
called out, "Mummy! Mummy!"

I can't take very much of this, said Liz to herself, as she
followed the staff nurse into an office, made an appointment to
call back the next day to speak to a specialist. Shirley, the
nurse told her, had been in that morning, would call back in the
evening. Yes, said Liz.

Charles was waiting in the foyer by a doll's tea party, a heap
of balding teddy bears, and a Christmas raffle stall. He was
gazing with some distaste at an ill-cast ill-painted plaster-of-
Paris snowman. Liz was very pleased to see him. "Come on,
out of here," said Charles, taking her arm, tucking it into his.
"That's quite enough for one day."

And off he drove her, despite half-hearted protests about
going to see Shirley, to the Open Hearth Hotel, out on the
Breasbrough Road. "This is all *completely* new," said Liz, at
first feebly, then with more interest, as they left the City Centre
and old Victorian suburbs of huge granite mock castles behind
them, and wound up towards the new, 1970s, plate-glass-
windowed, prosperous executive belt. Northam shone below

them in the darkening afternoon light, as they circled upwards. And there, gleaming its welcome, was the Open Hearth Hotel: long, low, bright, modern, crowded with palm and bamboos and bars, a swimming pool glinting from a jungle of tropical foliage at the far side of reception. "Good Lord," said Liz, "whatever is this place?" Charles smiled, proudly, as he checked in. Liz gazed in astonishment at advertisements for Jacuzzi, for sauna, for gymnasia, for beauty parlours, for conference suites. There was even, it appeared, a heliport facility. Liz, clutching her overnight bag, inspected the sequence of photographs and engravings that adorned the walls; they told the story of the open hearth process of steelmaking through artists' impressions of idealized nineteenth-century ironworks and steelworks, with tall chimneys bravely smoking, through historic early-twentieth-century photographs of furnacemen stoking and fettlers fettling. One wall was occupied by a large reproduction, in some strange laminated varnished material, of a Prospect of Northam from Chay Bank, taken from a mid-nineteenth-century oil painting. In the lofty rustic foreground, a group of village boys played with a whip and top, watched by an eager dog, while an old man smoked his pipe, leaning on a pile of millstones beneath a tree. In the distant scoop of backdrop, chimneys smoked; and beyond them rose again the barren hills. A curiously evocative landscape, thought Liz, as Charles appeared by her side and led her off to a carpet-walled lift.

"Charles," repeated Liz, over a cup of tea in the bedroom that she had, from two identical twin-bedded rooms, selected. "Charles, what *is* all this? I thought the north of England was in decline."

"I must say," said Charles, "it *is* a bit of a surprise. A mistaken speculation, I'd say. It's probably frequented largely by journalists and television crews making programmes about the decline of the north of England. But it may do well out of functions. Weddings, conferences, that kind of thing. There's still a lot of money around, even up here."

"I wish I'd brought my bathing suit," said Liz. "How ever did you find it?"

"Oh, I rang up a friend, last night," said Charles, vaguely. "A chap who used to be in Pennine Television. He recommended it. In fact, he owns it." Liz laughed briefly.

"I ought to ring Shirley," said Liz, "but I can't quite face it. I think I'll ring Alix, instead."

*   *   *

"A most extraordinary place," Liz was saying to Brian Bowen, in Shirley Harper's sitting room, eating a cold turkey sandwich and drinking a glass of wine. Pre-funeral baked meats. Brian had still been unable to bury his father; his father lay in the morgue in the Royal Infirmary, eleven storeys beneath the ward in which Rita Ablewhite uneasily reposed. "It has a heliport facility. I want to ask if it's ever been used, but I daren't," said Liz.

"Paralysed down the right side," Shirley was saying to Alix Bowen. "Apparently that means it's the left side of the brain. But they say her heart could give at any moment."

"They've fixed the housing committee, and the education committee," Cliff Harper was saying to Charles Headleand, "and now they're trying to fix the library committee, ordering books on Marx and Lenin. There's a chap called Blinkhorn, Perry Blinkhorn; he lost his seat on the Council at the last election, but he's been co-opted onto every sub-committee. It's a scandal, it's illegal, but what can you do? They'll ruin this city. Ruin it."

Alix Bowen was listening not to Shirley's description of Rita Ablewhite's stroke but, obliquely, to Cliff Harper's accusations; she was hoping Brian could not hear them too, for if Cliff and Brian were to engage, there would be trouble. Luckily, Brian seemed to be gripped by Liz's evocation of the Open Hearth Hotel; his grandfather had worked as a furnaceman with an open hearth furnace, he was telling Liz.

"Incontinent, and I couldn't find her spare set of keys," Shirley was saying.

Celia Harper, sixteen years old, perched on the arm of a settee and listened. Celia Harper never went out of an evening. Her brothers had left home, gone their ways, but she stayed, and sat, and listened, and bided her time. She was studying for her A levels. Other girls took time off in the First Year Sixth, even from the hard-working, well-disciplined Northam Girls High School, but not Celia Harper. She nursed her fantasies, she nursed her grudges, she coiled her springs. And now she dangled a pretty ankle, and toyed with a cheese biscuit (for she was very thin, unnaturally thin), and observed her relatives (her rarely, her uniquely assembled relatives) through cool, grey, expressionless eyes. This Christmas had produced surprises. Charles and Liz Headleand, Alix and Brian Bowen, summoned by Death, summoned by the corpse of shrivelled, sad little Uncle Fred Bowen, by the powerful will of that fat inert old woman. Celia had taken to visiting her grandmother of late; she had acquainted herself with the secrets of that time-locked house. She knew things that nobody knew. She kept them to herself.

"That Ideal Boiler hasn't been out in thirty years," her mother was saying to Alix Bowen.

Celia watched, and listened. The atmosphere was strange, hot, at once flat and feverish: the end of an era seemed to be at hand, barriers were low, the unlikely, the uncanny were loose in the air. Cliff opened another bottle of wine, recklessly: Liz lit a cigarette: Shirley, worrying about the house in Abercorn Avenue, toyed nervously with her silver locket. "It's nostalgia," Brian was saying to Liz, "nostalgia. The bookshops here are full of it. Old Northam, the Good Old Days, the wonderful old days of furnace and canal. You can buy all sorts of rubbish. Ashtrays, paper weights, calendars, even jars of marmalade with views of the Old Forge in Victorian times, and damn silly little fake cloth tops tied over the screwtop to make them look as though Granny made them. But can you buy a pair of nail scissors? I tried to buy a pair of decent nail scissors last week, and there weren't any. There was rubbish from Taiwan, and dinky little teenage doll's scissors with pink plastic handles called Judy and Belinda. Rubbish. No scissors. In the end I found a proper pair. It was made in Finland."

"Cliff's wing mirror pieces come from Taiwan," said Liz, holding out her glass as Cliff approached with the bottle, "don't they, Cliff?"

"You might as well have a mince pie," said Shirley to her ex-brother-in-law, Charles Headleand. "They're home-made."

Charles munched. "Excellent," said Charles.

Alix and Brian were not returning to Leeds that night, to Alix's parents'; they were spending the night in Fred's old flat, in Chay Bank. Sorting things out. Throwing things out. Parcelling things up. The cremation was arranged for the next day. "Could I give you some of the pot plants, perhaps?" Alix was saying to Shirley, looking round the long lounge, taking in a

forced white cyclamen, a forced pink azalea, a scarlet poinsettia, all Christmas-new: and, more promisingly, a well-
established begonia, a climbing vine. "It would be nice to find
them a good home."

"Aren't there people in the flats who would have them?"
said Shirley. "He had a lot of friends, in the flats."

"We must be off," said Liz for the third time. "I'll see you
in the morning, in Abercorn Avenue, Shirley. Come on, Alix;
come on, Brian."

They were giving the Bowens a lift, to Chay Bank. The
Bowens were without a car; the Renault 4 still stood in the
garage in Croydon. Cliff, Shirley, and Celia Harper politely
waved goodbye beside their privet hedge. "It's out of your
way," said Alix, apologetically, as Charles drove back towards
the City Centre. "Never mind," said Liz, briskly, on Charles's
behalf. Chay Bank loomed illumined, visible for miles around,
on the opposite hillside. Like a liner, moored in the night.
"Fred used to say it was like a liner," said Alix.

"Christ," said Charles, as he drove up the steep back
approach road, "what a wilderness."

"But I think it's beautiful," said Alix.

"Alix, you're barmy," said Charles, quite warmly.

"Jesus," said Charles, as the four of them stood in the dank,
graffiti-scarred, urine-soaked lift, on their way up to Fred's
flat. "And you say he *chose* to move up here?"

"Look," said Liz, pointing to a message on the grey-blue
wall, written in yellow in a childish hand. "I WANT TO FUCK
MR. LAMB," it read, mildly, innocently, a schoolgirl's appeal.

They made their way along the high skywalk towards
Number 412. Charles gazed downwards at the lonely, conspicuous parked hired Ford Sierra. "They'll strip it," he said,
"they'll siphon off the petrol and nick the tyres."

"Nonsense," said Alix, bracingly. "This is Northam, not
the Harrow Road. They haven't learnt bad habits yet, up
here."

"Ah," said Charles, "so you admit things are bad on the
Harrow Road?"

"Well, *sort* of," said Alix, as Brian opened the door of his
dead father's flat.

"But it's very nice," said Liz, looking round appreciatively,
admiring pot plants and bookshelves, a three-piece suite
covered in brown corduroy, a nest of tables, a Doulton vase, a
Wedgwood biscuit barrel. "And look at the view!"

Brian was pouring whisky. Charles could still see the Ford Sierra, alone, far, far below. "Why aren't there any other cars?" he asked, with not-quite-mock paranoia. "I don't like this sinister absence of cars."

"Do you want the good answer, or the bad answer?" asked Brian. "The good answer is that people don't need cars because public transport is so cheap in Northam. The bad answer is that unemployment in these flats is something like 85 percent. My father would have given you the good answer, Cliff would have given you the bad answer. You can take your pick. The statistics inform us that only 8 percent of households in this block have a car. That's why you don't see any cars."

"They didn't like the old estate, after Kathie died," said Alix, sitting back, tucking her feet up under her. "That's why they asked to be moved. Fred was on the housing committee. They liked it up here, didn't they, Brian?"

"I'm sure there are worse places than this in New York," said Liz. "It's just that you don't visit them, Charles. What's that on the wall there, Brian?"

"It's a circular saw. Well, it's a fake circular saw. In silver. It was his retirement present. Instead of a gold watch. It's got his name on it, and his years of service."

"The Good Old Days," said Liz.

"Well," said Brian, "at least he worked out his time. He wasn't made redundant."

"Small mercies," said Charles, who had just been made redundant, with the accompaniment of a golden handshake worth more than Fred Bowen had earned in his entire working life.

"Yes," said Brian, who was not at all clear about his own pension rights, and who occasionally found himself thinking glumly of Gloscley.

"I don't suppose anyone will ever give me a gold watch for long service," said Alix. "Or a silver saw. But if Polly and I get closed down, we've agreed to treat ourselves to lunch at Langan's."

Liz yawned.

"In my business," she said, "I don't think one has to retire. One gets wiser and wiser all the time. Until one dies. Dies into full knowledge."

"Is that how it will be?" asked Alix.

"I don't see what else," said Liz.

*   *   *

When Liz and Charles descended, they discovered that the offside wing mirror had been nicked from the Ford Sierra. "I told you so," said Charles, as he drove towards the Open Hearth Hotel. Both of them were amused, companionably amused, old comrades in mirth and crime again. "But Cliff has got thousands and thousands of wing mirrors," said Liz. "Thousands and thousands, a whole factory full of wing mirrors, tomorrow we can go and take our pick."

They staggered into the fervid foyer, worn out by the day's exertions, the day's emotions, warm with Brian's father's whisky. "Plastic," said Charles, waiting for their keys, picking discreetly at the bamboo trim of the reception desk. The thick-carpeted lift took them swiftly upwards. With no word spoken, they had agreed to spend the night together. Liz opened her arms to Charles, in the narrow bed. It was the beginning of nothing, the end of nothing: it was a night out of time, in a different sequence, in the sequence of the past, in the sequence of eternity. It meant nothing. It signified nothing. Charles entered her body, came instantly, as she came to meet him, and they both fell instantly asleep.

Henrietta Headleand lies under a mosquito net. She cannot believe that the Frenches do not have proper air-conditioning. Zambia is not what she had expected, not what she remembered from a visit twenty years ago with some great white hunter friends and her ex-husband, Peter Latchett. She had been looking forward to getting away from England for Christmas, for she dislikes Christmas, but here in Lusaka, at the Frenches', there is more of English Christmas than ever, a parody of an English Christmas, with a Christmas tree and crackers and cocktails, and a red-faced, sweating, drunken Father Christmas, and a lot of foolishly smiling black faces queuing up for silly gifts. The Frenches indulge their workforce. Henrietta disapproves.

At least the weather is too hot and wet for polo. That is a small mercy. Henrietta is deeply bored by polo. The Frenches are keen polo players.

She is bored by her new grandchild. She does not like babies. They make her feel old.

She is bored by the thought of Charles Headleand. He too makes her feel old. Charles is not what she expected.

Henrietta Latchett lies under her mosquito net, and tries to remember her trip into the bush, all those years ago, with Peter Latchett and Guy Hestercombe and Wally Lansdowne. She has lost something, some memory, some part of herself: what is it, where has it gone? She hears talk, now, at the Frenches', from her earnest son-in-law, of the dwindling of the elephant population, of the massacre of the rhinoceros. All the hunters have turned gamekeepers, or at least in the circle in which she now finds herself stranded. They speak censoriously of hunting, of poaching.

It had not been like this with Peter, Guy, and Wally, in the old days. They had sat in the evenings, by the blazing fire, drinking whisky and hearing the hyenas howl, telling stories of dangers survived, of risks run, of trophies snatched from nature. They had risen early, in the high bright light exuberant dawn. Henrietta had held her breath in the hide, as the shy antelope grazed and skipped, unconcerned, in the wet grass.

Henrietta tries to remember. The wild creatures have gone, have left her, she cannot summon them back.

And as she lies there under her net, far away, herds and herds of black lechwe graze, thousands and thousands of them, farther than the eye can see, were there any eye to watch them. Zebras smartly kick their heels, elephants walk slowly in single file, impala leap and skitter and run, and the emerald spotted wood dove cries in its heart-breaking, melancholy cry.

I lost my mother, I lost my father, and I am alo-one, alo-one, alo-one, flutes the dove, mourns the dove, in some dim recess of Henrietta's memory, while the heartless elegant little impala leap and jump and play.

Nothing had changed in the kitchen at Abercorn Avenue: there Liz and Shirley had once sat, at the white wooden kitchen table, doing their homework, and there they sat now, middle-aged women, with mugs of instant coffee in their hands. The Ideal Boiler was still warm: "But what can I do?" Shirley had asked. "I can't keep on stoking it, just in case. What can I do?"

The hospital had been vague in its prognosis. They never like to commit themselves, said Liz. It would be months, said Liz. She might even get better.

Was there a will? Shirley assumed there was, assumed it was in the desk in the front room. But the desk was locked, and she could not find the keys. She had only the house keys. "They must be somewhere," she said, vaguely, from time to time, gazing around as though they might discover themselves on a shelf, or hanging from a cupboard handle.

Neither of them wanted to go and look in the front room. Somewhere, in that front room, or in a wardrobe drawer upstairs, they might find knowledge they did not wish to possess. They both knew this. They said nothing; there was no need to speak.

"How is it kept so clean?" asked Liz, looking round at the old-fashioned white tiles, the exposed pipes, the well-dusted sideboard, the shoe rack with their father's polished shoes, the thick panes of frosted 1920s patterned glass in the window, at which she had so patiently gazed for so many years—a pattern of stars, or snowflakes? As a child, she had wondered; and wondered idly, now.

"She couldn't have kept it like this herself, surely?"

There was a Home Help, said Shirley. A nice woman. Three mornings a week.

"I suppose I'll just have to let the boiler go out," said Shirley. "But I somehow feel that if I do, it'll never start again."

Liz got up, crossed over to the boiler, lifted the hood, took off the metal plate with the metal handle, gazed into its glowing, fading crater. "It was always a bloody good boiler," she said, "you have to agree. All these years. Do they still make things like this? It used to burn anything, didn't it? Bones, banana skins, potato peelings, any old rubbish? Amazing."

She dropped in her cigarette end, dropped the lid.

"Sanitary towels," said Shirley, surprisingly, with a note of provocative elegy.

"Yes," Liz said to Shirley, "you'll just have to let it go out."

They sat in silence, for a while. Oppressed.

"If she were dead," said Shirley, "it would be different. If she were dead, we could get on with it."

"I suppose I'd better have one more look for the keys," said

Shirley, rising heavily to her feet. Liz followed her, slowly, into the narrow hall, into the back dining room; the air was stiff with their reluctance. Perfunctorily, they looked in vases, under mats, under the silent clock. There was nowhere to look, really. The objects were like funerary objects, dead for decades, the companions of the dead. Liz followed Shirley into the front room. They stood on the threshold, on the beige rose-patterned carpet, trespassers. In the corner stood the locked, roll-top desk. On top of the mushroom-tiled fireplace stood two Christmas cards: Shirley crossed, looked at them, passed them silently to Liz. One from Stella, one from Celia. To Grandma, with love.

Love. The word crackled, spluttered, died.

"I can't bear it," said Liz, wandering around the room, touching surfaces, fingering curtains, stroking the back of the settee. "No, I can't bear it."

Shirley felt under cushions, put her hand down the side of the armchair, came up with a thimble.

Liz paused in her prowling, by the strange silver and wooden object, which she had polished for so many years, so many years ago. There it was, with its device of a mailed fist uplifted, with its monogram entwining an S, an H, an O. She ran her finger round its rim. "But of course," she said, "of course. It's a wine cooler. A wine cooler. Wouldn't you say, Shirley?"

Shirley, tapping her front teeth with the thimble on her middle finger, contemplated the object.

"Well, yes," she said. "Yes, I suppose it is. I've never thought of it as being anything in particular before. But yes, I suppose it is."

Liz offered to stay, but there was no point, really. She sat for twenty minutes by her mother's side, but her mother did not know her. Go, said Shirley. I will ring when I need you. And Liz went, back down the M1, with her estranged husband, Charles; a heavy, physical, solid peace possessed them both, as though something serious had been settled. A bond; a non-sexual bond? A transsexual bond? Reaffirmed through sex? Liz wondered, as the car sped southwards. It was over now; she resigned Charles, willingly, to Henrietta. She had guessed it all, from the mutterings, from the ejaculations; she had guessed the delicate state of play with Henrietta; she had no wish to interfere. She no longer needed Charles. She would continue as she was, alone. With her tabby cat. A smile rose irrepressibly, at the thought of the tabby cat. The cat would be watching for her return, from her seat on the windowsill, her lookout place; she would run, eagerly, to the front door. Charles, I supposed, was the love of my life, thought Liz; and that is that. Love, sexuality, orgasm. I am monogamous at heart, thought Liz Headleand. I remain married to Charles. And as the curiosity of this notion struck her, she recalled, suddenly, the wild and handsome Dutchman, with whom she spent a night of sexual passion on a ferry on the North Sea in a Force Nine gale; where was he, did he recall that stormy passage?

"What are you smiling about?" asked Charles, as he overtook a red Golf GTI convertible.

"You," said Liz. "You, and my tabby cat."

"Thank *you*," said Charles.

On Eleventh Night, Otto rang Alix Bowen, back from Brian's father's funeral, for help. "Help, Alix," said Otto. "Help, I'm in the most terrible pickle."

Otto, a domesticated foreigner, often used words like pickle; they fell oddly, quaintly (in Alix's view, charmingly), from his lips.

"What kind of pickle?"

"It's Caroline's mother. She's had a fall, she's broken her hip; Caroline's had to go to Wolverhampton. She's left me with this shopping list. I don't know what it means."

"But you can't have a party, if Caroline's away?"

"She says she'll be back. She may be back. We can't stop everybody, we've forgotten who we invited. She left me this shopping list."

"Oh, dear," said Alix.

"Yes, oh, dear," said Otto, plaintively.

"All right," said Alix.

Otto and Alix stood with a trolley in Waitrose, talking about George Orwell, 1984, and the totalitarian state. Shoppers surged around them, collided with them, rebounded from them. Otto and Alix talked on, engrossed, as they drifted, shopping list in hand, to the Tinned Goods, then on to the Soft Drinks: their trolley filled, as they spoke of self-fulfilling and self-defeating prophecies, of the concept of "freedom," of the New Right's definition of freedom, of the difference between freedom and choice. Alix hesitated, before a dizzy range of packets of orange juice—which brand did Caroline favour, she asked Otto, but he reached for the nearest, he did not know, they were all the same, surely, he said. Otto, the new Otto upheld, these days, in theory, the advantages of competition in a free market (at least in non-essential commodities and services) but he was not, Alix pointed out, much of an advertisement for his own faith. "You would be quite happy," she told him, severely, "if orange juice came in cartons marked Orange Juice, and salt in packets marked Salt, and coffee in jars marked Coffee. You wouldn't be able to tell the difference."

" 'Produce of Several Lands,' it says," said Otto, staring, thus prompted, at the small print. "What can that mean?"

"Engraved on my milk bottles this morning," said Alix, as they made their way towards the girl at the till, "there was an advertisement for the *Sunday Post*. In red lettering, on the glass of my milk bottle. What can *that* mean? Does the dairy belong to a newspaper consortium? Does the newspaper consortium belong to the dairy? Does everything belong to something else? Is nothing what it is?"

"This is purgatory," said Otto, as someone in a hurry rammed, annoyed by their conversation, angrily into their trolley. "Is it always like this?"

Slicing cucumber, mixing yoghurt and mayonnaise, Alix described Brian's father's cremation.

"We sang 'The day Thou gavest, Lord, is ended,' " said Alix, "but it was eleven-thirty in the morning. I don't know if I'm doing this right, Otto, I'm sure this isn't what it looks like when Caroline does it."

Otto peered into the yellow pudding bowl.

"It looks all right to me," he said.

"I'm nervous in other people's kitchens," said Alix, squeezing lemons; an understatement, a polite generalization, for of course she was particularly nervous in Caroline's, which was full of equipment Alix did not know how to use.

Would Caroline come home and reprimand her for doing everything wrong? No, of course she would not, she would be grateful; but nevertheless, Alix felt herself to be an incompetent usurper.

"You're doing a wonderful job," said Otto, absently, as he dusted glasses, arranged them on a tray.

"You don't know where she keeps the grater?" asked Alix.

"The point is," said Otto, "that if they privatize British Gas as well as British Telecom, there's no logical reason why they shouldn't privatize the lot. Water. Trains. Hospitals."

"Prisons," said Alix, perched on a chair, opening a high cupboard over the sink.

"Exactly," said Otto. "Prisons. Law courts, police forces. Sewerage. The Post Office. The primary schools. The army. The monarchy. Why not?"

"Help," said Alix. "Help." A pile of unleashed saucepans, whisks, cake tins, plastic freezer boxes balanced precariously against her upraised arm; a soup ladle crashed to the floor. She tried to push the pile back in again, wobbled, clutched with her other hand at the cupboard door. "Help," she repeated. "I can't move, I'm stuck."

"Hang on," said Otto. He climbed carefully up on the chair beside her, pushed at the pile, shut the door on it, jumped down, took her hands, jumped her down to him.

They stood, facing one another. He held on to her hands.

"Alix," said Otto, "a Happy New Year to you. A Happy 1984."

He kissed her on the mouth.

Did he know what he was doing? She stood there. He kissed her again, less ambiguously, and then released her. She turned away, wiped her hands on Caroline's apron.

They said nothing. She cut another lemon in half, a lemon not needed, and squeezed it. He wiped another glass, a glass already wiped. It was nothing, said Alix to herself. There was nothing to be said.

But she knew it was too late to undo it. It was done for all time, done if he never touched her again, if he never looked her in the eyes again. He had been caught off guard, in his own kitchen. She had been caught off guard, off balance, perched on a wooden chair. Had he known what he now knew? Would he ever know what he now knew? They were two serious people, seriously married. Her lips burned, where he had touched them. Ridiculous, thought Alix: a grey-haired, middle-aged woman in an apron. But she knew she was not ridiculous, it was not ridiculous; extraordinarily handsome she knew herself to be, as she stood there in Caroline's blue striped butcher's apron.

"Yes," she said. "That's what they sang. 'The da-ay Thou ga-avest, Lord, is ended, The darkness falls at Thy behest.' " She sang, mockingly, sadly. "When I die," she said, brightening slightly, purposefully, "you know what I want you all to sing? Remember this, Otto. I'd like you all to sing Arthur Hugh Clough's 'Say not the struggle naught availeth.' It's Hymn Number 637 in *Songs of Praise*. Will you remember, Otto?"

"How," said Otto, looking away, folding in half his Map-of-the-Underground tea towel, "how could I ever, ever forget?"

Esther Breuer stayed on in Bologna. On Twelfth Night, she and Elena dined with Claudio's wife's sister. They returned to Elena's apartment at eleven, in time to take down the little silver tree. At its foot stood Esther's Christmas gift to Elena: a little dull silver-grey sequinned toad, with diamond eyes. Ceremoniously, Elena folded up the branches of the little false tree. Then ceremoniously, she turned to Esther, and kissed her on the forehead. Quietly, they lay side by side, in their white nightdresses, like effigies, in the wide, white-coverleted double bed. Quietly, they fell asleep. Time was on their side.

Twelfth Night. Otto Werner, waiting for the late arrival of Alix Bowen, wondering where she was, where she had got to, looking at the faces of friends as though they were the faces of strangers, forgetting names, mumbling apologies, knew that he had been in love with Alix Bowen for years—two years, three years?—and that it was a disaster. It was a wonderful disaster. Why had it happened? What was it for? Where was she? She had gone home to change; would she ever return, ever, ever, ever? Had she fled, forever? Had he frightened her away forever? She had driven off into the night, in the little blue Renault. "Imagine, Otto," she had said on parting, with what might be a new, an everlasting gallantry; "imagine, there was a *bird's nest* in the car's exhaust! Wherever did anyone find a bird's nest, in Wandsworth?''

"Come back soon, Alix," he had said, already dry with fever at losing her, sick with apprehension that she would not return. And she had wound down the car window to wave goodbye, and then had vanished. It was half past ten. Hello, said Otto vaguely to an ex-student, have a drink, he urged a colleague. Who were all these people, who had invited them? He listened for the doorbell, he listened for the sound of her voice.

Liz Headleand, in a corner of the large square Putney drawing room, was talking to Caroline Werner about old age. They spoke of their mothers, of hospitals, infirmities. "I suppose," said Caroline, "that we must study to be *good* old people. Good patients. Patient patients. So that our children will not resent us for surviving."

Caroline's children were still young: middle-sized children, halfway children, they politely and warily circled the adults, offering snacks, listening in on conversations. The youngest offered his mother a peeled carrot and some dip; she nibbled (too much lemon, perhaps? then, remembering she had not made it herself, no, no, delicious) and asked Liz a medical question, about hips. The child moved on, to a group by the piano, where Pett Petrie was explaining to a young economist the mysteries of literary success; he had just published a collection of essays and reviews called *Scraping the Barrel*—rubbish, Pett was boasting, cheerfully, utter rubbish, pieces on moles and blue tits, from ecological mags, a review of *The Importance of Being Earnest* in 1968 in Taunton, opinion pieces about Public Lending Rights from the 1970s—and they printed them, would you believe it, they printed them, in hardback? Are they selling? inquired the economist. I don't suppose so, said Pett, but who cares? I got the advance.

"Have a bit of celery," said the solemn child, to Alan Headleand, who was talking about his brother Jonathan's film about private schooling to a glamorous young, silver-sequinned, black-stockinged lawyer who said she worked for the GLC. "Thanks, chum," said Alan, and munched. The young woman said she was the niece by marriage of Alan's cousin Julia Rothenstein, who had appeared, sitting her university entrance examinations, in *The Radiant Way*. "Good Lord," said Alan, "then we must be sort of cousins ourselves, is that right? I saw some of *The Radiant Way* again over Christmas. What is Julia up to now?"

The child moved on, to politicians and civil servants, to television presenters and lawyers. Liz, speaking of artificial hips, followed his wandering trajectory, vaguely, remembering, as she spoke, the parties she had given, feeling herself a little old, perhaps (the attendant child so young, Caroline nearly ten years younger than herself); wondering if she would ever give another party, a big party, in her house in St. John's Wood. She thought of Esther, still in Bologna; of Stephen Cox, newly returned (for he had telephoned to say so) from Istanbul. Caroline—practical, well-organized, mild-mannered, decisive Caroline—was now in the centre. Matron, hostess; a fine cleavage, full firm breasts rising from her tight soft olive-green wool dress. Round her the room revolved, and Liz was on the circumference, on the edge. Why did this not alarm her? Why did it merely intrigue her? Am I *mad*? wondered Liz, as she observed her attention being redirected, fluently, calmly, towards an approaching military historian; as she exchanged preliminary murmurs, proffered notions, and continued, effortlessly, to converse.

"Look round this room," the young woman in sequins was saying to Alan Headleand, in whom she had found a soul-mate. "Look round this room and see if you can point to a *single person* in it who is engaged in primary or secondary production?" Her question was not wholly rhetorical; together they looked. "Bizarre, isn't it?" said Alan, as their eyes roved. "These are the experts," said the young lawyer from the GLC. "And we are of them," said Alan Headleand, for this was what they had been discussing: the anomaly of their own loyalties, their own lives. "Tertiary. All. A tertiary, terminal bunch." "Yes," said the young woman. Her gaze rested on Pett Petrie. "Now writing books," she said, "is that tertiary production? Or merely unproductive production, would you say?"

"Stephen Cox," said Liz to the military historian, "says he's writing a play about Pol Pot."

* * *

"A lot of slack in the economy," said the young economist to Pett Petrie.

"Slack in the economy," echoed Pett Petrie, a little drunkenly, "that's a good title."

An expert in criminology was speaking to Otto Werner of the increase in vandalism: the psychology of vandals, the, as it were, criminal responsibility of Utopian sixties architects and politicians, high rise, the Harrow Road estate, the status of sociology as a discipline. Otto was not listening, but the military historian's wife was: what did they make, she wanted to know, moving abroad away from home discomforts, of the recent art outrage in Ferrara? Somebody, it appeared, had covered the Jacopo della Quercia *Madonna* in gold paint.

Otto's heart was heavy. She would not come. Where was Brian, where was Alix? Had Caroline noticed they were not here? What had happened, what more in the way of death, illness, accident, disaster? Suddenly, listening with only half an ear, to the story of the gilded *Madonna*, Otto was convinced that Alix had been murdered by that madwoman from Garfield—what was her name, Fox, Jilly Fox—and that it was all his fault. Blood would be flowing, innocent Brian would be knee-deep trying to stanch the guilty pumping dreadful deep blood. He had found her and lost her. He, Otto, had himself killed her.

Abruptly, Otto left his guests in mid-sentence, and walked rapidly across the room to Caroline; Caroline must ring Alix, he had decided, must ring and enquire. But there was no need, for the door opened, and there she was.

Ah, there is Alix, thought Liz, bored by her military historian's description of the inaccuracies of a recent film on the atrocities in Kampuchea. There is Alix, looking extraordinarily radiant. What is it? A new dress?

Alix came into the room, sparkling, striding, turning heads, her own head held high. Waves crackled from her, sparks flew. Ah, thought Liz, that's what it is: a pin in her hair, a diamond pin. A fierce and fiery crown, emitting points of light.

"Alix," cried Caroline, crossing, embracing, "Alix, you angel, so much shopping, so much *work*, without you what would we have *done* . . ."

"Hello," said Alix, stooping to kiss the solemn child.

Across the room, Otto watched, dazzled. Alix glittered. She took a drink, ate an olive, inclined her tall head gravely to speak of Caroline's mother, to apologise for their lateness. Brian had been kept on the phone, his cousin from Northam, some matter of a death certificate wrongly dated—"But here we are," said Alix, "yes, here we are, at last. Alive, and well." The meaningless, superfluous words shone like jewels, shedding incandescent sparks. And there was Brian, grey, curly haired, affable, tired, smiling; yes, he agreed with Caroline, thank God it was all over. Waving at Liz, a newly friendly Liz, who felt an intimacy with Brian, now that she had seen his father's armchair, and his father's little silver circular saw.

Otto waited. For half an hour he waited, as Alix circled, as Alix laughed and shone. He had not detected the diamonds in her hair— which were not diamonds, as she was explaining to Liz, when finally he approached her, but paste, of course paste, a piece handed down from her godmother namesake Alix, who had died a year ago. "But marvellous quality," Liz was saying, as Alix said that she had never dared to wear them before but had thought, this night, this Twelfth Night, why not? Why not indeed, said Otto, kissing her hand; she turned to him, as he still held her hand, and looked at him with wide eyes. Yes, Alix thought, yes, it is as I thought. And Liz, observing a strange tremor in Alix's elation, excused herself, and moved tactfully, murmuring, away.

"Alix," said Otto. "I thought you were dead."

"Dead?"

"You took so long to come back, I thought you would never come."

She gestured helplessly, with her free hand. "The telephone . . ." she offered, apologetic.

"I thought you were dead," he repeated. "That woman, that woman who rang you just before Christmas, it was all my fault, you must take care, you must watch out for her—"

"Don't be absurd, Otto," said Alix, "she's harmless, at least she is harmless to me, that isn't part of the plot at all, I assure you."

"Then what is?" asked Otto, intently. He still held her hand.

"How will we know, until it has happened?" she asked.

"Alix. Dear Alix."

He gazed at her, as though looking at her for the first time, his old friend of fifteen years, and wife of an even older friendship.

Her nose prickled. The hair on the back of her head stood up, a shimmer of tears stood in her eyes, as she returned his gaze.

Slowly she withdrew her hand, stroked his sleeve; smiled; withdrew.

"I will take care," she said. "And so must you."

She backed away, and was gone.

Alix, driving towards Jilly Fox and the Harrow Road, three days later, remembered Otto and his warnings. Indeed, she never forgot him, though she had not thought much of them. What had done it? A touch, a kiss, a look? Or should she blame the decline in her support for the Labour party, her disapproval of Brian's dalliance with militants, and her confused reaction to Otto's marriage to the SDP? *Galeotto fu il libro e che lo scrisse*, she said to herself, aloud—always one of her favourite quotations. Paolo and Francesca, seduced by a book, seduced by reading of the adulterous passion of Launcelot and Guinevere. *La bocca mi bacio*. A pandar was that book and he who wrote it. *Galeotto fu il SDP e chi lo . . . ? e chi lo* what? *a fondato?* She wasn't good enough at Italian to make up the line: though she had studied Canto V of the *Inferno* at Cambridge, in Italian, as an optional text, and had been much moved then, all those years ago, by the plight of Paolo and Francesca, as moved as Dante had been by those weary spirits, perpetually adrift. Ludicrous, really, at her age. But yet not quite ludicrous. A dry fever, a burning. What was to be done? Nothing. Nothing. Was she still innocent? No, she had sinned in thought, if not in word or deed. Sinned? What a concept was that, in 1984, for the daughter of ardent atheists?

Alix, sitting patiently at Lords Roundabout in slow traffic, blamed the English Tripos at the University of Cambridge for the restless ecstasy and puzzled disquiet of her present state of mind, and wondered what Dr. Leavis would have had to say to *that*. Not what he had intended, surely?

She had taken the afternoon off work. Polly Piper had encouraged her. Polly Piper had no doubt but that Alix ought to try to help Jilly Fox. Polly Piper was a subversive. Moreover she had just that morning revealed to Alix that she had given in her notice, had resigned, was about to quit. She had been offered a new job, a highly paid executive post with a firm manufacturing ladies' underwear and home furnishings; it was branching out into romantic fiction publishing. I don't know what will happen to *you*, she had said to Alix, with a mixture of aggression and apology. You can apply for my job, but what's the point? Nobody ever takes up any of our recommendations. Nobody listens, ever. I don't know what's the matter with you, Alix, she had said. At your age, with your talents, with your experience, you ought to be the governor of Holloway or the mistress of Girton. But as you're not, why don't you apply for that post advertised by the Howard League for Penal Reform? It's not very well paid, but it's not a bad job. I'd write you an excellent reference.

Thanks a lot, Alix had said, with not very much irony. She had herself thought of applying for the job: but what would she do if she got it, and Brian had to move to Gloseley?

The traffic flowed through Maida Vale. *Amor che al cor gentil ratto s'apprende* . . . The canal brimmed full, as though with dark midwinter tears, glinting in the early afternoon darkness. Teatime, a safe time, Jilly had said. After Jilly, Alix had a rendezvous with Esther. She had taken the precaution of giving Esther Jilly's assignation address in Lykewake Gardens; had said she would be round by six. Thus, if she never reappeared, she guessed Esther might at least inform Brian? Esther was just back from Bologna; they could speak of Dante and Crivelli, of Elena and the Etruscans. *Amor, che a nullo amato amar perdona.* Love, which exempts no loved one from returning love . . .

What had Jilly written? "The winter solstice is now, and forever, and never." Very nicely put. And what had she meant about teatime being a safe time? What on earth was the rest of the daytime and nighttime like at Lykewake Gardens, off the Harrow Road? A ghastly address, but probably not widely known to the ghastly. The first stretch of the Harrow Road is an underpass. Lying to one side of it, dead, was an animal that looked, in the headlights, a little like a fox. A dog or a cat, probably, but it looked like a fox. An orange fox, under the hard belly of the soaring Westway.

Lykewake Gardens is a turning off Mortuary Road. Somebody's idea of a joke, Alix supposed, as she parked the car. Beyond rose the blocks and walkways of the Mozart estate, but Lykewake Gardens was an ordinary, shabby, late-nineteenth-century little terrace, with two-storey artisan houses. Some were boarded up, as though demolition were planned. Number 43 Jilly had appointed as their meeting place. Alix parked down the street, out of sight, round the corner, and approached on foot. Forty-three Lykewake Gardens bore an unwelcoming aspect. Ill-fitting curtains were drawn across the small bay front room, and one of the panels of the front door had lost its glass and was nailed up with a sheet of perforated zinc and some cardboard. Was there a light on indoors? It was hard to be sure. There was a slow, dull, blood-beat of music throbbing, but it might be coming from Number 41? Alix summoned her courage, and knocked on the door.

Nobody answered. She knocked again, louder. A curtain twitched at the window of the neighbouring house: a face looked out. Alix knocked for a third time, and thought she heard sounds within—shuffling, knocking, a clatter of metal like a falling bicycle. Alix tried the door knob, but it would not turn. The shuffling approached, the latch was cautiously lifted, the door opened a crack.

"I've come to see Jilly," said Alix. "Is that you, Jilly?" The door opened.

There stood Jilly Fox, in a tatty stained grey candlewick dressing gown, holding a candle in a brass candlestick. Her face was white, her eyes stared, her hair hung dishevelled, her feet were stubby and shapeless in layers of socks.

Alix stared at this apparition. The apparition stared at Alix.

"Jilly," said Alix. "It's me. You asked me to come."

Silently, mournfully, Jilly beckoned. Alix followed the candle's small light down a narrow corridor, smelling of damp, undound glue, wet plaster, chalk, mice. the floorboards were soft and uneven with layers of debris of newspaper and cardboard and bits of underfelt. Jilly went into a back room, a small back room, unfurnished save for two mattresses on the floor and a small table and some boxes. Jilly gestured to Alix, indicating that she should sit upon one of the mattresses. In the dim light Alix peered at it suspiciously. Impossible to tell how dirty it might or might not be. But what could she do? She sat. It was cold. A paraffin heater stood in a corner, but it was not lit. Alix shivered, and stared enquiringly at Jilly, who continued to stand holding her candle, expressionless.

"Jilly," said Alix, "you asked me to tea. Have you *got* any tea?"

"Look," said Jilly. "Look at these." And with her candle,

she attempted to illumine the walls of the room; the walls were covered in paintings, dreadful, psychotic paintings. Daggers, pierced hearts, severed heads, dripping blood, gaping wounds, severed limbs, floating eyes. Alix could see them, not clearly, but rather more clearly than she would have chosen. A rat gnawed a human foot. A monkey drank a jar of blood. A breast floated on a plate. A tooth was held aloft by pincers. A starfish flamed in the sky. They were crudely drawn, crudely painted, somewhat in the manner of 1970s London mural folk art, and they were vividly, all too vividly representational. Alix shivered again, and stood up, to look more closely at the detail.

"Who did all this?" she asked, in as normal a voice as she could summon.

Jilly shook her head. "I inherited them," she said, huskily.

"You mean they were here when you got here?"

"In a way," said Jilly. She pointed to the bottom left-hand corner. "But that bit's mine. I added that. My cockatrice."

And in the corner, indeed, stood a strange little monster, half-hatched from an egg: a twining serpent with a beaked cock's head, a red cock's comb. Alix stared, censorious.

"Do you *live* here?" asked Alix. "I can't think it's very cheerful, living with this stuff on the walls. And it's bloody cold, Jilly, haven't you got any kind of heating? No paraffin?"

"The electricity's cut off," said Jilly. "And anyway, what does it matter? I'm just waiting for the end."

"I want a cup of tea," said Alix forlornly. Then pursued: "What do you mean, waiting for the end?"

"The end," said Jilly. "If I just wait here, it will come soon. Can't you tell?"

Alix could indeed tell, but nevertheless took it upon herself to try to argue and reason with Jilly. She must see her social worker, get herself rehoused, get a job, even, perhaps, get in touch with her mother? *Do something* to get out of this—this macabre *dump*, said Alix, gesticulating wildly at the dance of death upon the walls. No, no, said Jilly, it is fitting, now, to wait for the end, the ordained end. Her language had taken on a Biblical colouring which had certainly not been apparent at Garfield: where had it come from? Some childhood scripture class, some folk memory, some mass dementia of yesteryear? How the rubbish does linger, thought Alix to herself, as her voice reasoned with Jilly, as she tried to ascertain why Jilly had summoned her.

"I wanted a witness" was Jilly's reply to this line of query.

"A witness to *what*? To the fact that you are sitting in this dump asking for trouble? Because that's what you're doing, isn't it? Asking for trouble?"

Jilly nodded, as her candle guttered.

"Oh, yes," she said.

"Look," said Alix, suddenly changing tack, suddenly thinking of a new light, remembering Liz's view that this was not necessarily a hopeless case, "look, why don't you see a doctor? A proper doctor? Somebody you can get on with? Are you still seeing anyone from Garfield?"

It appeared not. Alix wondered if Liz would see Jilly, if she could get Jilly referred to Liz; it gave her some hope, this thought, it gave her the energy to say she, Alix, must now get out, must go, must be on her way. Jilly accepted her departure; it's better you go, she said, before the others get here. They don't like me to see people from outside.

"What others?"

Jilly was vague. The others, she repeated.

"I think you need a proper, intelligent, sympathetic, interested doctor," said Alix. "It's no good just giving in like this. You were doing so well, at Garfield."

Jilly lit another candle, from the butt of the one that was dying. She lifted it and gazed steadily at Alix in its draft-flickering light.

"Alix," she said sombrely, "there is no hope for me. I am embarked upon the eternal night. You know this quite well, and you understand it quite well. I asked you here because you understand. To bear witness."

"I think that's rhetorical, melodramatic, self-important rubbish," said Alix, "and it's inconsistent, too, because in that Christmas letter you wrote to me you were going on about the light shining forever in eternal glory, not about the eternal night. You are also, I think, mixing your metaphors. Have I entirely wasted my time, trying to teach you the study of English language and literature and the techniques of practical criticism?"

Jilly continued to gaze steadily at Alix, with a small smile now gathering round her lips.

"I suppose you think I'm off my rocker," said Jilly.

Alix nodded, patiently, agreeably.

"Well, *I* think *you* are off *yours*," said Jilly. "I think you're mad. You're mad to have come here, for one thing."

"Actually," said Alix, "I suppose you could quite reasonably speak of embarking on eternal night. The image would be of a little boat upon the river of death? Or do you see it more as a sea? Setting off to sea?"

"You see," said Jilly. "Mad, quite mad."

"And now, I remember, you did say evil and good are one, so I suppose light and darkness might be one. So I take it back, about the inconsistency. But I still think it's melodramatic rubbish."

"I think you'd better go," said Jilly. "I should never have let you come here. And anyway, as you see, I am quite all right."

"Oh, yes," said Alix, picking her way carefully back along the dark corridor towards the front door. "Yes, marvellous, I've never seen anyone more comfortably installed."

Jilly laughed. "Alix," she said, "you are mad, but you are wonderful."

She unlatched the door, opened it. The light of the street lamp illuminated both their faces. And Alix had the impression that other faces appeared at upper windows of Number 43. The dull beat of blood seemed louder, in the open air.

"Goodbye," said Jilly. "Goodbye forever."

"I don't like all this terminal talk," said Alix. "I think it's very pretentious."

"This is rather a pretentious location," said Jilly, gazing down the desolate street. "It's well chosen, don't you think?"

"Yes, it is well chosen. I congratulate you."

"Remember me," said Jilly, as she laid a thin hand on Alix's sleeve. A gust of wind blew out the flame of the candle.

The two women embraced. The smell of Jilly's skin was acrid, sour. She was dry as a leaf.

Alix turned, and walked away, towards the corner, beyond which her car waited. Jilly watched her departure, and others watched too. Alix rounded the corner, and saw the Renault; she had the impression that somebody ran away from it, into the night, she felt that she half overheard a sound of laughter. A scurrying, a whispering, a taunting. Rat-faced people, fox-faced people. She held on to her keys, tight in her pocket; the metal bit into her fingers, comforting. Her getaway keys. She knew she was being watched from every side. She reached the car door, opened the car, collapsed into the safety of the driver's seat. But collapsed too far, too unevenly: something was wrong. She got out to look; the front two tyres had gone, they were as flat as the tyres of the old dumped car that had

resided for so many months outside the house in Wandsworth.
"Shit," said Alix, aloud, loudly. She knew without looking
that they had been slashed. She heard laughter, girlish laughter,
in the shadows, behind a wall. "Very funny," called Alix,
thinly, defiantly, to the empty air. Her words vanished. Alix
was angry, frightened, dismayed. Calmly she extracted her
briefcase, her shopping bag (Cumberland sausage for supper,
from Jermyn Street), locked the car, and began to walk,
calmly, carefully, indifferently, down the gauntlet of the street,
then faster, as she reached Mortuary Road, and faster still,
once out of sight of those mocking eyes, until she broke weakly
into a jog on the last stretch. There was the main road, the
Harrow Road. It was only five minutes from here to Esther's;
in the dark night, Alix Bowen ran, without looking behind her,
not daring to look back.

"Pierced hearts and severed heads and floating eyes?" asked
Esther, pouring Alix another large whisky.

"That's right," said Alix. "And a floating breast."

"Saint Agatha, that one," said Esther. "I wonder if it was
meant?"

"Well, what *does* Saint Agatha *mean*, come to that?" asked
Alix.

"A good point," said Esther. "I must say, considered
historically, which by me it rarely is, the sado-masochistic
content of Christian iconography *is* really rather startling.
Here, have a look at this . . ."—and she delved into a pile of
art books, and came up with *Painting in Naples: From
Caravaggio to Giordano*, which she passed to Alix, open at
Guarino's *Saint Agatha*. The saint suggestively clutched to her
concealed but mutilated bosom a blood-stained white cloth,
and her face wore an expression of ecstatic dreamy erotic
intensity.

"I forget if you went to that exhibition," said Esther. "I
know I kept telling you to go, but I bet you never got round
to it. You didn't? I thought not. Liz went. Liz said that picture was menstrual. I don't quite see what she means, do
you?"

"The red and the white?" suggested Alix, tentatively,
gazing at Agatha's voluptuous disarray.

"I must say," said Alix, "the paintings in Lykewake

Gardens were rather less oblique. They were more like the paintings by that chap in Broadmoor who murdered his mother.''

"Look," said Esther, momentarily distracted, turning the pages. "Look at this wonderful *St. Mary of Egypt*. The bread and the skull. Brown, brown. Look at the texture. Wonderful.''

"Were they all psychotic, the Neapolitans?''

"I don't know. They're not my lot, really. I asked Liz what it meant, this severed-head business, and she just said it was something to do with fear of castration. Or rather, to do her justice, she said she thought that that was what a proper Freudian would say.''

"I can't possibly ring the AA,'' said Alix. "Not twice in a month. They'll think I'm dotty.''

"And did you say floating wounds? That's what that chap in Broadmoor painted. Great bleeding wounds, floating around all by themselves.''

"Didn't Crivelli paint wounds?''

"All sacred art is full of wounds. But yes, he did. You're quite right. Very odd ones.'' Esther heaved around amongst various other large volumes, and abstracted her own Crivelli catalogue. "Is this the kind of thing you mean?''

She pointed at a *Pietà*, where the incision in Christ's bosom resembled a little open mouth, with lips; a little mouth, about to speak. Or a vagina. Yes, decided Alix, it more closely resembled a vagina. A wounded vagina, about to speak. *Vagina implorans.*

"Yes,'' said Alix. "Pretty odd, isn't it?''

"I suppose it is,'' said Esther.

Alix gulped at her whisky.

"I can't ring the AA now anyway,'' she said. "I've had too much to drink. It'll just have to stay there until the morning. I wonder if Brian wanted to go to Milton Keynes in it tomorrow? He's got an examiners' meeting.''

"Give him a ring,'' said Esther.

"And I'll have to buy another spare. Oh God,'' said Alix. ("Forty pounds'' said Alix.)

"Tell me more about the cockatrice,'' said Esther, turning the pages of Crivelli, pausing before a *Madonna of the Passion*, where a brave cock crowed proudly, aloft on a marble pillar.

"I suppose a cockatrice is a male-female symbol?'' said Alix. "But I'd have thought it was a *dead* symbol. As dead as

the proverbial door nail. I'm amazed by the way people keep
on with the same old vestigial stuff. It dies hard.''

"You would have expected us to have marched forward into
the new light by now? The rational, radiant light?'' asked
Esther.

"Well, yes, I would,'' said Alix. "Wouldn't you?''

"I suppose even I would have expected a little better,'' said
Esther. "A *little* more light.'' She sighed.

"Tell me about Bologna,'' said Alix.

"Ah, Bologna,'' said Esther. "Well, that was radiant, in its
way. But I paid the price. Look, look at my palm. My poor
palm. It missed me.''

"Not too well, is it?''

"Not really. It didn't like my being away at all. It'll have to
go, soon. I keep hoping it might put out some final exotic
expiring blossom. But I don't think it will, now. Do you?''

The palm stood stiffly to attention, rigid in death.

"No,'' said Alix. "I don't.''

Alix left the Cumberland sausage at Esther's. She also had to
wait three quarters of an hour for a bus. She stood there,
inventing stories to tell Brian about the car, inventing excuses,
like a guilty wife.

"Never mind,'' said Brian. "Never mind. What a horrid day
you've had,'' He stirred the scrambled eggs, the ideal husband.

"I'll collect it tomorrow, at lunchtime,'' said Alix. "I'm not
going there in the dark again. I'm so sorry.''

"I'd have gone on the train anyway,'' said Brian.

"And with the poor car out of action for so long over
Christmas,'' said Alix, miserably, a little drunk still from
Esther's Scotch. She had confessed one tyre only.

"That wasn't your fault either,'' said Brian, reasonably,
distributing egg on buttered toast.

"No, no,'' said Alix even more miserably, vehemently,
hopelessly, "it wouldn't have been so bad if it *had* been my
fault; it wasn't my fault, it was the fault of other people.
Wanton, idle, pointless, awful people. Deliberate. Malicious.
The fault of the people.''

"Now then," said Brian. "Come and eat your eggs. It'll all be all right tomorrow."

But at lunchtime the next day, as Alix Bowen and Polly Piper, armed with a spare tyre and some sandwiches, approached Lykewake Gardens in a taxi, they could see from afar that it was not all right. The road was full of police, cordoned-off: disaster, quiet, drab, uniformed, muttering disaster called quietly down the shabby street through the cold air. Alix's heart lurched, sank. "I knew it," she said to Polly, "I knew it."

The taxi driver slowed, stopped, some twenty yards from the cordon: sensing trouble, he was caught between the desire to see more and the desire to retreat. He turned round, questioningly, to his women passengers, who earlier had taken rather ill his jollity about the spare tyre, and who were now gazing ahead, transfixed. "Do you want to get away?" he said, in a not helpful manner (for they were, after all, his fares, and under his protection), but it was too late to retreat, for the police had sighted them, were upon them, in a little cluster.

Alix got out of the cab, gestured at her car, standing beyond the cordon, explained: yes, that was her car, with the two flat tyres; yes, she had come to fix it, to pick it up, with her friend Miss Piper; yes, it had been parked there all night. Polly paid the driver, but he hung around almost, as it were, against his will, allowing himself to be sucked into the vortex of danger. Questions came at Alix from all sides. She tried to walk towards the Renault, but was restrained; someone asked her for the keys, she declined to hand them over. What is all this, demanded Polly, magisterially, dauntingly, but she was not answered. The car itself, they could now see, was the object of attention, the fatal attraction, the source of the shifting and mumbling and staring: Polly, put on her mettle by the confused officers, attempted to stride towards the Renault, speaking as she did so of the Home Office, but they called after her in horror, they interposed themselves and restrained her: don't, Miss, don't go near, they cried, with such conviction that even Polly faltered. "What is it? Is it wired for a bomb?" she demanded. But Alix knew already that it was not a bomb. She knew that there, in her car, was the head of Jilly Fox.

And so, of course, it was. Well, obviously, as Alix later

conceded. The configuration of the street, the hard white January light, the police vans, the disorganized officers, the faces staring from upstairs windows, the air of subdued horror and illicit excitement; what else could it mean? Where else had the narrative of the previous tea-less teatime been tending?

No, not a bomb, said one of the policemen. A head, a human head.

Is that what he said? Neither Polly nor Alix could, later, be certain, but both remembered clearly that at some point (at roughly this point?) Alix was heard to declare, "I know whose it is," and Polly was heard to say, "Shut up and ask for your solicitor."

Both agreed, later, that this was the most incriminating remark Polly could, in the circumstances, have uttered: but both agreed that, in the circumstances, it was hard to think clearly, even though trained by a Cambridge degree to do so at all times.

Nobody seemed to be thinking very clearly: nobody seemed to be in charge. The discovery, whatever it was, was new: the situation was as yet fluid, unresolved. Alix continued to repeat that it was her car, but that she wouldn't hand over the keys until somebody explained what was happening; gradually she edged her way up the road towards it, step by step, one or two of the reluctant officers shuffling along with her. "Surely I can look inside my own car?" Alix heard herself saying, plaintively, innocently; and at this moment the group's attention was distracted by the arrival of a newer, darker, smoother, superior official vehicle, and Alix took the opportunity of crossing the last two or three yards to look inside the Renault. Polly had flinched and fallen behind: Alix found herself curiously fearless. And there indeed, reposing upon the driver's seat, loosely wrapped but only partially concealed, in a piece of mutton cloth, was the head of Jilly Fox. The eyes were open, and stared. Alix gazed at them, at Jilly's livid face, at the dishevelled hair. So this was it: death. Alix stared, and was not turned to stone. Her lips moved, drily. Goodbye, Jilly, said Alix Bowen, standing there on the cold pavement. Goodbye. A policeman, a young bearded policeman, stood silent in a shocked respect at her elbow, too shocked to interrupt this brief obsequy. And when Alix Bowen turned back to the living, turned back to Polly Piper, it was Polly who appeared to have been petrified, Polly who, at one remove, through the shield of knowledge of Alix, stood there pale and frozen, aged and motionless, appalled and death-blasted.

"It's all right, Polly," Alix is alleged to have said. "Don't worry, it's all right." Although, clearly, it was not.

For ages of time they stood there, in the cold, dull white noonday glare, transfixed. Nothing moved. Far down the street, the taxi driver stood by his cab. Faces watched from windows. A young woman with a push chair and baby stood motionless, outside Number 18, arrested by her own front path, unable to proceed with her day's shopping. Polly stood like a statue, in her leather coat and boots, in her fur hat. The young policeman stood, uncertain. A cold frame held them.

And then, suddenly, there was action. A man who appeared to possess authority descended upon Alix and Polly, full of questions, assurances, respects. Meekly Alix, recognizing hierarchy, handed over the keys, told her story of the previous day. Yes, she could identify the victim. Yes, she knew her well. Yes, she had seen her alive the day before. Where? Here in Lykewake Gardens. Which number? Could she tell them precisely where, when, why? Polly again suggested caution, spoke of solicitors, but Alix, armoured by innocence, shook off these warnings. It occurred to Alix that the body of Jilly Fox had not yet been located. Was the body of Jilly Fox lying, even now, in 43 Lykewake Gardens? Should she lead them to it?

"Number 43, it's just round the corner," she heard herself saying. "No, I don't know who lives there. I think it's some kind of squat."

The man in authority suggested that Alix and Polly should sit in his car, out of the cold, while he went to look at the house. Polly said she had to get back to work, but he indicated that this might not be possible. Polly asked if she could ring the Home Office to let it know where she was. Alix smiled at this, suspecting that the Home Office had little interest in the whereabouts either of herself or of Polly Piper, and that some of it might be surprised to learn that they still existed. To whom would you wish to speak? asked the man. Polly named the most important person she could think of, and was told she could speak from the car radio. "Harry," Alix heard Polly say, "Harry, this is me, Polly. What? Yes, *me*." (Intimacy established.) "No, I'm in the back of a police car. I won't be back in the office this afternoon. What? No, I can't tell you now. I'll speak to you later. I'm with"—she consulted through the car window—"Chief Inspector Nicholls. And my col-

league Alix Bowen. Yes, I'll ring you this evening. Bye for
now.''

Chief Inspector Nicholls appeared suitably impressed by this
interchange. He departed, assuring them he would be back
soon. And he was; looking, Alix fancied, a little grim round
the mouth, and rather important. He had, she imagined, just
seen the rest of Jilly Fox.

Alix spent the rest of the day helping the police with their
enquiries. Polly was allowed to leave after a couple of hours;
indeed, she was obliged to leave, somewhat against her will.
She said she wanted to stay with Alix, but was discouraged
from doing so. She left, sweeping out of the police station in
a cloud of voluble reassurance; now she had recovered from the
initial shock, she was thoroughly enjoying herself, as Alix had
known she would. She even had the presence of mind to carry
off the spare tyre. "I don't suppose it's needed as evidence, is
it?" she said, as she reclaimed it. "I'll keep it for you, Alix.
God knows when you'll get your car back. Don't worry, I'll
ring Brian as soon as he gets back from Milton Keynes. I'll tell
him all.''

And she vanished, the tyre under her leather-jacketed arm,
like an instrument of torture robustly carried by a healthy saint.

Alix continued to make statements, give names, addresses,
telephone numbers. The admonitory presence of the crudely
invoked Sir Harry Hoggett hovered over her interviews,
protectively, and she was treated with some courtesy—chau-
vinistic courtesy; but courtesy nonetheless. After a while, as
she began to realize the possible implications of publicity in the
press about her post-Garfield relationship with Jilly, she began
to wish she had followed Polly's advice and asked for her
solicitor, but it seemed too late in the day to demand to speak
to her now. The day wore on, punctuated by cups of tea. Alix's
mind wandered. Severed heads, floating wounds, teeth in
pincers, cockatrices. Why did she not grieve, at the horror of
Jilly's death? Because Jilly had willed it so. A martyr, she had
become, and had died serenely. But a martyr to what? To
what?

Alix was cross-questioned about the slashed tyres. Yes, she
had thought she had heard noises, giggling, scuffling, as she
approached her car the night before. Girls' voices?

Alix hesitated. Yes, she had thought so. But should she *say*
so?

"I can't be sure," she said.

Why had she parked so far from the house, they wanted to know. I don't know, she had said—some kind of caution, perhaps? So what had she been expecting to happen? Oh, she didn't know. But in an area like that . . . What did she know of the area? What were Jilly's contacts in the area? Had Jilly mentioned any names?

On and on it went, with long and tedious intervals. The Horror of Harrow Road strikes again, the headlines would declare. The second attempt in a month. Alix could not remember who the first of this second series, the pre-Christmas victim, had been.

They had been girls' voices, Alix was almost certain. But girls could hardly have hacked off Jilly Fox's head.

Bizarre, ironic, yet not quite coincidental, that she should find herself here, contemplating the nature of female crime and female contributory negligence, subjects so central to the professional concerns of herself and Polly Piper. They had been drawn to the scene of crime as by a lodestar. Had Jilly Fox asked to be murdered? Well, yes, obviously, but we must not say so.

Alix recalled the dark street, the whisperings, the scuttling. Criminals and victims. Painful, painful. I am in danger of submitting, thought Alix, to the "moral panic" which Adler was accused of evoking when she proposed (*Sisters in Crime*, 1975) the emergence of a new kind of female criminal, the production of the feminist movement of the 1970s. With what dangerous delight feminist sociologists have turned their attention to these things. What was the study of a female gang in New York that Polly had recommended so warmly? College girls and corner girls. Were she and Polly guilty of admiration for the criminal? for the streetwise, the cunning, the careless, the brave? Why else had she herself, Alix Bowen, Cambridge graduate, found herself in Lykewake Gardens off the Harrow Road? She had chosen to implicate herself, as surely as Jilly Fox had chosen to meet a violent death.

Alix, sipping strong tea, tried to fix her mind upon the image of that woman with her baby, emerging from their hallway in Lykewake Gardens. A young black woman, wearing a long grey cloth coat, and a woollen hat; a nylon net, plastic-handled shopping basket over her arm: her baby well wrapped and bonneted, sitting in a chipped blue old-fashioned push chair. An ordinary woman, an ordinary baby. Not well-off, or why would they live in such a dump, but warmly dressed, respectably dressed, against the cold: and the brickwork of their house painted quite smartly, albeit in a somewhat violent deep salmon pink. *1867*, it said, on a cheap plaster flourish over the doorway. A home, a private place. No painted monsters, no gnawing rats. Once, thought Alix, I had a sense of such lives, of such peaceable, ordinary, daily lives. I could envisage interiors, clothes drying on fireguards, pots of tea in the hearth, a pot plant on a windowsill. Now I see them no more. I see horrors. I imagine horrors. I have courted horrors, and they have come to greet me. Whereas I had wished not to court them, but to exorcise them. To gaze into their eyes and destroy them by my gazing. They have won, they have destroyed me. There is no hope of a peaceable life, of a life for the people, of a society without fear. Fear grows, flourishes, is bred, blossoms, flames. That woman and her baby, they pause forever on their front step. The street will destroy them.

I am defeated, thought Alix. We are defeated. But how *can* I admit defeat? Is it the wrong battle I have been fighting, all these years?

Chief Inspector Nicholls returned, in the late afternoon, to ask Alix if she would object to accompanying him to the hospital mortuary to give a formal identification of the remains of Jilly Fox. I'm sorry, Mrs. Bowen, he said, but if you could come along now, I could let you go home. We haven't been able to contact the parents. It seems they're abroad. On an off-season package holiday in Marrakesh.

Of course, said Alix, unable by nature and nurture not to sound obliging. A world of normality Nicholls offered, in comparison with her own thoughts. They sat together in the back of the car, and Nicholls explained that the coroner's mortuary was closed, for its biennial clean: therefore, they were to go to St. Andrew's Hospital. They chatted, as they passed through the dark streets. There were the *Standard* placards. *Horror Victim in Dumped Car*. Got that a bit wrong as usual, said Nicholls. I needn't urge you to discretion with the press, Mrs. Bowen, said Nicholls. No, said Alix, after all, I *am* a civil servant. Well, a sort of civil servant.

"When will I get my car back?" asked Alix, as they pulled up outside St. Andrew's. "My husband *will* be annoyed. I hardly dare to tell him."

It was a joke. He laughed. Polly Piper, Alix reflected, would not have descended to such a joke. Polly Piper was probably even now making different jokes, modern, murderous jokes, while drinking whisky and soda with Sir Harry Hoggett at their club in Pall Mall.

The hospital was old, red-brick, Victorian. They walked along corridors, descended in a creaking old-fashioned metal-grid-doored service lift. They walked along more corridors. Doors opened. "Hello, Stanley," said Chief Inspector Nicholls to an elderly nicotine-moustached man in a white coat. Stanley looked suspiciously at Alix. "One of the bereaved," said Nicholls. In code Stanley nodded, ushered them into another, smaller, cubicle room. Dark blue Dralon drapes hung across the end of the cubicle. A young man wearing a hastily donned black tie over a hastily buttoned plaid Viyella shirt hovered, nervously. Alix caught his eye; he looked away, embarrassed. He looked rather ill. He somewhat resembled Alan Headleand. Alix half expected music, but there was none. In the nineteenth century, she told herself sternly, people used to go and gape at the victims in the Paris morgue. English gentlemen, English poets, English novelists went on purpose to stare. Géricault collected heads from the guillotine, took them back to his studio to paint, or so Esther had claimed. Who was she to flinch? And anyway, she had seen the worst already: Jilly's head, yellow white, staring, handsome, livid, wrapped in grey muslin, mystic, wonderful.

"Ready, Mike?" asked Stanley, hovering officiously. Mike nodded. "Ready, madam?" Stanley enquired, rather unpleasantly, of Alix. Alix nodded.

The Dralon curtains swished back to something of an anti-climax: there lay a recumbent form, but it was covered with a sheet, and a delicate white serviette lay over its head. Stanley nodded at Mike; Mike gently removed the serviette. And there again was the head of Jilly Fox, her eyes now decorously closed. The pallor was remarkable; its greenish-yellow hue and texture unreal, like wax. Mike looked very happy. The snake-like tresses had been combed into neatness: had poor Mike been obliged to comb them himself? Had his fingers closed those accusing ecstatic eyes? Alix knew Mike, instantly, for what he was: a college boy, doing his stretch as a corner boy. Earning money, toughening his spirit. She wanted to speak to him. She wanted to touch Jilly. She wanted Stanley to make the crude, comforting jokes she knew he

would have been making had she not been there. She did not
have the courage to ask if she could touch Jilly. Instead, she
found herself, for the first time in her life, crossing herself—
the wrong way, probably, if there was a wrong way for a
gesture. The Black Mass way? Stanley, Mike, and Nicholls
stood back respectfully, but somehow suspiciously. Alix gazed
at Jilly, as though she were a finished work of art. She nodded
authentication. Yes, she asserted, this was, or had been, Jilly
Fox. She searched in her mind for a farewell, for an epitaph.
For words, any words. For flights of wordy angels, to sing her
to her rest. There lay Jilly Fox, with her three A levels, upon
a mortuary slab.

Nicholls cleared his throat. Stanley nodded at Mike. Ap-
prentice Mike stepped forward to cover her face, but Alix
stepped forward too, and without asking permission, gently
touched Jilly's icy forehead. Icy? Yes, icy. She had clearly just
come out of a refrigerator. A refrigerator chest, with shelves,
Alix imagined. Stanley, Mike and Nicholls closed in on Alix.
Alix stepped back, deferentially. A ridiculous scene—the
bruised much-fingered Dralon curtains, the black tie, the white
coat, the serviette, the extraordinary blend of solemnity,
menace, and irreverence.

"And what did they use," Alix heard herself saying, "to
chop her head off? A Black and Decker?"

But not even Alix's indelicately correct guess at the instrument
of decollation could convert her into a prime suspect. Or even
a secondary or tertiary suspect. She was allowed to go home.

The Jilly Fox episode put an end to Mike Gitting's spell as a
mortuary assistant. That very evening he told Stanley (of
whom he had grown quite fond) that he had had enough of bits
of bodies arriving in bin liners. B.I.D. Brought In Dead.
B.I.V.D. in this case, agreed Stanley, adding Longlife milk to
his tea from the carton he kept in the mortuary refrigerator, but
don't let it put you off, Mike, these police cases are always
unpleasant, it's just a bit of bad luck they had to come in while
you were here. It's a good life, a secure life, let me tell you.
You can get a diploma, make a career of it. No, thanks, said

Mike, who had already got a history degree from Sussex and was waiting for an interview with a provincial subsidiary of Global International Network. No, I don't think so, really. I don't think it's quite me. But despite this prompt decision, Mike Gitting's dreams were to be haunted for years to come. He had been educated at a Quaker school in York, and as a boy had been disturbed by descriptions of heads displayed above the city gates, displayed and left to rot, the hair falling away, the teeth bravely grinning at the weather; now they returned to grin at him. Heads, haunches, forequarters, set upon poles. No, no, no, thank you, said Mike Gitting, tossing in his history-troubled sleep.

"My God, poor Alix," said Liz Headland, when Polly Piper rang to tell her the exciting news. But she reflected, shortly after, as she tried to ring Esther, that Alix of all people was unlikely to be deeply upset by such a ghastly event. Why? she wondered, why?

Otto Werner was not so confident. When he heard the story, guilt exaggerated his fears. The encounter had been of his making. What if Alix's own head had been chopped off? What if he had unwittingly sent Alix to her death? What of the grief Alix must now be suffering? Did she blame Otto for this grief? No, Alix did not blame Otto. It did not occur to her to do so. Nor, as Liz had rightly guessed, was she apparently much disturbed by the more sensational aspects of Jilly's death, or indeed much grieved by the death itself. It would have seemed to her a sentimentality, to grieve over so determined a departure. She was forced, over the next few months, to take a considerable interest in the case, as police questions continued, as various kinds of post-mortems took place (on Jilly Fox's body, on Alix's friendship with Jilly, on Alix's position at Garfield, on the mini-quango in Nightingale Terrace), and she was overheard, at one point, to declare controversially, provocatively, that she felt very sorry for Jilly Fox's murderer, who had been forced to play a role in a drama not of his own making (his: sic).

Alix had lunch with Edgar Lintot, at Liz's suggestion, and

described her impressions of Jilly, and of the murals at Lykewake Gardens. No, she had agreed with Edgar, Jilly was not mad at all. But the man that murdered her, he is mad. Poor chap. Yes, poor chap, agreed Edgar. Interesting case, said Edgar. Yes, interesting, agreed Alix. I don't think it can be very nice, to go around possessed of a compulsive urge to chop off people's heads, said Alix, accepting another glass of wine. I entirely agree with you, said Edgar. Thus spoke the outdated voice of reason, in a small Greek restaurant just off Charlotte Street.

The post-mortem on Alix's marriage was less easy to conduct. The roles of victim and murderer were less easily allotted. Alix had no confidantes in this investigation: loyalty to Brian, to her own past self, to the whole network of the past, made it impossible for her to speak, even to Liz, even to Esther. Because of this, she saw less of Esther and Liz at this time. Nor did she speak to Otto. She and Otto continued to meet, as before, in company. Nothing passed between them, save looks, glances, moments of consciousness. Nothing. Was it a consolation, occasionally to catch a glance, to clasp a hand on parting? Yes, perhaps.

Difficult times. Brian did not get the job at Gloseley, which Alix had almost begun to look upon as some kind of solution. Alix's classes at Garfield were suspended, cut like the table-cloths, ostensibly for economy reasons. But, in fact, as everyone quite well knew, suspended because of the Jilly Fox scandal. Alix was not surprised. Work at Nightingale Terrace ground slowly to a halt, as Polly prepared for her new life. Alix handed in her notice too. There was some talk of finding her a new job within the Home Office but nothing was offered. She and Polly sat at their desks with their feet on the table drinking coffee, talking endlessly of the Fox affair. Polly, unlike Alix, was obsessed with the murderer's identity, and came up with some wild suggestions of well-known sexual perverts in high places, suggested by the one escaped victim's allusion to a possible moustache. Alix, outclassed, scoffed. Thus they passed the time, unprofitably, in the spring of '84.

Brian spent nearly all his spare time attending political meetings, supporting the miners. He collected money, distributed leaflets.

Alix watched images of the miners' strike on television. She watched the police in their riot gear. She watched charging horses. She listened to miners' wives speaking of solidarity.

She heard the leader of the miners' union speak of certain victory. She saw blazing cars, upturned vans. Alone, she sat and watched and listened, hour after hour. What was it she felt? A kind of terrible grinding disaffection. As though the plates of her mind were rubbing and grating against one another. Arthritically, incurably: an invisible, internal inflammation. If she sat still and did not let her mind move at all, the pain would ease, but as soon as she tried to think, to react to what she saw and heard, the pain would start up again. And yet (and this was where her mind would wince in protest, would tell her to be still)—and yet, Brian was right, of course he was right. The cause of all this pain, this grinding, this deep misery, was the economic system itself. This system under which she lived. There was no hope in it, so why did her common sense, her rational being, her education all scream out in protest against the folly of Brian's newly wasted life? Against the vacuous pointlessness of the slogans of his new-found, moustached, thin-lipped, polytechnic chums? Because of her class background, no doubt, Brian's chums would say. Did say. But she did not believe this.

Or if she did believe it, what then? Where should she go then? So sat Alix Bowen, and many thousands like her, as the year wore on, as she watched the grim images that filled her little screen, and heard the righteous voices of unreason in the terminal struggle of warring factions in her own land. Where was a voice to speak to her, for her, for England? Where was Cromwell, where Whinstanley? Was the country done for, finished off, struggling and twitching in the last artificially prolonged struggles of old age?

The miners went on holidays by the Black Sea.

The miners pawned their wedding rings and their silver photo frames.

The miners ate well in soup kitchens, on food parcels from rich Marxists in the Home Counties.

The babies of miners suffered acute malnutrition.

Miners threw bricks through the windows of miners.

Miners were peaceful, home-loving folk who loved their old grannies.

Miners beat their wives.

The wives of miners stood bravely on picket lines.

*   *   *

What I can't see, said Esther to Alix, is what any of this has got to do with you. Or with me. It's simply not our problem. We didn't make it, and that's that. I've never met a miner, and I'm sure a miner wouldn't want to meet me.

It's not as simple as that, said Alix.

Alix and Brian were obliged, at last, to get rid of the old Renault 4. They did their best to keep it going: they patched it up, after the Lykewake Gardens episode, and it chugged gamely on for another few weeks, but then it suffered another ignominious disaster. Brian, going down one morning, discovered that the passenger window had been shattered and the radio nicked. Oh dear, oh dear, said Alix. Her view was that thieves should not vandalize or steal from such evidently unfortunate old vehicles: they should go for the B reg. Brian would not give in easily, and he and Alix went off to the breaker's yard in Stockwell, where you could pick up spare parts for next to nothing. Alix gazed, saddened, admiring, as Brian clambered around the towering heaps of old scrapped cars, searching for his own car's siblings. The weak spring sun shone on rust and chrome, on sodden upholstery and fractured glass, on weeds struggling from corners of brickwork, as Brian, agile, picked his way through the mechanical junk in search of a spare window. His failure to find one the right size depressed him. All the Renaults on the scrap heap were of a later model than his own. I give in, he said to Alix, wiping his hands on his grey trousers: we'll have to get rid of it, it's just not worth spending any more on it.

"What shall we do with it?" asked Alix, as they drove home. The thought of selling the car to the breakers for a tenner upset her. She had never gone in for whimsy about the car, had always thought people silly when they gave their cars pet names and talked of them as people, but nevertheless she did not like the image of the car in the breaker's yard, piled high amidst the corpses. She knew that Brian did not like the idea either, though they were both too sensitive to share this somewhat dubious emotion.

"I'll take care of it," said Brian, gallantly.

And they returned home in drafty silence, subdued, as their thoughts turned to the cost of replacement. The finances of the Bowens were not flourishing, their prospects were not bright.

Rita Ablewhite lay in a hospital bed, staring at the ceiling. Sometimes she muttered to herself. Sometimes, but not often, Shirley went to sit with her. The nurses said she understood more than she let on, and that if only she'd cooperate she'd be able to feed herself, dress herself, maybe even walk again. Rita Ablewhite did not, at this point, choose to cooperate. A most unsatisfactory position.

Deborah Manning died. She had lingered on longer than anyone had expected or hoped, but the end, Nicholas assured Alix, was not too bad. Was he saying this to protect her? Alix did not know. She went to the funeral, in the little church at the foot of the Downs. The leaves of the chestnut were unfolded. Broad green spring. There were bluebells in hedgerows. Ilse presided over the funeral party, the lady of the manor. With extraordinary grace. The gypsy, settled. Sam vanished into the garden, and lay gazing into the depths of the pond. Yellow irises rose, stately, festive. The bulrushes, according to Nicholas, were getting out of hand. He would cut them back, now Deborah was gone. What is it, this grace, wondered Alix? Is it natural? Is it of nature? Is it a free gift? She remembered Sebastian, who had been destined to a life of ease. And she with her questions, her doubts, her difficulties, her withdrawals, had destroyed him. Thus she now read the plot of the past. She had not, it seemed, destroyed Nicholas. Not even her great love had destroyed him. She resolved to keep away, to stand out of his light, to let him be.

Esther Breuer's palm died. She offered it painless euthanasia, by putting it out on the front steps one frosty night. She repented the next morning and took it in again, under the influence of the silent young man upstairs—well, not so young, now, but she always thought of him as the silent young man.

As he saw the palm on the steps upon leaving the house, he addressed to Esther perhaps the only complete sentence she had ever heard him utter in some thirteen years. "You'll kill the poor thing," he said, "if you leave it out there." "Yes, I know," said Esther humbly, apologetic, "but it wasn't really doing very well indoors. I thought I'd—I'd give it a change."

And she put it back in her front window, but the deed was done, and its withering accelerated. Esther felt unaccountably guilty whenever she saw (which was not often) the silent young man.

She was not at all surprised to receive, a week after this exposure, a phone call from Elena in Bologna informing her that Claudio was ill in hospital and was asking to see her. I think you should come, said Elena.

So Esther went, responding to this last summons. She had never in all these years met Claudio's wife, and did not necessarily expect to do so now, but wondered, nevertheless, as the Alitalia plane descended, what was she *really* like? And what kinds of tales, if any, had he related to her of his friendship with Esther Breuer? She had little doubt but that he had lied of each to the other; delicacy had prevented her from cross-questioning Elena too closely on this subject, but nevertheless she had gathered, indirectly, that the bitter hypochondriac Claudio described as his wife was as much a figment of his imagination as the werewolf. Roberta Volpe was patient, pleasant, mild, forebearing, Elena implied. She and Elena liked one another. As one normal person might like another. So Elena implied.

Esther thought of Claudio Volpe, who had been the great love of her life, and wondered what had happened to that love. Now she did not feel it any more; had it ceased to exist? Because she did not feel it any more, did that mean it had never existed? These thoughts tormented her. She had wasted her entire adult emotional life on a fantasy. On a werewolf. On a non-person. Was there any recovery? And how could she face the sight of the non-Claudio, the shell-Claudio, the real Claudio?

Esther Breuer was quite well aware of the fact that her emotional relationships throughout her life had been based partly on her desire to avoid normal sexual intercourse. She did not need someone like Liz Headleand to tell her this, nor would Liz ever have had the impertinence to suggest it. For both she and Liz knew that such knowledge was irrelevant. Nevertheless, Esther Breuer, approaching Claudio's hospital bedside after a fortifying coffee with Elena, was obliged to pause, to take stock, to hesitate, on the polished linoleum; her blood sang in her ears. What *was* it that was relevant, what was this obsession that she had accepted, willed, encouraged?

Claudio lay there, yellow, shrunk, sharp, in a private room. Flowers, books, fruit, bottles of spirit surrounded his bedside. A crucifix hung on the wall. He looked up at her, sharply, as she entered. Sharply, fretfully. An old man, a sick old man. But she was relieved to sense that he was not yet harmless; from him emanated still a faint potency, an odour of malice. *"Siediti,"* he instructed her, and she sat. *"Ascolta,"* he said, and she listened.

He spoke of the soul, and its journey through time; of the material and the immaterial; of the *spiritus mundi,* the *anima,* the *stella marina,* the *deus absconditus.* He had been reading Jung, he said, Jung the old faker; but it was interesting, nevertheless, to look back at books he had admired as a boy: look up the Medusa, he said to her, look up the *stella marina,* the fish that burns like a star in the midst of water, the starfish that burns at the North Pole.

Esther listened, relieved. Relieved to find him as mad as ever, madder than ever. Finding him so, indeed sublimely so, even for him, she acknowledged that what she had most feared was to find a fretful, reduced, humbled old man; complaining about hospital food, stupid nurses, pain. But no, Claudio was far, far beyond and above all that, still encouraging himself with dreams of hidden power and forbidden knowledge. He spoke of Gorgon and the Medusa and Géricault and Demogorgon and Salome and the Bessi of Thrace. He spoke of a witch he had known in Sofia. He spoke of a fool of a Dominican priest who visited him every evening to talk theology. To entertain him, Esther told him the story of Jilly Fox and the cockatrice. He was entranced, as she had known he would be. It is not a mortal murderer, said Claudio, it is a spirit. It is a mass hallucination, unleashed from the fear of the people. By disbelief you can disarm it. If you decide so, Esther, there will be no more deaths.

I don't see how I can undo a mass hallucination by single will, said Esther. Everybody else would have to join in.

You do not recognize your own power, said Claudio, solemnly. If you will it, there will be no more deaths.

Really, said Esther, gazing at the white lilies, the yellow

roses, thinking that shortly she would ask Claudio to offer her a drink, and then she would run back to Elena's for comfort, to laugh, to weep, to recover, in the outside world of health.

She was sipping a stiff gin and amaro when another visitor was announced. There was a tap on the door: it's that imbecile of a priest, said Claudio, suspiciously, eagerly (she could tell he enjoyed his nightly confrontations), but it was not; it was a dark, curly-haired, handsome Englishman bearing a potted orchid. Esther did not at first recognize him, so much out of context, so far from home, but he recognized her. "Esther Breuer, I think," he said, having greeted Claudio and deposited his orchid, and she saw that it was art historian and Minister for Sponsorship Robert Oxenholme.

"Pour Robert a drink," Claudio instructed Esther, in English. He never sounded quite as plausible in English.

"What are you having?" asked Robert, inspecting Esther's dark glass.

She told him.

"I'll have the same," he said.

And so they drank, and chatted—a little party, by the sickbed. Esther felt she should make her escape, and leave the two men time together, although it was another half hour before Elena would return from work, but Robert Oxenholme insisted on leaving as she left. They assured Claudio they would return another day, and left him to his crucifix and his priest. In the corridor, Robert Oxenholme took hold of Esther's elbow. "I don't like death," he said. "Come and have a drink. And anyway, I have things to say to you. Have you time?"

"I don't like death," he repeated, in a bar on the Via Castiglione. "But maybe Claudio is immortal. Have you been long in Bologna?"

Robert Oxenholme, it emerged, had come to Bologna principally to see Claudio. "To pay my last respects to the old fraud," said Robert, affectionately. "A great man, Claudio. In his way."

"Yes," said Esther.

"And you, Esther—if so I may call you—what are you doing here?"

"I am on a similar mission."

"Not working?"

"Not really working. Though I thought I'd go and see Angellotti at the Institute tomorrow. And have a look at the Cossa. That kind of thing."

"Are you free for dinner?"

Esther laughed. "This is the kind of conversation I used to have in Italy when I was twenty-five," she said, in explanation. "No, I'm not free. I'm staying with Claudio's sister Elena, as you must have gathered, and she's expecting me home."

"Home," he echoed, playfully, wistfully.

"You're in a hotel?"

"I spend half my life in hotels."

"How sad."

"Could you dine with me tomorrow?"

"I don't know." She hesitated, not sure if he was serious. "Perhaps Elena . . ."

"Might invite me *home*?"

She laughed, again. She asked where his home was, what his family was, why he travelled so much: surely you know people in Bologna, she told him, firmly, a man in your position knows people everywhere. I know Claudio's wife, Roberta, said Robert. She's a very nice woman. But I can hardly impose on her at a time like this. Poor Robert, said Esther.

"I heard you lecture once," said Robert. "In the Royal Institute. It was one of the best lectures I've ever heard in my life."

Esther blinked, then hit back.

"What was it on?" she asked.

He told her, at some length, and quite accurately, what it had been on. She had spoken on the ideal Renaissance city in art and philosophy. An unusual subject, for her. She remembered it well. She had worked hard on it.

"Did you ever publish it?"

She shook her head.

"Why not? Why don't you publish?"

Again she shook her head.

"You waste your talents," he said. "You bury them in the ground instead of investing them."

"That's what people say, these days," she said. "We all choose our own parables. And yours is in vogue at the moment."

"You prefer the parable of the sower? You prefer to cast your thoughts on stony ground?"

"You heard me."

"And here I am again, fully sprouted. To tell you not to waste your talents. A full circle."

"And what would you advise?"

"Something a little more ambitious, perhaps? Is it because you are a woman that you lack ambition? Or because you despise money? Or because you don't need money? Or because you despise your audience?"

"I get along, after my own fashion," said Esther.

"I wrote a book on Signorelli," said Robert Oxenholme. "Nobody asked me to, nobody paid me to do it, but I did it." He ordered another drink.

"Yes," said Esther. "I read it."

"Well, more of a monograph than a book," he said.

"Yes," she said.

"I don't understand your attitude," he said. "You *ought* to want to publish. It's very English, the way you don't bother."

"I'm not exactly English," said Esther. "More Austrian-Jewish, to be precise. But go on, tell me what it is that I ought to be doing that I'm not doing. You have my attention."

Robert Oxenholme explained to her what he thought she ought to be doing with her talents. She ought to be productive, ought to be ambitious, ought to commit herself to a lasting work. Esther pointed out that even the evening classes which she had taught had been taken away from her by cuts in public spending effected by the government he represented (an exaggeration, but he was not to know that), but he brushed this aside impatiently as an irrelevance: evening classes for old ladies, he said, a waste of time for someone with your record, your gifts . . . No, she ought to be working on quite a different scale, as she knew quite well herself, and it wasn't too late, there was time to make a lasting contribution to the world of scholarship, what right had she to disdain it? He grew eloquent. She was a loss to the nation, he suggested, a casualty of an education system that prized modesty above self-esteem, that encouraged dilettante dabbling, that scorned profit, achievement, success. He pulled out of his briefcase a guide to the Caracci frescoes of the Palazzo Magnani, issued by the Credito Romagnolo. There, you see, is the proper relationship of art and commerce, he said, as she leafed through it, looking at Romulus and Remus suckled by the she-wolf, at the happy *Rape of the Sabine Women* and *Romulus Overcome by Pride*. Here is twentieth-century patronage, enlightened patronage, art and industry hand in hand.

Yes, said Esther. Are you suggesting that I approach the Nat West or the Midland Bank for a grant to write a book on Crivelli?

He halted, drew breath, and repeated his invitation to dinner. "Ring your friend, tell her you won't be back," he said. "I can make some interesting suggestions. Not the Nat West or the Midland, I agree, but some really interesting suggestions . . ."

"You are the devil, tempting me with the riches of this world," said Esther.

"No," said Robert, a little sadly. "Claudio is the devil. I am just a salesman trying to sell you a new ideology, but I don't expect you to buy."

"Why are you trying so hard? To convince yourself?"

He shrugged. "Perhaps." He sipped his Punt e Mes. "My great-grandfather was a collector, you know. Not a bad collection, as English collections go. We've had to part with quite a lot of it."

"If one lived here"—she gestured up the street, at the façades, the balconies, the red blinds, the crumbling glories— "one wouldn't need to collect, it would be on one's own doorstep to walk through, every day."

"Ah, but who built it, that we tiny creatures can walk in its arcades, we afterthoughts, we puny little men?"

She could see that this notion moved him. It had never occurred to her to think personally in quite such terms before. She told him this.

"I must thank you," she said, "for a new perspective."

"Red Bologna," he said reflectively. "A Communist city. A well-run city. A civilized city. Well, I must be getting back to my lonely hotel."

"Poor Robert," she said. "I liked your book on Signorelli."

"Too kind," he said. "Hardly a monumental work, but my own, my own."

"I don't see what's *wrong* with being a dilettante," said Esther, vaguely, as she rose. Her thoughts had turned to Elena, and the evening ahead. "It doesn't harm anybody, does it?"

"That's rather a negative aspiration," said Robert Oxenholme, following her out onto the pavement. A light rain had begun to fall. "Not to do harm."

"Oh, I don't know," said Esther, her concentration span over, suddenly eager to be rid of him. "One could aim for worse."

She thanked him, shook his hand.

He stood on the pavement, irresolute. Esther walked briskly

away from the temptation that he had offered. Whatever it was, she said to herself, it had come too late.

"Why don't you come and live here with me?" Elena asked Esther, later that night.

"Because it would be too pleasant. Because it is too beautiful. Because you are too beautiful," said Esther.

"Think about it," said Elena.

There was a little lizard in the bottom right-hand corner of the painting in Sala XIV. Blood from Christ's feet dripped into a skull, but the little lizard paid no attention. It sat, sunning itself. Esther stared. She stared so hard that she fancied she saw it move, but of course it did not move; it was merely the shadow of Robert Oxenholme that moved, as he silently approached her, and stood behind her. "Hello," he said, "I thought I'd find you here."

That night they had dinner.

The next day, Esther met Claudio's wife, Roberta. She was a short, square woman, with straight white hair, and a brown face, and very blue eyes, and a practical, almost bluff manner: very unchic, very un-Italian, thought Esther, as they robustly shook hands in a comradely manner, in the hospital corridor. Anyone less like a hypochondriac it would be hard to imagine. She had a manner of great sweetness and motherliness; she treated Esther as though she were a child, warmly, impersonally, protectively. "*Cara*," she called her, from this their first meeting, and was to continue so to address her for the years to come. Esther felt instantly safe with Roberta. A good woman, a worn and weathered woman, an outdoor woman. Her face was brown from the sun, her eyes were blue like flowers.

Claudio died three weeks later, a fortnight after Esther's return to Ladbroke Grove. Esther did not go to the funeral; she decided she could not afford the fare. She had wasted enough of her slender resources on Claudio Volpe. But she read the obituaries, which were handsome and lengthy. A great man, Claudio, as Robert Oxenholme had said. A great man, with an international reputation. Fame is the spur that the clear spirit doth raise, / That last infirmity of noble minds, / To scorn delights and live laborious days. . . . She pondered the lesson of Claudio Volpe. He had achieved greatness through the intensity of his commitment to his own folly. Where reasonable men fail, Claudio had succeeded. He had seventy-seven lines of obituary in the London *Times*. She counted them. In the Italian papers, of course, the tributes were even more fulsome. One of them claimed that he had died in the arms of a Dominican priest; a more sensational journal counter-claimed that he had requested that a stake be driven through his heart. Poor Signora Volpe, was Esther's only response to this bit of malicious embroidery. One of the papers showed a photograph of Elena and Roberta arm in arm at the funeral. His mistress and his widow, the paper suggested, salaciously, and, Esther hoped, inaccurately.

Alix and Liz Headleand commiserated. Neither of them had ever met the wicked Claudio, and Alix could not think of much to say, but Liz, remembering the conversation on the canal bank about monomania, was more forthcoming. Mad, yes, she agreed with Esther, mad he had probably been, but only, as it were, north north-west. Usefully mad, manipulatively mad. Esther described Signora Volpe. Liz listened with professional interest. As a matter of fact, Liz said, Charles has gone mad too. He imagines he hears voices in the sky. He imagines the sky is full of voices.

She laughed, Esther laughed.

The dish receiver had driven Charles mad, said Liz, with relish.

Claudio died, but Liz Headleand's mother began to recover. Nobody was very pleased about this; she was not very pleased about it herself, or so it seemed. But slowly, inexorably, she improved. Why, Liz wanted to shout, as Shirley described this unfortunate process over the telephone. Why? Oh, all right, said Liz, barely bothering to disguise her irritation, I'll come up and have a look at her.

And off she went, in the early summer of '84, cancelling a
few meetings, a few appointments, driving up the M1, fiddling
with the knob of her radio, trying to avoid what seemed to be
a seamless, circular, continuous, endlessly repetitive discussion of the miners' strike, and settling at last for a Norwegian
song cycle of the late nineteenth century. She had a new car
and wasn't quite sure how to tune in; where, for example, was
the World Service? Had it vanished, overnight, amidst the
threatened cuts? Had it been sold to Albania? Liz thought of
Alix Bowen and the old Renault 4. She had thought of trying
to sell her old car at a give-away price to Brian and Alix, but
had been unable to find an appropriate formula for the offer.

She had booked herself into the Open Hearth Hotel. She
didn't want to stay with Shirley, and was sure Shirley wouldn't
wish to have her. Abercorn Avenue, as Shirley had pointed
out, stood empty, but nobody in her right mind could want to
sleep in Abercorn Avenue. Supposing Rita Ablewhite recovered, and wanted to go home? The thought appalled Liz,
appalled Shirley.

Liz hung her clothes in the hotel wardrobe. She had booked
in for two nights, and already was wondering if she need stay
so long. Time dragged, faltered, stopped.

Liz stood by her mother's bedside. Yes, it was true, she was
recovering. She appeared to know Liz. A kind of distant
recognition animated her semi-paralysed features, and she
almost appeared to be trying to smile. This so shocked Liz that
she sat down smartly. Then she proceeded to speak, as she had
done for years, over the telephone. She told her mother about
her new car and her new car radio. She told her about the
endless reporting of the miners' strike and about the Norwegian
song cycle: did she detect a faint sympathetic tremor of distaste
at the mention of this item? Liz ploughed on, moving on to the
affairs of her stepsons and her daughters, on to the projects of
Charles. The old woman had probably forgotten that she and
Charles were divorced, and anyway, at this point, what did it
matter, what difference did it make? For three quarters of an
hour, she talked. For fifty minutes. The academic hour.
Enough, enough. She gathered her bag, her Northam evening
paper, and took her leave. Her mother lay in a long pale ward,
with old ladies on either side of her, and a neat locker by her
head. Liz had brought no flowers. The next day, she would
bring flowers.

Liz walked the streets of Northam, in the light summer night. A knot of men stood on Hag Bank Corner with placards and buckets, collecting for the miners. An out-of-date boy skate-boarded elegantly down a wheelchair ramp. A group of girls in mini-skirts and plastic sandals giggled in an alley. She gazed into shop windows: modern shops, chain stores, high street shops, the same as any city. Where was the Regent Café, where mothers and bored daughters had sat long over coffee and cakes? The waitresses in black with white aprons had smelled human, of heat and sweat. Everybody had smelled more, in the old days. Only deep poverty and eccentricity smell, these days. Was this improvement? Liz wondered.

Rumour had it that Brian Bowen had been offered a job in Northam, was thinking of accepting it. As the rumour came direct from Alix Bowen, it was probably authentic.

Northam is a small city, and Liz in a quarter of an hour had wandered from the shopping centre into the old industrial district. For Sale, To Let, read posters. She had heard of this, but had not seen it with her own eyes. Willow herb and buddleia grew, as they had grown in the aftermath of the Second World War, in the bomb craters of Liz's childhood. She stood and stared. The canal was green with weed. An old man walked his dog. No, there was nothing here for her, nothing at all.

Her pace quickened as she returned, up the hill, to her new Japanese car in the hospital car park.

Watching television late that night, alone in her hotel room, Liz noted that a group of British television journalists had been captured and taken hostage in the Middle East. One of the group was Dirk Davis, who had once, long ago, been a friend and colleague of Charles's. A friend, and then an enemy. She resisted the temptation to ring Charles in his Kentish Town flat. Charles would know this bad news. Charles knew everything, and, anyway, the mention of the very name of Dirk Davis for some reason filled him with ungovernable rage. But Liz had shared many a bowl of spaghetti, many a plateful of chop suey with Dirk Davis in the old days, and she did not like to think of him bound, blindfolded, threatened. Buckets, gags, guns. No, she did not like it.

*   *   *

Shirley and Liz sat at the kitchen table in Abercorn Avenue, drinking mugs of instant coffee. "This could go on forever," said Shirley, glumly, gesturing vaguely at the silent room.

They spoke of power of attorney, of selling the house. But they knew that they would do nothing. Nothing at all.

"I think," said Shirley, "that she's trying to communicate something."

The two sisters looked at one another, with wild surmise, appalled.

"Oh, God," said Liz.

She drove home that night, and was cautioned for speeding on the stretch between Northampton and Milton Keynes.

Shirley sat by her mother's bedside, holding up pieces of white card with the letters of the alphabet clearly printed upon them in large, bold script. *C-A-T*, she spelled. Her mother, imperceptibly, nodded. *D-O-G*, she tried. Another semi-nod. Shirley's imagination staggered. *C-E-L-I-A*, she tried, and was sure she was met with blankness. *M-U-M* received, perhaps, faint recognition. So that was it, begin again at the beginning. What did that *mean*? Was it worth it? Well, it was better than sitting there knitting, anyway. Shirley persevered.

Otto Werner rang Alix Bowen and asked her out to lunch. This was an unprecedented invitation. They never met, alone, the two of them. Alix did not lunch, except occasionally with Polly Piper, with whom she liked to keep in touch. She suspected that Otto did not lunch much either. Her suspicion was confirmed by his uncertainty of what place to propose for this rendezvous. "But where will you *be* at that time of day?" he repeated, plaintively, to which she kept saying, in the end rather irritably, "I won't *be* anywhere, I'll come to where you say."

"Oh, all right," said Otto, and suggested an Italian restaurant off the Kingsway where he had once been taken by a historian from Aberdeen.

He sat there impatiently, waiting for Alix. He had arrived twenty minutes early, through anxiety, and was too worried to concentrate on his copy of the *New Statesman*, which he had begun to annotate, as was his habit, for Alan Headleand. The waiters pestered him with offers of drinks, and in the end to keep them off he ordered a tomato juice. He was sipping it cautiously when, at last, she arrived. It was raining; she was wearing a pale blue raincoat with a hood. The waiters wrested it from her in the narrow hall. She stood there, blinking, wiping her glasses, adjusting to the indoor light, as the waiters attempted to jostle her in his direction. She took her time. Oh, God, thought Otto, looking at her; oh, God. Otto loved her. Though that was not why he was here. Not quite. She was clutching a briefcase, bulging with papers. She refused to let the waiters have it. What he loved about her, one of the many, many things he loved about her, was the look of puzzled certainty, as she held on, obstinately. She held on.

"Otto." She advanced upon him. The table was so cramped he could not get up to greet her. She squeezed his hand, sat. "It's wet," she said, superfluously, shaking her wild grey hair.

"Alix." He gazed at her. This at least he was allowed to do. The waiters hovered, flocked, pestered, offered drinks.

"I'll have what you're having," said Alix. "Is that a Bloody Mary?"

"Yes," said Otto.

"On second thought," said Alix, "perhaps I'll just have a tomato juice. With a lot of Worcestershire sauce."

Outwitted, Otto smiled at her, a little blindly. She was wearing a blue jersey. Her eyes were a very interesting deep grey-blue. Dazzled, he stared.

"What's news, then?" asked Alix, gaily eating a piece of roll. They incompetently ordered a meal. "I wanted to talk to you about Brian," said Otto, eventually. "Well, what I mean is, I wanted to ask you about Brian. About what I should say to Brian. I don't know how to put this. Alix, I'm putting it very badly."

Alix drank a spoonful of *stracciatelle*.

Otto cleared his throat.

"Brian tells me he's been offered this job in Northam."

"Yes," said Alix.

"He asked me what I thought."

"Yes," said Alix.

"So I'm asking you what you think, in order to know what I think. If you see what I mean."

"I see."

"Do tell me, Alix."

Alix laid down her spoon. "Eat your spaghetti, Otto, it will go cold," she said, firmly. Then she told him what she thought about the job that Brian had been offered.

"Of course, on paper, it's just the kind of thing Brian can do," she said. "It's just the kind of thing he ought to be doing. A community programme, good public money, left wing Council, a lot of support. It was Perry Blinkhorn that thought of Brian. Do you know Perry? And there'd be a real social mix in the classes, not the kind of self-selecting bunch Brian's been teaching at the college for the last few years . . ."

Her voice trailed away, miserably.

"So what are the snags?" asked Otto.

"Oh, I don't know," said Alix, suddenly forceful. "It seems disloyal to mention them, but I'm going to. Well, for one thing, I don't trust Perry Blinkhorn, and I don't trust the back-up. I think they might put the money in for a year, and if it didn't work out, they'd scrap it. I don't like the look of the contract they've offered him. And of course none of that would matter, I mean I'd be in favour of Brian taking a gamble on it, if it were *really* the kind of thing he wanted to do. But I don't know that he does. Brian's a good straight orthodox teacher; you know, he wants to teach great literature, he doesn't want to spend his time transcribing the reminiscences of the unemployed and trying to publish them in a cooperative magazine. He may *think* he does, but he doesn't. I'm better at that kind of thing than he is. Oddly enough I've got more patience with people than Brian has. One of the reasons why he's a good straight teacher is that he gets the best out of people, he makes them work, he insists on proper work, whereas I just let people chat along . . . Oh, I know there's room for both, I know I'm useful in my own way—or I have been, in my time—but I can't really see Brian fitting into this cooperative, community set-up, can you? His standards are too high." She laughed, and continued. "Yes, his standards are too high. He'll annoy them, and they'll annoy him. But even *that* wouldn't matter, if I myself had more faith in the whole thing. Look, Otto"—and she dived under the table, into her briefcase, and produced a brochure, and thrust it at him, over the chicken and rosemary and sautéed potatoes—"look, this is the kind of stuff the Council promotes. This is what it puts its money into." Otto turned the pages of the Northam Directory of Worker Cooperatives. His eyes fell on the smiling faces of young vegetarians promoting ethnic restaurants, on the dashingly dreadlocked intense stares of Rasta men promoting Afro-Caribbean sound ("our stocks include reggae, soca, funk, soul . . ."), on smart young women offering secretarial services to small businesses, on brawny young men offering panel beating at record prices, on the inventor of a mechanical implement for cleaning top-floor windows, on street theatre groups and children's play centre carers, on gravestone restorers and conference promotion material designers, on home knitwear and home computer groups, on an actors' cooperative agency, on the editors of an alternative newspaper and the manufacturers of experimental High Flavour Foods for the Elderly; his eyes fell on a desolate advertisement for a Sport and Social Centre which economically and perhaps ironically portrayed an empty table, two empty chairs, an empty beer mug, and a single cigarette burning in an ash tray.

"Yes," said Otto, and would have smiled, had it not been for Alix's expression. She took the brochure from him, turned the pages, and drew his attention to another advertisement: two youths, one white, one black, smiling with the greatest possible charm and diffident optimism at the camera, with a touch of nonchalance and a touch of anxious appeal. The caption proclaimed that they were experts on the rearing of rabbits, hamsters, gerbils, guinea pigs, and other small mammals, that they would advise on breeding, diseases, hutch building, diet, and all relating matters. The last sentence read, "At the time of going to press our premises are not yet finalized." A harmless hamster nibbled in the foreground, as the boys leaned across a table towards the lens. At the sight of them, Alix's eyes filled with tears.

"I mean," said Alix, her eyes bright, "this is the kind of thing *I* believe in. *I* believe in it. So why does it, when printed like that, on that nice expensive shiny paper, so well produced, so plausible—why does it make me want to *weep*?"

He reached out his hand for hers. They held hands, on the pink tablecloth.

"It's despair, that's what I feel," said Alix, sniffing, as a tear brimmed. "Despair. It's all hopeless, hopeless. Sandbags against the tidal wave. Patching up holes in the dyke before the deluge. Little boys, with their thumbs frozen. And drowning, drowning.''

She wept, for a moment, then wiped her eyes. "Sorry," she said. "Sorry. And anyway, I'm not so sure that I want to go and live in Northam. That's a terrible thing to say, but it's true. I'd rather have gone to Gloseley. I could have sat on Gloseley Heath and picketed the air base. Crouching by a fire. With the Gloseley women. I could have been a real outcast, in Gloseley!''

"You don't believe in all that," said Otto.

"No, I don't. I don't believe in anything. I believe it's all hopeless. Hopeless. It's all over. There's no way back, and no way forward that we can go. We're washed up. You know quite well what I mean, Otto, you feel the same yourself.''

"Alix," said Otto, reaching again for her hand, "I don't know that I could bear it if you went to Northam. I know I don't see you all that often, but I need to know you are there. It means more than I can say, to know you're there. Only four miles away. There.''

"Don't," said Alix.

"But I must," said Otto. "And I must also tell you what I haven't even told Brian. I've been offered this job in Washington. Yes, Washington. Not for this year, for 1986. I don't know what to do. I ought to accept. I can't afford not to accept. The money—well, you can imagine what the money is like. Think of a figure and double it, that's what the money is like. So how can I know what to say to Brian?''

They gazed at one another, in this parody of an adulterous lunch. The waiters took advantage of the lull to offer dessert. Otto absent-mindedly said he would have a trifle. He spooned at it, thoughtfully, as Alix attempted to reply.

"You should go," she said, predictably. "There's no point in your staying here. When even *I* say things are finished here, then they must be well and truly finished." She paused, pursued. "What does Caroline think?''

"She's not keen to go. She doesn't really like America. But she would. If I wished.''

"Oh, dear," said Alix, "I don't know what to say."

"Of course you don't.''

The waiters brought the coffee.

"And I don't know what to say to Brian," said Otto.

"No, of course you don't.''

They drank their coffee in silence, holding hands.

* * *

Alix, sitting on the bus on the way home, stared blankly through the streaming pane at the wet shoppers of Oxford Street. Despite terrorists, despite unemployment, despite the horror of Oxford Street itself, still they thronged. Perhaps anywhere, thought Alix, would be better than London. The traffic crawled, halted, crawled again. Alix cleared a little round space in the misting window, and there, on the corner of Bond Street, standing by the florist, was her husband, Brian Bowen, and two of his chums. Brian was holding a yellow plastic bucket, and a handwritten placard which said HELP THE WIVES AND FAMILIES OF THE MINERS. The rain fell steadily on the hood of his anorak as Brian jangled the coins in his bucket. He stood stolidly, cheerfully, smiling when anyone threw in a coin. The brotherhood of man. Most people smiled at Brian, even the hard-bitten shoppers of Bond Street and Oxford Street smiled. But Alix did not smile. Brian and his bucket were more than she could bear. She bowed her head and took out her handkerchief, and all the way to Wandsworth Bridge she wept.

Stephen Cox was of the opinion that Brian and Alix should go to Northam. He could not see anything wrong with the job on offer in Northam. He was working on a play about Pol Pot, and was of the opinion that the extremism of Northam City Council had been much exaggerated. Nor did he think Northam was very far away from London. It was a damn sight nearer than Tokyo or Seoul or Singapore, he pointed out reasonably, as he rolled a little cigarette.

Esther, Liz, and Alix had supper at Esther's place. It had been months since they had seen each other all at once, as it were. They exchanged news, and there seemed to be a lot of it.

Esther spoke first, of her dalliance with Robert Oxenholme, which had flourished in the months since Claudio's death. He took her out to dinner, invited her to the opera, asked her to go with him to functions. Esther, grinding pepper into her *zuppa di verdura*, confessed herself flattered. Quite disgracefully charming, she proclaimed him, sinisterly charming. I am, kind of, fascinated, said Esther, watching him at work, in a crowded room. And what does he want out of me? Oh, I don't know, I think he sees in me his own lost promise, his lost opportunities. He's very bright, is Robert, and I suppose he feels he's wasted his talents in all this sponsorship nonsense, and that I've wasted mine in a quite different way, and so he's trying to corrupt me.

Perhaps he thinks you haven't wasted yours at all, suggested Alix.

Well, I don't know, said Esther. I don't know about that myself, so I don't suppose he does either.

And are you being corrupted? enquired Liz.

I quite like the dinners, said Esther, cautiously. But I'm not so keen on the receptions. The opera, I can take or leave. Although *Boris Godunov* was rather wonderful. He has this box, and you can drink all the way through, if you want.

And what happened to his wife?

His wife, Esther explained, had gone off with a racehorse trainer.

Esther collected the soup plates, started to dish up the next course.

Charles and Lady Henrietta were to be divorced, Liz informed them, as Esther handed round the fish stew. Amiably? No, not very. Expensively, more like. My money-learning capacity is more prized now than once it was, said Liz. Rumour, or rather Ivan Warner, claimed that Henrietta was having an affair with an elderly actor; but really, at her age, I think that's a bit unlikely, said Liz. Charles had started a new enterprise, with his one-time partner; they were both full of enthusiasm, almost like the old days, starting from scratch again, making their own coffee in the office. Rejuvenated. Charles's old enemy Dirk Davis was still being held hostage, which seemed to be worrying Charles disproportionately. How many months was it now? Three, four? Of course, he might be dead by now, said Liz, fishing a bone out of her plate. I don't know, I think in some way Charles feels if Dirk gets out, he'll survive himself. It must be five months, because I remember hearing about it on the news when I was up in Northam seeing my mother in June. And how was her mother? God knows, said Liz. As you both know quite well, I wish she'd die. But Shirley says she can make herself understood, a bit. She can't speak, but she can spell things out with these cards Shirley made for her. It's ghastly. I wish she were dead.

Alix could not be so frank about her own feelings, being still a married woman. She could not tell Esther and Liz that she was in love with one of her husband's closest friends, Otto Werner. As she could not tell Otto or Brian this either, she had to keep it to herself. Instead, slicing a piece of Cheddar, taking a biscuit, accepting another glass of wine, she told them that she had started house hunting in Northam, and described the kinds of houses she had already seen. Property prices were considerably lower than in London, of course, and some of the Victorian houses were very charming. There was one on that rustic little lane down by the Botanical Gardens . . .

Perry Blinkhorn, Alix had to admit, was making himself very pleasant. Perhaps he wasn't such a bad lot after all.

I think it's awful that you're going, said Liz. And Esther keeps threatening to go and live in Bologna. What shall I do, if you leave me on my own?

You could marry Charles again, suggested Esther. Or Ivan Warner.

Funny you should say that, said Liz. Do you know, I actually think Ivan has thought of proposing to me. And I'll tell you something even funnier. I've got quite fond of Ivan. I've even found myself wondering what it would be like, being married to Ivan.

Liz, really, remonstrated Alix.

Well, of course I *wouldn't*, I'm much happier on my own than I've ever been, but it's interesting that I even thought of it, isn't it? Well, perhaps it's not very interesting. Perhaps I only thought of it because he was thinking of it. And anyway, he decided not to ask.

A silence fell, as Liz lit herself a cigarette. Alix was wondering about Stephen Cox. There had once been a feeling, a sense of possibility, that Liz and Stephen might marry, but it seemed to have faded, although they still saw each other. Too well matched, perhaps.

The candles flickered, the gas fire flickered, the room was warm and intimate. It had heard many confidences. The red wallpaper had absorbed them. Alix remembered running here, for safety, from Lykewake Gardens. Nearly a year ago, now. She supposed one could still come to London, have supper, stay the night at Liz's. But would it be the same? Should she be in the way at Liz's? Alix did not like to be in the way.

The silence prolonged itself, peaceably. Liz mentioned, briefly, her cat. The traffic hummed quietly along Ladbroke Grove. Alix spoke of Ilse and Nicholas, of the strangeness of seeing them at home, adult, in so serious a house. Esther offered dried apricots. A police siren wailed in the distance. A dog barked. And gradually, stealthily, as they sat there, they became aware of a change in the quality of the street noises— a change, was it possible, in the quality of the light? Esther, going to the kitchen to put the kettle on for coffee, glancing out of the first-floor window down the side street, noticed a strange group of cars, a knot of policemen. She returned to the front room, could see that both Liz and Alix were listening, though to what they did not know.

The curtains were drawn, the room glowed, comfortably. The little figurines marched along the bookcases, as they had always marched. The little mosaic fountain of Cambridge days was in its rightful place. The palm was gone, but Esther had purchased a new plant, an umbrella tree with big deep broad-fingered leaves and new delicate little opening pale green uplifted hands in its crown: a more friendly plant, a less bristly plant. Lilies stood in a deep red vase: a present from Robert, Esther had said. So Robert sat in the red room, where Claudio had once sat before him?

Esther cleared her throat. "I think something's going on in the street outside," she said. "Shall I look?"

They were reluctant to look, reluctant to allow the street to impinge on their evening. They were safe in there, they had created their own safety. They could read one another's reactions; they saw the same images.

"I don't know," said Liz.

"I don't know," said Alix.

So for a little while they sat there, becalmed, en-isled. Outside the tension mounted, Esther went through to her bedroom at the back of the house, and, without turning on the light, looked out into the October night. At the back, there was a small narrow London garden, one of a row, the end of a row, a corner garden. It seemed to be full of people. Esther went back into the front room, the first-floor front room, and very slightly twitched the heavy curtain to peer out.

She looked back into the room, at Liz sitting curled up in a chair, at Alix lying back on the couch with her feet on a low table.

"The house is surrounded," she said, flatly.

"What on earth can be happening?" asked Alix, at last, in a tone of mild and indulgent curiosity.

"I don't know," said Esther. "Should I go out and see?"

"I wouldn't do that," said Liz. "If it's the police, they'll shoot you." They all laughed.

There was only the one front door to the house, Esther explained, and a garden door from the basement-garden flat, where old Mrs. Finchley had lived for decades. "They can't be after Mrs. Finchley," said Alix.

"Perhaps the top floor is an IRA bomb-manufacturing hideout," suggested Liz, helpfully.

"I don't think he's Irish, that quiet young man," said Esther. "I don't know what he is, or who he is, but I don't think he's Irish."

"Well, we'd better just sit here and have our coffee," said Alix. "I agree with Liz, if we try to be helpful they'll only shoot us. Much better to keep a low profile, if you ask me."

So Esther made the coffee, and they waited, not entirely in silence; they chatted in a desultory fashion. Alix looked at her watch. "Will they shoot me for trying to go home?" she asked. "I really ought to be thinking about leaving."

And then the telephone rang. They all jumped, guiltily. Esther answered it. Yes, she agreed, cautiously, she was Dr. Breuer. Yes, she was at home. With friends. Then she listened for a short while. Then she said, yes, I see, and put the phone down.

"They're trying to arrest that silent young man upstairs," she said. "How very odd. They didn't say what for."

"He's probably the Harrow Road murderer," suggested Alix, belatedly, for this was what they had all been thinking.

"Yes, probably," agreed Liz.

"Oh, dear," said Esther.

"Well, what are we meant to do about it? Is he up there?"

"They think so."

"And what do they want us to do?"

"They weren't very clear about it. They don't know if he's armed, but they do say he's dangerous."

"Dangerous? Surely not?" said Esther. And I am sorry to say that they all laughed.

"Well, there's an awful lot of them and if we've noticed them by now I imagine he has too. Why don't they just knock on the door and ask for him?" said Alix, who had peeped through the curtain.

"Too simple," said Liz. "They like to make a big deal out of this kind of thing. Perhaps they're hoping he'll take all three of us hostage and they can have a big shoot-out. They like that kind of thing."

"That's the kind of irresponsible talk that Brian's friends go in for," said Alix, with interest rather than censoriousness.

"Well, quite right too, the police are a bloody disgrace," said Liz robustly. "And you'll be the first to agree when they shoot you dead through that window. Move away, Alix, move away."

Alix moved, obediently, but continued to argue the cause of the police: it wasn't their fault if they'd learned confrontation, their position in urban society was increasingly untenable . . .

"Alix," said Esther, "is this you I hear? What has happened to your political outlook? How will all that go down in the Socialist Republic of South Yorkshire? That's the kind of line *I* take, not you."

"Oh, I don't know," said Alix feebly, "I suppose it's to do with my father, and my respect for authority, or rather my desire that authority *should* be respected and respect-worthy, which my father was—well he was respect-worthy but not respected, if you see what I mean."

"I suppose it would be unwise to have another bottle of wine," said Esther.

"Yes," said Liz, "it would."

"Did they tell us not to leave?" asked Alix.

"Yes, apparently they're negotiating with him on the telephone. From their radio car."

"Did they give you their number? So we could ring them? If anything happened in here?"

"No."

"Incompetent fools, I told you," said Liz with satisfaction.

"Liz, you surprise me," said Esther. "This anti-police line. Where does it come from?"

"I suppose I learned it from the kids," said Liz. "Aaron got into a bit of trouble the other day. He was stopped—OK it was four in the morning, but that's not a crime—and searched, and because he gave them a bit of lip they turned him in for the night."

"He probably enjoyed it," said Esther.

"Rubbish," said Liz. "He was furious. OK, it reinforced his prejudices, which is always gratifying, but he was quite properly outraged."

"Was he drunk?" enquired Alix.

"I suppose so, but what's that got to do with it? He was on his feet, not in a car, and he was walking along minding his own business. Reciting poetry, according to him."

"That probably *is* an offence," said Esther.

"Cinna the poet," said Alix. "No, no, I am Cinna the poet."

"I wonder if he's threatening to commit suicide?" said Liz. Her face suddenly brightened with expertise. "Did they really not give you a number to ring? If they had, we could have told them that one of your guests is a fully qualified psychiatrist and willing to intervene—for a fee of course—in her professional capacity."

What a wasted opportunity, they all agreed.

"We could dial 999," said Alix. "Or the local police station."

"No, they've missed their opportunity," said Liz. "But tell us about him, Esther. Who is he, this monster under your roof?"

"Well, to tell you the truth," said Esther, "I know absolutely nothing about him. He's lived here years—eight, nine? more even—and he's called Whitmore. P. Whitmore. I don't know what the P. stands for. He never gets any post, only circulars. I don't know where he works. We never speak. He never makes a sound. He never has anyone in, or not that I've noticed. The only time we've spoken in the last few months is when he told me I was being cruel to the palm when I left it out on the front steps to die."

"Not much to go on," said Liz.

"I suppose," said Esther, "there's absolutely no reason why he *shouldn't* be a criminal psychopath. But then there's no reason that I know of to suggest that he is one. Or that he's committed any kind of offence of any sort."

A slightly bleaker silence fell.

"The world is full of mad people," said Alix, "and I suppose we all come across them from time to time."

"Poor chap," said Esther. "Now I think about him, I feel I've never said more than hello and good morning. But he never looked as though he wanted to be spoken to."

"If you'd asked him in for a drink," said Liz, "you'd probably have ended up with your head in a flowerpot. So it's just as well you didn't."

"Do you think I ought to go upstairs and see how he is?"

asked Esther. "I could persuade him to come down. I'm quite good at calming people, and after all, he does know who I am."

"I don't think you should do anything of the sort," said Alix. "They said he was dangerous."

"You're in no place to talk. Look at you and Jilly Fox."

"Poor Jilly," said Alix, and sighed. "Poor Jilly."

Esther made another pot of coffee. "And as we're hanging about, I think we could risk just a small drop of Strega," she said.

Over the Strega, to entertain them she recited the story of the Dutchman on the aeroplane, which she had never before had occasion to relay. As she told it, she and Alix noticed that Liz was reacting to it with a peculiar excitement, indeed she was turning uncharacteristically pink, and when the anecdote was over, she pressed Esther for more details. How old had he been, the Dutchman? How tall? What was his job? Where did he live? Did Esther know his name?

Flattered by the reception of her tale, Esther was able to satisfy all these queries.

"In fact," she said, at the end of her interrogation, "I can tell you a lot more about that man from a two-hour flight than I can tell you about a decade of living in the same house as P. Whitmore. But he was rather a memorable man."

"Yes," said Liz, and took out her powder compact, looked at herself, and powdered her nose.

"Whereas poor P. Whitmore is quite insignificant. Does insignificance turn people into murderers, Liz?"

"Not always, fortunately," said Liz. "But sometimes, you."

Again they were silent, listening to the silence upstairs.

"This is ridiculous," said Liz, as the night wore on. "I've got to be up at seven."

"I suppose I could ring Brian and tell him what's happened," said Alix, "but there's not much point in worrying him, really, is there?"

The phone rang again. The police informed Esther that they were about to move in, and that Esther and her guests should move into the back room and stay there with the light off until told to move.

"How will we know when to move?" Esther wanted to know.

The question caused some confusion. "We'll knock on your door," said the police.

"How will I know it's you," said Esther, "and how do I know it's you anyway? And anyway, who *are* you? I can't see your number, or your warrant, or whatever it is you're supposed to identify yourself with, can I?"

Liz and Alix were much amused with this interchange. Esther put the phone down. "*I* don't see the point of going into the bedroom in the dark," said Esther.

"We'd better do what we're told," said Alix.

"They're as thick as two planks, I told you so," said Liz. But they agreed with Alix.

So the three of them progressed into the dark bedroom and sat in a row on Esther's white crocheted bedcover, admiring her bedroom décor in the half light. I like your mirror, whispered Liz. Esther, in whispers, described its acquisition. She had bought it in a junk shop on the Seven Sisters Road. This is like being back at school, whispered Esther.

"I'm going back for my cigarettes," said Liz, after three minutes. "They didn't tell us not to smoke, did they?"

She came back, reported she could hear steps in the hallway, raising her voice defiantly to its natural level.

A couple of minutes later, there was a knock on the hall door.

Esther opened it. It was all over, a policeman said. The man upstairs had agreed to go quietly.

Alix, standing by the window, pulled back the curtain, and saw P. Whitmore being led down Esther's front steps. He was, as Esther had said, an unremarkable man. He looked slightly puzzled. He was put in the back of a police car, handcuffed.

So that, thought Alix, is the murderer of Jilly Fox.

Esther's peaceful life in Ladbroke Grove was ruined by this incident. She insisted on staying there that night, despite the offers of accommodation from Liz and Alix, but the harassment over the next few weeks was more than she could bear. Once the story reached the press, the house was perpetually surrounded. Photographers, television cameras, police, journalists, sightseers. The very worst of human nature, said Esther to Liz over the phone, amidst her suitcases. She was off to

Somerset, to stay with Peggy and Humphrey. The house appalled her. It was not so much the personal danger that ill-meaning friends suggested she had herself suffered; it was more the revelation by association of the horrible nature of other people's curiosity. And she herself was horrible, was curious. What had he been doing up there, what had he been thinking? What had the police found, just above her own ceiling? Why had she not more civilly wished him the time of day? Had she asked him in for a drink, could she have saved the life of Jilly Fox?

There will be no more murders, Claudio had said, and Claudio, it seemed, would be right.

"They stand out there gawping," she said to Liz. "It's like Rillington Place. I can't go on living here. It's like that story about the house with the Golden Windows. You know, where you find your own house is the one that shines in the distance. But this is the other way round. You find the rot was within."

"But not in *you*, Est," said Liz. "Not in *you*."

Esther laughed, but uncomfortably.

"In all of us, I thought we thought," Esther said. "Newspapers have approached me," said Esther, "for my story. What story, I ask them? I haven't a story. Anyway, it's all *sub judice*. I'm off to Somerset. And eventually, perhaps, to Bologna."

"But what about your things?" asked Liz. "It's so lovely, in your flat. I've known your things all my adult life."

"I'll ring you from Peggy's, when I've calmed down," said Esther.

P. Whitmore was charged with seven murders.

P. Whitmore, despite the evidence of his alleged penultimate attempted victim (an attack, in fact, never proven), had never had a moustache. Nor was he by any stretch of the imagination a practising member of the aristocracy. Polly Piper was disappointed.

"I suppose he must be guilty," said Alix to Hannah Glover over a nice cup of tea. "Otherwise the whole thing would be too bizarre. I hear he's going to plead guilty. So Edgar Lintot told me."

"Well, my dear," said Hannah Glover, "your friend Esther Breuer had a very lucky escape."

"Oh, don't be absurd, Hannah," said Alix, staunchly; although, of course, secretly, she agreed that this was so.

Alix and Polly Piper had their promised farewell lunch at Langan's. Alix was in bravely high spirits. She drank a dry martini straight up and the other half of a bottle of white wine, ate a spinach soufflé and a plate of fish in a greeny-yellow sauce adorned by some flat leaves, and finished with a small tartlet and a Calvados. Polly outpaced her, and had a second Calvados. They spoke of the murderer and of Esther, of the satanic Claudio Volpe. Perhaps he possessed the spirit of poor P. Whitmore, suggested Polly. Murder by remote control?

They moved on from death to love. Alix tells Polly, as she cannot tell Liz and Esther, that she is in love with Otto Werner. What will you do about it? asks Polly. Nothing, says Alix.

Polly accepts this. She can think of nothing to suggest. She tells Alix of her own passion for an unlikely much-married somewhat disreputable antiques dealer. He's nothing, really, says Polly, I don't like him, I don't respect him, I wouldn't be seen out with him, but I can't help going to bed with him. He's a sort of gigolo figure, I suppose. What does that mean?

They discuss the complications in the sex lives of emancipated women today. Alix becomes confidential. She rarely talks about such matters. Polly nods, smiles, sighs.

"God, I shall miss you, Alix," she says, sentimentally, tearfully. "It was great, working with you. We were a good team, weren't we, Alix?"

And she waves, commandingly, absently, for the bill.

Esther walked up Crowsfoot Hill in the dark December afternoon. It was a sharp, dry day, and there was an occasional small dry patter, as one acorn after another fell onto the crisp earth. In the failing light, a shepherd was gathering sheep in the steep field above her. The hanging wood rose even more steeply. The sunken lane, in spring and summer edged with ferns and primroses and pennywort and wild strawberry, showed now its complex irregular stony little wall pattern, of man-made, nature-embraced antiquity. The roots of the trees gripped the stones. An owl hooted thrice. The nights were long, in the country.

Long, too, to Alix, seemed the provincial winter nights, and long the evenings in the newly rented house. She stood by the front window, looking out over suburban Northam. The lights twinkled down the slope. Ironic, it was, as others did not fail to point out, that Brian had returned to Northam so soon after his father's death. Too late had come the summons from Perry Blinkhorn. Too late to cheer the last years of old Fred Bowen. But in time for Alix to pop over to Leeds to see her ageing parents.

Brian worked nights. Alix sat alone. Sam was on holiday, with Nicholas and Ilse: in January, he would start at his new school.

Alix was, in theory, settling in. Buying lampshades, tea towels. Alix was very bad at this kind of thing. They had let their London house. Brian had agreed that it would not be wise to sell. Who knew what the future would hold? A property in London (accepted Brian the extremist) was not to be parted with lightly.

Brian was behaving with a heart-breaking, a humble consideration, treating Alix with a respectful delicacy that she returned in good measure. Very careful they were with one another these days, Alix and Brian. Little was said about the difficulties they might encounter, that even Sam might encounter, but much was thought, much implied.

Alix sat alone through choice. Overtures had been made, social overtures: Sally Blinkhorn had asked her to supper, she had been to a Christmas party at the Town Hall, she had met Northam's elderly historian at a university event, she had been asked to drinks by the director of the art gallery, who proved to be an ex–Feldmann Institute student of Esther's. Shirley Harper had asked her to supper. She had taken the initiative herself and visited old Mrs. Orme with a paper bag of pikelets. She had been invited to a poetry reading and a lecture. She had been asked to a party to meet Northam's poet.

But on the whole, she declined her invitations. She preferred to sit here, alone, in a rented house. A solitude, profound, intense, filled it and her; she was afraid, but behind the fear lay what? A sense of expectation? So she had sat alone, as a young woman, all these years ago, and nursed baby Nicholas in a basement.

Now her baby Sam had taken his O levels and was staying with his half-brother, Nicholas, in Sussex. None of them needed her. Even Brian did not need her much. He was engrossed with his new colleagues, his new work. He talked of this to her, rather than of other things. He was finding it more interesting than either of them had dared to hope.

Alix stared into the dark night, straining her eyes as she searched for the future.

She missed Liz and Esther. In another, sharper, more sickening way, she missed Otto. Otto had accepted the post in Washington. He rang her sometimes of an evening when Brian was out. There was an urgency in his voice when he spoke to her, but Alix would not acknowledge it. The time for urgency was over. He wanted to know if she was all right, he wanted to know when next she was coming to London, he wanted to know about her house, her garden, her peace of mind. Oh, it is peaceful here, said Alix, gazing across the back garden to a patch of suburban wasteland. Otto did not transgress.

I need a job, said Alix to herself sometimes. But a kind of numbness constrained her.

She would have isolated herself completely had she been able. Brian understood this. He understood her well. Silently he gripped her hand over their supper of leeks vinaigrette and fish pie.

"The fish is wonderful up here," said Alix, faintly. "The market is wonderful. There isn't any fish like that in London. Not even in Harrods."

"A very good pie," said Brian.

"Shirley rang again," said Alix. "She invited us to supper, again. We'll have to go."

"Yes," said Brian, "we'll have to go."

"But Cliff will drive you mad," said Alix. "And he's so tactless."

"Never mind," said Brian. "Never mind."

"And then we'll have to have them back," said Alix, "and then they'll ask us back. And on, and on, and on."

"But you might get to *like* Shirley," said Brian, doubtfully.

"I don't think Shirley approves of me," said Alix.

"How could anyone, ever," said Brian, warmly, "*disapprove* of *you*?"

Liz discussed Alix and Brian's move with Stephen Cox over dinner in Bertorelli's in Notting Hill. Stephen was going up to give a lecture in Northam, would stay the night with Brian and Alix. "Do you know what Alix said?" Stephen asked Liz. "She said, 'Oh, God, now we've moved out of town I suppose *everyone* will want to come and stay the night, and now I'm not working I really haven't got the time to be making and unmaking b-b-beds all day. You'll have to bring a sleeping bag,' said Alix."

"In what *tone* did she say that?" Liz enquired.

"Oh, spirited. Spirited. Nothing to worry about. Or not much."

"Alix is a hero," said Liz. "I couldn't face it. If I had to move to Northam, it would be the end of me. I *love* London. This is one of those days when I love London. I love this restaurant, I love the restaurant cat, I love Notting Hill, and I thought that was a great movie."

"You *are* in a good mood," said Stephen, admiringly.

The restaurant cat, comically obese, ostentatiously whiskered, black and white and smiling, purred around their ankles. Its portrait adorned the far wall.

"Yes," said Liz, smiling. "I am."

"Tell me what's happened to Esther's house," said Stephen.

"Not even the thought of Esther's house can depress me at the moment," said Liz. "I banish the Harrow Road. But if you really want to know, we'll drive back that way. It's quite interesting, what's happening to Esther's house. It's being eliminated. Utterly eliminated. As though it had never been. Cut out of the city, like a cancer."

"And when does the trial of Paul Whitmore begin?"

"In a month or two, Edgar says."

"And what is Edgar's opinion of Esther's friend Paul Whitmore?"

"Oh, he thinks he's mad. Barking mad."

"Edgar, you say, doesn't believe in evil."

"No. He rather dislikes talk of evil. You should talk to him one day about Pol Pot."

Stephen smiled, gently, questioningly, as he stirred his coffee.

"I still rather regret that missed opportunity," said Liz. "I wish I'd gone up and knocked on P. Whitmore's door. I was a coward, not to go up."

"We are cowards all," said Stephen.

Alix and Brian Bowen sipped their sherry, politely. Shirley nervously, aggressively, offered nuts. Cliff lit a cigarette. Celia sat in a corner and watched. Sam sat in another corner and watched.

They spoke of fish and house prices, of pot plants and the weather, of Shirley's mother's health.

It was, as Alix had known it would be, difficult to avoid politics. Everything, in a room like this, at a time like this, with men like Brian and Cliff, seemed political, politicized. They could not speak of education, although Alix would have been interested to hear more of the reputation of Sam's prospective state sixth-form college: education was a divisive issue. They could not speak of Brian's job, for that would have involved mentioning the Council which financed it, and the high rates paid by Cliff, domestically and commercially, which were in his view financing that finance. Even house prices were tricky, as a topic; Alix and Shirley steered Brian and Cliff away. And Shirley's mother's health offered potential contention, although fortunately Cliff refused to see it. Rita Ablewhite was, thanks to Shirley's half-hearted persistence, gradually improving, and although she still could not speak comprehensibly, she could hear a little better, could indicate understanding, could answer questions by spelling out Y-E-S and N-O. She might eventually reach a stage of mobility where a return home would be possible, so good were the social services in Northam. She wouldn't be able to manage the stairs in Abercorn Avenue, but there was already a downstairs toilet out the back, and the Council offered generous grants for conversion . . .

No, pot plants were a safer subject. Those that Shirley had inherited from Fred Bowen were flourishing. Alix admired them, several times.

The conversation limped, lumbered, well-meaning, hamstrung.

The two young people stared. Alix sensed from Sam an acute boredom, a restlessness, with which she had the deepest sympathy. Celia was too polite to betray any emotion at all. Celia reminded Alix of evenings of her own childhood. She sympathized with her too.

The house was tidy. Its tidiness was oppressive. Unnatural.

Of Liz, who would have provided a natural point of contact, they could not speak. Shirley's resentment of Liz was too naked, too raw. Liz had treated Shirley, her mother, and Abercorn Avenue badly. Alix agreed with Shirley's unspoken proposal that this was so. But nevertheless was cheered, in the back of her mind, to think that selfish, bracing, energetic Liz existed, that she continued to inhabit the other world, the old world, the familiar London world. And the house in Wandsworth was only rented, after all. Not sold.

Alix ate her pork chop. Family supper, Shirley had offered, and family supper it was.

Alix took in the décor. Curtains with pelmets. Things matching. A hotplate, a trolley. No books, in any of the rooms. Perhaps Celia had books, upstairs?

Sam cheered up when he saw the pudding: an excellent selection, pie and cream, trifle, a mousse. Sam had some of everything. Shirley smiled at him, with her first warm smile of the evening. "Yummy, really yummy," said Sam, reaching out his plate for more. Pudding-starved Sam.

Celia nibbled, coldly. When interrogated by Alix, she admitted that she was taking her A levels, and had already sat her Oxbridge. Yes, she had been offered a conditional place To read History and Ancient History. Yes, she was pleased about this, as her school had been discouraging about the chances of its girls, suddenly forced to sit Oxbridge in the fourth term. Alix longed to know more about this, to know what Shirley and Cliff and Celia thought of the fourth-term Oxbridge ruling, but she dared not pursue the topic; it was nothing if not political.

So Celia would have a year off, between school and university?

"No," said Celia, primly. Her docility was sinister. She can't wait to get out, thought Alix. Her two brothers had already vanished, one to London, one to Australia. Celia was the family's white hope. She could not wait to leave the family. And she was, as she conveyed in the menacing crossing of her ankles, only a girl.

Over coffee, coffee made in an electric machine the like of which Alix had never seen, her mind drifted back to her own entrance examinations, to Flora Piercy's room, to her year off. Her time as an au pair girl, her lonely nursing of a friendly French baby, her exhilaration at finding Liz and Esther again. Esther, during this time, had fallen in love with Italy. Liz had sat at home, here in Northam, filled with expectations, great expectations. Alix had done nothing much. Young she had been, and with her life before her.

"Thank you for a lovely evening, Shirley," said Brian, politely, the true born gentleman, as they stood in the hallway, putting on coats and hats. He had got off lightly: nobody had mentioned Auntie Yvonne.

Rita Ablewhite died that night, in her hospital bed. Quietly, politely, without a sound, she suffered a heart attack, and died.

Liz rang Alix with the news. "I'm driving up this afternoon," she said.

"Come and stay the night," said Alix.

No, said Liz, she'd already booked herself into the Open Hearth Hotel, but could she come to supper? Of course, said Alix.

"Dead," said Liz. "Yes, dead. At last. I can't believe it."

But Charles was not listening. He had just received news that Dirk Davis had allegedly been executed by his captors. The news had flashed through onto his teletext when he was looking for something quite different. There the message had been, in flashing green teleprint. No confirmation as yet.

"Dead," he echoed, to Liz's statement. But he was not listening to what she said, as she rambled on over the phone.

"Shirley hates me," said Liz, over her second whisky, to Alix and Brian. "She hates me. I don't hate her, but she hates me."

"Well, so what?" said Alix, robustly. "Why should sisters love one another?"

"You like yours."

"Yes, but I don't see much of her, do I? Not much more than you see of Shirley. I wouldn't like to have to *live* with her. Or even very *near* her, come to that."

"I'm frightened," said Liz. "I'm frightened, of that horrible house."

Rita Ablewhite was cremated, with the minimum of ceremony. Only her two daughters and Cliff and Celia Harper were in attendance. No hymns were sung, no music played.

Liz took a week off work, to help Shirley sort out the house. She stayed, resolutely, in the hotel. Shirley seemed to respect this.

They agreed on a plan of campaign. Together, they would search the house for a will, for any indication of communication with solicitors. If they failed to find anything, they would approach Cliff's solicitors. "Not that I think they're much good," said Shirley, "but at least they're local."

Together, Liz and Shirley stood shivering in the front porch as Shirley turned the key; together they shivered in the damp hall. The house was very cold. It smelled deadly. A few circulars lay on the mat. Shirley picked them up. Shirley had been paying the bills; not much arrived for Rita Ablewhite.

They felt awkward, incompetent. They had to break their way into the desk like thieves, with implements from Shirley's car tool kit. The nicely polished wood splintered, the lock gave.

Shirley stared at the pigeon holes full of scraps of paper and old envelopes. "I kept trying to get up the courage to ask her if there was a will, but it seemed so—tactless," said Shirley. Liz laughed. Somehow, here in this house, things were not so bad between them. Laughter was possible, in extremis.

"Right," said Liz. "You begin at that end, and I'll begin at this."

They kept on their overcoats and scarves, despite the single-bar electric fire. It was the same electric fire that had warmed them in their girlhood. Before it Liz as a schoolgirl had dried her knickers, nearly forty years ago. The wiring was antiquated, the plug was of a rounded, round-pinned variety not often seen in the 1980s.

Shirley found the will quite quickly. They went to make themselves a cup of coffee before they opened it.

"The last will and testament of me, Rita Ablewhite, of 8 Abercorn Avenue Northam." It was dated 1949. The solicitors were her executors. It left everything, in so far as they could establish from a cursory examination, to her two daughters equally, with provision for grandchildren should the daughters predecease her. A proper will, a solicitor's will. It revealed nothing. Liz and Shirley did not know whether to be relieved or disappointed. They looked at one another questioningly. Neither gave anything away.

"I don't suppose the house is worth much," said Shirley, after a while, "in the condition it's in. But it's better than a poke in the eye with a burnt stick."

"It's such a *normal*-looking will," said Liz, wonderingly.

Both sisters sat there, fingering their silver lockets reflectively.

Then they returned to the desk, in an upsurge of energy. They emptied the pigeon holes, threw old bills in wastepaper baskets, discarded thirty-year-old accounts with implausibly small totals from the fish shop, kept one or two more serious items—a co-op book, a savings account book. Bored with the desk, they went upstairs, and started stuffing old clothes in black bags. Their father's suits, preserved in moth balls. The Salvation Army would take them, said Shirley, and what wasn't fit for them could go on the Council tip. Wildly, they packed and sorted. Laughing, at last exhilarated. A good day's work.

Just before leaving, Shirley returned to the question of the will. We ought to get in touch with her solicitors, she said. Enderby and Enderby. She tried to look them up in the telephone directory, but they seemed not to be there. "Oh dear," she said to Liz. "They've moved, or died, or something. What happens when solicitors disappear?"

"Mm?" said Liz, absently. She was not listening. She was crouching on the floor, over the open bottom drawers of the desk. Drawers stuffed with newspaper cuttings.

"I said, how do we track down the solicitors?"

Liz shut the drawer, and staggered stiffly to her feet; her

head was spinning slightly. She was not as supple as she had
been, could not crouch on her knees as easily as she had once
done.

"I don't know," said Liz. She was not focussing at all. She
stood there, gaping at nothing.

"That's enough for today," said Shirley. "I've got to get
home. I'll have a go at tracking down the solicitors tomorrow,
shall I?"

"Yes, fine, yes, of course," said Liz.

"Are you feeling all right, Liz?"

"Yes, yes, fine, I just feel a bit dizzy, that's all. I stood up
too suddenly."

Liz passed a hand across her brow.

"I'm fine," she repeated, uncertainly. And then, a little
more robustly, "Perhaps you could let me borrow the keys,
Shirl? I could come along tomorrow and do a bit more sorting.
You did say you had to stay at home tomorrow, didn't you?"

"Yes, I've got the plumber coming," said Shirley. "But I
will try to get hold of the solicitors. Somebody must know
what happened. Look, this is the front-door key. It's a bit stiff,
and you don't want to push it *right* in . . . not *quite* in, for
some reason—try it—yes, that's right."

"Thank you," said Liz on the cracked asphalt of the front
path.

And thus she made her rendezvous.

The dark drawers and the bottom drawers of the wardrobe were
stuffed with them. Newspaper cuttings, going back to the
1920s, the 1930s. Nothing very personal, no letters, no family
photographs, mainly cuttings. Marked cuttings. Dated cuttings.
From local papers, national papers. Mingled in with them were
a few apparently random documents: school reports for Liz and
Shirley, vaccination certificates. What am I looking for,
wondered Liz, as she spread them before her on the floor. A
marriage certificate or a death certificate? Some pre-Northam
memory? A photograph of my father?

Her heart was beating very loudly in the silent house, and the
blood was singing in her ears. This was from her cramped
position, she told herself.

She remembered her mother, cutting up newspapers.

Many of them were related to the Royal Family. A harmless,

a common obsession. There was a whole package connected with the Coronation of 1937, another packet documenting the Coronation of 1952. On the brown cover of the 1937 bundle her mother had written: "We were in London. It rained."

We? Who was *we*? Liz had been an infant, in 1937, and Shirley had not been born.

A bundle in an old elastic band was stuffed with references to Dr. Alethea Ward, who had endowed and named the Cambridge scholarship which Liz had been awarded. A complete file, from Dr. Ward's obituary in the Northam *Daily Telegraph* onwards. She had died in 1935, the year of Liz's birth, a fact of which Liz, in the deep selfishness of youth, had hitherto been oblivious. Alethea Ward had meant as little to her as the names of benefactors inscribed on benches in public parks. Yet here was Alethea's life story, preserved and haphazardly, posthumously, updated. There was no hint of the nature of Rita Ablewhite's interest in Alethea Ward.

Rita also seemed to have been obsessed, less normally, by cases of sexual crimes against children. Liz, coming across these packages, had to force herself to look. The mess of paper jumped and swam before her eyes. One could make any story out of these fragments. Her mind jumped. And why had her mother, all those years ago, also been collecting newspaper cuttings about the Hestercombes and the Oxenholmes? Why were there so many newspaper photographs of Stocklinch Hall? Had it been there that Rita Ablewhite had toiled below stairs? One could rearrange these pieces as one wished, like the jigsaw scraps of an experimental novel. A man had killed himself in Stanhope Wood with a penknife, reported an item in the *Evening Star*. A man had been charged with the murder of a six-year-old girl. Suspicious behaviour on school premises. Claimed to be depressed because of operation. Committed an offence on the railway bridge. Sentence reduced on appeal to three years. Suicide while of unsound mind. Found hanging in slaughterhouse, after police alerted neighbours. Stocklinch Hall to be opened to the public on Saturday afternoons. A Pleasant Day Out from Leeds. Van Dyck sold to pay for death duties. Attempted an offence in school bicycle shed.

Liz staggered to her feet, walked up and down the room, lit a cigarette. Patience could assemble the parts, but Liz was not a patient woman. She walked up and down, up and down. Was there gathering, in the back of her mind, in the farthest reaches of her memory, an image, a recollection, a sensation? An overheard, uncomprehended conversation? She sank once more to her knees, opened more bundles of cuttings. Could the answer be here, simply, in one of these shabby packets?

More suicides, more paedophiles. On balance, more suicide than murder, more minor offences than major offences. There was a chronological order, of a rudimentary sort. Liz tried to think, to reason. Her father had left—to join the army, according to ill-defined family assumption—in 1940, had been killed abroad, again according to ill-defined family assumption, in 1944. She turned to the more likely cuttings. Any of these victims she could choose for her father. Any of these outcasts, these perverts, these penknife suicides. The story had a remorseless logic. It made narrative sense. Of the silence, the seclusion, of the barrier of secrecy, the fear that had possessed the daughters. Liz's heart beat so wildly that she wondered if she was about to die. Keep calm, she told herself, keep calm. She turned the yellowing scraps. Of her own infancy, she had hardly a recollection. In vain had her analyst Karl probed, offered suggestions, hypotheses. Before the age of four, nothing. Was this the explanation?

She could not look. She leafed on, finding a harmless cutting, paperclipped on to a shot of the Marquess of Stocklinch and an article about Princess Margaret Rose and Crawfie: an advertisement for the good services of the friend of her mother's one and only friend, Miss Featherstone, LRAM, ARCM, ALAM, ATCL, LGSM(Eloc.), MRST, Authorized teacher of P. G. Waley's System of Sinus Tone Production. Large Miss Featherstone, and the diminutive Miss Mynors. Yes, she remembered them.

Liz stood up again, lit another cigarette. History, fact, memory, fantasy. Truth, belief, faith, delusion. She had spent her entire professional life attempting to investigate the relations of these concepts.

She walked to the window, gazed down the cold February suburban street. The leafless trees stood against the dark sky.

Her whole body was throbbing, thudding, beating; her head seemed about to split with the effort of recollection, of accommodation. How purposefully she had deceived, all those years ago, the innocent Karl. False clues she had offered him, she had knowingly misled him, half-hoping he would detect her falsities. And now the clues were all around her. The end of the thread was in her own hand.

She could not follow. Breathing heavily, exhausted, she felt knowledge slip from her, she felt herself let go. She looked at the littered floor. *What is the nature of the effort required of me?* She spoke the words, aloud. They sounded in the empty house. *If I knew what it was, I would make it,* she said to herself, silently, in good faith.

No, there would never be knowledge, there would only be fear, uncertainty, suspicion. Knowledge would be death. Liz's breath came quickly, as she skirted revelation. *Is it fear in me, is it necessary fear?*

A great sun was burning dully, in the back of her mind, just beyond vision.

She knelt down again, started to turn over the pitiful records of pitiful lives. An impulse told her to burn them, to shove them in the Ideal Boiler as she had shoved the guilty secrets of her childhood, and set fire to the lot. Her skin was very hot. Shame? Guilt? She was very near these monsters; she could smell them in their caves, she could smell them in the cave of her own body.

Liz crouched in a dark landscape, reading police news, reading of royalty. Princess Elizabeth, Princess Margaret Rose. Lord Filey of Foley, the Hon. Roy Oxenholme.

I am exhausted, thought Liz. Defeated, she began to push the clippings back into their folders, into their envelopes; already the record was jumbled, already the pieces had strayed from sequence, inconsequentially. What did it matter who her father was? She opened the drawers, began to stuff the papers in again, at random. *What does it matter who I am?*

She would leave, go back to the safety of the anonymous hotel, the hotel without history. To the plastic canework and carpeted lift. To the hotel with its forged, fake history.

A life of drudgery, a life of concealment, a life of silence. A life sentence of silence.

Liz picked up the wine cooler, fingered its silver monogram. She thought of Henrietta Latchett. A silver shine, a pewter shine.

She wandered over to the bookshelf. Her mother's books. The old favourites: Victorian novels, Edwardian novels, Penguin detective stories. A row of Liz's own school prizes and textbooks. Children's stories. School anthologies. Liz took one or two down, opened them, gazed at their once familiar inscriptions. And right at the end, pushed between two larger volumes, a slim volume, a children's primer, limply bound.

Liz held it in her hand, regarded it with mild astonishment. *The Radiant Way*.

She had no recollection of it, at first sight. She gazed intently at its jacket: two children, a boy and a girl, running gaily down (not up) a hill, against a background of radiant thirties sunburst. Charles had learned to read from this: had she too so learned, nearly half a century ago? It had been a popular pre-war title; were she and Charles bound by a common recollection? A Jungian recollection? And Charles had chosen the title for his series?

She opened the book cautiously. Yes, there was her own name, inscribed in an unknown hand. *Elizabeth Ablewhite. The Radiant Way, First Step*, 1933. She turned the pages. Was she perhaps beginning to remember? Did she recognize these nice children? Pat and Ann. Pat, Ann, and Mother. Sing, Mother, sing. Mother can sing. Sing to Mother, Ann. Pat has a cod. Ann has a fan. The illustrations were evocative: fuzzily tinted, delphinium-towered, hollyhock-adorned herbaceous borders round a vast middle-class lawn, Mother sitting young and decorous in an armchair, reading, with a glass-fronted bookcase, a fringed standard lamp. Mother kisses the children good night. Ann sits in bed with a pug dog. Nursery simplicities, childhood idyll. And where was Father? Ah, there he was, coming home from work in his belted overcoat, in his thirties jacket with its sharp lapels. Liz stared at the features of Father. Smooth, clean-cut, very slightly sinister. A bit of a con man, Father. A weak con man. No match for ever-present, smartly frocked, ever-smiling, competent Mother. A shadowy figure, Father. He appeared in only three sequences: Coming Home, On the Train, and The Picnic.

Father. Yes, she had sat upon her father's knee, learning to read from this very book. She had rubbed herself like a kitten up and down, sitting astride her child-molester father's knee. Spelling out words to Father. Enjoying the coarse fabric of his trousers. Enjoying his illicit smell. Giggling as he tickled her and played with her. Damp between her innocent infant's legs.

Guilt. Shame. Infantile sexuality. Liz gazed at the white-ankle-socked children, in their sunny, monosyllabic garden. The children in the garden. The serpent hissed, sweetly. The children aged, slowly. They skipped downhill forever, along the radiant way, and behind them burned forever that great dark dull sun. Liz shook her head, slowly, smiled to herself, slowly. It was beautiful, it was necessary, she said to herself.

She touched her locket, she laid her fingers on the images in the book. She had been very near to knowledge. She would go no further, today; she would nurse her strength, for the next encounter.

She needed strength that evening, when Charles rang. Charles was in a state of near hysteria. He had been informed that the terrorist group had executed Dirk Davis, and thrown a video cassette of the event over the British Embassy gate. It purported to show Dirk Davis standing against a wall, blindfolded; Dirk Davis being shot by two masked gunmen; Dirk Davis's body lying twitching, then inert, at the foot of the wall.

"Christ, how ghastly," said Liz, sympathetically. "Whatever did they do it *for*?" Charles did not know: why did anyone ever do such things? They were making some crazy demands about release of terrorists in Israeli jails; nothing to do with Britain at all, Charles said. Liz didn't know what to say to calm him down, didn't know how to point out that Dirk Davis's death was nothing to do with Charles either. Because she knew Charles felt it was. And maybe, to do him justice, all telejournalists felt themselves to be implicated by this death: comradely sorrow?

What haunted Charles most, she could tell, was the notion of the video. Death by technology. Death by the new Do-It-Yourself News programme. Death over the teletext. Perhaps Charles was culpable. He had loved these things, was still obsessed by dish receivers. He had envisaged a world in which people, whenever they chose, could receive real moving pictures of the deaths of old comrades. All over the world. Perhaps it served Charles right.

Charles walked up and down the only large room of his flat in Kentish Town, gesticulating nervously to himself, talking to himself. Perhaps the video was a fake. Henry Adamson, who had seen it, said it could conceivably be a fake. Charles felt sick, because he knew that he could not rest until he had seen the video, until he had witnessed the shooting of Dirk Davis. Until he had authenticated, for himself, the dead body of Dirk Davis. Until he had seen Dirk Davis die a violent death, and lie twitching at the bottom of a brick wall. And not once, but again, and again, and again, and again. He was doomed to watch, again and again and again. Enslaved by death. Hooked on death. Again, and again, and again. The car park in Acton, the brick wall in Baldai. Again, and again, and again.

Liz Headleand woke at five in the morning, in the Open Hearth Hotel, feeling ill. Shaking with psychic fever, with a blinding headache. She took a couple of Panadol, and waited for dawn. There was nothing to do but to sweat it out.

She was too ill to get up. She drank a cup of tea, declined medical assistance. She lay and sweated. Fruit was brought to her, and toast. The day passed. Shirley called, for the keys to Abercorn Avenue. Liz lay, speechless, hot, shading her eyes with her hand. Shirley tried to explain that she was on the track of the solicitors, but Liz would not listen. Not now, she whispered, not now.

For twenty-four hours she lay there, as memory worked its way through her body. Dimly she remembered her calm of the day before, when confronted with the evidence. Why had she not been more shocked then? In self-protection, no doubt. A well-known trick. Now was the day of reckoning. A lifetime of memory, in a day. How can one know and not know, simultaneously? How often had she asked herself this simple question, when unknotting the tangled threads of the memories of others? How can the utterly unexpected be *the same as* the expected? How can it be?

Repression. Trauma. The skeleton in the cupboard. Something nasty in the woodshed. A classic case. A banal case. No wonder I feel so rotten, said Liz to herself, rousing herself at the end of the day to watch the ten-o'clock news. The shock was subsiding, the fever abating. So Dirk Davis was dead, and Jilly Fox was dead, and Claudio Volpe was dead, and Rita Ablewhite was dead, and she, Liz Headleand, was still alive. Her forehead had turned cold and damp. Clammy. She was beginning to feel hungry. The organism, the machine, was beginning, despite all, to restore itself. She rang room service and ordered an omelette and chips and half a bottle of Beaujolais. Propped up, alone, in her white five-year-old nightdress, she studied the unsatisfactory nature of knowledge. The anti-climactic nature of knowledge. So this was it. A night of bad dreams, a day of sweat, then a desire for omelette and chips. Already she was losing interest in the riddle that had teased her for decades. Tomorrow she would go and stuff that old rubbish in the Ideal Boiler and put a match to it. Why bother Shirley with these shabby little speculations? Let them go up in smoke: guesses, suspicions, half-truths, the Royal Family, Stocklinch Hall, Miss Featherstone's credentials, Dr. Alethea Ward, and those pitiable paedophiles. She would remember no more. She would no longer gaze at the past, she would no more question her own wicked heart. On she would go, relentlessly, into the dark red sun, down the radiant way, towards the only possible ending.

Liz was relieved, over the following week, to recall that she had formulated the notion of necessary anti-climax for herself, independently, in her day of sweat, for it emerged, anti-climactically, that Shirley's daughter, Celia, had known the facts about her grandfather for years. They did not seem to have done her much harm. Shirley and Liz, chewing over the solicitor's revelations, discreetly stoking the Ideal Boiler with incriminating papers, pondered this discovery.

"Well, she used to spend a bit of time with her," said Shirley, puzzled, as she prodded a smouldering bundle of old school reports from Battersby Grammar, "but I'd no idea they *talked* to one another. Or not about that kind of thing."

"And Celia never mentioned any of it?"

"Not a word. But she's always kept herself to herself, has Celia."

They pondered the mysteries of heredity. Shirley essayed one or two delicate questions about the possible nature of their father's aberration, but Liz diverted them, claiming not to know much about that kind of thing. Their mother's solicitor, or rather the successor of their mother's solicitor, a go-ahead, lively young thirty-five-year-old in Dilke Street, had produced the will, looked through a few old papers, bracingly reassured them: yes, he was well dead, their father, Alfred Ablewhite; yes, as far as he knew Alfred and Rita had been legally married; Alfred had been arrested in 1939 for a minor sexual offence (exposing himself on a railway bridge to primary school children on their way to St. John's C. of E. Infants' School), had been acquitted, and had shortly afterwards committed suicide, though suicide was not proved. So that was it, the mystery. A sad case. Accidental death. There had been a good claim on the insurance.

Rather a shabby little mystery; every family has one. So declared Liz, as she watched the papers blacken. No, she repeated, she didn't know much about that kind of thing, it was not the kind of sexual deviation with which she associated herself, professionally.

Liz did not say so to Shirley, but she could not help associating this kind of offence with inadequate and retarded lonely young men of the lower middle class. She remembered one such from her own childhood, in the alley off Jubilee Road, near the Alhambra. He had shaken his big limp thing at her. She had no idea what it was, that big brown unnatural trunk of an object; not very nice, she had thought it at the time.

She must ask Alix about sexual deviation and class. Alix would be sure to be able to provide a sociological reference.

"I suppose you could call it a relief, really," said Shirley. "That it wasn't worse. It could have been worse."

"Oh, easily," said Liz. She regaled Shirley with one or two worse cases that had come her own way. Stunned children, reeling from confrontation with bull-headed minotaurs.

And their conversation passed, naturally enough, to the Horror of Harrow Road, Paul Whitmore, whose lengthy trial was even then in progress, even then hitting the headlines of the tabloid press. It was no longer a question of whether he had committed the crimes: more a question of why the police hadn't picked him up earlier, and whether he would be found not guilty by reason of insanity. If he were, Liz predicted—and in her view clearly he might in be—there would be an outcry. People seem to think life in a psychiatric hospital is all prawn cocktails and sirloin steak, said Liz. Well, isn't it? said Shirley. Not even at Garfield, said Liz, did they have prawn cocktails.

Liz wasn't very interested in why Paul Whitmore was a murderer. She had lost her chance for involvement by failing to go up and knock on his door that night at Esther's. She was more interested in the fact that his crimes had driven Esther out of London and, as it appeared, out of the country. Esther was off to Bologna in the summer, off for good. Or so she said.

"But don't you believe in evil?" Shirley said, as she tried to tie a knot in a black plastic bag full of old shoe polish, ends of sauce bottles, ancient tins of wartime powdered milk.

Liz reflected, poked the ashes of police reports into sullen flame. "No," she said after a while. "And I don't believe in good either. I believe in suffering, and the alleviation of suffering. I believe in pleasure. And I believe in death. I think belief in evil has caused immense suffering. I don't see the point of suffering. I'd like to do away with it."

"I don't follow you," said Shirley.

"I'm not sure I follow myself," said Liz.

"I suppose we could get someone in to clear all this," said Shirley.

"Yes, we could, but it would be too shaming, don't you think? Like exposing dirty washing," said Liz.

Shirley laughed. "I must say," said Shirley, "I do think you behaved appallingly to Mother." She opened a jar of pickles, sniffed.

"She behaved appallingly to us," said Liz.

"Smell that," said Shirley, handing over the jar.

Liz sniffed. "Jesus," said Liz.

Alix Bowen sits on the top of a double-decker bus, on her way to work, reading the Northam *Daily Telegraph*. The sentencing of Paul Whitmore has been driven into second place by the end of the miners' strike. A new villain has been released to the crowd. The gallant miners have been defeated; in the inelegant words of the Prime Minister, they have been "seen off." Alix does not know what to think. The right-wing *Telegraph* rejoices, but soberly enjoins its readers to count the cost. Alix sits there and obediently counts the cost. The cost is incalculably great. The nation is divided as never before, the Labour movement is in ruins, the self-deception of some of Brian's friends has reached the proportions of mass psychosis. Some argue—Liz Headleand's daughter Sally argues, for example— that all is not lost, what though the fight be lost, for the wives of miners have seen the light, have become articulate, have been radicalized, are moving forward into the brave new world of matriarchy. Alix doubts this. Alan Headleand believes it is possible to fall back in order to leap forward. Yes, maybe, thinks Alix, but Alan is young and he has time in hand. Otto Werner thinks the whole thing has been an unmitigated, irreversible disaster. He is leaving the country. He will not return.

Alix looks up, from her paper, at the passing streets. She is growing accustomed to the perspectives of Northam. Here is Bard Road, with its condemned council flats. Blind windows, nailed up. Plyboarded. Empty, not quite derelict. Blind bard. Hear the voice of the bard, who present, past, and future sees. The Council have been talking of restoring this street for months. There is no money, the Council says. The Council fights the government. Money.

Alix is on her way to see the bard of Northam, who is not yet blind, though he is somewhat deaf and certainly ageing. She has a new job, with Northam's famous poet. It is, like all her jobs, a dead-end job, but at least it is not socially useful; in that, at least, it is a new departure, and she takes some pleasure in this. She has had enough, for the time being, of trying to serve the community. There is no point in it. The community does not want her, and she does not at the moment much care for the community. There is no hope, in the present social system, of putting anything right. The only hope is in revolution, and Alix does not think revolution likely.

Stephen Cox has gone to Kampuchea. Alix hopes he is all right.

Alix stumbled across her new job by accident. She met Northam's poet at a party given at the Holroyd Gallery by Esther's art gallery director friend. They got on famously, Alix and Beaver, after they happened to discover that Northam's poet had known Sebastian Manning's father in the old days. "Yes, I knew him in Paris," said fierce, whiskery old Beaver. "In Paris, in the thirties." And they had reminisced, in front of a pleasant dullish painting by Rigby Saunders, a painting of a bulrush fringed pond in Sussex. Alix spoke of young Nicholas, Beaver spoke of his days as an office boy on *transition*. And so here she is on her way to Beaver's home, to catalogue his papers, perhaps to edit his *Letters;* who knows, to write his biography? Beaver, who is a bad-tempered, cantankerous, disillusioned old monster, has taken to Alix. She has become quite fond of him. (She does not feel obliged to pity him. He repels pity, rudely; he is on the far shore.) His house is in chaos. His wife has died, the rooms are stuffed with papers. Time has passed him by and, by its natural revolution, has caught up with him again. He is in fashion, with the younger generation. His works are being reprinted. He is interviewed, solicited. *transition*, Beaver points out, was a periodical that proclaimed "the revolution of the world." Not much sign of *that*, grunts Beaver, as he thrusts at Alix another box full of letters from Joyce, Pound, Gertrude Stein, Ford Madox Ford, of sketches by Duchamp, Miró, Picasso, of pebbles painted by Man Ray. Alix, despite herself, is entranced by the stuff. "This is worth a fortune," she tells him. "You're an irresponsible old fool, not to have got in touch with Ellmann, with all those people appealing for letters in the *TLS*," she tells him.

Walrus Beaver snorts, threatens to burn them, regales her with anecdotes. He writes her rude poems and threatens to publish them. She laughs, and kisses his forehead.

The revolution of the world. In a dusty attic in Northam, Alix sits and reads of dead aspirations. But the poems live. Beaver's poems are good. They are high art, and good. Alix has found her corner in immortality, in Beaver's attic. She is in a position of power: Beaver has conferred power upon her. She can destroy, edit, publish. She can rejoice scholars and biographers, or deny them. She could even lunch them, at Beaver's expense.

She finds a cutting of a review of Beaver's second volume of verse, published in *Scrutiny*. The review praises Beaver as one of the best poets of the rising generation. She shows it to Beaver. Beaver laughs and laughs. He tells her stories about the Leavises. They both laugh, until tears stand in their eyes.

So this is where my privileged education has brought me, thinks Alix, as she sits on top of an extremely heavily subsidized double-decker bus, on her way to a northern suburb of Northam. I sit in an ivory attic, while Brian toils at the coalface with the disadvantaged, the illiterate. Paradoxical.

Brian thinks Beaver's work is élitist. This is a new word, from Brian, one he never employed at his old job with the Open University, in the Adult Education College in South London. Can he mean it?

I have been driven into paradox, thinks Alix. I have not chosen it. I have been driven into it. It is not satisfactory. But what else can I do? She thinks of the two youths with their hamsters, in the glossy brochure. Their premises not yet finalized.

*   *   *

June 1985.

It is Esther's fiftieth birthday. Alix and Liz congratulate her on having arranged the only sunny weekend of a dismal damp year.

"But it won't be sunny anywhere else," says Esther, lying on the grassy hill beneath the blue summer sky. "I can only arrange the weather for this valley. Everywhere else, it is raining still. There is a limit to my powers."

Alix and Liz beg leave to doubt this. Her powers, they claim with admiration, are limitless, supernatural; had they not been sublimely manifested in her summoning up, the evening before, the solid, fleshly apparition of their old Cambridge friend Flora Piercy? Esther laughs, at the recollection of their astonishment. She had not herself been astonished to see Flora Piercy walk into the garden, for she had arranged that arrival, had stage-managed it with some care, had been planning it ever since she had discovered that Flora lived up the combe from Peggy and Humphrey, with her second husband, Basil Penarth. "You must come down for a drink and surprise Liz and Alix," she had said to Flora, and Flora had obeyed her summons and materialized at the garden gate, bearing a bunch of ragged white roses and a Camembert cheese. They had sat in the garden, under the cherry tree, at the wooden table, drinking champagne, exchanging three decades of news. Births, deaths, marriages. Flora claimed two grandchildren, and was now a JP, having settled down, as she put it, after a rackety early career as courier and travel agent in the south of France. Time, said Flora Piercy Penarth, is an illusion. She was accompanied by a springer spaniel.

"That spaniel," said Esther reflectively, lying on the grassy hill beneath the blue summer sky, "is a bloody nuisance. That's why I wouldn't let Flora come on this picnic. She wanted to, but I draw the line. It doesn't know how to sit still, that spaniel."

Esther bit into an egg and anchovy sandwich, held out her beaker to Liz for another glass of thermos-chilled Berry Bros. Saint-Véran '77.

"This is the perfect day," says Alix. They eat, drink, talk, lie there in the sunshine. The grass is rich with buttercups, with clover, daisies, vetch, and speedwell; the hedgerow is thick with foxgloves, honeysuckle, campion, red dock seed, forget-me-not, stitchwort. The grass in its own kind, in itself, is rich:

bromes, fescues, oat grasses, quaking grass. Esther points them out, idly, inaccurately. Even Esther is not very good at grasses. She misses a rather unusual rye brome. It evades her notice.

The green hill slopes up behind them to the brilliant azure. Large pink lambs, surreal, tinted from the red earth, stand outlined on the hill against the blue. An extraordinary primal timeless brightness shimmers in the hot afternoon air. A slight breeze moves the grass like waves on water.

Alix and Liz have never before been invited to Esther's Somerset retreat. All this is new to them. Esther has kept them away from Peggy and Humphrey; she does not like her friends to mingle. Peggy and Humphrey are away, now, in France, so Liz and Alix are allowed to visit. It is a farewell party, as well as a birthday celebration. Esther is off to Bologna, in July. She will live with Elena, and write a book in collaboration with Robert Oxenholme. So it has been arranged.

"You can come and see me in Italy," says Esther, when Alix and Liz express regret at her departure. And who knows, maybe they will go. Maybe the invitation is good.

The sun begins to drop down the sky, towards the west, towards the green steep hill. The grass is loud with insects.

"Strange," says Liz, dreamily, "that little wood we walked through, and the clearing. And the smell of artichoke soup."

"There is another wood, down by the river," says Esther, "that smells of curry and burned jam."

Esther describes to them the secrets of the landscape. She tells them of the snake by the trout pond. She tells them of the heron in the reeds. She tells them of the bleeding lamb. She tells them of the lonely calf. She tells them of the woodpecker in the grove. She tells them of the primroses of March, of the rosebay willow herb of high summer, of the purple and gold of autumn. She tells them of the sliding fountain that appears, mysteriously, welling up in the green field, and disappears as mysteriously, regardless of rainfall. A secret spring, a hidden source, a sacred fount.

Alix's eyes are shut.

"Alix is asleep," says Liz. They listen to her breathing, deeply, heavily.

"No, I'm not," said Alix. "Not really."

They all shut their eyes. Perhaps they all, briefly, sleep, and dream.

Then they rouse themselves, and pack their basket. Alix puts the Ordnance Survey Map into her old string bag. Liz replaces her old clogs. Esther sticks a flower behind her ear.

They make their way on, along the footpath, the devious way home. The sun descends. A fox watches them from the edge of a clearing, sits its ground for a moment, then runs away into the hazel coppice.

At the top of the last steep, homeward ascent, they pause for breath, leaning on a gate. Below them lie the deep wood, the grove, the secret valley, the cottage, the wooden table, the cherry tree. Beyond are the hills, and beyond the hills, the sea. Where they stand it is still, but above their heads, high in the broad leaves of the trees, a high wind is passing. It shakes the leaves, the branches. The leaves glitter and dance. The spirit passes. The sun is dull with a red radiance. It sinks. Esther, Liz, and Alix are silent with attention. The sun hangs in the sky, burning. The earth deepens to a more profound red. The sun bleeds, the earth bleeds. The sun stands still.

ABOUT THE AUTHOR

MARGARET DRABBLE is the author of nine previous novels and a biography of Arnold Bennett. She lives in London.